BELLADONNA

DONNA

ADALYN GRACE

LITTLE, BROWN AND COMPANY
New York Boston

Little, Brown and Company
Hachette Book Group
1290 Avenue of the Americas, New York, NY 10104
Visit us at LBYR.com

First Edition: August 2022

Little, Brown and Company is a division of Hachette Book Group, Inc. The Little, Brown name and logo are trademarks of Hachette Book Group, Inc.

The publisher is not responsible for websites (or their content) that are not owned by the publisher.

Library of Congress Cataloging-in-Publication Data
Names: Grace, Adalyn, author.
Title: Belladonna / by Adalyn Grace.
Description: First edition. | New York : Little, Brown and Company, 2022. | Audience: Ages 14 and up. | Summary: Nineteen-year-old orphan Signa Farrow confronts Death—and her own deathly powers—when she investigates the mysterious murder of a relative at the Thorn Grove estate.
Identifiers: LCCN 2021039601 | ISBN 9780316158237 (hardcover) | ISBN 9780316158459 (ebook)
Subjects: CYAC: Orphans—Fiction. | Ghosts—Fiction. | Haunted houses—Fiction. | Death—Fiction. | Mystery and detective stories. | LCGFT: Paranormal fiction. | Thrillers (Fiction)
Classification: LCC PZ7.1.G6993 Be 2022 | DDC [Fic]—dc23
LC record available at https://lccn.loc.gov/2021039601

ISBNs: 978-0-316-15823-7 (hardcover), 978-0-316-15845-9 (ebook), 978-0-316-52660-9 (Barnes & Noble special edition)

Printed in the United States of America

LSC-C

Printing 1, 2022

There's a house in the woods
with an Arthurian table and a
never-ending charcuterie board.
This story is for those
I've sat with at that table,
who make writing feel
like magic.

PROLOGUE

IT STARTED WITH THE CRY OF A BABY.

Swaddled in a crimson gown bold as blood, Signa Farrow was the most striking two-month-old at the party, and her mother intended to prove it.

"Look at her," her mother crooned, lifting the fussy infant for all to admire. "Is she not the most perfect creature you've ever seen?" Rima Farrow sparkled as she twirled her baby around the crowd. Every part of her was draped with elegant jewels, each of them a gift from her architect husband. Her silk gown was the deepest shade of cobalt, bustling over crinoline wider than anyone else dared to sport in her presence.

The Farrows were one of the richest families alive; all who attended this party sought to dip their toes into even a fraction of their wealth. And so they plastered their faces with the grins they knew Rima hungered for and cooed at the child she held with such affection.

"She's beautiful," said a woman who watched Rima rather than the baby as she fanned her sticky skin in protest of the summer's heat.

"Perfect," said another, purposely overlooking Signa's crooked little nose and wrinkled neck.

"She'll be like her mother, I'm sure. Feasting on the hearts of unsuspecting suitors in no time." This was spoken by a man who ignored how deeply Signa's eyes unsettled him—one a winter blue, the other melted gold. Both too mindful for a newborn.

Signa never stopped crying—she was flushed with fuss and her skin was clammy. All who saw her thought this typical—summers in Fiore were a hot, wet blanket. Whether indoors or out, bodies glistened from sweat that coated skin like a veil. Because of this, no one expected what the baby already knew: Death had found his way into Foxglove manor. Signa could sense him around her like one might sense a fly that brushes too close. Death was a buzz upon her skin, alerting the fine hairs on her neck. With his presence Signa settled, lulled by the chill that blossomed with his nearness.

But no one else experienced the same comfort, for Death came only where he was called. And that night he'd been called to Foxglove, where poison laced every drop of wine.

First came the coughing. Fits of it overtook the party, but guests would cough into their pretty white gloves and pardon themselves, thinking the cause was something they ate. Rima was one of the first to show signs. Cold sweat prickled her temples, and she passed her baby to a nearby servant girl as her breaths thinned. "Excuse me," she said, a hand to her throat, fingers pressing into the sweat that pooled into the crevices of her collarbones. She coughed again, and when she drew her hands away from her lips, blood the color of her baby's dress stained her satin gloves.

Death stood before her then, and the infant watched as he laid his hand upon Rima's shoulder. With a final inhale, her corpse fell to the floor.

Death didn't stop with Rima. He swept through the grand estate, collecting the poor souls whose faces purpled as their chests seized with uncooperative breaths. He tore through dancers and musicians, stealing their breath with a single icy touch.

Some tried to make it to the door, thinking there must be something in the air. That if they could get into the gardens, they'd be spared. One by one they fell like stars, only the lucky few who'd not yet tasted the wine able to make their escape.

The servant girl barely managed to get Signa into the nursery before she, too, fell, lips bleeding rubies as Death slowed her heart and cast her body to the floor.

Even as an infant, Signa was unfazed by the stench of death. Rather than stir from the panic around her, the baby focused instead on what no one else could see—the bluish glow of translucent spirits who filled the estate as Death plucked them from their bodies. Some went peacefully, taking the hands of their partner as they awaited an escort into the afterlife. Others tried to claw their way back into their bodies, or to flee from a reaper who did not give chase.

In the midst of it all, a dead and glowing Rima stood silently in Signa's room, watching with a deep frown and vacant eyes as Death crossed the threshold. His footsteps made no sound as he approached the baby, his shape nothing more than ever-moving shadows. But Death did not need to be seen; he was to be *felt*. He was a weight upon the chest, or a collar buttoned too tight. A fall into frigid, lethal waters.

Death was suffocating, and he was ice.

And yet when he reached to collect Signa, who was full and settled with her mother's poisoned milk, the baby yawned and curled herself against the touch of Death's shadows.

He fell back, shadows retracting. Once more he tried to claim her, yet his touch did not show him flashes of the life this young child had led. It showed him instead something he'd never before seen—glimpses of her future.

A brilliant, impossible future.

His touch could not kill the baby he circled around, as confused by her as he was fascinated by what he'd seen.

Though Rima wished to stay—wished to wait for her child to join her—Death stepped back and offered his hand. To Rima's surprise, she drew close and took it. "It's not her time," he said, "but it is yours. Come with me." There were too many souls in need of ferrying to remain any longer. He'd be back, though. He would find this child again.

Hand in hand with Death, Rima's spirit cast one last look at the baby they left behind, alone in a house with nothing more than corpses for company. She prayed that someone would find Signa soon, and that they would protect her.

Just as the night had begun with the cry of a baby, it ended with one. Only this time, no one was around to hear it.

4

ONE

IT'S SAID THAT FIVE BELLADONNA BERRIES ARE ALL IT TAKES TO KILL someone.

Just five sweet berries, eaten straight from the foliage. Or, as Signa Farrow preferred, mashed and steeped into a mug of tea.

Her dark brows were slick with sweat as she leaned over the steaming copper mug, inhaling the fumes. Certainly eating the berries straight would have been easier, but she was still learning the effect belladonna had on her body, and the last thing she wanted was Aunt Magda finding her passed out in the garden with a bright purple tongue.

Not again, anyway.

It had been weeks since Signa last saw the reaper. Only a final breath would draw him out from hiding, and he never left empty-handed. At least, that was the way it was supposed to be. But Signa Farrow was a girl who could not die.

The first time Signa remembered seeing the reaper, she was five and had fallen down the stairs of her grandmother's house. Her neck had snapped and was crooked as she'd watched him sideways from the cold floor. She understood, vaguely, that her young body was not meant to endure such things and wondered if he'd arrived to take her. Yet he said nothing, watching as her bones snapped back into place, and disappearing when she recovered from a fall that should have killed her.

It was another five years before she saw Death again. Signa had watched from her grandmother's bedside as Death took the woman's hand and eased her spirit from the body. She'd been ill for months, and she smiled and kissed Signa's forehead before letting Death guide her into a peaceful afterlife.

Signa begged for Death to return. To bring her grandmother back as Signa held the corpse's hand and cried until there was nothing left in her. No one else was able to see him or the spirits he led, and she wondered if it was her fault this had happened. If she was to blame because she was the girl who could see Death.

She didn't remember how long she remained in that house before someone had smelled the body and came to find Signa, hair matted and clothes unwashed, curled at her grandmother's bedside. They'd whisked her away from the house, shepherding her off to the first of many new guardians to come.

She spent the next several years testing her odd abilities. It'd started with pricking her finger on a thorn and watching the blood bubble and then disappear, as though the skin had never been blemished. From there the experimentation shifted into jumping off stones high enough to break bones upon falling. Signa came to realize she would feel only a sharp snap, then be fine for a cliffside stroll minutes later.

But the belladonna berries were never meant to be an experiment, just something she plucked from her aunt's unkempt garden after arriving several months prior, thinking they were wild blueberries. She'd had no idea they were poisonous until she fell upon the weeds, vision swimming. Death made an appearance then, watching from behind the bend of an oak tree. Even if Signa hadn't recovered too quickly to speak with him, she'd been too distracted by Aunt Magda, who found her in the garden clutching deadly nightshade, her mouth stained purple. The woman nearly had a heart attack when Signa bolted upright from the ground, the poison out of her system within minutes.

Signa had learned something that day—how to draw Death out of the shadows. And with that knowledge, she refused to let him hide from her a moment longer.

Signa lifted the tea to her lips, though her tongue only grazed the warm steam before the copper mug was knocked from her hands. She stumbled from the rickety wooden bench she was perched upon as the mug clattered to the floor and the violet tea spilled onto the worn gray stone of the kitchen.

Signa whirled to find Aunt Magda scowling. That was an expression she wore often, though if one was to look deeper, they'd see that her thin bottom lip and leathery hands trembled in Signa's presence. They'd see dilated pupils and a thin sheen of sweat upon her wrinkled forehead.

"You think I don't know what you're up to, demon-child?" Aunt Magda scooped the mug into her hands. She sniffed and peeked inside, scowling at the mush of berries. "Filthy girl, doing the devil's work!"

Aunt Magda threw the mug at Signa, who reeled back but couldn't avoid being struck on the shoulder. There was enough liquid left in the mug to burn her, and for the purple juice of the berries to stain her favorite gray coat. "I warned you what would happen if you brought that witchcraft into my home."

Signa ignored her searing skin and looked her aunt hard in the eye. "It was tea." Her voice was so firm that anyone who didn't know better might believe Signa was telling the truth. But unfortunately, Aunt Magda did know better. She thought herself too smart and too godly of a woman to be tricked by a "witch."

Not that Signa truly believed she was a witch, of course. Though she did have a love for botany, and often found herself wishing that she knew a few spells. How wonderful it'd be to have a spell to tidy the dust from this hovel, or to feed herself something other than stale bread and whatever concoction she could think to cook up with the sparse ingredients Magda left for her.

"Pack your things," Aunt Magda snapped as a draft of autumn air hissed through a slit in the kitchen window. She pulled a coat tight around her frail body. Her skin was graying, and every so often her chest rattled with a wet, hacking cough. There was a moment when Signa looked past her aunt and into the shadows, waiting to see if Death was coming to claim Aunt Magda as she'd feared ever since that cough started a week prior. "You'll sleep in the shed tonight." Magda's words were spoken so coolly that Signa's insides withered, and she found herself wishing she'd never had the misfortune of being taken in by the awful woman. It was a shame she had so few alternatives.

Because of the inheritance she was to claim on her twentieth birthday, and the allowance that her caretakers received from it, Signa had once been warred over by potential guardians. Her grandmother had won the first war, not out of greed but of love. When she'd passed away, Signa was sent to live with her mother's brother—a young and healthy banker with a fine estate and fruitful love life. Though he often left her alone to care for herself, Signa didn't despise her years with him. She'd even had a friend to keep her company on romps in the woods and on espionage missions through the neighborhood—Charlotte Killinger.

Her uncle's love life proved to be *too* fruitful in the end, however—at the age of thirty, he died from a disease he'd contracted from one of his many partners. Signa had hoped to be taken in by Charlotte's family after that, only to discover that her friend's mother had passed from the very same disease. That scandal was effectively the end of the girls' friendship, and Signa hadn't received so much as a letter from Charlotte since.

Signa was twelve when the whispers began, made worse when her third guardian died in a tragic carriage accident on his way to pick her up, then when her fourth guardian drowned in her own bathtub after a sedative and too much liquor. *The child is cursed by Death*, some said. *The wickedest of witches, spawned by the devil himself. Wherever she goes, the reaper will follow.* Signa never said a word to dissuade them because she wasn't certain they were wrong.

She pretended she couldn't see the spirits she passed on the streets or even shared homes with, hoping that if she didn't interact, perhaps they'd one day disappear altogether. Unfortunately, ignoring spirits wasn't so easy. Sometimes she thought they knew she was hiding from them and were the worse for it, howling through the house or haunting mirrors, always trying to catch Signa surprised and frightened by their antics.

Fortunately, there were no spirits living in Magda's house, though that didn't much improve Signa's situation. Aunt Magda was the sort who would lose herself in gambling halls for days at a time, always to return with empty pockets. She didn't worry herself with silly things like keeping the kitchen stocked or ensuring that Signa could breathe properly in the dusty hovel she claimed was a home, and she cared only about the allowance that housing Signa provided.

Signa understood her aunt's fear of her—expected it, even—but it made for a miserable life. Only months from turning twenty, she would soon be able to claim her inheritance and finally build a home of her own. One filled with light and warmth and, most importantly, *people*. She would parade through that house in a beautiful gown, catching the eyes of a dozen handsome suitors who would proclaim their love to her. And Signa would never again be alone.

But to claim that future, she needed to confront Death. That very night, preferably, before he claimed yet another guardian and damned her further.

"Pack, girl," Aunt Magda demanded again, her bony hands trembling. "I'll not have you in my house tonight."

Pausing only to pick up her mug from the floor and examine

the newest dent in the copper, Signa hurried out of the kitchen. The rickety wooden staircase groaned as she climbed, trying to think only of how the floor creaked as if offended by the weight of her steps and the grime that covered the house from the floorboards to its craggy roof. She tried to think of the orb spider that lived upon a perfectly preserved web in a corner of the ceiling, out of reach but always in view. Anything to get the dark thoughts out of her head— that there was something terribly wrong with her. That she was a monster. That everyone and everything would be better if only she were normal.

Magda believed Signa carried the devil within her very soul, and perhaps that was true. Perhaps the devil *was* nestled comfortably within her, and that's why it was impossible for Signa to die. Regardless, that notion didn't change what Signa knew she had to do.

Aunt Magda's cough rattled the house, and Signa moved faster. In her tiny bedroom in the attic, she slid her trunk toward the bedroom door to block anyone from an easy entry and tiptoed back to the center of the room. Gathering up her skirts, she took a seat on the floor and removed her coat, taking the belladonna berries from a pocket. She set them before her, then retrieved a rusty kitchen knife from a second pocket and wrapped the tarnished handle in the folds of her skirts for easy access. Signa picked up five berries, and though she couldn't say why, she smoothed down her dark tresses and adjusted her collar to ensure she was presentable before letting their sweetness explode on her tongue.

The poison began in her chest, as though someone had torn her open with a hot iron and seized hold of her lungs. Her skin was a leaking faucet, fat beads of sweat rolling from her pores. Signa heaved as bile burned her throat, shutting her eyes against the shadows that swarmed in and cast strange hallucinations.

Only moments later, the effects of the belladonna were slipping away—it was a dose that should have killed a person, though one Signa could recover from in minutes. But she needed to stay in this moment for as long as possible because this was what she was after; this was her chance to chase the reaper, and to stop him once and for all.

Finally, ice spread its way into her veins. It was a familiar presence that seared her from within and demanded to be acknowledged. Signa opened her eyes, and Death was there before her.

Watching.

Waiting.

His presence was intoxicating and familiar, and it took Signa by surprise as it always did—writhing shadows cast into the vague shape of a human. So dark and void of light that it was painful to look at him. And yet looking at him was all Signa could do. All she could ever do. She was drawn to him like a moth to a flame. And so, it seemed, was he to her.

Death no longer waited at a distance but bent over her like a vulture before its prey, shadows dancing around him. Signa looked up into the endless abyss of darkness, and though her eyes stung, she refused to look away.

"I'd prefer you not summon me whenever the urge strikes." The voice was not what she expected. It wasn't ice, nor gravel, but the sound of water in a meadow, slipping over her skin and inviting her in for a midnight swim. "I'm a busy man, you know."

Signa stilled, breathless. More than nineteen years she'd waited to hear Death's voice—and those were his first words? She folded her fingers around the knife's hilt and scowled. "If your intent is to ruin my life, it's time you tell me why."

Death retracted, and as he did, warmth swept in, biting into her numbed fingers. She hadn't even realized she was cold. "You think that's what I'm doing, Signa?" The disbelief in his voice mirrored her own. "Ruining your life?"

There was something concerning about those words. Something overly familiar that sent chills shuddering across her skin. "Don't say my name," Signa told him. "Upon Death's tongue, it sounds like a curse."

He laughed. The sound was low and melodic, and it had his shadows writhing. "Your name is no curse, Little Bird. I just like the taste of it."

It was strange, the things his laughter did to her. Though Signa had spent years building her words for this moment, she found that now she had none. And even if she did, what was the point? She couldn't let herself be swayed by curious words—not when his actions had all but ruined her life, stripping her of every friend, guardian, and home she'd ever had. And so she didn't let herself think any longer; it was time to seize her opportunity and see if Death had a weakness.

With trembling hands she clutched her knife tight, fighting the heaviness in her limbs to gather all the strength she could muster. And then she struck him square in the chest.

TWO

THE BLADE SLIPPED THROUGH THE SHADOWS, AND SIGNA CURSED.

Death peered down at his chest, and the shadows tilted as though he was cocking his head. "Now, now, aren't you a curious thing. Surely, you didn't believe something so trivial would work on me?"

Her lips soured at his amusement, and she withdrew the knife. She'd hoped the blade would do *something*. That it would deter him or let him know that she was serious about him staying away from her. She wanted Death to see her as dangerous. As someone not to be toyed with. Instead, he was *laughing*.

And because of that laughter, Signa barely registered the persistent banging at her bedroom door. She stilled only at the screeching of her trunk sliding against the wooden floor and Aunt Magda's yelling as she stormed into the room, sheet white and with the fear of the devil in her eyes. The woman wasted no time, trembling as she grabbed a fistful of Signa's hair and hoisted her from the floor. Her eyes darted toward the window, as though she intended to throw Signa out.

Beside Aunt Magda, Death bristled, choking the air from the room. Ice bit into Signa's skin as she tried to pry herself away from her aunt's grasp. And though Signa knew she should tell him to stop, she didn't. Her aunt's eyes burned with hatred, and as the woman lunged for her neck, Signa gritted her teeth, took her aunt by the shoulders, and threw her off-balance.

The moment Signa's skin touched Aunt Magda's, it was as though a fire burned through her veins. Her aunt fell back as if stunned, breaths thin and reedy. The color drained from her skin, as though Signa's touch had leeched it all away. Aunt Magda tripped over a corner of the trunk, tumbling backward with a silent scream, lungs emptying themselves.

She fell upon the floor with a smack, silent for perhaps the first time in her life.

By the time Signa understood what had happened, it was too late to help Aunt Magda, whose glossy eyes stared hollowly at the ceiling. Death hovered above her, bent to inspect the body.

"Well, that's one way to shut her up." His tone was light with mirth, as though this were all a joke.

Signa's breaths then came not in sips but in panicked gasps. "What have you done?"

Only then did Death straighten, recognizing her panic. "What have *I* done? I'm afraid you're mistaken, Little Bird." He spoke with the same slow inflection one might use when instructing a child. "Take a breath and listen to me. We haven't much time—"

Signa heard none of it. When she looked at her hands, they were the palest blue, as translucent as a spirit's. She tucked them behind her with a low moan. "Stay away from me!" she pleaded. "Please, just stay away!"

There was an edge in Death's voice when he replied. A hint of darkness looming in the meadow. "As if I don't already try." He turned from her, and Signa could only watch as Death reached through her aunt's corpse and tore the spirit from her body.

That spirit took one look at Signa, then at Death, and her eyes widened with understanding. *"You rotten witch."*

It felt as though the ground were falling out from beneath Signa's feet. Already her mind was crawling in on itself, her vision tunneling as she stared down at her trembling hands. Hands that had betrayed her. Hands that had stolen a life.

"What have I done?" she whispered, her body curling into itself. *What have I done, what have I done, what have I done?* And then, with dawning horror, "What do I *do*?"

"First, you take that breath." For some reason it eased her nerves to hear Death speaking and not Magda, who sat staring at her translucent body in shock. "I assure you, I did not expect this—"

"What do I care for your assurances? You're the reason this happened!" Signa didn't know whether to laugh or cry, so the sound that escaped her was a mix of both.

Death's shadows tripled in size as darkness enveloped the room. *"You* summoned *me.* I've done nothing but come where I was called. I'm not your enemy—"

At least at this, she knew to laugh. "Not my enemy? You are a perpetual cloud upon my existence. You're the reason I've spent my life in places like this, with people like *her*, surrounded by spirits! You're the reason I'm miserable. And look at what you've done now." Her eyes fell to the corpse in front of her, and Signa buried her face in her translucent hands as tears burned hot. "You've damned me. Now no one will ever want to marry me!"

"Marrying?" Death stared at her incredulously. "That's what you're crying about?"

She sobbed harder, the words doing nothing to ease her spiraling mind.

Had Signa been looking, she would have seen that Death's shadows wilted. She would have seen that he reached out for her, only to draw back before she could reject him. She would have seen his shadows wrap themselves around Magda's mouth, silencing the woman before she could say another cruel word.

"I never meant for this to happen." His voice rang genuine. "Our time is limited, and I know that whatever I say right now, you won't hear it. But I'm not your enemy. In two days' time, I'll prove it to you. Promise me you'll wait here until then."

Signa made no such promise, though it wasn't as if she had anywhere else to go. Still, she didn't look up until Death was gone and warmth crept back into the room, bringing feeling back into her fingers and toes as life once again colored her skin. The effects of the belladonna had worn away, leaving a pulsing headache and the seething spirit of her aunt as the only reminders that Death had visited.

Signa took one look at her through watery eyes, and Aunt Magda scowled. "*I always knew you had the devil inside of you.*"

Without argument, Signa fell back upon the floor to stew in her misery.

Signa stood before the crooked door of her dead aunt Magda's house later that evening, hugging herself as she waited for the coroner to finish his work.

He made haste—not because he was unnerved by the body but because he was fearful of Signa with her raven hair and oddly colored eyes, and of the crowd of neighbors who watched from a distance with knowing looks.

"You never asked for this to happen," Signa whispered to herself as she braced against anxious onlookers. "You may have *thought* it, but thinking is not the same as doing. You are good. People could learn to like you. This is his fault."

His fault, his fault, his fault. It was her new mantra.

Signa hated Death even more now than she did before. Hated what he'd somehow caused her to become. Though . . . she couldn't say she was sad that Aunt Magda was gone.

Or at least mostly gone.

"Are you going to let them take me?" Aunt Magda's spirit croaked, angry even in death. *"You owe me, girl! Are you going to let them stuff me into a bag like that? Do something, you little witch, I know you can see me!"*

"Unfortunately, I can hear you, too," Signa grumbled, realizing she'd spoken aloud when she earned a surprised blink from the man lifting her aunt's bagged body into the back of a black carriage.

Unsure what to do, Signa stared between him and her aunt's floating spirit until the man grew uncomfortable and excused himself, sputtering on about how sorry he was for her loss and how he'd be in touch.

All the while, neighbors held their crosses tight around their necks, whispering that they always knew there was something off about the girl. Telling anyone who would listen that Signa was a bad seed, and that Magda should have known better than to invite the devil into her home. There was even a spirit among them in a loose white tunic, who crossed themselves over and over again as they stared at Signa with empty, hollow eyes.

She tried not to scowl. It didn't matter that their gossip bothered her. It didn't matter that she would have given anything to have just one person to confide in—because they weren't wrong to fear her. Signa had used the powers of the reaper.

She just needed to figure out how it had happened.

Signa's skin prickled as she backed away toward Magda's house, hoping neither the neighbors nor her distracted aunt—who was busy making a fuss about her body as the coroner's carriage disappeared down the street—would follow as she sneaked away and into the garden.

The term *garden*, in this case, was used loosely. Over the years the land had decorated itself with weeds and wildflowers Magda had often complained about, and that Signa spent hours tending to as well as she could without so much as a shovel or shears. If there was anything she'd miss about Magda's home, it was the garden.

She made her way beneath a willow, knocking the overgrown

foliage to one side so she could lean against the tree's trunk. But she wasn't alone.

Beneath the leaves, covered with dirt and clover, was a hatchling. It was so new to the world that its eyes were shut tight, its skin pink and fleshy, without a single feather.

Signa stooped to inspect the poor creature, which was covered in soil and hungry ants that had every intention of devouring it alive. The insects overtook it, ruthless in their pursuit. Signa couldn't help but sympathize with the creature; it was like her—cast out of its nest and expected to fend for itself. Only it was not as capable as Signa; for it could not cheat death. It would be a mercy for the creature to die swiftly and be put out of its misery.

But Magda's death had been an accident. If Signa took another life, on purpose this time, what did that make her?

She didn't want to give any consideration to the thought, yet she knew that she needed an answer before she was face-to-face with anyone else she risked hurting.

Tentatively, she peeled her gloves off and brushed the tip of one finger along the hatchling's spine, sweeping away some of the ants and debris that had collected. She held her breath, waiting to see if its death would come. Curiously, the hatchling continued to writhe on the ground, its heart pulsing.

Again she pressed a bare finger upon the bird, longer this time. When she pulled her hand away, the creature was still breathing.

She leaned back against the trunk of the willow with tears of relief prickling her eyes. Her touch hadn't killed the poor bird. Her touch wasn't *lethal*. Unless... unless there was more to it.

She remembered the belladonna in her pocket, and with a shaking hand Signa drew five berries from it. Ensuring that the foliage would conceal her from anyone who might wander by, she popped the berries into her mouth and let them burst upon her tongue. The symptoms came fast—the nausea, the swimming vision, and there across from her, Death himself stood once more. Though she knew he'd come, she refused to acknowledge him, glad that he waited at a distance. She reached out once more to stroke her finger along the bird's spine, and this time its heartbeat ceased and it stilled with a final relieved breath.

Signa drew her hand back and clutched it to her chest. There was no denying it—with just a touch, she could bring death. But that death would come, it seemed, only when the reaper was in her presence. Only when Signa was in this strange space, teetering between life and death.

She had so many questions, yet not once did Signa spare Death a glance as she forced herself from the ground, leaving the dead hatchling upon the soil for the ants to claim as she stumbled toward the house.

She was glad, at least, that the hatchling would no longer feel pain. Glad that if she was to be a monster, at least she could deliver mercy.

THREE

A POLISHED IVORY CARRIAGE ARRIVED TWO DAYS LATER.
The barking of a neighbor's hounds signaled its arrival, and Signa's chest tightened as she glanced out the kitchen window to see the commotion. She'd practically been living in the garden since her aunt's death, saying her goodbyes to the plants and waiting for the days to pass while she ignored the spirit who rampaged through the house. Aunt Magda was atrocious even in death, rustling the curtains and howling her frustrations whenever she wasn't telling Signa how much of a pest she was or snooping on the neighbors.

Signa had received a letter the day prior—one with a red wax seal and signed by a Mr. Elijah Hawthorne, extending her an invitation to his home, Thorn Grove. It was with surprise that Signa recognized the name as the husband of Magda's granddaughter, Lillian. She'd heard Magda complain about the young woman before, telling stories of the wealthy socialite who'd cut off Magda's allowance with no warning.

Signa had spent all day and well into sunrise the next morning staring at the letter, unconvinced it wasn't a figment of her imagination. She didn't want to consider how Death must have managed it, and though she had half a mind not to take this offering, Signa was no fool. Setting off for Thorn Grove was the best option she had. There was little choice but to put aside her tea, clutch Elijah's letter tight, and hurry outside.

The carriage didn't buckle as it clattered over the thick vines and damp moss that erupted between the splitting cobblestones. The two horses that pulled it had dark black coats slick with sweat; their nostrils dripped from the exertion, but their bodies were healthy and coiled with muscle. Signa couldn't help but think of her own bony wrists and scrawny legs, and be a little jealous of these horses whose diet was surely superior to her own. The massive stallions huffed as they halted before her, and an elderly coachman shimmied down. He was a rail-thin man, tall and fair-skinned.

"Morning, miss." Tipping his top hat, he propped the carriage door open. "I presume you're the lass I've been sent to pick up?"

"I believe I am." Signa trembled like a hummingbird. Someone had truly arrived to retrieve her. To whisk her away to a family high within the social hierarchy, with whom she might wear beautiful gowns and sip tea with other women and have the life she yearned for. It seemed too good to be true; she kept glancing toward the shadows, waiting for Death to appear, laughing as he told her it was all a ruse.

"My orders are to bring you back without delay," said the coachman. "We've got a bit of a journey ahead of us. Have you got any belongings?"

"Just a trunk, sir. It's right inside. I can get it—"

The driver waved away her words with a smile so bold it was alarming. Signa couldn't remember the last time she'd seen such an honest smile. "Nonsense, miss. It's my pleasure." Unused to such politeness, she could only nod as he toddled toward the house and wonder whether she was meant to stand there or get into the coach.

Signa didn't have to wait long for her answer; a cough from the coach signaled that the driver hadn't come alone. A boy younger than anyone she'd expected—in his early twenties at most—emerged from the carriage. The young man was dressed handsomely, fitted in a frock of the deepest black and matching leather boots. He was tall as a willow and broad as an oak, with a full head of soot-black hair that curled behind his ears. His skin was tanned from the sun, and there was a whisper of freckles dusted beneath eyes that reminded Signa of smoke—a pale and wispy gray, with a halo of dark coal around each iris. He had a small scar cut diagonally through the arch of his left brow.

"Just look at the gold lining on that carriage! Of course my grand-daughter, Lillian, felt the need to show off her wealth. It's not as though the wretched girl ever thought to help me out. She's a silly, awful thing, just like you." Magda's words dripped with bitterness as she circled the boy, but for once Signa didn't care.

There were two rules Signa knew about spirits—the first was that Magda could haunt only the land where she had died, and the

24

second was that should her corpse be burned, her spirit would be torn unwillingly from the earth.

It was the first rule that relieved Signa, for it meant that she would never have to see her dreaded aunt again.

"It's a pleasure to meet you, sir. I hope your journey was comfortable." Signa cleared her throat and gathered every bit of politeness she could. She even attempted a curtsy in her heavy bombazine gown and black feathered veil, which was itchy and the only attire she seemed to wear lately.

The young man didn't return her formality. He cut a severe look around the withered porch and the unkempt garden, too full and crowded to walk through without stepping on overgrown weeds. "I'm Sylas Thorly, and I'm here on behalf of Mr. Elijah Hawthorne to escort a Miss Farrow back to his estate, Thorn Grove." His voice was the low rumble of an approaching storm. "I assume you're she?"

Having expected a Hawthorne, Signa noted his name with interest. "I am."

"Wonderful," he drawled, taking more interest in smoothing out the dark leather gloves that fit his hands like a second skin than he did in her. "Into the carriage we go. It's as Albert said, we've quite the journey ahead of us."

"If you need to rest, I could make tea—"

Sylas adjusted his cravat and paid her little mind. "I'd prefer we not linger at this hovel for a second longer than necessary."

She clenched her teeth but pressed on. "What about the horses? Do they need watering?"

Sylas tipped his head toward the sky and squinted. When he

inhaled a long breath, Signa got the sense that he was searching the clouds for his lost patience and was coming up short. "You're kind. But the horses have informed me that they, too, would prefer not to linger at the risk of catching a disease. Come now, Miss Farrow." Sylas motioned toward the carriage, offering a gloved hand to help Signa into it.

The carriage was small, and Signa had to keep her tense body pressed against one side so she didn't accidentally bump Sylas's knees, which were spread widely and far too comfortably in such tight quarters. A moment later—when her travel chest had been loaded and Albert had climbed back onto the coach—the snap of the reins sounded and the horses took off.

Sylas's smoky eyes found Signa's briefly before he picked up a newspaper and spread it across his lap. Uncertain of what she was meant to do, she looked for another copy or anything else she might read, but found nothing. "You're not a Hawthorne, then?" Signa asked, feeling it necessary to say *something* when before company. From what she'd gathered in a book her mother had left behind for her, *A Lady's Guide to Beauty and Etiquette*, it was scandalous for an unmarried woman to be left alone with any man. Yet, given the grand carriage and all she'd heard, there was no doubt the Hawthornes were wealthy and of high society, and thus quite respectable. Perhaps, then, Signa's book was out of fashion? "Could Mr. Hawthorne not come for me himself? Or Lillian?"

Sylas blew out a quiet breath and stretched his long legs the best he could. He was far too tall for such a space, having to sit hunched like a crow perched upon a log. "Lillian is dead and Mr. Hawthorne's daughter, Blythe, is sick. So no, they couldn't."

Signa stiffened. Death, it seemed, had beaten her to Thorn Grove.

"I'm sorry no one was there to see you off," Sylas muttered, seemingly as uncomfortable with making small talk as Signa.

"It's no bother, I'm quite used to handling myself." Besides, the only one who could have been there for her was Aunt Magda, whom Signa would prefer to never see again. Every spirit that walked the earth was tethered to the world by some sort of intense emotion, like anger or sorrow. She'd seen weeping women staring out windows and spirits arguing back and forth, stuck in an enraged loop. Signa had gotten used to their patterns and was skilled at avoiding them, for spirits frequented the same spots until they eventually decided to pass on from this world.

In all her years, Signa had known only two spirits to pass on. Most—like the raging Aunt Magda, who was beating on the door of the carriage and shouting, *"Don't you dare leave, you witch! Don't you dare just leave me here!"*—could spend years roaming the earth, feeding off their most pressing emotions.

But leave they did, down streets of cobblestone where the scent of cinnamon and apple lay thick in the autumn breeze. Signa sighed her contentedness the moment they were too far for Magda to follow, listening to the occasional swish of Sylas turning the pages of his newspaper.

"You seem relieved to be leaving," Sylas noted after a moment, eyes on his paper.

She grunted without thinking, for how true the words were. "Anywhere is better than this place," she said as she tipped her head against a window, settling in.

She didn't notice that Sylas's fingers had stilled on the pages. Did not see the dark look that crossed his face as his jaw tightened and he buried himself in his reading.

If she had, perhaps she would have thought twice about Thorn Grove and all that awaited her.

FOUR

SIGNA HADN'T EXPECTED THEY'D NEED A TRAIN TO REACH THORN Grove. When she'd first smelled smoke in the air, she'd shut the coach's windows, thinking they'd pass it by. But as the coach slowed, Sylas pressed a thin yellow ticket into her hand. She'd never been on a train, though she'd read in the papers of how fast they were: the new way of travel; a modern luxury. It took Sylas clearing his throat for her to catch her bearings and slip out of the carriage. The moment the heels of her boots hit the ground, Signa was swept into another world.

The station was a massive building of slate gray, adorned with the face of a clock that was so large it could only be described as imposing. It struck the hour, the sound like a gong reverberating through the station.

Inside, the weathered floors were yellowed. Flies swarmed over-stuffed trash bins, and the distinctive scent of musk from too many rushing bodies hung in the air. A spirit was present, too. A man in a long black coat with worn holes in the bottom sat upon a bench and watched the passersby solemnly. Signa averted her eyes, giving him a wide berth.

Dirty as the station was, there was something grand about it. There were men in business attire who held the most luxurious walking sticks, and women in bonnets and cotton day dresses bustled about, all of them with somewhere to be. A few took to benches set up at each platform, skimming a newspaper or puffing on cigars. Others hurried through the station, clutching their belongings as their eyes skimmed up to the giant clock that lorded over them.

An older gentleman with a proud chest escorted a grinning woman who couldn't stop staring down at the ring on her finger. Pulled in by a habit from too many days spent alone, Signa filled out their story in her head, imagining that they were newly married and off to start their honeymoon. She envisioned all the beautiful gowns that were packed away in the woman's travel chest, made from the lightest fabrics so that she would feel the salty air upon her skin as she and her beloved traveled seaside. Desire curled within Signa, so fervent that she forced herself to turn away from the couple. What might it be like to be a woman like that? To be swept away across the country by a handsome man she couldn't stop grinning at, silly with happiness?

Beside her, Sylas murmured something under his breath. Signa nodded and pretended to listen, lost in her daydream and a sea of more people than she'd ever seen. She barely managed to weave around them all as she and Sylas made their way through the station, led by a helpful young attendant who'd taken one look at her ticket and offered to carry her chest. It was solid and heavy, yet Sylas didn't offer the boy his help. In fact, he kept stone-faced and silent, as if making a point of not looking at the attendant.

"You'll have the compartment to yourself, miss." The attendant's voice was breathy from his struggle with the weight of the luggage. "The finest one on the train."

Signa had never wandered through a place so busy, and where everything around her felt grand and vast. Where it felt like she'd be lost forever should she make one wrong turn. Though Sylas perpetually looked like someone who'd swallowed a sour tart, she was glad to have him there with her in the event that she got lost. "Have you traveled often?" she asked.

The response came from the attendant beside her. "Not often, miss. I'd love to, if I could manage it between work, but they keep me busy."

Signa turned to glance at the spot where she'd last seen Sylas, only to discover his absence. Sucking in a breath, she scanned the crowd until she saw him—there, straight ahead, stepping onto the train.

A moment of panic struck, and she spun to the attendant, scooping her hands beneath the travel chest he carried. "Here, give me that," she said. "I'll take it the rest of the way."

The attendant flinched but tightened his grip. "It's really no bother, miss. This is far too heavy for a lady—"

Fearing there was little time to argue, she pried the chest from his arms. It was, indeed, extraordinarily heavy, made from pure mahogany and fastened with iron locks. It certainly wasn't intended to be carried by a woman in heels and mourning wear, but she'd manage. The tightening of her lungs—the worry of being separated from the sole person who knew where she was headed and could help her if she got lost—was far worse than the extra weight.

"Thank you so much for your time. I can manage from here" was all Signa said to the attendant before hurrying after Sylas, attempting to take long steps despite her swaying back and shaking arms. Several people offered to help, but already the conductor was calling out for final boarding, and Signa could focus only on getting herself and her belongings where they needed to be and not getting separated from the devil that was Sylas Thorly. By the time she made it to the train, her skin shone with sweat and her breaths were so heavy that no one looked her in the eye.

Even burdened by the weight of her belongings, Signa had to take a moment to admire the beauty of the train. It was finer than she'd expected, with black-iron handrails and sturdy wooden tables that had red-leather benches on either side. Her ticket indicated a private room where Sylas waited, lounging upon a plush velvet seat with his boots kicked up onto the matching maroon seat across from him. He took one glance at Signa and wrinkled his nose.

"My God. I had no idea a woman could sweat so profusely."

If Signa truly were a witch, she might have boiled Sylas alive. "I wouldn't be sweating if you hadn't decided to run ahead without me, *sir*."

At this, Sylas scoffed. A foul, repulsive sound. "I should have known you weren't listening to me. Had you not allowed yourself to fall prey to distraction, you'd have heard me say that I was going ahead to ensure that our compartment was in order."

Signa bit her tongue. Now that he had reminded her, yes, she *did* recall that Sylas might have said something, and that yes, she *had* nodded. Still, he should have been louder.

Choosing not to respond, Signa set about storing her luggage in the overhead bin. Heavy as the chest was, her arms trembled as she tried to lift it above her head. She was grateful for an excuse to keep her back to Sylas, but she couldn't quite manage the maneuver. Her muscles seared, and after several solid minutes of pushing through and ignoring the aching, they eventually gave out on her entirely.

Signa stumbled back, momentarily convinced she would soon be paying Death another visit after being crushed by the travel chest. But before she could fall, Sylas was on his feet, bracing her from behind. From head to toe, Signa flushed as his chest pressed against her back. She'd never been so close to a man.

Sylas didn't appear to share her surprise. While she was still focused on the firmness of his chest, he stepped to the side and took the luggage from her, placing it in the overhead bin. "Why would you choose to carry something so heavy?" he asked. "Had I not been here, that chest might have fallen upon your face. What would you have done then?"

"I suppose I would have been faceless," she answered, indignant. "And again, I wouldn't have needed to carry it if I hadn't had to race to keep up with you. I feared you'd left me."

Sylas threw himself into his seat with a snort, legs insufferably outstretched. "You should have told me you walk so slowly. I might have thought to carry you, had I known."

She took her seat across from him, wondering if his unbearable personality was some sort of test for her patience. Holding her knees together so that they wouldn't bump his, she flashed a razor-thin smile at her escort and asked, "Would you mind sitting a bit straighter, Mr. Thorly?"

Sylas peered down at himself. "Am I sitting oddly?"

Good God, she would need strength to deal with this man. With the toe of her gray boot, Signa tapped one of his knees, then the other—they were too far apart. "You're sitting like you're the only one in this compartment."

His blink was slow, and though Signa knew he understood, he didn't right himself or apologize. Sylas only laughed and shut his eyes, as if he intended to take a nap. "You're certainly forward."

She'd tried her hardest to have good manners, but there was something exasperating about this man. Something about his aloofness and constant staring—as though he'd already decided Signa was a nuisance—caused those manners to waver and harsh words to slip out. Signa could barely stop herself as she took hold of her dress and hiked it up to her knees, freeing enough room for them to spread apart like Sylas's. "It would seem my manners are as impeccable as yours. I expected someone in your position to be more polite."

"And what position might that be, Miss Farrow?"

"The position of escorting a lady."

"A lady?" He cracked open his eyes, assessing her unseemly posture and the hiked-up dress before shutting them again. "Let me know when we find one, and I'll happily escort her."

Ignore him, she told herself, forcing her lips into a smile that could burn. *You are to be a lady. Poised and graceful and demure.* She folded her hands together and patted her dress back into place.

Feigning calmness, Signa inspected their compartment. Beside Sylas was a trolley stuffed full of sugary treats and baked goods. There was sweet sea salt toffee, boxed sticky buns that dripped with thick syrup and golden walnuts, tiny pastries that oozed plum jelly, and so much more. She was so busy feeding her eyes that she nearly jumped when Sylas whispered, "Could I interest you in a handkerchief, Miss Farrow? I believe there's some drool on your lip."

She did everything in her power not to cast him a loathing stare, then inquired, "Are these for us?"

He looked to the trolley, but no light shone in his eyes. There was no delight upon his lips, nor a hunger roaring from his stomach. "They must have come with the compartment" was all he said. Flat. Factual. As though there wasn't a feast of sweets before them. Signa found herself wondering if perhaps this man was inhuman.

A Lady's Guide to Beauty and Etiquette claimed that there were important rules when it came to dining in front of others. There were certain forks to be used and a particular order of eating things. Yet Signa longed for the treats so fiercely that her stomach protested her resistance. Loudly.

She froze, waiting in horror to ensure that Sylas hadn't heard. Luck, however, was too infrequently on her side.

Sylas arched one fine brow as he leaned forward and took hold of Signa's hand. Though both her hands were gloved, Signa stiffened when Sylas slid a handkerchief into her palm.

His voice was coy when he spoke. "You look as though you're in pain."

She wrapped her fingers tight around the handkerchief, thinking through a million things she'd like to say, not one of them proper or polite. Instead, she said, "I had a large breakfast. It would be rude for me to indulge."

Sylas's smile was a scythe. A surprising thing, curt and cleaving. There one moment and gone the next. "It would be offensive to waste so much food, Miss Farrow. Especially when it was bought for you. Show some respect to Mr. Hawthorne and eat."

Perhaps Sylas wasn't the absolute worst after all. Signa didn't need to be told twice to pull the trolley toward her. She reached immediately for a tart with bright yellow custard and glazed strawberries, the top sprinkled with powdered sugar. Because there was no cutlery or plates, she slipped off her gloves and tucked them at her side, eating with her fingers.

"Will you be rude to Mr. Hawthorne, then?" she challenged Sylas between bites, doing everything in her power not to groan from the tart's deliciousness. It'd been ages since Signa had eaten something so overwhelmingly sweet. She polished it off within a minute, moving right on to a sticky bun.

Sylas blinked at the sweets, as though the idea to eat one had never occurred to him. He peered at the cart, scanning over each item before selecting a tiny tea cake drizzled with orange marmalade. As he ate, his posture became less severe and his furrowed forehead less grim. The moment he finished his tea cake, he glanced back at the cart for another.

"Tell me more about your work with the Hawthornes," Signa said while he chose a small fruit tart. It seemed like a simple enough subject, nothing too personal or too taxing. Even so, Sylas hesitated before answering.

"I used to work closely with his wife, but I'd be surprised if Elijah even knows I exist."

"He sent you to escort me," Signa pressed as she tried not to lick her fingers. "Surely, he knows who you are."

Sylas took perhaps the largest bite Signa had ever seen anyone take, then said, "I was sent by one of the staff. Mr. Hawthorne's daughter is dying of the same illness that took his wife—he's not in the right state of mind to know anyone's name right now."

She was glad for the excuse of toffee in her mouth as she pondered what her future would be like at Thorn Grove. Perhaps this journey was little more than a cruel trick; perhaps she'd arrive only to find Death had already staked his claim upon everyone there. Maybe this was his next move in an elaborate game of chess, and she was stuck playing a pawn. Or . . . maybe he really was trying to prove himself to her.

"It's my turn to ask a question," Sylas said. "Do you know what you're getting into by coming to Thorn Grove?"

She knew so little about the place, and though his question was unnerving, it didn't change her answer. "It doesn't matter. I've nowhere else to go."

Sylas faced the window next to him, where distant paved streets gave way to a glistening ocean. It made her wonder: Would there be an ocean close to Thorn Grove? Or perhaps there'd be a forest, or nothing but sprawling, rolling hills.

"Your arrival is what Lillian would have wanted," Sylas said eventually. "She wasn't someone who could refuse an orphan."

Orphan. Signa hated the word—hated how it was something

that, to most people, defined her and her situation so thoroughly. "What about the estate itself?" she asked, hurrying to change the subject. "Has it been there long?"

"Thorn Grove is a beautiful place. I'm told it's been passed down for many generations."

Signa tried not to grimace as she polished off a tart. Places that old were likely crawling with the very spirits she was trying to avoid. "And Mr. Hawthorne is a businessman?" she asked rather than let her thoughts linger. "Does he work in banking?"

She was surprised when the corners of Sylas's lips quirked. "Not banking, no. The Hawthornes own the most popular gentleman's club in the country. Its members are dukes and earls. Princes even, so I've heard. The wealthiest and most affluent people only. It keeps him a busy man."

At this, Signa scrunched up her nose. The idea of a club for only wealthy gentlemen seemed ridiculous. "Do they have a club for women as well?"

Lines of confusion etched into Sylas's forehead. "For women? Of course not."

"What about one for all people, then?"

Even more lines. "There's not one of those, either."

"That's a shame." Signa rested her head against the window. "Were they more inclusive, the Hawthornes could be twice as wealthy." Her words came easier, for it was comfortable in this compartment, even with Sylas. He was rude, certainly, but not cruel. And over the past hour, his brooding had undergone significant improvement. "Is that your business, too, Mr. Thorly? The club?"

His eyes shifted to the trolley cart, skimming over the remaining items. "No. I used to work in the garden, but it was closed after Mrs. Hawthorne's death. Since then, I've been tending to the horses."

Signa looked to Sylas's boots—too fine a leather and not nearly so worn as she would expect of someone who spent his time in a stable. The leather of his gloves appeared new, too, as did his coat, with its polished silver buttons and tiny ruby cuff links. It didn't seem as though he'd have any reason to lie, and yet Signa found it difficult to believe that Mr. Hawthorne would send a stable boy to retrieve her. For now, she made no comment, deciding it was better not to sour the mood.

"Why would they close the garden?" Signa plucked another toffee from the trolley and leaned back against the velvet seat cushion. Though excitement burned in her blood, the sugar was making her tired, and her eyes would drift shut anytime she looked out at the ocean.

"Because that's where Missus Hawthorne would often spend her days. She's buried there, beneath the flowers." There was something calming about the evenness of his voice. No surprising inflections. No emotion seeping through. Just a steady lull that she found herself relaxing into.

"Was her death a pleasant one?" The question hung oddly upon her lips, and she wished at once that she could take it back. *Pleasant* was a word few would associate with death. But Sylas, fortunately, understood what she was asking.

"I presume you've seen a flower wilt, Miss Farrow? That's what watching Lillian was like. She was like a beautiful flower, cherished by everyone who knew her. Even the illness loved her so greatly that it gave her little reprieve. It wanted her to itself, and so it stole her life suddenly."

"And what was that illness?"

His brows lowered. "It was such a mystery that the doctors could never give it a name. One day Lillian was fine, healthy, and the next she was vomiting blood. A few days later she lost her ability to speak. Her mouth had festered with the disease, and eventually she lost her tongue to it."

Signa turned to the window again, though she could see Sylas fidgeting from the corners of her eyes. "I'm sorry if I've offended you." His words sounded genuine. "Such conversations are not suitable. My apologies."

He couldn't see that Signa's hands were fisted tight, buried in the folds of her dress. "I take no offense, sir," she said. "It's just that I sometimes find myself wondering why death is so needlessly cruel."

Something twisted in the lines of his forehead. "I think, for someone in as much pain as she was in, death might have felt like a reprieve."

Signa tried to find some truth in the words. But all she could see was the blood on Aunt Magda's lips and the hollowness of her eyes as she fell. All she could think of was how her aunt's hatred had kept her from journeying to the afterlife and had tethered her to Earth for who knew how long. "Perhaps," she said, voice barely a whisper, "but I don't believe that makes death any less cruel."

"And why do you say that?"

She folded her hands upon her lap, trying not to let the bitterness creep into her voice. "Because death is only a reprieve for the dead, Mr. Thorly. It cares little for those it leaves behind."

FIVE

THERE WAS SOMETHING STRANGE ABOUT THE MAPLE LEAVES. THOSE
that lay scattered across the lawn of Thorn Grove were deeper in
color than any Signa had seen before—some of them rich as coffee,
others the burnished red of dried blood.

The pitted roads their second carriage had traveled upon since
arriving by train morphed into manicured cobblestone, so white
and pristine it looked as though someone had dropped to their knees
and scrubbed each stone. Tall, manicured hedges lined the endless
stretch of road that led to the estate, some of them twisted into elegant spirals or trimmed into the shapes of horses or swans.

The exterior of Thorn Grove was grand—a massive brownstone
manor like the kind she imagined her parents had once owned, sit-
uated upon rolling hills that were fading to yellow to welcome the
shift into autumn. There were windows at least three times her size,
pointed red rooftops protected by sculpted winged beasts, and finely

lacquered carriages pulled by muscular horses that trotted through an iron gate strung with jasmine and ivy.

Dozens of people meandered across the lawn. Gentlemen and ladies in their finest suits and most eye-catching bustles filtered in and out of the manor with flutes of champagne balanced gingerly between fingers and laughter upon their tongues.

It was certainly a far cry from Aunt Magda's; there was wealth everywhere Signa looked. Dignified pillars surrounded the courtyard, inlaid with whorls of gold. On the second floor of the manor, delicate stained-glass windows of a million colors shone over a balcony. Even the soil itself looked rich, and the grass somehow wilder and more vibrant than what lay beyond the gates. There were no weeds to be seen, and tiny orange and yellow wildflowers bloomed across the hills, stretching toward a thick grove of trees in the distance—the start of the woods.

No place had ever stolen her breath so thoroughly; Signa found herself pressed against the carriage window, fogging the glass as the landscape unfolded before her. She felt like a minnow in a springtime pond, small and insignificant among such beauty.

As the carriage rolled to a stop, it took everything in her power to remember her manners and not throw the door open so that she might hurry and explore, but instead wait for the coachman to clamber down and open the door for her. When he did, the brisk autumn air grasped Signa around the shoulders, carrying the scent of sap and earth and twirling leaves underfoot. It wisped through her dark tresses, and she breathed in its greeting as she made her way up the path toward the magnificent estate.

Waiting upon the massive porch, three people watched Signa at a distance—a portly older man, a gentle-looking woman, and a young man with the most severe expression she'd ever seen. The younger man stood upon the threshold of Thorn Grove in a fine navy suit that fit him like a glove, his shoulders squared as he observed the guests filtering in. He was far too young to be Signa's guardian, yet the pride in his frame spoke of his comfort at the manor.

It'd do her no good to simply stand there, yet Signa waited a beat longer, wishing at once that she had a mirror. Even a large body of water or a polished stone would do—anything she could see her reflection in—so that she might ensure she looked presentable. She fussed with her mourning dress, smoothing out the bombazine to make it more presentable. "That couldn't be Mr. Hawthorne, could it? Oh, he looks so young. Tell me quickly, am I presentable?" She looked to Sylas, whose smoky-gray eyes skimmed over her just once. At the worry in her voice, he softened a little.

"That isn't Elijah," he said. "And you look fine, Miss Farrow. Given how far we've traveled, I'm certain they wouldn't mind if you arrived haggard."

She wondered whether that was meant to reassure her. "If you could introduce me, Mr. Thorly, it'd be much appreciated."

But Sylas drew back with a dip of his head. "Believe me when I say it would be better if I didn't. Mr. Hawthorne didn't give the staff much notice of your arrival, and not everyone will take kindly to someone of my status being sent to escort a lady such as yourself. You'll have to handle introductions on your own, I'm afraid."

There wasn't time to press for further details, as Sylas was already escaping down the hill behind her and toward the stables.

Left standing alone among fallen maple leaves with panic in her chest, Signa swallowed and tried to quell her fretting by recalling the introductory lessons in her mother's etiquette book.

1. *A woman should always wear a smile.*
2. *A woman should never shake the hand offered to her but accept it with cordial pressure.*
3. *For a woman, meekness and modesty are considered two of the most respected virtues. They're to be practiced at all times.*

Signa had trouble believing the third rule was one anyone should adhere to. Though, for the sake of her future, she'd try. Skirts in hand, Signa started up the path to the manor. Curious eyes and pointed whispers followed her, and step by step, Signa found herself wishing only for a deep enough hole in which she might hide.

It was impolite to be seen dressed in mourning wear at a soiree, yet what choice did she have? It seemed a poor day for her new guardian to hold such an event, though she was in no position to comment.

When she approached the young man at the door, Signa could see from his smooth face and intense eyes that he was even younger than she'd assumed, in his early twenties. Up close, he reminded Signa of a fox, with bright green eyes that were friendly but a little too squint as they peered down at her. The sun had leeched away color from his hair. It wasn't red, nor was it blond, but somewhere odd and in between. A rich harvest orange, brassy and bright. There was a hitch in his jaw as he looked her over, clearly attempting to level his disapproval.

"Miss Farrow?" asked the older man beside him. He was stout and of an olive complexion, dressed in a fine black suit. Though a smile lingered beneath his full black mustache, his eyes were dark and tired things. "Welcome. I'm Charles Warwick, the butler of Thorn Grove."

"It's a wonder you've arrived," said the younger one, his chin dipping as he inspected her. "Father told us of you just this morning. Welcome, cousin. I'm Percy Hawthorne."

Signa extended a hand, and when her cousin accepted it after a beat of hesitation, she squeezed with her best effort at cordial pressure. Percy's lips pressed into a thin line as he drew his hand back, tucking it behind him. Perhaps that was too much pressure, then. Or maybe not cordial enough? Or was this a situation that warranted a curtsy and no handshake at all? *A Lady's Guide to Beauty and Etiquette* really ought to have been more specific.

"We're glad to have you staying with us, Miss Farrow." Signa was relieved to turn her attention to a curvy woman who had soft strawberry-blond curls and was wearing a dress the color of blue forget-me-nots. "Do you not have an escort?" The woman glanced behind Signa, as if expecting someone else to appear. When no one did, she took Signa by the shoulder. "Never mind that. I'm Marjorie Hargreaves, governess to the master's daughter, and now to you as well. Your room is already in order." Her voice was soft as a song. "Should you need anything, I'd be happy to—" She jumped as glass shattered somewhere near the estate's entrance, followed by laughter that sounded . . . inebriated, to put it kindly.

Percy's eyes flashed, though that lasted for only a moment before he rectified himself. "Warwick will see to it that your belongings are moved in promptly. You should have no trouble settling in."

Marjorie motioned for her to follow them into Thorn Grove, and once inside, Signa knew that her cousin was right. The estate was grander than anything she could have imagined; they could have put her in a stall with the horses, and she would have been just fine. Anything was better than living at Aunt Magda's, but Thorn Grove was on a level of its own. Still, there certainly were a lot of people.

"Is Mr. Hawthorne celebrating something?" she asked, hoping for an indication that this was a rare occurrence. Percy scowled, and though he opened his mouth to respond, Warwick cut in with a swift, "It's nothing to pay any mind to right now. If you're wanting to attend, then worry not. There will be plenty of soirees for you to join in the future when you're properly dressed and prepared."

Signa brushed a clammy hand over her gown. "Come," Marjorie said with a kind smile. "You must be tired after your travels." She jumped at the sound of another crash, followed by even rowdier laughter in the ballroom ahead, but she never once looked away from Signa.

Percy's focus, however, was divided. "I look forward to getting to know you better, cousin. Welcome to Thorn Grove." Hat in his hands, he bowed to her before turning on his heel and heading off toward the sound of the breaking glass, Warwick following behind. And though Signa's curious mind lingered, Marjorie allowed no time for her thoughts to fester.

"Come," Marjorie said again. "I'll show you to your suite."

Marjorie escorted Signa up one of the two grand mahogany staircases that led to the second level of the massive three-story estate. The governess made polite small talk but kept peering down, craning her neck to sneak glances at the party below. So distracted was Marjorie that she hadn't noticed the man who leaned upon a banister that had been sculpted to look like the branches of a gnarled tree and twisted up the entirety of the two staircases.

Signa noticed him, though. Noticed he had hair black as pitch, a long, pointed nose, and sinister eyes that cared only for Marjorie. When the stranger leaned forward to snatch hold of her hand, Marjorie practically leaped from her own skin.

"How are you such a difficult woman to find, Miss Hargreaves?" His voice was low and unpleasant, as if he were speaking around something lodged deep in his throat. The man wore shoes of the finest leather Signa had ever seen, and his rich black suit appeared to have been custom made, with buttons of melted silver. In his hands was a walking stick he grasped tightly—a stunning piece of rosewood, with a brass handle that was carved into the shape of a bird's skull. "I've been looking for you everywhere."

"Lay a hand on me again and I will push you over this banister, Byron." Marjorie ripped her hand away, placing it instead upon Signa's back with some force. "Come, Signa. Pay these guests little mind. They're forbidden on the upper levels."

"I am no guest, Miss Hargreaves—" the man tried again, but

Marjorie didn't spare him so much as a second as they hurried up the stairs, much to Signa's disappointment. She rather disliked puzzles, for she had a bad tendency to need to solve them. Life, she believed, would be much simpler if one had the answers all laid bare before them.

It'd been only an hour since she'd arrived, and already Thorn Grove was filled with curiosities. It was odd that Mr. Hawthorne would hold a soiree the same day as her arrival, let alone that he'd sent a stable boy as her escort and kept her coming a secret until the last moment. And what were they celebrating downstairs at such an early hour, with the echo of laughter and shattering glassware? Signa wanted to ask, but the tension pulsating in Marjorie's neck warned this wasn't the time. Signa was a beggar, not a chooser, and she needed to play what few cards she had carefully.

Her skin itched, and she wondered if this was all some sort of trap. Some clever ruse of Death's. Had he known Elijah would invite her to stay? Had Death been the one to pull the strings, and if so, how?

It took what felt like ages of walking through long stretches of dimly lit halls before they arrived to Signa's new room, a space nearly the size of Aunt Magda's entire house, with a sitting room, bedroom, and her own bath all attached in one suite. In the sitting room, the wallpaper was beautifully latticed in varying shades of green, with velvet gold curtains draped across glass doors that opened onto a balcony.

Rich mahogany floors were covered with an oversize Persian rug decorated in emerald and gold, and Signa wanted nothing more than to curl her toes into it. The ceiling itself was a brilliant white, with thick molding embellished with expertly carved vines and flora. It matched the fireplace, where yellow peonies blossomed from thin glass vases upon the mantel. Plush reading chairs were meticulously placed around it, while a dainty wooden drawing table sat behind, close to the window. Light shone upon it like a halo from the gap in the curtains, warm and inviting.

Signa's heart squeezed as she took it all in. This was the most beautiful space she'd ever seen, and somehow it was *hers*. "Will I be able to meet Mr. Hawthorne this evening?" she asked. "I'd like to thank him for allowing me to stay here."

"The master is a busy man," Marjorie said as she helped a distracted Signa out of her coat. The woman moved to put it in the armoire, but upon seeing the stain of belladonna berries upon a more thorough inspection, she scrunched up her nose and draped the coat over her arm for laundering. "But I will speak to him of his plans for you, and I assure you that you'll be well taken care of. You'll be fitted for new dresses in the morning, after your lessons."

Signa's hair whipped into her face as she spun to face Marjorie. There was no filtering the excitement from her voice. "My lessons?"

Marjorie's laugh was smooth as silk. "You're a young woman, Miss Farrow, and I am the governess of this estate. I'm not certain what your education was like before, but while you're here, it's only fitting I help prepare you for marriage, and for one day managing a home of your own. I assume you've not yet made your debut?"

"You assume correctly." Again, there was that hopeful edge. The thrill of being presented with exactly what she'd yearned for: To debut into society. To attend parties and be courted by handsome suitors, and then to gossip about them with friends over tea. The idea of it alone threatened to burst her heart. It was all there within her grasp.

"Then I've plenty to teach you, and very little time to do it." Marjorie set her free hand on her hip, still smiling. "Shall we start tomorrow?"

Weary as she was, Signa would get started now, should Marjorie allow it. A fluttering in her heart made her impatient and wanting. But there were six more months until she would receive her inheritance, and if she was to last at this estate—if she was to have the freedom of the life she wanted—then she needed to ensure that Death couldn't get his hands on anyone at Thorn Grove. Not to mention she'd have to watch her own hands, too.

Though she knew they would not hurt anyone right now, she tucked her hands behind her back all the same and smiled. "Tomorrow is perfect."

"Wonderful." Marjorie readjusted the coat in her arm. "You may take the rest of the evening to settle in, then. You're welcome to explore any of the upper floors, but I ask that you keep off the first level while the guests are here. Tonight, dinner will be brought to you, so please relax. I'm sure you're exhausted."

She was. But as Marjorie saw herself out, letting the door shut quietly behind her, Signa knew there would be little relaxing. The moment the woman's footsteps disappeared down the hall, Signa cracked the door open again.

Marjorie *had* suggested she explore after all.

SIX

S IGNA WAS NO STRANGER TO FINDING WAYS TO PASS THE TIME. LEFT
with little to do during her days and few to converse with, she'd
spent many afternoons stealing glances out the windows or wandering outside, curious to know more about the neighbors of whatever
house she lived in. Some were more interesting than others, sneaking in strange company when their partner was away, or sharing
the latest gossip over tea with a friend, which Signa would casually
overhear as she just so happened to be taking a walk near an open
window. She never spent any time with such people and could do
little with the information she gleaned. But for Signa, the point was
always to fill in the gaps in their stories. She was intent on solving
the puzzles she'd formed in her head, and mentally crafting stories
for people she'd never be close to.

Thorn Grove was already a puzzle, and far too much of one for
her not to investigate. Signa counted down from sixty before she
crept along the dim halls, sticking close to the walls and relying on

their shadows to conceal her as she tiptoed toward the staircase. Technically, she'd be breaking no rules so long as she remained on the landing.

Signa crouched and peered down the banister—through the crafted branches that adorned it—and into the party below. From this angle, she could see only glimpses of what was happening, and she had to strain to hear voices over the swell of a piano and violin. The details of the gathering came to her in pieces—in bright lights and flashes of golden walls and silver serving trays. Crystal flutes filled with bubbling champagne, and miniature gilded cakes that were offered to women in beautiful gowns and men in their proper tailcoats. Those who didn't eat either busied themselves by drinking or by dancing to the music that swept through the ballroom. Their dancing, however, was not at all what she expected.

Signa's grandmother had often relayed stories of her daughter's fondness for parties. It was at a ball where Rima met Signa's father, and her grandmother had always promised that Signa would have the same fortuitous fate. They never discussed how it was Rima's love for parties that ultimately stole her life, focusing instead on romanticizing her time alive. For years Signa had listened to stories of her mother, told to her with great softness as her grandmother brushed through her hair or tucked her into bed, as though speaking the stories aloud would keep them alive. Signa had loved hearing the stories and imagining that she would soon follow in Rima's footsteps. But her young life had not gone as she'd hoped, and those stories now filled her with a deep envy for the women adorned in silks and lace, with their delicate curls and rouge on their cheeks. They made her wonder where her beautiful stranger was, the man who would sweep her away into a waltz (which she'd of course be perfect at, despite never having danced outside her bedroom).

But if the etiquette book Rima left behind was any indication of what a party should have been like, the one happening at Thorn Grove was all wrong. Parties were meant to have dance cards. Varying music for each different dance, with a myriad of rules for every one of them. No woman was to drink more than a single flute of champagne, laugh so boisterously, or dance so freely. Yet at Thorn Grove, no one paid etiquette any mind.

Flushed were the women who stumbled from the ballroom for fresh air, hiccupping as they fanned themselves. They used those fans to swat away the eager hands of those who tried to pull them in for a dance, and instead hunted down the lavish cakes with rosy frosting and golden glitter. No one seemed to pay any mind to the two women who were tucked away in the far corner, their bodies pressed so close that blood rushed to Signa's cheeks; she'd never seen two people embracing so thoroughly.

Either her etiquette book was more outdated than she thought, or this was far from polite society.

It took Signa a moment to notice that there was a familiar face in the crowd—Percy, standing outside the ballroom with his hand fisted around a champagne flute as cheers erupted from inside. With everyone distracted, Signa lowered herself down the first step for a better vantage. She could barely make out a man standing upon the highest point of a chairback, making a show of balancing himself as the chair tipped. The man clapped, demanding everyone's attention.

He seemed to be enjoying himself, just as the guests of the party appeared to be enjoying his show.

Percy, however, was glowering. So was the long-nosed older man beside him, the one who had grabbed Marjorie's hand earlier. Byron. "Someone needs to put a stop to this," Percy demanded. His expression was so severe that Signa thought to slink back into the safety of her room, knowing she shouldn't get involved. But still no one had noticed her, and curiosity kept her grounded, pressing closer to the shadows to observe.

"It will be worse if either of us makes a spectacle," said the man, his lips thinning as Percy stepped out of his reach.

"How many months must we stand by and watch? How long must we allow him to play at this fantasy? My father is no child, and this house is no circus! It's been half a year, Uncle." Percy's fist was balled so tightly that if he hadn't slammed his crystal flute to the floor at that moment, it might have shattered in his hand. The dark-haired man sighed and drew back several paces while Percy surged forward, demanding the attention of every eye that turned curiously toward him, including that of the man on the chair—who, Signa now understood, was Elijah Hawthorne.

He was rosy cheeked and glossy eyed, with a tall, willowy frame and a head of blond waves. There was a grandness to him, an air of exuberance that said he was someone who could crack the world open with his smile. Someone who kept company with earls and princes, and somehow seemed even grander than them.

"Given how much time they've been spending in our home, I thought it only polite to say some words to your guests, Father."

Percy's smile was thin as he glanced past Elijah to a roomful of guests who looked entirely disinterested in having to observe anything so serious. "I wanted to take a moment to thank you all for coming for this continued celebration of my dead mother."

Elijah stepped down from the chair as the music quieted, eyes tight on his son, who did not falter amid surprised gasps.

"Seeing as my mother could not eat, dance, be merry, or so much as breathe in her final days, I'm sure she would have appreciated how you all do so endlessly." Percy squared his shoulders. "And thank you to my father, for continuing to throw these soirees in her honor, so that we may continue to celebrate her death together." He raised his champagne flute for the toast.

No one dared to move, waiting for the lord of Thorn Grove to speak. To punish his son for his outburst, or somehow mend this disgraceful situation. But instead, Elijah found a platter with a miniature cake upon it and took the plate in his hands. Removing one of his gloves, he plucked the dessert up with his fingers, taking a bite as he approached his son. So quickly that anyone who blinked would have missed it, Elijah shoved the rest of it into Percy's mouth.

"Come, Percy." Elijah laughed. "You're too uptight. Would it be so bad to relax for a single night?"

A crowd Signa could not see gasped as Percy stumbled, spitting the cake out and wiping pink frosting from his lips with a snarl. She couldn't hear what Percy said to his father; could see only that his mouth moved to spit the words before he shoved away from Elijah.

Laughter rose as Percy reeled back and Elijah stretched his hand out for another flute of champagne. "Now," he said as he stepped back onto the chair—the music swelling again, as though it had never missed a beat—"where were we?"

Percy stormed out of the room, bolting toward the stairs even as Byron reached for him. He was so quick that Signa hardly had time to stand, unable to retreat to the shadows before he noticed her. Percy's bitter eyes landed upon Signa's.

"Nice to see you again, cousin." He spoke through clenched teeth, trying to still his shaking fists as he looked over the black dress Signa had yet to change out of. "Come to enjoy the party?"

"I'm sorry. I've never seen a ball before, and I . . . I thought . . . I just wanted to see what it was like." Signa didn't have the heart to tell him that frosting smudged his chin. She barely had a voice at all; it felt as though anything above a whisper might break him.

Percy didn't share the same issue. His voice was a loaded pistol, ready to strike anyone in its path. "Well, now you know. My mother died months ago, and he's been throwing these ridiculous parties ever since. They last for days, sometimes. Or hours if he gets into one of his moods and has everyone escorted out. I'd wonder why people keep bothering to show up, if not for the fact that these social-climbing deviants have nothing better to do with their time."

Signa couldn't tell if talking was helping him blow off steam or was building up even more of it. Either way, she didn't think it fit to stop him. "I'm sorry—" she began, cut off as he held up a hand.

"It's no matter, cousin." Wiping the frosting from his chin, he pushed past her and up the stairs. "Think of it as your welcome to Thorn Grove."

SEVEN

IT WAS A RELIEF THAT PERCY HADN'T LINGERED. CLUELESS AS TO how to console him, Signa had only watched as he climbed the stairs, muttering that he needed to clear his head. Having decided it best not to loiter—lest she be caught snooping by anyone else—Signa left her hiding place in the shadows. She had every intention of returning to her room to try to clear her own head of the bizarre situation she'd witnessed. Only, the moment she stepped upon the landing, a wash of glowing white flashed in the corners of her eyes.

It was with dread in her chest that she turned, blinking clarity into her vision. When she looked again, nothing was there.

Perhaps she was more exhausted than she'd realized. It had been a long journey after all.

At least, that's what she told herself as she paced the halls, struggling to find her room in what seemed to be an endless maze of hallways. Thorn Grove was eerier than she'd anticipated. She rubbed her arms, forcing her feet ahead one step at a time.

Though the manor was bustling on the lower level, the deeper into the second story Signa ventured, the emptier and gloomier the estate became. There was no sight of gilded cakes, and nothing more than the faint hum of a distant violin. Gone were the white marble pillars that had ghosted her reflection as she passed. In their place were strange iron sconces that reminded Signa of bird's nests. Like the branches along the banister, they were intricately designed, with several thick twig-like pieces of iron stretching from them and a dimly lit candle towering in the center of each.

She looked behind her, and again a wash of white flickered just out of her view. This time, Signa could have sworn she saw a face.

She turned away at once, holding her breath. If it *was* a spirit, hopefully it hadn't realized she'd noticed it. Continuing forward, she was determined to ignore it and to find her room again. It was difficult, though, to ignore the cool buzz on her skin as she journeyed past endless walls of paintings that were twice her size, each of them adorned with a gilded frame and featuring a person who must have once lived at Thorn Grove. The sheer number of them was less than reassuring; this estate was surely crawling with spirits.

She came to a painting of a well-decorated man with hair nearly as orange as Percy's. He had a rifle slung over one shoulder, while his other hand rested upon the back of a whippet. The painting hung next to a large room with two leather couches the color of burnt molasses and shelves stuffed with musty books that took up the entire left wall.

Signa crossed the thick red rug to the shelves and scooped up one of the volumes, disappointed to find it was nothing more than a book about finances. She couldn't remember the last time she'd been surrounded by books—when she lived with her last uncle, perhaps?—and grumpily shoved the book back onto the shelf.

Next, she examined a large rosewood desk scattered with jars of ink and sheets of parchment. There were newspaper clippings, too. Some about Grey's Gentleman's Club, and an obituary for Lillian Rose Hawthorne. She picked it up, though the moment she touched the parchment, moss sprouted from the paper and curled around her fingertips. She'd never dropped something so fast.

Clutching her hand to her chest, Signa silently cursed herself for being so foolish. If the spirit hadn't already realized Signa could see it, it certainly knew now. She had to be more careful.

Deciding the room, with its desk and ledgers, must be where Elijah worked, Signa left the office without touching anything else. The moment she stepped into the hall, the buzzing, prickling sensation was back like a gnat on her skin, and as she passed the next portrait, she could have sworn its eyes trailed her every step. This feeling was one she was familiar with, and one she refused to have any part of, especially with the possibility of normalcy so close within her reach. Determined to grasp it, she hurried on. Yet no matter which way she turned, the halls stretched on. The farther into them she ventured, the more goose bumps flared across her skin. She spun around only to find that no one was behind her. No humans. No spirits. Not even the reaper himself.

It's in your head, she told herself. *You're just not used to such a large manor.*

Signa had seen many spirits in her lifetime—too many, in fact— and knew that being in their presence would make one tired, and cold in a way that not even fire could ease. It was the same cold that sank into her bones in that moment.

A cold that came from the next room, waiting for her.

The painting outside the door was of a woman with pale skin and hair like a sunburst. Her smile was warm and rich, though her eyes were what made it impossible for Signa to look away—one blue, one hazel. So similar to her own that Signa found herself sucking in a breath. She'd never seen someone with eyes like hers, had never even imagined such a thing.

Signa reached for the doorknob, but the moment her skin touched the brass, she heard the dreadful sound of wet coughing from a room behind her. She turned toward it, and at once the chill in her body shattered, the spell broken. Warmth seeped back into her skin, and yet she shivered. Who else, she wondered, would still be upstairs, like her, and not at the party below? Her curiosity stronger than the pull of the dead, Signa crossed to the door where the sound came from and pushed it open without a knock.

Aside from its coloring, the suite was a mirror image to her own—with a beautiful reading room in pale blues and silvers, cast in a golden glow from a fire that roared beneath the polished ivory mantle above the fireplace. The space was lovely, but perhaps a little cold. It hardly seemed lived in, either. There were no books at the reading table, nor any quills or parchment strewn across the desk.

She crossed the floor slowly, careful with her steps as she approached the adjoining bedroom. The door hung open, and try as she might to be quiet, whoever was inside heard her.

"Who's there?"

Signa hovered at the threshold between the rooms. There was a waifish girl in the bed, nearly a skeleton; her skin was so translucent, it seemed she'd never seen the sun in her life. The girl's hair was the pale yellow of dried straw, the color leeched away. Her eyes looked as though someone had carved the life out of them, hollowing them into empty, fathomless things. When the girl furrowed her brows, the full outline of her skull was visible.

"Who are you?" The girl frowned, her lips the palest shade of pink, like a winter-faded rose.

"You must be Elijah's daughter." Signa stepped inside the room and shut the door, glad for an excuse to leave behind the eerie hallway and the spirit that waited for her. "I heard you are ill." Though she hadn't quite realized the severity of the situation.

The girl's laugh was brittle. "I have a name. It's Blythe." She didn't seem to have the energy to lift herself from her pillows, though her glare never tired. "What are you doing in my room? Servants are forbidden from entering without permission."

"My apologies, but I'm no servant. I'm your cousin, Signa Farrow." She knew it wouldn't be hard to make up an excuse to slip away. Blythe looked like she needed very little push until she was knocking on Death's door, and Signa refused to play any part in it. Yet something about Blythe fastened Signa's feet to the floor. Perhaps it was because the last time Signa had spoken to a girl near her own age had been years prior, back when she knew Charlotte Killinger. Or perhaps it was the desperation in Blythe's eyes, and the fact that she seemed as starved for company as Signa. Whatever the reason, Signa remained.

"It's rather dreary in here," Signa said, pausing as she skimmed the shadows for any sign of Death. When she didn't spot him, she relaxed, satisfied. "Shall I open a window?"

"Do you think I cannot manage a window on my own?" Though she made no effort to kick Signa out, each of Blythe's words was clipped and deadly as poison. Signa suspected she could ask Blythe to sing a hymn, and the girl would somehow wield it like a weapon.

Signa had nothing to say to that. So much as a wrong breath would quite possibly get her head ripped off her neck and tossed out the window. Rather than answer, she took a seat on the edge of the four-poster bed. Her curiosity felt like the buzz one gets from coffee, making her fingertips twitch and fiddle at the hem of her dress. Signa looked her cousin over, assessing her. Pale skin, glum eyes, frail body . . . But Blythe didn't smell like death. She didn't smell like the spoiled sweetness of rot and disease. Her fingernails were cracked but not yellow or gray. And her giant blue eyes, despite their venom and the tired shadows that weighed them down, were clear of fog. "What are you sick with?" Signa asked.

"How bold you are," Blythe scoffed. "If we knew that, perhaps I wouldn't be stuck in this bed all day." She dropped her head onto a pillow and sighed. "God forbid they send in someone tolerable to keep me company."

Signa had the vague impression that Blythe knew no one had

sent her and just wanted to take a jab at her. She ignored it and looked toward the door, thinking of the painting of the woman with two-colored eyes like her own. "I never imagined a place this large could feel so empty, even when there are so many people visiting," Signa said absently. "Who else lives on this floor? I thought I heard someone in the room across from yours."

The air went so frigid that Signa found herself wishing she hadn't let Marjorie take her coat. Blythe's eyes were icicles, ready to impale.

"You couldn't have," she whispered. "It belongs to my mother. No one's been in there in ages."

Before Signa could think about what the words might mean to someone not as closely associated with Death as she was, she asked, "You mean *belonged*, right? Your mother was Lillian Hawthorne?"

Those words were enough to melt the ice from Blythe and drown her. She turned a ghostly shade of white; even her lips paled. Her mouth opened as if to speak, but surprise halted her words. It took Signa too long before she realized her crassness.

"Oh, Blythe, I didn't mean—" The apology was halfway out of her mouth when Blythe literally kicked her off the bed, grinding her heel into Signa's thigh.

"Get out!" she spat. "You wicked girl, get out of my room!"

Signa scrambled from the bed, cursing herself for her insensitivity. "I'm sorry!" She reached to set a hand upon Blythe's shoulder. "I didn't mean—" Again her words cut off, but this time it was with an abrupt intake of breath. The moment she set her hand upon Blythe, all she could see was Blythe, and all she could feel . . . Well, she didn't quite know how to describe it. It was unlike anything she'd ever experienced—an all-encompassing sort of feeling that tethered her there and made her breathing unsteady.

Whatever this feeling was, Blythe didn't appear to be sharing it.

"Get out of here," Blythe snarled. "You stupid girl, get out—" Her eyes went wide, and she doubled over without warning, chest rattling and body shaking as she was taken over by a violent fit of wet coughs. Blythe covered her mouth with the sheets, staining them a deep crimson. With each cough, the sheets grew darker.

The hairs along the back of Signa's neck stood on end as a flood of coolness swept into the room. She knew full well what that coolness brought—*who* that coolness brought—and anger flared inside her.

"Oh no you don't," Signa growled in warning. Perhaps she'd been a fool to come. Perhaps the whole thing really was a ruse to damn her further. Regardless, Signa didn't linger to confirm Death's arrival. Instead, she turned on her heel and ran as fast as her legs would carry her—down the hall, down the stairs, and to the first servant she could find. Down to whoever might have a chance at saving Blythe and halting Death.

All she needed was to last six months. *Six months*, and yet she couldn't last even a day without bringing Death into Thorn Grove.

EIGHT

FORTUNATELY, SIGNA FARROW KILLED NO ONE THAT NIGHT.

After hours of people floating in and out of Blythe's room, things were beginning to settle. Signa watched through the crack in her bedroom door, surprised to find that her room was just down the hall from Blythe's—either the spirits or her own paranoia must have been toying with her earlier to make her lose her way.

Now when Signa peered into the hall, only a handful of silhouettes lingered in the candlelight outside Blythe's door. She squinted to see if Death was among them, relieved to find him absent. There was, however, someone else there that Signa was increasingly curious to meet—Elijah Hawthorne. His back was turned to Signa, but she could see more of him than she'd been able to earlier. He was exceedingly tall and alarmingly thin, with blond hair brighter than anyone's. Brighter than even starlight, perhaps.

Signa drew a long step past her doorway to get a better look, and the moment her foot pressed down upon the floorboards, they creaked so loudly that Elijah and the servants fell silent and turned to find the source of the sound. Signa couldn't move. Could hardly even breathe as their eyes snapped to her. All it took was four long steps from Elijah, and she could finally see his face clearly.

It was a stern face. A tired one that was without so much as a hint of the exuberance she'd witnessed earlier. It was hard to believe this was even the same man.

"Who is this?" His voice was hard as he spoke to the servants, just a hint of a slur lingering at its edges. Then he turned to Signa. "Who are you?"

It was Marjorie who responded, emerging from behind Mr. Hawthorne and taking a firm hold of his shoulder. "This is Signa Farrow, your new ward." There was something familiar in the way Marjorie touched him. Something comfortable. Something, Signa noticed, that was entirely out of place between a governess and her employer.

"My ward?" Elijah braced his swaying body against a wall while Marjorie heaved a sigh. The look she cast Signa was purely apologetic.

"Yes, sir. Your ward. She arrived just this morning, with the letter you wrote her?"

"Ah, that ward." Pulling free from the wall, Elijah closed the rest of the space between himself and Signa, who stood as tall as she could, chest so tight she thought she might burst.

"Hello, sir." Her voice was meeker than she meant it to be, weaker than even etiquette demanded. So she tried a little louder. "I appreciate your hospitality."

Elijah grimaced and squinted his eyes shut, pressing a palm to his temple. "Quiet, girl. Are you trying to wake the dead?"

She stuttered, hardly having a response for such a ridiculous question. "O-on the contrary, sir, I quite prefer them asleep."

Elijah drew yet another step closer so that he could peer down at Signa. The moment he did, he fell back with a hiss of breath. "My God. Your eyes."

Signa flinched and pressed a hand to her cheek, just below the golden eye. It was a typical enough reaction—she was used to the surprise. But Elijah didn't seem surprised; he seemed almost afraid.

"I can cover them if they bother you, sir," she said, readying to turn and search for a cloth of some sort. Anything to wrap around her eyes. But before she could retreat into her room to find one, Elijah seized hold of her wrist.

"Are you here to show me my sins, child? Are you my past, here to haunt me? A ghost, to remind me of what I've done?" His words were breathless. At once, Signa remembered the portrait in the hall and understood that the woman featured on it was Lillian. But what about the spirit that had been calling her to that room? The one who had followed her. Had that been Lillian, too?

Behind Elijah, Marjorie's shoulders sank. "Let the girl go, Elijah. She's no ghost. She merely shares your wife's blood."

His face turned colder then, each line sharp as glass. Slowly, he released his grip on her. He took another moment to assess Signa, taking in her hair—so much darker than Lillian's golden curls—and her skin, so much sallower. "Forgive me," he said, though his tone far from begged forgiveness. "It's possible I've had too much to drink.

For a moment, I thought perhaps you were someone I once knew. But if it's true you're my ward, then I suppose it's my duty to chastise you for being up at such an unreasonable hour."

The lump in her throat was impossible to swallow. Somehow, Signa spoke around it. "I had some difficulty sleeping. I wanted to make sure Blythe was..." Healthy? Alive? "Safe, for the night."

Elijah's mouth tightened. "You've met my daughter?" This seemed to surprise Marjorie as well. The woman's eyes creased at the corners.

"Only briefly, sir. I heard coughing, and I went in to check on her."

"So it was you that got her help, then."

Though it was perhaps not the most honest thing to do, Signa nodded, leaving out the part that Blythe's coughing attack was *because* of her.

"Then be sure to do it again, should you hear anything." Elijah would no longer look at her. "Now get to bed, child. We're approaching an hour made only for ghosts."

Signa shivered. "Yes, sir."

He again braced himself along the wall as he departed, and the firm look Marjorie shot her told Signa that she should do the same. She turned the knob to her suite and disappeared into it. Oddly enough, it wasn't the memory of Elijah grabbing hold of her or his reaction to her eyes that Signa's thoughts lingered on as she crossed the plush rug of the sitting room and moved into the bedroom. It was the words he'd last spoken: "an hour made only for ghosts."

She took a seat on the edge of her four-poster bed. Her travel chest sat beside it, still sealed tight. After having her belongings shut away for so long, she wanted nothing more than to unpack the chest. But try as she might, Signa couldn't convince herself to so much as crack it open. After tonight, she had no doubts that her time at Thorn Grove would be cut short. If there was one constant that Signa could count on, it was that no matter where she was, Death would find her. She didn't know how or why, or whether this was all an elaborate game meant to drag out her torture while he watched and laughed and enjoyed the show.

She would find out, though. And, even if it was the last thing she ever did, she would stop him.

It was late into the witching hour when Signa roused to the sound of crying and the rustle of maple leaves blowing in through a window. She didn't remember leaving it open, yet open it hung, carrying in the scent of rain and damp soil.

Signa pried herself from the warmth of the bed to peer out into the night. When minutes passed and the crying had not returned, she drew the window shut and made her way back to bed. Yet she noticed from the corners of her eyes as she passed her vanity that the reflection in the mirror remained still. Neck prickling, she paused to examine the mirror, hoping the image was a trick of the light. But when her reflection stared back at her, its edges fuzzy and a smile that Signa wasn't wearing curling at her lips, she knew this was no trick.

Signa smothered a scream as she threw herself from the vanity, where a burst of white light escaped and fled through the bottom of the door. She knew at once it was the spirit from earlier, and this time there was no denying that she'd seen it.

Signa didn't bother with a coat or her boots, wasting no time as she threw open her door and chased the light down the hall. Now that the spirit had confirmed it could be seen, Signa had no choice but to confront it. If she didn't, who knew if the beastly thing would ever leave her alone.

Thorn Grove didn't so much as creak from the weight of her steps as she hurried down the staircase, and the hinges were silent as she swung the front door open into the cold night. At once she threw her arms around herself, for her flimsy white nightgown did nothing to stop the pervading chill from creeping into her skin.

"Hello? Is anyone here?" Step-by-step, she forced her numb feet toward the cries that ate their way up her skin, gnawing at her bones. The louder the crying became, the more the world beneath Signa withered. The moss along a maple tree dried to a dark brown while fallen leaves wilted and scattered in a sudden wind. It was as though the very earth were warning her of what lay ahead, and that she should turn back. Yet Signa didn't stop moving until she saw the source of the sound.

A woman with translucent skin and soft white hair that trailed behind her like the embodiment of wind itself sat beneath the bend of a tree, wearing a dress silver as the low-hanging moon. The spirit's cries ceased as Signa approached, head snapping up to look at her. Signa's footsteps faltered along the dead bramble as the spirit's eyes crawled over her body, assessing. She tried not to show that fear was clawing at her, urging her to run.

The spirit glided forward without warning—without a sound—and when Signa tried to fall back, dead roots ruptured from the ground and snaked around her ankles to hold her tight. She fell flat on her back, shivering and cursing her luck as the spirit hovered over her.

The spirit was beautiful, with smooth skin and pale hair that fell in loose waves. But the longer Signa looked at her, the grayer the spirit became, with bluish-black lips and fingernails to match. Yet it was her eyes that Signa couldn't turn away from—one blue, and one hazel. Two different colors, like hers. Like the woman from the portrait Signa had seen earlier that day.

Lillian Hawthorne.

From so close, Signa could see that the spirit's mouth was something from a nightmare, filled with pus and bleeding sores that festered over her gums. Her tongue was a useless purple mush, as though it had burned away. Lillian tried to speak, but all she could do was moan, and the louder Signa screamed at the monster to get away from her, the louder the monster moaned back.

Lillian reached out as if to snatch at Signa, but Signa dug her fingernails into the roots and tore at them, ripping them from her ankles. Enraged, Lillian screamed as Signa scrambled to her feet.

"Stay away from me!" Signa snarled at her. The spirit flinched at the steel in Signa's voice. But the pause was only temporary, and with a deep frown Lillian started forward again.

Signa bent to scoop up a handful of soil and tossed it at the spirit's face. "I don't care who you are, just leave me alone!" So as not to awaken all of Thorn Grove, she had to hiss words she wanted to yell, and she hated the spirit for that, too. "Leave me alone, or I'll find your body and burn it until you're nothing more than a pile of ash!"

As Lillian brushed the dirt away, her blackened lips twisted into what Signa thought must be a sneer. But the threat kept her at bay.

"What do you want?" Signa grumbled. "Why did you draw me here?" Lillian wasn't anyone Signa wanted to get involved with, and yet Lillian had died in a way that, admittedly, made Signa more than a little curious. And curiosity was a hungry, persistent thing.

Lillian's spirit hesitated, then pointed to her black lips.

"You can't talk?" Signa asked, and the spirit shook her pale waves with a grunt. It wasn't the first time Signa had seen a spirit unable to speak. Some streets were filled with soldiers or warriors from ancient wars she didn't care to know more about, and too often the spirits were riddled with holes in their chests or faces.

"I know who you are." Signa drew several steps back for her own assurance. "I know it was you waiting for me inside the house earlier. What do you want from me?"

Spirits didn't need to breathe, but it looked as though this woman was drawing in a long breath and attempting to gather her patience. She didn't move toward Signa but snapped a frail branch off a tree. For a moment Signa debated running, but instead of skewering Signa's flesh, Lillian lowered herself to the ground, kicked a clear path in the dirt, and used the branch to write words upon the earth. When she was finished, Lillian tossed the branch away and pointed at her work.

Though Signa knew her nosiness could very well be her undoing someday, she obliged and read the words. Her stomach twisted the moment she did, and she looked to Lillian for an explanation. The spirit's body was flickering away at the ends like little tendrils of smoke. If Signa's years seeing spirits had taught her anything, it was that they weren't free to wander. The farther they ventured from where they had died, the more they struggled to remain on Earth.

Clearly, Lillian's spirit was far from where she had passed, and her time here was running out. She retreated toward the woods at the outskirts of the property, until the only remaining trace of her was the words she'd carved into the earth:

Come to my garden and save her.

Signa knew at once that Lillian was referring to Blythe.

Blythe, who Death had proven he was after.

Blythe, who Signa had felt tethered to for reasons she couldn't explain.

Blythe, whose death would make rumors surge. Whose death would likely put Signa out of yet another home she could not afford to lose.

The realization struck: If she could stop Blythe from dying, then she would stop Death. She would *beat* him. And if she could manage that, perhaps he'd finally leave her alone and allow her the life she yearned for. A life out of the shadows, where she'd never have to deal with him or these God-awful spirits again. A life with people and parties and companionship, and where she could just *be*.

Foolish as it was to get herself into a bargain with a spirit, if it meant beating Death, Signa would do whatever it took.

NINE

Marjorie was true to her word that Signa's mourning wear would soon be a thing of the past.

The modiste arrived at dawn, dragging a trunk full of fabrics into Signa's suite.

Signa had gotten hardly a wink of sleep, and—coupled with the past several days of traveling and the fact she'd spent the previous night being haunted—there was little she wanted more than to curl up in bed for the remainder of the day.

Until she remembered that today marked the start of her lessons.

"Come now, Signa. Only the dead sleep at such an hour." Marjorie sighed as she followed behind the modiste. "The master won't have you walking around looking like the grim reaper. It's time we add a bit of color into that wardrobe of yours and prepare you for the season."

Signa roused like the dead resurrected, limbs heavy and her eyes stinging against the waking sun. It felt like only minutes had passed since she'd fallen into bed. Only minutes since she'd had the misfortune of meeting Lillian's spirit. And yet she summoned all her wakefulness at the promise of new clothing and shuffled into the sitting room. A pleasant young woman who Marjorie introduced as Elaine, Signa's new lady's maid, took to combing Signa's dark waves out of her face as the modiste fussed over her waist with a measuring tape.

The modiste was old, with as many wrinkles as the years she'd lived carved into her face. Beady brown eyes were covered by round spectacles, though they seemed to be of little help, given how closely the woman bent toward Signa, stooping to read the numbers on the tape.

"You are too thin, girl," the woman tutted. "Nothing more than a twig with breasts."

Signa turned toward the window, determined not to let them see the shame upon her face. Her sheer nightgown did little to disguise the sharpness of her ribs, and she brushed anxious hands over them. Marjorie glanced at them, as well, those too-sharp bones protruding from her skin. Signa had done what she could, living with Magda, but she was too young to access her inheritance on her own, and the modest allowance Magda had been given from it went straight to the gambling dens. That woman likely would have been *happy*, should Signa have starved to death. All she'd cared about—all most of her guardians had ever seemed to care about—was how to claim a piece of Signa's fortune.

"Leave room in the gowns," Marjorie told the seamstress, looking away from Signa's ribs and pretending to busy herself by helping Elaine fix her hair. "She'll be baby cheeked in no time."

The seamstress grunted, satisfied. Once she'd jotted down Signa's measurements in a leather pocket notebook, she held swatches of fabrics in a wide array of colors to Signa's face. They worked before an ornate silver mirror, which Signa used to sneak glances at herself, half expecting to see her reflection begin to move on its own as it had the previous night. There was soil beneath her fingernails still, as well as on the soles of her feet. It was all she could do to feign ignorance when the modiste inspected them with a frown.

Though Signa knew little of the cost to have a wardrobe made, she could imagine. And it was far more than any guardian had spent on her, ever. Elijah truly must have wanted Signa out of her mourning wear. While Marjorie gasped over muted tones like blush, champagne, and periwinkle, Signa's eyes strayed to greens dark as the forest and reds deep and rich as blood. Yet she said nothing of her opinions, for what did she know of fashion? If she wanted to fit in with society, surely she should trust Marjorie to make the decisions and settle for the dull tones without complaint.

The modiste left behind a gown upon her departure—a pale yellow day dress, with ribbons of blue and lace of white. Signa wanted to balk at its gaudiness, but she lifted her arms as Elaine helped her into it. If this was the style, it didn't matter whether she felt it suited her or how comfortable she was.

"This will have to do for now," Marjorie said as Elaine laced the corset. "At least until your own are made."

The kindest word Signa could think of for the dress was *hideous*. It was also incessantly cheery, given the state of Thorn Grove. She may have looked like a walking banana, yet she minded her tongue and did not complain once it was on, asking only, "And when *will* those dresses be ready?"

Marjorie's laugh was polite and demure, a textbook example of how *A Lady's Guide to Beauty and Etiquette* stated it should be. Signa made a mental note to practice mirroring it, later. "The modiste makes quick work. Now come, it's time for lessons. The master would have my head if he saw us dawdling."

From what she'd seen of Elijah, Signa very much doubted that. Regardless, she followed Marjorie out of the room and down the hall, trying to ignore the prickling of her skin that came from the feeling of being followed by the eyes of several dozen portraits.

The prickling stopped once they'd descended to the lowest level, and Signa was relieved to find that Thorn Grove felt like a new place that morning. Gone were the music and ball gowns that had filled the halls, and the laughter that had lingered close behind. Left in their place was the quiet sweeping of a broom upon marble.

"Remember, no dawdling," Marjorie prodded when Signa lingered for too long upon the staircase, studying the odd decor that prevailed throughout the estate. The staircase that looked as though it was carved from a tree. Iron sconces shaped like bird's nests. And, as Signa kept looking, one also shaped like the head of a fox, and a chandelier with arms that looked like spikes.

Whoever designed this place was an odd soul. A soul, Signa decided, that had been begging for this house to be haunted.

They'd certainly gotten their wish.

Signa could still feel the press of exhaustion on her body from the previous night's haunting as she followed Marjorie into the parlor—a room as grand as any other in the estate but perhaps better lit with its two bay windows. The walls were a buttery yellow even brighter than Signa's awful dress, and they were perfect for capturing the light. Feminine touches adorned the room, entirely out of sync with the more masculine second floor. There were elegant whorls carved into the molding, a bright patterned rug, and dainty floral cushions with lacy trim. It was upon those cushions that Percy and Blythe sat, sipping steaming cups of tea.

Blythe looked no better than she had the night prior, with her sallow skin and sunken frame, but there was a sharpness in her eyes. A will to sit upon the couch and sip her tea and not be stuck alone in her room, even though her hands trembled every time she lifted the cup to her lips.

"My dear sister said she awoke feeling rejuvenated," Percy said the moment Marjorie's surprised eyes rested upon the girl. "I thought some fresh air and company might do her well."

Marjorie's mouth formed a tight line. Rather than argue, though, Marjorie turned and opened the windows, letting in the fresh breeze. "Very well, then. Perhaps you're right."

Signa stood straighter in the presence of her cousins. One day at Thorn Grove, and already she felt like she'd made such a horrid first impression on them both. She wanted to prove herself to them, though was struggling to do so between her heavy eyelids and the urge to yawn.

Stubborn, awful old spirits. She didn't want to think about Lillian, or the dead, or anything other than her lessons and the new family she was now living with. She wanted to study, to impress them, and to prove her readiness to debut into the next phase of her life. One where she hoped to have far more connections with the living, and far fewer with the dead.

Batting her hair behind her shoulders, she refocused herself and smiled at her cousins. "I'm glad to see you're both well this morning."

"You as well," Percy said while Blythe set her teacup upon its saucer and balanced it on her lap.

"Have you had a governess before, Miss Farrow?" Marjorie asked as she took a seat upon a tiny round pouf in front of Signa.

"Given her manners, I would assume not," Blythe muttered under her breath, taking another sip when Marjorie flashed her a look.

"Are you claiming that yours are any better?" asked the governess.

Blythe scrunched up her face as Signa felt a rush of shame, hot and searing. She'd be damned, though, if she let Blythe see that her words had struck. "I've had a governess in the past," Signa told them. "...On and off."

Whatever Marjorie thought of that answer, she didn't betray it. "What about lessons?"

Rather than admit how much time had passed since she'd had a proper lesson, Signa said, "I can read, and I know my lettering. Arithmetic, too." Only the basics, given that no one had ever stayed around long enough to teach her more than that.

Marjorie's lips curled into a smile that one could envy. "And what about music?"

Not wanting to give her cousins any additional fuel to taunt her with by admitting she'd rarely played, Signa said, "I suppose I'm a wonderful listener."

Blythe coughed into her drink while Percy nudged her with his elbow, hushing her between his own snickering.

Marjorie ignored both Hawthornes. "Duly noted. Why don't we begin there, then? With sight-reading and lessons on the piano."

Frustrating as it was, Signa had been taunted enough throughout her life to ignore her cousins. She nodded and instead let herself imagine sitting in the manor she would one day own, seated at the bench of a pianoforte, playing with a perfect grace. Her daydream was short-lived, however, as a wave of coolness jolted over Signa's spine.

"Miss Farrow?" Marjorie's voice was distant.

Signa could not *see* Lillian, but the faint sound of crying fought to steal her attention.

No spirits, Signa told herself, pretending she didn't hear it. *Think of your future. Of the work you must put into debuting. Normal people do not speak to the dead, Signa.*

Yet she couldn't stop listening. It seemed the others heard the sound, too, for Blythe had gone deathly still. The porcelain cup slipped from her hands and dropped onto her lap, hot tea staining her dress. Percy sat up with a jolt, as did Marjorie.

"Heavens, Miss Hawthorne!" The governess motioned for Percy. "Help your sister back to her room and fetch Elaine. Blythe will need to change into a new dress. And while you're at it, find a better use of your time, too, Percy. You both are far too distracting."

Marjorie waited for Percy to help his sister—whose eyes were still dazed and anxious—out of the room before she turned to Signa. "Now then, never mind all that, and pay no mind to the sound. It's merely the wind." She took Signa by the hand and led her to the sleek black bench of a beautiful grand piano that likely cost as much as Aunt Magda's entire house, if not more. There wasn't so much as a trace of dust on it. "It's always louder this time of year. Sounds like the devil himself is stomping about outside."

Signa knew full well that the wind had nothing to do with the sound, though she had no choice but to nod. She sat, fighting the urge to make herself small in her seat as Marjorie straightened her back and lengthened her neck, placing Signa's hands at the starting position upon the keys.

"Now," Marjorie said, "let's begin by practicing your scales." Signa's bones protested holding such a stiff posture, already aching. But if this was what it took to bring her vision to life and secure her place in society, she would do it. Signa pressed down upon the first key and had to swallow a grimace when her finger came away wet. Every inch of her stiffened, muscles coiling tight, for there was nothing on the piano. Yet when she lifted her finger, she saw mud caked upon it, and tiny worms sprouting from between the keys.

"Your scales, Signa," Marjorie urged without any acknowledgment that she could see what was happening beneath her pupil's fingertips. She didn't see that Signa's feet were sinking in dirt that wasn't there or that her fingers became a perch for the worms to curl themselves around.

Lillian's message was clear as the day—Signa needed to hurry and find the garden, or this spirit would never rest.

But until then, Signa steeled herself and pressed down upon the muddied keys. She refused to stop playing.

TEN

I**T WAS HOURS BEFORE** S**IGNA MADE HER WAY OUTSIDE, STRETCHING** her aching back as the wind lashed at her. The air was crisp, but it was nothing her scarf and a belly full of warm tea couldn't fend off. Her body welcomed the chill after spending so long at her lessons.

In only a day, she'd nearly forgotten the stark contrast between the estate's interior and exterior. Here, surrounded by endless moors of yellowing grass, wildflowers pocking the earth, and the golden blanket of leaves scattered along the ground, was a place of fantasy. The afternoon was peaceful; no bodies danced in or out of the house. No strangers in their finery. Though Signa knew not what the cooks were baking, something sweet and doughy warmed the air around her, and her stomach roared despite Marjorie having fed her more scones than she'd been able to eat.

But there would be time for sweets later, when her hands weren't muddied with dirt and worms and earth not truly there.

Come to my garden and save her.

Signa *would* go to that garden, but she needed to find it first.

Behind the estate were steep, endless moors. Before it, manicured hedges and a grove of maple trees. And far beyond Thorn Grove was a line of trees that marked the start of the woods. Not one garden in sight.

Signa might have believed she was being toyed with if not for her conversation with Sylas two days prior—he'd told her he'd once worked in the garden with Lillian. Though Signa despised the idea of asking him for help, he was the safest option. With the class difference between them as stark as it was, surely he wouldn't dare report her for sticking her nose where it didn't belong.

And so Signa hiked up her hideous yellow dress and made her way across the trimmed lawn to the stables, her grip on her skirts tightening as she approached snorting beasts and stomping hooves. The horses of Thorn Grove were massive creatures, all with glossy coats in a spectrum of colors—solid black, pure white, a rich chestnut brown. They seemed comfortable in their roomy stalls, but Signa had little trust in the wooden barriers confining them. If these beasts wanted out, they were clever enough to free themselves.

Signa peeked into stalls as she tiptoed through the stables, surrounded by horses that stretched their necks toward her in an attempt to win her attention. One of them went as far as to nip at her shoulder, and Signa reeled back to bop it firmly on the nose. "There will be none of that!" she admonished, smoothing out the shoulder of her dress. "Being handsy with a woman is no way to get her attention."

The horse snorted, indignant. He was smaller than the others, though appeared no younger. Where the others' coats gleamed, his was a dull brown, the color of burnt caramel. Compared with the others, this one was lanky and odd. "Well now," she said, hands on her hips as she watched it, "aren't you a silly thing?"

In response, the horse stretched its neck to nip at her shoulder once more. She was mid-step, stumbling back to tear the fabric from the horse's mouth, when someone laughed. It was a rich sound, one that sent tiny shivers up Signa's spine. She recognized it instantly.

Signa whirled around, not having heard Sylas approach. He was as alarmingly tall as ever, and his dark hair was slicked back now, showcasing the beautiful contours of his face. Despite the cool autumn air, Sylas wore only trousers and a long-sleeved cotton tunic. It was open at the collar, sleeves rolled up over strong arms as though he'd been working, though his boots and dark gloves had hardly a speck of dirt on them. They were of so fine a leather—and so well maintained for a stable boy.

Sylas leaned his forearms against a stack of hay bales. At his side, a large gray hound sat alert, ears erect and head tilted.

"I didn't know the Hawthornes had a dog," Signa said for lack of anything else, hating that her tongue felt hopeless and numb around this young man. Rude as he could be, the lack of any available male company in her age range ... ever ... made Signa more tongue-tied than she cared to admit.

"Oh yes," Sylas said. "He's a beastly thing, too. Trained to kill anyone who trespasses onto the estate."

Signa drew a nervous step back. But the moment she did, the

hound's tongue lolled out, and the dog flipped happily onto its back. Signa glanced at Sylas.

"I said he'd been trained," Sylas said. "Not that he listened. And he belongs to me, not the Hawthornes. His name's Gundry."

Signa stooped, scratching Gundry's offered belly. She laughed as the hound panted and twisted to lick her hand. Signa had always wanted a pet—any creature would do, really. She'd dreamed of having a cat, or a hound. Even a rat would have sufficed, so long as it kept her company. But considering how often she moved, she'd been too afraid to ask for one for fear that something might happen to it— or that one of her guardians would refuse to let her take a pet with her to a new home. She'd never given much consideration to a horse given the animal's sheer size, though she supposed one would be an equally wonderful companion.

"Do you ride, Miss Farrow?" Sylas's voice was cool as the breeze around them, teasing her as she swatted the pesky horse away from her hair. "You seem like a natural."

"Ah yes, I'd nearly forgotten how astounding your manners are." Signa smoothed a hand over her hair to ensure it was secure in its fastenings. "It's been a long while since I've been around horses. My late uncle had a few, but they were sold when he passed, and he was never keen on me riding them. Though his weren't quite so large."

"Riding was a passion the two masters shared." Sylas crossed to the horse toying with Signa and pressed a flat hand upon its snout. It settled at once, exhaling a contented breath. "Master Hawthorne rarely comes to see them now, but he is the one responsible for these horses. He's always loved beautiful things."

Signa took one look at the pesky, smallest horse, and Sylas laughed. "That creature is Balwin, beautiful in his own right. It's said he charmed Lillian back in the day—they bought him from an inn they visited during a summer holiday. He's an entertaining enough horse but flighty. Has a mind of his own."

Sylas Thorly, the man who'd terrorized her for a full day with his oddities, was fond of a strange horse and a large gray hound that looked to be part wolf. She never would have guessed it.

"I've come to ride," Signa said, determined. "I want to see Lillian's garden."

A flash of surprise crossed Sylas's face before he nodded. "Pick a horse, then. Not Balwin—he's due for a ride, but he likes to test his riders."

"What about that one?" Signa pointed to a gorgeous black stallion whose coat was so shiny it gleamed as if wet.

"What do you say we try one of the older mares? Like the white one there, on the right?" Sylas gestured to a solid white horse, but Signa's eyes wandered instead to the magnificent golden mare beside it. This horse was a little taller, and her eyes far livelier. She snorted and stomped a hoof in a pleasant greeting, as if inviting Signa to step over and greet her.

"What about her?" she asked, obliging the horse by offering her palm for it to smell and lip at.

Sylas dipped his chin. "She's . . . a friendly horse, but she hasn't been out in a while. Maybe pick another—Miss Farrow, what are you doing?"

"I want this one." Signa was already undoing the locks on the stall and stepping inside to claim her horse, pulled to the golden mare in a way none of the others inspired. The mare blinked her chocolate eyes at Signa and huffed, dipping her head as if in an offering. Signa took the offer and ran her fingers over the horse's velvety neck, scratching her behind the ears.

"Is there something *wrong* with this one?" Signa asked, and the mare looked to Sylas, as if demanding a polite answer.

"Of course not." Sylas sighed and grabbed equipment from the side of the stall before following Signa into it to get the horse saddled up. "It's just that Mitra was Lillian's horse. Though it's about time you got a solid ride, isn't it, girl?" He stroked the mare's neck more gently than Signa expected. She found herself staring, the lightness in his tone warming her skin.

"Wait outside." Sylas's voice held none of that same gentleness when he spoke to Signa, who flinched. "I'll get her ready."

ELEVEN

When Sylas ventured out of the stables fifteen minutes later, he wore a thick navy cloak and led not one horse but two and a hound that panted at his side. Next to her golden beauty stood Balwin, the pesky chestnut stallion that was fixated on trying to eat Sylas's hair.

"Have you brought me options?" was all Signa could think to ask.

Sylas was not too busy swatting Balwin away to snort. "I'm coming with you. Lillian's garden is in the woods. You've clearly not ridden in a while, and if I were to let you ride there without an escort, Mr. Hawthorne would have my head."

Signa fought her clenching jaw. As if sensing her annoyance, Mitra closed the space between them and nudged Signa with her shoulder. Signa, in turn, wrapped her fingers around the horse's neck, stroking her soft hair. She could feel its fierce pulse of life beneath her fingertips. The quickness of the mare's heart and her impatient, uneven breaths.

They were a well-suited match, each of them as eager to break free and roam as the other. But when Signa went to mount the horse, she faltered. Tall though she was, the stirrups were out of her reach. She wrapped her arms around Mitra's neck and tried to haul herself up, but the horse whinnied and shook her off.

Behind her, Sylas asked with mirth in his voice, "Do you need assistance?"

Head held high, Signa ignored him and tried again, hanging on to the horse for dear life while trying to swing one foot into the stirrup. Mitra scuffed at the ground as Signa hung from her, slipping, refusing to admit defeat.

"My God, you are a stubborn one." This time, Sylas didn't ask before he set his hands upon her waist and lifted Signa onto the mare. He did it with a single sweeping motion, as though she were as light as a feather. Though Signa's own heart fluttered, Sylas appeared to think nothing of such an intimate touch as he patted Mitra's rump, ensured Signa's feet were fully secure, and hauled himself up and onto Balwin.

Beneath Signa, Mitra shuddered with anticipation. She didn't wait for a command before starting off in a trot so jarring that Signa began to slip from the saddle. She fisted the reins, bending forward at the waist to steady herself. Then Sylas was next to her, slapping a stick on Mitra's rump. Signa wanted to snarl at him as his swat made the horse whinny and move faster, though the jarring subsided within seconds.

Signa sat up straighter, casting a glance at Sylas, whose eyes danced with mischief as he and Signa raced across the moors, over rolling hills of wildflowers and through wetlands that slowed their steeds. Closer and closer to the woods they traveled, until Signa's chest burned with the desire to reach it.

Come to my garden. Lillian's spirit pulled her, guiding her.

Come to my garden.

Goose bumps rose along the flesh of Signa's arms and legs. She had never seen a spirit so angry, and the last thing she wanted was to be terrorized by Lillian Hawthorne. Even more than that—though she had no desire to admit it aloud—Signa could feel the curiosity sinking its claws into her. An unsorted mess of puzzle pieces she wished to make whole.

She had to know what the spirit wanted with her, and how a woman so young, so beautiful, had died in a secret garden tucked into the woods far behind Thorn Grove.

Signa gave Mitra a gentle nudge in the side, and the horse responded at once. She'd been Lillian's horse after all; perhaps she felt the pull, too.

Sylas fell behind them in their haste, calling out, trying to stop them from rushing headlong into the woods. Though Mitra handled the moors expertly, never faltering from her path, Sylas struggled to urge the unruly Balwin forward. His voice sounded hollow in her ears, his protests fading with distance. Signa didn't wait—*couldn't* wait. The woods beckoned her, and she dove into the belly of the beast, letting its jaws clamp shut and swallow her whole.

The woods consumed her, embracing her so fiercely that Sylas's frustrated cries and Balwin's hooves cut away, the only sound a soft rustling in the autumnal trees, the leaves a mix of harvest orange and midnight green.

It didn't take long for yellowing grass to tangle around Mitra's white stockings. The woods tugged at Signa's skirts, at Mitra's mane, scratching and scraping against their skin, hungry for blood. Signa tried to cover the horse as best she could, but the branches were low and savage, clawing against Mitra's side.

In the corners of her vision came a flash of white so fleeting that she'd have missed it if she blinked. It came again seconds later, whisking away toward the right, where trees had snapped in half or been cleared away. Signa followed after what she knew was Lillian's spirit, which led her into a clearing and to an iron gate set into a weathered stone wall. She pushed upon the gate to find that there was a lock in its center, covered by ivy and vines.

She was glad there was no one around to hear her very unladylike curse as she looked upon the garden wall, three times her height and impossible to climb even if she stood upon Mitra's back. She pried at the lock, frustration mounting when it didn't so much as budge.

How was she meant to find a key to a garden that had clearly been abandoned for months? It wasn't as though she could ask Elijah for it, and Sylas probably already knew the place was sealed and had led her on this wild-goose chase for a laugh. Hands tight on the reins, Signa was about to turn back to find Sylas and give him a piece of her mind when another flash of white flickered in the corners of her vision.

Lillian was there, watching, hiding in the shadows of the iron gate. Her hair was pale as butter, and her face was covered with moss, with rotting vines woven into and out of the gaping hole where a mouth should have been. Hollow eyes watched from between the ivy leaves. Hollow eyes that looked not at Signa but behind her, to the ground.

Signa turned to the familiar sight of tiny black berries—belladonna—and understood so well that her chest felt like it was being cleaved in two.

The night she'd last eaten belladonna—the night she'd spoken to Death—she'd used his powers as her own. What if she could do it again? She'd seen him pass through walls. Seen him disappear into the shadows, and then re-form himself at his will. Was it possible that she, too, could do that?

Signa dismounted, gritting her teeth at the sight of the belladonna berries that waited at her boots. She'd not wanted to approach Death again until it was with a way to destroy him and end her blasted curse. But if she wanted Lillian to leave her alone, it seemed there was no choice.

With dread in her belly, she stooped and plucked the berries, filling her pockets and her palms.

Death loomed in the air like an approaching storm, dark and heavy. Signa felt the weight of him choking her, warning her. Even the sound of the wind was as biting as a blade when the world slowed around her, as if time was coming to a standstill.

But Death wouldn't touch her. He never did.

Signa pressed five berries onto her tongue and waited as her blood burned and chills shot down her spine. It didn't take long for the poison to clench her insides. For her vision to swim while illusions of the woods tunneled around her, for a power unlike any other to form within her, beckoning her to come and sample it.

Death had arrived.

TWELVE

DEATH'S PRESENCE WAS FROST THAT BURNED INTO SIGNA'S VERY bones—an icy lake she'd plunged into headfirst. But rather than allow her to come up for air, he embraced her in those frigid waters with no intention of letting go.

"Hello, Little Bird. Come to stab me again?"

His voice was a balm for the gooseflesh along her skin, and Signa's insides twisted in annoyance at her body's response to him. Not anger nor fear but a deep, festering curiosity she couldn't seem to shake.

"Tell me whether I can use more of your powers," she demanded. If he would not hesitate, then neither would she.

She lifted her chin and turned to face him. Or at least she believed she was facing him. It was difficult to know, given his form. Death was little more than the shadows of the trees. The darkness lingering in the corners where light couldn't quite reach. He was nowhere and he was everywhere, until slowly his shadows began to contract along the ground, consuming the forest floor and bathing it in darkness until he was there. No face, no mouth, but the form of a man who loomed over her.

"Tell me, Signa," Death began, ignoring her question, "are you afraid of me?" His shadows drew closer until his form was smaller, less imposing. "Most people fear death. They fear it all their lives, though they never see me until their final breath. There are a handful of humans out there with a keener eye, of course. Those who spend their lives trying to bridge the gap between the living and the dead, and who catch glimpses behind the veil. But when I stand before them, even they are wise enough to fear me. Yet you have called me time and time again. You have questioned me. You have even gone as far as to attempt murder." Though they were dark words, Signa didn't miss the hint of humor within them. It lit a blazing, angry inferno inside her.

"Am I amusing to you, *sir?*" She clenched her teeth as the shadows danced among the trees.

"At times." His voice was little more than a whisper in the roaring wind, though she heard it as clear as though it came from her own thoughts. "And other times you are an endless annoyance. Always, though, you are a fascination."

Talking to Death felt like listening to a riddle. She could barely resist rolling her eyes at how long-winded he was and had to press two more berries to her tongue.

"Tell me whether I can do more with your powers," she said, firmer this time but keeping her voice low in case Sylas was nearby. "You said that night that you could explain, so do it. Quickly." If Death had eyes, she imagined she was glaring straight into them.

The trees fell quiet when he spoke. "Here, in this space between the living and the dead, it would seem as though you are able to do more than pester me, Little Bird. I don't know the extent of your abilities, but I do believe you've barely scratched the surface."

Signa swallowed down the fear that festered in her throat, her suspicions confirmed. "How is that possible? What have you done to me?"

When the ground beneath her feet trembled, Signa understood she'd asked the wrong question. "Because you are so quick to blame me," Death said, "let it be known that *I* have not done *anything*. I am not responsible for your gifts. I am not responsible for what happened to your aunt, though sometimes I wish that I was. The things she put you through... Had you not wanted her alive, I might have taken her long ago."

"My wanting someone alive has never stopped you before." Her body was a tensed coil ready to spring. "Am I to believe you had nothing to do with the deaths that follow me wherever I go? That I alone am responsible for them?"

Night pulled closer as Death drew forward. "You bear no responsibility for those deaths. Magda's was the first life you took. Even I was not expecting it."

If what he said was true, and even he hadn't been expecting that to happen, then... "*How?*"

The wind itself seemed to whisper the response. "There's a reason you can see spirits, Signa. There's a reason you're able to cross the veil between life and death. Though I've not been able to confirm *why*, it seems your suspicions are correct. When you're here—when you have crossed the veil and are able to see me—it seems you have access to an arsenal of skills similar to my own."

So strange was the mix of relief and horror that Signa felt. Bile rose to her throat at the confirmation of what she'd done. None of the other deaths were her fault, which of course was a relief. Yet Magda's death *was* her fault. Her aunt had died by Signa's hands, and the thought alone made her want to curl up against the nearest tree and let herself be sick.

"Listen," Death whispered. "Important rules were broken that night. Life and death is a game of balance, Signa. A balance that must always be maintained, otherwise you will bring chaos into this world. Magda was not meant to die that night. When a life is taken, another must be spared. Do you understand?"

His words, yes, but the actuality of them? Signa was barely comprehending any of it. Death's sigh blew across her cheeks as his shadows drew around her. "When you killed Magda," he explained, voice tiring, "I had to give life to another who was meant to die that same night. It was Blythe who I gave it to."

Her eyes snapped up. "Blythe would have died?" Though their meetings had been short, Signa had seen how fiercely Blythe's soul blazed. The girl was too young, too innocent, and too full of will to die before she'd gotten the chance to truly live. Though Signa knew it shouldn't have—knew it wasn't right—knowing that Aunt Magda's death had saved Blythe made her feel . . . better.

Like something she'd be willing to do again, if given the choice.

"You saved Blythe?"

"*You* saved Blythe," Death corrected her. "Though you killed another to do it. Do you understand what I'm telling you, Signa? There is a cost to everything."

For a long moment Signa was too hung up on his words to speak. She had saved Blythe.

She hadn't doomed Blythe to a sudden death. She hadn't cursed her or killed her or been the reason behind her suffering. Rather, for the first time ever, Signa had *saved* someone.

Mind reeling, she pressed her hands to her thundering chest as though to still her heart. In this space between life and death, she had the reaper's powers. If that was true enough to both take and give life, then what else could she do with such powers? In the back of her mind an idea was brewing, though she needed to learn more before she could act on it.

"Lillian contacted me last night," Signa admitted suddenly, whispering as though her spirit might overhear.

"I'm not surprised," he said. "Your actions already saved her daughter once. You and Blythe are connected now."

"Did you know this would happen?" Signa asked, braver than she'd ever felt as she peered into the depths of his shadows. "Did you know I'd end up here at Thorn Grove?"

"I knew Blythe would die that night, just as I knew the Hawthornes were your last remaining family. I spared her so that you'd be welcome here, though I cannot take her ailments away."

Perhaps it was unwise to challenge Death, but she didn't care. "Am I truly welcomed, or are you the reason I'm here? What sorcery must you have cast upon the Hawthornes for them to accept me?"

"There was no sorcery," he told her. "I merely helped speed along the process with a letter. Despite what you may think of me, I want you safe and in a stable home. Had I chosen someone other than Blythe, that opportunity would have been lost."

Signa digested the information, uncertain what to believe. He didn't *sound* like he was lying, but then again, he was Death. It was likely he who invented deceit.

"Lillian's waiting for me." She turned to face the garden gates. "There, inside the garden." The *locked* garden.

"And how do you intend to get in?" Again, the most aggravating amusement stirred in his voice. "Climb up the ivy? I think I might enjoy watching that."

Signa ignored him. If what he said was true and she really could possess his powers, then there was a way. If he could become incorporeal—if he could become the very shadows themselves— what was stopping her? Her only hesitation was that she wasn't quite sure how to *use* such powers. The night she had killed Aunt Magda, she hadn't meant to do anything to the woman but keep her away.

"Can you walk through walls?" Signa asked, though she thought she already knew the answer.

"I can walk through anything," came Death's response, voice lifting with intrigue.

"So if I wanted to walk through the garden gate—"

"You'd simply have to summon the power, make clear your intention, and do it."

"And what of my body?" she asked. "Will I remain whole, or will I turn into a spirit?"

Death's chuckle was a low rumble that shook the ground. "You will remain wholly yourself. You need only to be here with me, on the other side of the veil. Why don't you give it a try?"

It wasn't as though she had another choice.

Drawing a breath deep through her nose, Signa tried to gather her powers—which felt ridiculous, considering she couldn't feel anything and still half believed this was all some cleverly contrived lie—and ran straight into the thick iron bars of the garden's door.

To her surprise, she did not smack headfirst into the gate. But she didn't quite get *through* it, either. At least not entirely.

The trees shook, and the earth quaked as Death's laugh shuddered through Signa's bones. She hadn't even been sure he could make such a sound, though upon hearing it, she felt heat rising to her cheeks. For she was stuck in the garden gate, her front half inside the garden and her back half still with Death.

It felt like there was something hard *inside* her. Cold, biting metal that grated against her insides. Her hands trembled at the wrongness of it all, as though she'd been sawed into two parts.

"I forgot to mention," Death added in that clear-meadow voice of his, "if your powers are the same as mine, then our skills are centered around intention. You can do anything you want, yet if you doubt yourself for a second ... Well." Again he laughed, and Signa couldn't help noticing that the stars winked with the sound, as if they, too, found her ridiculous.

Just how much power, she wondered, did Death have? How much power did *she* have?

Signa hurried to shove several more berries into her mouth, not wanting to discover what might happen should she return to being fully corporeal in this state—or perhaps worse, discovered by Sylas. "Are you going to help me," she hissed, "or will you simply stand there and continue to laugh, you useless heap of shadow?"

Slowly, Death's laughter ceased. "Now, now, Little Bird. You need only ask for help, and it shall be yours."

Annoyance boiled within her, spilling over. "Just get me out of here before—"

"Before your berries dwindle away and you're fully mortal once more? Or before that boy finds you bottom up?" Though Signa couldn't see him, she stilled at the brush of shadows that chilled her skin. "No one has dared speak to me in the way that you do. Why is it you are so polite to others? So demure and soft, and yet so bullish when we speak? Ask me kindly, Signa Farrow."

She rolled her eyes. "Perhaps it's because whenever you're around, someone always ends up dead." But there was more to it than that. Perhaps it was because Death couldn't exist—because he *shouldn't* exist, and Signa wasn't fully convinced that he wasn't part of her own imagination. Someone she'd manifested in her loneliness, as a way to explain the strange things happening around her.

Or perhaps it was because Death was real, and near him Signa grew too comfortable. With all her pretenses lost, her words became sharper and more venomous. Possibly, it was because there was no need to impress him. No need for social graces and second-guessing her every thought and action. With him, there was no pretending. Perhaps this was simply who she was.

"You've been watching me?" she asked.

"I find that you make the time pass quicker. Otherwise, I grow bored and weary, and who else can I taunt?" His response surprised her—so brazen, so forward.

She hated how flustered it made her. "Considering that you find me so fascinating, you'd better help me out of this before I solidify and bleed internally from the *iron bars* that are piercing my *organs*." Death waited, still and patient and significantly more amused than he ought to have been, until Signa bitterly added a terse, "*Please.*"

"Ah, that's better. I'm glad to see you're learning." He was before her then, shadows reaching toward her. Reaching...A hand? Signa had never seen anything remotely human about Death, but it was indeed a hand swathed in shadows. A hand that hesitated in the air for a moment before his fingers curled around hers. Life around them stilled, taking a breath.

And the world exhaled again as Death pulled her into the garden.

THIRTEEN

T HE GARDEN WAS NOT SO DEAD AS SIGNA HAD EXPECTED.

The first thing she heard upon entering was the quiet rushing of water, joined by a choir of croaking frogs. The soil was rich and ripe for autumn, bearing an abundance of wolfsbane, fragrant orange and red chrysanthemums, pansies with a deep purple that bled into their yellow petals, blooming witch hazel, and dozens of striking plants she'd never before seen. Across from them were rows of browning, unharvested herbs and, farther back, bushes of nightshade. Though untended, the garden didn't feel unkept like Aunt Magda's. Aglow in the setting sun, this garden felt alive and wild with magic.

Signa tried to imagine what it might look like during a warm summer day, the way Lillian would have enjoyed it with birds singing and the soft buzz of insects as she lay out in the grass, sunbathing. Or perhaps having a picnic.

Lillian, Lillian, Lillian. The name buzzed through the air as if the garden were paving the way to her, ushering Signa forward.

"Was it a peaceful death?" It was similar to the question Signa had asked Sylas. This time, however, she went right to the source.

Death lingered beside her, and tension prickled the air. "Despite what you seem to think of me, I'm no monster. Though pain cannot always be avoided, I try to make death peaceful when I can. I cannot take everyone at their happiest state, but I do try."

To her surprise, she found that she believed him. "Then what about Lillian?"

"I don't remember every life, Little Bird, for there are far too many, and I cannot tell you much. What I do know is that this was her favorite place in the world, and that she's buried in the back, near the pond. Shall I take you to her?"

Signa shivered. "Please do."

Death led Signa through the garden as though he'd traveled there a hundred times before. As she followed, she wondered how long Lillian had been sick. How many times had she been so close to Death's door that he'd sat in this garden with her, waiting to see if she'd finally call to him?

Though green with algae, the pond buzzed with life. It was a gentle place, with fallen maple leaves and lilies sprouting outside the bank. Tiny brown frogs burrowed themselves in the damp soil or hid between the pebbles lining it. In the water were tiny minnows, and facing the pond were two oak benches, both overtaken by damp moss. Behind the benches, tucked toward the back, was the grave littered with a decayed bouquet and more moss.

"Be careful when you speak with Lillian." Death's voice had lost all hint of amusement. "It takes spirits a great deal of energy, so they won't often communicate with the living. If a spirit is angry enough, though, it might try to possess you."

Never before had Signa even known that was *possible*. Then again, she'd never met such a malevolent spirit as Lillian. She had to gather herself, taking a few heartbeats before she closed the space between herself and the grave. On her way to it, she plucked one of the lilies from its stem and gingerly placed it next to the withered bouquet.

"You told me to come," Signa whispered, patting a hand to the soil. "Here I am, Lillian. Come and tell me what you want."

Her heart seized as the cold flooded her skin like a thousand needles stabbing into her. Bile burned her throat.

When she looked up, Lillian was floating over the water's edge.

No longer was her mouth a gaping black hole; her lips were full now, and shaped like a heart. It was covered in blisters and sores, and Signa was certain the woman's tongue would still be a pulpy mass of rotted flesh should she attempt to speak, but ultimately, she looked more human.

Assuming humans could glow bluish-white and hover above the ground.

Death stepped forward, offering the spirit his hand, but she drew away from his touch as though it were poison, resisting his call. His offer of an afterlife.

"You can't just take her?" Signa asked, and Death stiffened, as though the suggestion alone was disgraceful.

"I won't do such a thing against her will. She'll come when she's ready." He bowed his head, and with that retreated into his shadows.

When it was just the two of them, Lillian's lips curled into a thin smile. But her lips were too cracked and raw to handle the movement, and one of the sores opened, oozing a trail of black blood down her chin. If the spirit noticed, she didn't care.

Signa was glad that none of the Hawthornes were able to see Lillian like this. Everything about her was a reminder that the dead did not belong in the world of the living. Lillian would terrify even those who loved her most.

"Lillian," Signa whispered. If the spirit wasn't able to use words, they'd need to keep this simple. "Do you realize that you're dead?"

From her experience, many spirits never acknowledged that fact and went on acting as though they were still alive. Yet to her surprise, Lillian nodded.

Good. This was a good start. "The doctors said it was an illness. Were you sick for long?"

The spirit's face contorted, a dark shift in her demeanor. She floated to her grave and stooped to the ivy coating the ground, taking a piece of it in both hands. Glancing up at Signa beneath iridescent lashes, Lillian didn't so much as blink as she tore it to shreds, until the muscles of Signa's throat tightened.

"Death," Signa called, though she never took her eyes away from Lillian. "Do you know how Lillian died? Did you see the illness?"

He took shape, leaning against a tree, and responded with a tone that betrayed nothing. "I'm afraid I don't know anything more than she does."

Some help he was. She groaned, trying to soothe her racing heart as Lillian kept tearing at the ivy, then jerked to a sudden halt at the sight of a pebble near her grave. Lillian grabbed for it, and with trembling hands carved a single word into the dirt, the script so messy it was barely legible: *kill*.

So reassuring was the word that it took every ounce of determination Signa had to keep herself grounded even when her mind urged her to run. "Did you... kill someone?" she asked, to which Lillian scowled. The spirit pointed to the sores on her lips, then to herself, and Signa gasped when the realization struck.

If Lillian was saying what Signa thought she was... the situation was going to change too much and be far more complicated than Signa wanted anything to do with. Part of her ached to turn and escape now, before they went any further. Before she learned a secret she didn't care to learn.

But Signa couldn't draw away. Couldn't get her feet to move even if she wanted them to. So rather than flee, she forced herself to ask, "Lillian, are you trying to tell me that you were killed?"

Tossing the pebble, Lillian spun to Signa with a fervent nod. At once, Signa began to piece it together. The sudden death, the failed doctor visits, the angry spirit, and now...

"Blythe. It's happening again, isn't it? Whatever—*whoever*—killed you is back for your daughter. Is that right?"

Lillian blinked away, then reappeared beside a small bush of berries on the opposite side of the garden.

Signa sprinted toward her and opened her fist, where she still held a small handful of the berries, now half mushed into her palms. She stretched them out toward Lillian, whose eyes went black as Signa asked, "Poison? You think you were poisoned?"

106

Lillian's spirit rocked with a violent twitch. Quelling her trembling, Signa dared to add, "Was it by someone at Thorn Grove?"

Another violent shudder. The sores on Lillian's lips festered, turning from purple to a vicious black before they tore open with blood that ran from her lips, down her chin, and soiled the top of her gown. Her body spasmed, head bobbing in a furious and terrifying nod. "Who?" Signa demanded as Lillian's eyes brightened, glowing. "Was it one of the cooks? A maid? The tutor? Was it someone you trusted?"

"Enough!" Death was there beside Signa, his shadows consuming her, drawing her back. "Do not press the dead, Signa. She doesn't know."

His warning came too late. The spirit's neck bent and snapped as she jerked it from one direction to the next, shaking, nodding, twisting. Blood poured from Lillian's mouth, and the moonlight caught the pulp of her shredded tongue as she threw her head back and screamed a sound so shrill and grating it brought Signa to her knees. The wind whipped the water from the pond and tossed the croaking frogs into the trees, marring the clean branches with their blood.

Death was before her, his shadows like armor blocking her from the carnage.

"What's happening?" Signa gritted out, hands clamped tight over her ringing ears as she tried to see around him.

"You pushed too far." The darkness expanded around them, creating a barrier. "Wayward spirits aren't meant to recall their final moments. You never know how they might react."

Signa leaned around the shadows to watch as Lillian reached

down the back of her own throat and grabbed the awful heap that was her tongue. She clawed her grimy, soil-stained nails into it, ripping off pieces of flesh. She tossed the bloodied heaps to the ground and then went for another, as if trying to remove her own tongue in its entirety.

But then the wind stilled, and Lillian's neck twisted back to its rightful place. Her eyes snapped to Signa, to the shredded bits of her tongue that were already fading. To the bloodstained trees where several frogs lay impaled.

She looked to Death then, and tears flooded into her eyes, black and bloody.

And then Lillian was gone, and the static in the air followed.

Death retracted his shadows from around her as Signa clawed toward the nearest tree and threw up. There was an iciness in her body she couldn't quell, and her hands shook even as she pressed them against the trunk to steady herself. Outside the garden, Mitra whinnied at the sound of another pair of hooves in the distance.

"It's time to go" was all Death said as he took hold of her shoulder, pulling Signa to her feet and back through the garden.

"Do you know who did it?" The words tumbled from her, a little slurred.

"If I did, I would tell you. I'm not all-knowing, Signa. When I touch a person, I see glimpses of the life they've lived. But I know only what they know, and while Lillian suspects foul play, she doesn't know who's behind it." Gundry pawed outside the gate. He ceased his sniffing at once and looked up, tongue lolling out when he saw

Signa stumble through the gate. He looked at Death, too, and his tail began to wag.

"He can see you?" After all she'd seen that day, she wasn't sure why it was so surprising. She'd seen spirits interacting with animals before, but Death had always felt like a step beyond that. Like someone who shouldn't even be real.

"All animals can see me," Death said, patting the hound on the head. She almost thought she could see a hint of a smile peeking out from his shadows, but when Signa blinked again, he was gone.

There was so much. So much she didn't know. So much happening that she could barely process.

She had Death's powers.

Lillian had been murdered.

And now, to save Blythe, it was up to Signa to discover who had done it.

FOURTEEN

B Y THE TIME SYLAS FOUND HER, SIGNA WAS LEANING AGAINST
Mitra, gripping the reins to hold herself upright. Sylas's hair was
mussed and peppered with twigs, like he'd taken a tumble into the
bushes. Beneath him, Balwin seemed delighted and not at all out of
breath.

"Miss Farrow!" Sylas exhaled a relieved breath. "You shouldn't
have taken off like that!"

"It's not my fault you couldn't keep up," she managed. She
wiped her mouth with her forearm and sucked in gulping breaths
of the cool air, letting it flood her lungs and cool her skin. She hadn't
realized before that interacting with a spirit took so much of a toll on
her, but as it was, she could barely lift her hands. No longer could she
feel Mitra there beside her, holding her up. No longer could she feel
anything.

"Signa?" Sylas's voice was faint. "Are you ill?"

"Quite," she managed to say. "I believe . . . I believe I must have eaten something foul." She couldn't stop shivering, couldn't stop the press of cold deep within her bones. Couldn't think of anything other than how they needed to hurry because Blythe's killer was on the loose somewhere within Thorn Grove.

Signa groaned as Sylas hauled her atop Balwin. She had half a mind to protest as his arms wound around her waist to secure her in front of him on the saddle, though as it was she could hardly see straight. She tried not to flinch from his touch. Tried to accept the help and let herself remember that she couldn't hurt anyone now that the belladonna had faded from her blood.

"If you're going to lose your stomach," he warned her, "make sure it's not on my boots."

She made no promises. It felt like someone had taken a cricket bat and bludgeoned her in the temple. Her stomach threatened to empty itself at any moment, and though Sylas had shed his cloak and settled it over her, she couldn't stop shivering.

"What happened to you?" As kind as his actions were, Sylas's voice had a hard edge. "Do you get ill like this often, or only when you disappear to frolic in the woods?"

"I would hardly call this a frolic," Signa countered, curling her fingers in the offered cloak. "And no, it doesn't happen often. I think I saw something in the forest." She decided to slip a piece of truth into her next statement, just enough to sound a little bewildered. "It felt as though something in the woods was calling to me."

With his chest against her back, she could feel his body become taut against hers. Her cheeks warmed, and she tried not to think about the inappropriateness of this situation or how strong his thighs felt around her, and instead on how he didn't appear to be breathing. "Is something wrong?"

"It's nothing you should worry yourself—"

"I can judge that for myself," she cut him off, feeling brave with Sylas in a way she didn't often get to be. "Whatever it is, tell me."

There was a moment when the only sound was the crunch of leaves beneath the horses' hooves. Signa twisted to look at him, and when his smoky eyes met hers in the dim moonlight, her mouth went dry.

Everything about this man had grated her nerves when they'd first met. Now, however, things were frustratingly the opposite. Her attention fell to the tunic that was rolled up on his arms, to his broad shoulders, down the deep neckline that revealed a glimpse of his chest.... And then she averted her eyes like the proper young lady she was and pretended he didn't make her skin hot while simultaneously making her want to pummel him.

Sylas, fortunately, didn't appear to notice her struggle. "There are rumors about Thorn Grove." His whisper was as unnerving as the dark forest surrounding them. "Rumors I wanted to tell you the day I picked you up but didn't know how. Had you anywhere else to go, I might have." They had to duck beneath branches that clawed at them, and when one threatened to tear at the sleeve of her borrowed cloak, he paused to help her untangle it with deft fingers. The moment she was freed, she swayed forward in the saddle and cleared her throat.

"You were saying?" She could only pray that her skin was not flushed pink.

He frowned a little but continued nevertheless. "I was saying that, at night, the servants claim they can hear a woman crying. Some refuse to wander the halls after dark, for there are whispers of a ghost. A blond woman in a white dress, watching them one moment and gone the next. And Master Hawthorne... He's the worst off. I think he hears her, too. I think that's why he doesn't sleep, doesn't eat, doesn't do much of anything anymore."

"Other than throw soirees," Signa added. The most lavish and risqué ones she'd ever heard of.

"To drown out the sound of her cries, I imagine," Sylas defended. "To keep her at bay, and to forget. I've known the Hawthornes for a long while, and I assure you that he was not always like this."

They knew about Lillian's spirit, then. They may not have been able to see her, but they knew she was there. Signa's body sagged against his as she blew out a breath. So relieved was she that, had she the energy, she'd have thrown her arms around Balwin and kissed him between the eyes. Death had told her there were people who could see glimpses behind the veil of the living. While they likely couldn't see Lillian as she could, they knew they were being haunted. If anyone suspected Signa of seeing Lillian's spirit, they wouldn't bat an eye. Luck, it seemed, had finally decided to throw her some favor.

"What about you?" She was becoming far too comfortable slumped against Sylas but could do nothing about it as exhaustion sank into her bones. "Do you believe in ghosts, Mr. Thorly?"

"Don't take me for a fool, Miss Farrow. In a place like Thorn Grove, how could I not?"

The words were like fairy music; never had Signa heard anything so sweet. "Then you will understand when I say I was forced out of the estate and into the woods tonight."

"Whatever your reason, you need to be more careful. You've not stopped shivering since I found you." He adjusted the cloak he'd thrown around her for emphasis. "If it's discovered that this happened and that I didn't report it, I'll lose my job. My loyalty is not to you but to my employer. So if you want me to take that risk, you're going to have to give me a good reason."

Signa willed her brain to spin a story so believable and so masterfully told that she'd be able to escape the situation with him none the wiser, but her temples ached and her mouth burned with the desire to just *say* it. To tell someone else what was going on, so that she didn't have to do this alone. There was something about Sylas and the way he spoke—so factual and direct—that made Signa feel as though he might believe her. It was for the same reason that, around him, her petals unfurled a little. She'd been able to speak her mind to him without him running away. Not to mention that Sylas had already admitted to believing that Lillian's spirit was haunting the Hawthorne estate.

The breath she drew was so sharp that Mitra flapped her ears. "If I tell you," Signa whispered, "you must swear not to tell another soul."

Sylas, it seemed, was every bit as ruled by his curiosity as Signa. A smile in his voice, he leaned into her and said, "I promise."

"To *anyone*? No matter if you think me ridiculous?"

"I already think you're ridiculous," he mused before Signa turned and fixed him with a glare. "Fine, yes, I agree to not tell a single soul upon this earth whatever it is that you have to say. Now, are you going to continue with this suspense? Out with it."

"I wanted to find her grave."

He stared at her blandly. "Are you fascinated with the macabre, Miss Farrow?"

There was no simple way to word it. Signa did the only thing she could—squared her shoulders, and said, "I have a reason to believe that Lillian didn't die of natural causes. That she was murdered, and if we don't find out who did it, Blythe will die, too."

For a long while, the distant hoot of an owl was her singular response. Signa curled into herself as she listened, expecting as they crossed the moors that Sylas would flee to the nearest doctor and ask for her to be taken away. To her surprise, though, the first thing he asked was, "*We?*"

Signa brushed her fingers across Balwin's mane. She hadn't meant to say it, but now that she had ... It was becoming apparent this was a situation greater than anything she could handle on her own. She needed help, and Sylas knew about Thorn Grove. He knew about the *Hawthornes* and had access to the staff in a way she never would. He could help.

She was spared having to answer until they arrived at the stables. As he helped her off Balwin, she caught Sylas by the hand. He jolted, and for a moment Signa feared that the effects of the belladonna were still potent. That perhaps she still had access to her powers and had stolen his life. But they both wore their gloves, and he was blinking at her with dark, curious eyes.

"I need you to tell me everything you know about the Hawthornes," she urged, realizing she'd grown louder in her excitement when Sylas leaned forward to quickly press a finger to her lips, the touch intimate enough that her mouth went dry.

"Miss Farrow, I work in the stables." He looked behind her, ensuring no one was watching as he pulled her inside. "It's not my place to gossip about those who pay me—"

"I've seen your boots, Mr. Thorly. I've seen the way you dress, and it's apparent to anyone who looks at you that you want to be more than a stable boy." Something in his eyes flashed. Something Signa latched on to and pushed against. "Imagine what could happen if you save Blythe. If you put an end to Lillian's hauntings and give Elijah peace of mind. If you ever step into the stables after that, it will be to mount your own horse. You'll never have to work again."

Sylas undid the horses' bridles and saddles, and his pinched forehead told her just how much the gears in his head were turning. "Should you be found out and let go for any reason," she added to sweeten the deal, "I will employ you myself the moment I claim my inheritance. Use your position to help me, Mr. Thorly. Be my confidant, be my ears, and your future will be so much more than working in the stables."

"You've a clever tongue," he replied. With the horses shut back in their stables and their gear put away, he propped himself atop a bale of hay and asked, "You'd pay me out of your own pocket to help you solve a murder for a family you've only just met?"

"The Hawthornes have been kind to me," she said in spite of his scrutiny, staring at the little scar upon his brow. "Besides, it's not as though I'm wanting for money."

His laugh was little more than a bewildered puff of breath. "I suppose you have a point. Very well, then. You have yourself a deal, Miss Farrow."

She tried not to let her surprise register. She'd always known money held power. It was everything in this world. Yet this was her first time experiencing for herself just how much sway it carried. She allowed herself the tiniest sliver of a moment to relax her shoulders and bask in her relief over the fact that she would no longer be alone in this. She knew too little about the Hawthornes and had too little time to deal with this on her own. She *needed* someone like Sylas, and there was plenty for him to gain as well. Money had always been what people wanted from her, and if that's what it took to get his help, then so be it.

"Tell me everything you know," she urged him again. "Is there anyone who disliked Lillian?"

"There was an entire society who disliked Lillian." He smoothed a hand through his hair, inky as the night. "You've seen the family's wealth yourself. And I'd wager you've seen what jealousy and greed can do to people. People didn't have to know her to dislike her."

With great bitterness she thought of what had become of her parents, then of all the ways her guardians had treated her over the years. Though her friend Charlotte had made the time she'd spent with her uncle full of fond memories, the older she'd gotten, the more she thought about how often he'd left her alone. About how he would use the money meant to care for her on imported clothing and lavish gifts for his lovers. She'd spent most nights locked in her room, trying to drown out the strange noises of the guests she'd never been allowed to see.

It was Signa's grandmother alone who had truly loved her, while the others craved only her fortune. Some of them had been decent enough to keep her fed and warm, but she'd never felt like a person to them. Never felt like anything other than an invisible girl dragging a hefty sum behind her.

Seeing the answer upon her face, Sylas nodded. "Lillian was a wonderful woman, but the Hawthornes will always be a target no matter how kind they are. There are people who would kill for money, Signa. People who will spin lies into sweet words and even sweeter smiles. You'd be wise to remember that."

She doubted that would be an issue. There'd been times in her life when strangers showed her kindness, certainly. Until they'd seen her talking to a spirit or heard the rumors and would flee. Even when she had her inheritance, she couldn't imagine that changing unless she secured a proper husband and made a name for herself among society.

Could it?

"If what you're saying is true," Signa said, "then why should I trust you? You agreed to take my money quickly enough."

His response was simple. Firm. "You shouldn't trust anyone but yourself, Miss Farrow. But for Blythe's sake, I'm going to help you. First things first, we'll need to get you back into Thorn Grove without suspicion." Sylas stood and offered his gloved hand.

Tense in the shoulders, Signa accepted. He led her to a stall where his hound, Gundry, lay curled in the hay. The hound growled as Sylas motioned him aside and bent to shuffle several hay bales out of the way. Signa couldn't help noticing the contraction of the muscles in his back as he worked, taking his distraction as an opportunity to observe the male physique. More and more, she found her interest in it stirring.

"Press your hand flat against that panel." There was a stone wall hidden behind where the hay had been. Signa followed his orders and pressed the stone. It clicked and shifted beneath her hand. "Now turn it," he said.

When she did, the wall slid open to reveal a pathway bathed in darkness. No lights, no sound, just a draft and an endless maze ahead.

Sylas grabbed hold of an oil lamp on one of the stable's workbenches. Gundry rose, stretched himself out with a yawn, and padded to his master's side. "Has anyone shown you the tunnels into Thorn Grove?"

As Sylas held up the lamp, Signa peered into the nothingness before her. The hairs on her arms stood on end. "Never. Where do they lead?"

"These? Into the kitchen pantry," Sylas answered. "Though I'm sure there are a dozen more paths, I know of only a few. I don't believe they're used anymore, but this one was intended to be an escape route for the servants in the event of a kitchen fire. There are others that servants used to keep out of sight of those living at the manor. The tunnels are dark, but they'll get you inside the estate undetected. Should anyone find you emerging from the kitchen, tell them you were roaming the property and lost your way, and found yourself in need of a late-night snack since you missed dinner. Now"—he ducked beneath the entrance and stepped into the tunnel, extending a hand—"do you trust me to escort you?"

The words felt like a trap. Sylas had warned her not to trust him. Not to trust *anyone*. And yet she reached to him, eager to feel the brush of his hand upon her once more. "Not even a little."

"Very good, Miss Farrow. Now let's get going." His fingers curled around hers, and he drew her into the tunnels.

According to Sylas, parties at Thorn Grove were no rare occurrence.

"She loved few things more than company and a reason to celebrate," he said as they took slow, cautious steps through the tunnels. The way he spoke of Lillian made Signa imagine someone so much grander than the ghostly spirit she'd encountered. It made her think of how she envisioned her own mother—as someone made for the spotlight. The type of woman who came alive beneath the dazzle of lights and music. One whose body was made to wear a ball gown, and whose smile charmed all who beheld it.

That made it easier to believe Sylas when he said that all who met Lillian fell in love, and that Elijah was no different. "There's gossip that he wasn't always known for his chivalry, or for being a man who belonged to only one woman," he whispered. "That changed when he met Lillian."

"Could the murderer be one of his jaded ex-lovers?" Signa squinted, using the dim glow of the lamp Sylas held to see where she was going.

"Maybe." He lifted the lamp higher, trying to better spread its light. "I've heard Elijah's brother favored Lillian as well, though it was rare to find a soul who didn't. Lillian always said Thorn Grove was too magnificent a place to keep to themselves. Guests were in and out constantly."

Signa nodded, though in her gut she knew there was more to it. Lillian had died of poison, alone in her garden. If there was one thing Signa knew about belladonna, it was that death came swiftly if enough was consumed. Yet Lillian had been sick for months, which meant someone had been slipping the poison to her in small doses, skillful enough to make her death slow and painful. They weren't looking for a random passerby with a dislike for the Hawthornes; they were looking for someone with the time for precision. Someone with frequent access to the estate.

"Did any of the staff hold grudges against Lillian?" she asked, rearranging the puzzle pieces in her head.

"No," Sylas answered with confidence. "Everyone who worked at Thorn Grove during her time here loved Lillian."

Signa wasn't sure she believed that someone could be so well loved and admired. Surely, the woman must have had bad blood with *someone*. "And what about Elijah?"

Sylas bobbed his head and considered. "They enjoyed him less so. It wasn't that they didn't like him; Elijah was always a business-man first, and everything else second. He spent the majority of his time in his office or at the gentleman's club."

Signa remembered one person who clearly didn't dislike Eli-jah. It hadn't gone unnoticed by Signa how Marjorie had caressed his arm, or how she'd spoken to him with a familiarity unbecom-ing of a member of the staff. But that didn't prove anything. If something was going on between Marjorie and Elijah, it could be a new development.

Signa braced one hand against the tunnel wall for balance, her thoughts racing too quickly to pay attention to her steps. "Tell me more about his job."

"Grey's is a family business," he answered. "I think the Hawthornes are so invested in it for the pride, more than anything. It was started by Elijah's great-grandfather Grey Hawthorne, and has been in the family for generations, allowing them access to some of the most affluential people in and out of the country. As the eldest son, Elijah inherited it from his father. He runs it with his brother, Byron, and one day it'll pass to Percy."

It took a moment for Signa to recall the name; for her to remember the man who had stopped her and Marjorie on the stairs the first night at Thorn Grove. The one who'd drawn out the sharpness of Marjorie's tongue—Byron. It was Elijah's brother who Percy was speaking with that night. The same brother who'd favored Lillian.

"Does Byron not have any children?"

"Even if he did, Percy is Elijah's eldest and everything will go to him," Sylas said. "But no. He never married."

More and more puzzle pieces shuffled around in her head, not a single pair of them fitting together. There was more to all this, something Signa wasn't seeing. Fortunately, this was only the second night. Now that she'd accepted Lillian's task, perhaps she'd have a chance to sleep without the spirit bothering her. To *think* and check in on Blythe to figure out how the poison was being administered.

"I met Byron on my first night here," Signa mentioned. "He seemed angry, though I never figured out why."

Sylas grabbed the back of Signa's borrowed cloak and steered her to the side before she could trip over a small pit. He did it effortlessly, and Signa was glad that he would not be able to see her embarrassment in the darkness. She glanced sideways at his black hair strewn around him like a dark halo, noticing again how large he was. Like a walking tree trunk, really. A tree trunk with muscles. It was astounding.

"Elijah hasn't been back to the club since Lillian's death," he said, the corner of his lip twitching upward when he caught Signa staring. "There's been talk that he's no longer fit to run it, yet its ownership belongs solely to him and he refuses to let Byron take over."

If what Sylas said was the truth, then perhaps that's why Byron had been at Thorn Grove, talking to Percy, the night she'd arrived. Was his relationship with Percy a way to take control of the business himself? She was about to voice the question aloud when the toe of her boot caught the edge of another dip in the ground. She should have tripped—she felt the momentum of herself falling and prepared for the impact—yet Sylas was there before her, using his free hand to brace her by the shoulders as her face smacked into his chest.

For a long moment she stood frozen in place, contemplating whether this was an appropriate condition under which she might fake her own death to prevent further mortification. Eventually, she decided it was worth the embarrassment to glance up at him, ever so slowly, only for every bone in her body to seize when she saw that his smoky gray eyes were peering right back down at her.

"Don't you ever watch where you're going?" His voice was low and brisk. "You could have hurt yourself."

"I'm quite fine, thank you." This close, she couldn't help but stare at the faint smattering of freckles that were dusted beneath his eyes.

"Then would you mind releasing me? We're here."

Not having realized she had her hands fisted in his shirt, she released her hold at once. The fact that she had not simply melted into the ground from sheer embarrassment was a true testament to her inability to die. "Thank you for accompanying me, Mr. Thorly," Signa announced as she drew back and smoothed her dress. "I'll try to visit Blythe tomorrow and see what I'm able to find out."

"And I'll search the kitchen tonight and speak with the cooks." He tilted his head down at her, his right cheek sporting a dimple that Signa hadn't noticed before. "If I find anything, I'll contact you." There was a door before them, small and built into the wall. "This will take you into the pantry," he said. "Sleep well, Miss Farrow. Rest assured, we'll get to the bottom of what's happening in Thorn Grove."

FIFTEEN

SIGNA PUSHED PAST A SACK OF POTATOES NEARLY THE SAME SIZE AS she was to crouch through the small opening into the kitchen pantry. As she shoved it aside, it tipped over and sent nearly a dozen potatoes toppling onto the floor. In the silence of the night, their tumble seemed loud enough to shake all of Thorn Grove. She cursed her poor fortune as she stuffed everything back into place, concealing the tunnel door into the pantry. Tearing off her gloves, she stuffed them into her bodice and tried to look at least halfway like she'd been ready for sleep in case someone came for her. When no one did, Signa gathered her skirts and tiptoed out through the kitchen and past the parlor. She'd reached the edge of the stairs when a gruff voice called, "What in the devil are you doing up at this hour?"

Signa spun to find Elijah Hawthorne staring at her through the open door to the parlor. He was dressed in his nightshirt, though the exhaustion upon his face made it clear he'd not slept. Perhaps not even in days, given the shadows under his eyes.

She wrapped her borrowed cloak tighter, thankful to the darkness for concealing her. One look at her muddied skirts, and Elijah would realize Signa had not yet been to bed. "Good evening, sir." Her mind raced through a list of every possible excuse, all of them feeling heavy on her tongue. "I was having trouble sleeping."

"So you took to wandering?" His clever eyes flickered behind her, toward the kitchen, and Signa's blood ran cold—he knew. Or at least he suspected. This was his home after all. He probably knew of each and every one of the tunnels. Yet, if Elijah did realize, he said nothing of it. Rather, he waved Signa over to where he sat at a small round table before the buttery-yellow walls. Though Signa detested the color, she had to admit that the room was cozy overall, which said a great deal given that she could admire it even beneath the weight of Elijah's severity.

"Come sit, child." There was a checkerboard before him, and as Signa joined him, he adjusted the pieces. "Do you play?"

"I do," she answered without specifying that she'd only ever played against herself. She had a feeling there was a correct answer and didn't want to risk losing an opportunity to speak with the man she was most curious about. And so she reached for the black pieces, careful to keep her skirts tucked under the cloak.

"I understand the inability to sleep." Elijah let her make the first move, not watching her as he observed the board. "This is no welcoming home, I'm afraid. Though I must caution you against any exploration, especially at such late hours. Nights in this manor are often difficult for those faint of heart."

Signa waited for him to move his checker toward the middle of the board, then moved her own before responding. "I'm aware of the rumors but be assured that my heart is not faint. Are these ghosts the reason you're up as well, sir?"

There was a tick in his jaw. One so quick she would have missed it had she not been watching him so closely. "Do you hear her, too, child?" He jumped one of her pieces, capturing the middle of the board. "Do you hear her crying?"

No matter how she strained, she couldn't hear even a whisper of noise within Thorn Grove. "I hear no one, sir. Not at the moment."

Elijah was unfazed as she tried to surround his pieces. "So you see the problem. I cannot sleep when I hear her roaming about, haunting these halls, and yet I cannot so much as shut my eyes in her absence, for I wonder if I will ever hear her again."

He captured another piece of Signa's in her distraction, for in the darkness of the shadows she finally saw who she was dealing with— not a fool, as he'd seemed the first time she'd seen him, nor a drunk, but a man who was fraying at the seams. One who was hardly able to keep himself together. Elijah ran a hand over his face, his graying scruff too long and untamed for societal standards.

Too late she realized that even in this state, Elijah was the one steering this conversation. "Had I felt like there was a choice, I would have never taken another ward." He looked not at her but to the pieces laid before him, like he was sorting out his own puzzle.

Signa was taken by surprise at the bitter sting she felt at his words. It made sense Elijah wouldn't have wanted her—she came with too much baggage, and for someone with such wealth, there was no benefit for Thorn Grove to take her in. Still, hearing it aloud hurt more than she cared to admit.

"There is a cleverness in your eyes, girl," Elijah said. "You are not so dense to realize that I am a man who wouldn't remember to put on my coat if I didn't have someone to do it for me. A day here is enough for you to know, I'm sure, that my wife is gone and my daughter not so far behind. And my son—God, my son. I've failed the poor boy in too many ways. Yet, had my Lillian known of your situation when your grandmother passed, she'd have demanded we take you in. It was a misfortune that we were unaware until recently, for she would have given you a wonderful life. That was her way, God rest her soul. She took in whoever, and she would love them. In her memory, I had no choice but to bring you here."

Elijah's jaw snapped shut, as if deciding he'd spoken too much on the topic. A shadow crossed his face, and he let Signa capture two of his pieces.

"I've gone nineteen years without a parent, sir," she told him. "I've no interest in obtaining one now. I am grateful for what you've provided, and for me, that is enough. I am quite well suited to being on my own."

To her surprise, Elijah laughed. It was a quiet sound, little more than a hiss of air. "I used to believe that, too."

Signa had no chance to say anything more, for Elijah cleared the board with one final move. Her mouth gaped open as he captured every one of her remaining pieces in one fluid stride. "Those who play a defensive game of checkers will always lose." He didn't wait for her to stand. Didn't offer a hand to help her up. "Good night, Signa. I pray that sleep will find us well, and that we do not meet here again tomorrow night."

It seemed that if she was going to meet up with Sylas after hours again, she'd need to find another tunnel. That, or perhaps learn to walk through the walls after all. Signa waited, staring at the board and retracing her moves until the sound of Elijah's footsteps disappeared. When they did, she headed up the stairs.

To the surprise of her poor heart, she found she was not alone. Percy sat on the top step. Had his hair not been bright as a flame, she might have tripped over him in the darkness.

"Percy!" She clutched her chest. "What are you doing?"

"I didn't mean to frighten you." His voice was a low whisper. "I was coming down for a drink when I heard the two of you, and I just...Forgive me for eavesdropping. It's been so long since my father and I had a real conversation. I'd nearly forgotten him capable of it." His shoulders caved inward like a wilting flower. "That was her favorite room, you know. That's the reason he goes in there so often. This house has always been so strange and dreary, and she wanted a space that felt entirely her own. Father fought her on the color for the longest time—he hated the yellow. But my mother was always good about getting her way. Sometimes I see him in there just staring at the walls, remembering."

Signa could almost picture Lillian gliding through the halls, taking tea in the parlor and mulling over the decor. It seemed like she had such a different life—such a different family—than the one Signa was coming to know. "Do you ever speak with him?" she asked, heart heavy. It seemed to her that, though he might refute it, Elijah was in great need of company.

Percy's face soured. "My father wasn't often around. Marjorie gave me my lessons, and Uncle Byron taught me to be a gentleman. My father and I only ever spoke of two things—the business I would one day run and my obligation to keep up appearances and maintain the status of the family. For twenty-two years that was our connection. And now he has severed it with no explanation. So no, we no longer talk, for we don't even know each other."

It took a moment before Signa could respond. As someone with a different and overall frustrating experience with death, she took a great deal of care with her words. "Grief is a strange thing, Percy, for no two people experience it the same." It was a foreign thing, to have someone to comfort. She didn't know if what she was doing was right as she reached out and set her hand upon his; she knew only that this was what she'd always wanted for herself. For someone to sit with her and take her hand, and to know that they were there for her.

Percy needed someone—it was clear in the way he glared at the floor, and the slump of his shoulders—and Signa was glad to be that person for him. She took a seat beside him, patting his hand gently as she said, "I'm sorry for what you're going through. It sounds like he loved your mother very much."

He stared down at her hand with a frown. "More than anything or anyone. But that doesn't give him an excuse to disappear when the rest of us still need him."

Signa understood all too well. She'd spent years watching

everyone she knew become ghosts—even those who were still living. "It doesn't," she agreed. "But he is a smart man, and I believe he'll find his way back to you. He may simply need more time."

Percy turned his hand in hers. "Thank you, cousin. For the sake of this family, I do hope you're right."

Drawing himself up onto his feet, he offered his hand to help pull her up as well. Yet as he did, his eyes caught the sight of Signa's muddied skirts peeking out from under her cloak. Though he said nothing of it, deep lines creased Percy's brow as he set his hand upon the small of her back and guided her deeper into the house, as though she might otherwise flee. "Come, cousin," he pressed, "whatever troubles we must endure, they will still be here after a night's rest."

SIXTEEN

THE PAST WEEKS HAD KEPT BLYTHE IN ISOLATION, HER ONLY VISI-
tors Elijah and the doctor who cared for her. Every day, Signa tried
to slip unnoticed into her cousin's room to check on her, only to be
met with a locked door, pulled away by lessons, or scrutinized by
Elijah's watchful eye when he spent his evenings by Blythe's bedside,
ensuring nothing happened to her while she slept.

This particular morning, her plans were thwarted when Marjorie burst into her suite dragging an armful of gowns—tea dresses
and traveling dresses meant for daytime use and others with extra
ruffles and richer fabrics made for parties. They were far better than
the yellow day dress she'd been forced to wear so often, though she
couldn't help but feel a knot of sadness at their dull, muted hues.

"You'll want to ready yourself quickly." Marjorie handed Signa a
soft periwinkle tea dress. "You have company arriving soon."

This roused Signa at once—how could she have company when
she knew no one?

"I've arranged a tea for you, with young ladies your own age," Marjorie said. "I thought you might like to have friends here after being forced to leave your other ones in such a rush. All of these girls are friendly with Blythe and come from affluent families. All are unmarried and are perfectly suitable company."

Signa had no doubts that they were, but still she asked, "And they have to visit now?"

Marjorie's face was stern. "What do you mean *now*? I was under the impression that this was what you wanted."

"It is!" Signa said hastily. Of course it was what she wanted—company and a foothold in high society was all she'd *ever* wanted—though she would have preferred it any other day. "I only meant that I'd hoped to see Blythe today."

This seemed to appease Marjorie, whose smile was sympathetic. "I see. Unfortunately, the doctor is with Miss Hawthorne. You're welcome to visit her later this afternoon, after your lessons."

Signa wanted to demand that she be allowed to pay her cousin a quick visit, though when Elaine arrived to help Signa hurry and dress, she realized any such effort was futile. Blythe would have to wait a little longer.

The dress slipped over her skin like silk, made from imported fabrics with little expense spared. It was color coordinated to compliment the parlor in which they'd be having tea, and laced in the back, leaving Signa room to grow into it with a more sufficient diet. For now it was a touch loose, which made it one of the more comfortable things she'd ever worn, given that one was not expected to wear a corset beneath a tea gown.

By the time Signa finished getting ready, she certainly *looked* respectable, but she was contemplating every which way she might possibly sneak *A Lady's Guide to Beauty and Etiquette* into tea with her. It sat upon her writing desk, and she trailed a delicate finger down its immaculate spine. Would her mother be proud to see her like this? Would she have dressed Signa similarly? Pinned her dark tresses the same way Marjorie did, to show off her delicate face and slender neck?

"They'll be here by now," Marjorie chided. "Come along."

Signa withdrew her hand from the book. She knew its contents by heart, had studied its pages front to back more times than she could count. Now was the time for execution.

She followed Marjorie down the stairs, walking between fretting maids who dodged her in their hurry, setting up Thorn Grove for another party. Her heart pattered with every step. She wouldn't allow herself to slip up like she had with Blythe—wouldn't forget her tongue for even a moment.

Three young women waited for her in the parlor, seated at a circular table that seemed absurdly small and intimate. Marjorie introduced them as Lady Diana Blackwater, a rather plain girl with fair skin, mousy hair, and beady rat-like eyes; Lady Eliza Wakefield, with a long alabaster face and blond ringlets, and . . .

Signa didn't trust her own legs to hold her up when she saw the hazel eyes that stared back at her. Charlotte Killinger wore a blue-and-white-striped day dress, her shoulders back and her neck long and delicate. Her old friend was even more beautiful than Signa remembered—her rich umber skin warm and glowing, cheeks warmed with the tiniest hint of rouge. She was taller and less baby cheeked, but still every bit the girl that Signa had once known. The friend she still thought of to this day, but one whom she'd not spoken to since the scandal between Signa's uncle and Charlotte's mother all those years ago.

Charlotte's mouth hung ajar, her eyes wide as a doe's before she bowed her head in a gracious nod. "It was kind of you to invite us."

"It certainly was! We've all been so curious about the Haw-thornes' new ward," Diana chimed in after a cursory dip of her head. Her voice was strident, but Signa paid it little mind for her heart was busy beating a mile a minute. For so long she'd wished to see Char-lotte again. But why did it have to be now of all times? Now, when she'd finally let herself believe that she could start fresh and where the rumors of the past would not haunt her every move.

Signa stumbled, legs numb, as Marjorie gave her a gentle nudge toward her chair. One of the servants poured steaming tea into their cups while another set out teacakes and pastries. While Charlotte thanked them, the other two girls ignored the help. Their fascination rested solely with Signa, and their eyes glinted with it the moment Marjorie was out the door.

Eliza smiled at her from across the table. "Well, aren't you a tiny thing." Whether it was a compliment or an insult was impossible to tell. Eliza leaned forward, her long curls brushing the tablecloth. "How are you enjoying your time with the Hawthornes? They truly are the most interesting family."

"Interesting?" Signa echoed, her throat so painfully dry. "How so?"

"The parties, for one." Eliza laughed, as though the question was ridiculous. "Not to mention the wealth, the rumors, the mystery. I suppose you wouldn't know considering you've only just arrived, but the family you're staying with is the talk of the town."

Signa dared to look sideways at Charlotte, who sat erect in her chair, wordlessly sipping her tea. She hadn't said one word and busied herself by staring up at a landscape of a beautiful spring garden.

A Lady's Guide to Beauty and Etiquette was very clear about gossip: *Do not speak idly.* Signa agreed, not caring to gossip about those who had shown her such grace. But Eliza's eyes were lit with mirth and her tongue was ready to seep poison, and so to get the information she sought, Signa took the bait. She reached for a blueberry scone and leaned forward with a quiet intake of breath.

"Rumors?" she asked in a tone that conveyed she'd never once imagined such a heinous thing to be possible. "Surely, you're mistaken? What sort of rumors are they?"

"All sorts," Diana chimed in. "That ghosts haunt Thorn Grove. That perhaps Missus Hawthorne—poor thing—took it upon herself to end her life after discovering her husband had had a series of torrid affairs and too many illegitimate children to care for. They even say the help is in cahoots to rally against the family."

The allegations seemed to be all hearsay, though Signa tucked the information away as more puzzle pieces to be sifted through at another time. "The Hawthornes are curious people," Signa said, choosing her words with care; she had no assurance that whatever she said wouldn't leave this table or that she wouldn't be branded a gossip. "But they're also very generous to welcome me into their home when they've suffered such a great loss."

Diana made a noise in the back of her throat. "I'm sure your fortune helped with that." She leaned back in her seat and examined her frilly white gloves. "My father says Mr. Hawthorne's business is failing and that you're to inherit a fortune grander than even theirs."

Signa wasn't shy about the butter she spread upon her scone, heartbeat so fierce that even her neck was beginning to perspire. When she'd imagined this conversation, it'd been much more informative and relaxed.

Charlotte peered up then. "She only just arrived, Diana," she said in a smooth voice between sips of tea. "I doubt she knows much about the Hawthornes at all."

Eliza's lips tightened, and Signa took hold of another scone. She figured if she didn't know what to say, then—so long as her mouth was full—she could bide her time and let the others speak.

But that was before a flood of cold air washed into the room.

"Is there a window open?" Eliza shivered. "I wouldn't have thought I'd require a coat at tea."

Signa knew too well what that draft meant and choked mid-bite. She tried to be discreet as she turned her head around to see Death was there beside her, sitting in a chair of shadows next to Diana. He folded one shadowy leg over the other, and in his hand, more shadows had formed an imaginary cup of tea, which he raised to her in greeting. *Apologies, I forgot to bring my dress and gloves.*

The words were not spoken aloud but seemed to reverberate in her head.

He was in her head.

She clenched her skirts and paced her breaths. *No. No no no no.* None of this was going according to plan.

First Charlotte, and now . . . no. Signa had eaten no belladonna; she'd not journeyed to the place between the living and the dead to access him. All her life, she'd been able to see Death only when there was reason for it—when someone near her was dying. She'd sooner try to kill Death again than let him take one of these girls, and she tried to convey every bit of that in the glare she shot at him. He seemed to enjoy it, a low laugh rattling in her head and filling her chest.

Relax, Little Bird. I only came for some rousing gossip.

Diana took a delicate bite of scone, unaware of the monster pretending to sip steaming shadow tea beside her. One touch, just a graze of his shadows, and these girls would be dead. Signa's throat was too tight to swallow the hunk of scone that had lodged in her throat. She choked on it, grabbing for her tea and sucking down half the cup in one go.

Although Charlotte made a point of not staring, Diana laughed. "Good God, don't tell me you're not fed here? You eat as though you've not seen food all week. And those collarbones of yours . . . So very sharp."

Signa's shoulders wilted. She knew better, certainly. Knew to take her time, to take small bites, to pretend she didn't find the food delicious and that she felt no desperate call to devour it all, and instead pretend she was delicate and barely knew the meaning of food.

Beside her, Death set down his tea. *How do you feel about this woman? I could infect her with a light plague, perhaps. Or we could give her the pox? Blemished skin may do her vanity some good.*

Recognizing the levity in his voice, she fixed him with a brief, angry look, to which he sighed. *Fine, ruin my fun.*

Between Charlotte sitting on one side of her and Death on the other, it was a fruitless endeavor to attempt to focus. Diana and Eliza dominated the conversation, and when they noticed Signa had gone some time without even a murmured response to any gossip, Eliza turned her flat brown eyes to her to pry: "Have you a suitor already, Miss Farrow?"

Death stood and loomed over Eliza, so close that Signa's throat grew tight. *Don't mind me*, he said. *Go ahead and answer. Is there someone you've got your eye on, Little Bird?*

Her fists clenched. She wanted with everything in her to demand that he leave, but she had no way to convey that with the others scrutinizing her. Noticing her struggle, Death said, *You should be able to respond to me, you know. If you hear me, I'd wager you can respond.*

She tried, eager to tell him to leave her alone long enough for her to glean information about the Hawthornes, or at the very least to find a way to speak to Charlotte in private. Yet as hard as she strained to send those words to him, he didn't react as though he could hear her.

"Do you intend to make your debut here, Miss Farrow?" Charlotte asked, a wary edge to her voice.

Signa held her porcelain teacup in both hands as she stared at her friend. Despite the nerves, despite what Charlotte knew and could do to undermine her . . . she was still relieved that Charlotte was present. That she'd finally found her old friend again and could see firsthand that she was safe and healthy and beautiful. "I'm hoping to join this season, yes," Signa told her, liking the way the announcement felt when she spoke it aloud.

Eliza clapped her hands. "Oh, you must have a party to celebrate! Invite us, and we'll ensure you know everything about every man in town—" She clutched her throat, losing her breath for a moment when Death stepped around her.

Will I be invited to your party? I do love a good dance.

He would be invited to nothing, and though Signa wished she could tell him as much, she kept her smile and asked Eliza, "What men are thought to be joining this season?"

The commotion at the table was immediate. Eliza leaned in, brandishing her fork as she spoke. "I believe you'll want to keep your eye on my cousin Lord Everett Wakefield."

Charlotte perked up at the name, her eyes brightening. "He's arrived?" she asked, to which Eliza nodded.

"Just three days ago. He'll be joining us through the summer to see if he might find a suitable wife. I do wonder, too, who *your* cousin Percy might seek out, Miss Farrow. He's set to inherit the family business, and its fortune, you know."

Eliza was correct, assuming Elijah didn't ruin his prospects. Signa thought back to two nights prior, when she'd watched Elijah shove a cake into his son's mouth. She couldn't imagine Percy's embarrassment, couldn't imagine how it must feel to have a father lose himself so fully in his mourning.

The Hawthornes were fraying at the seams. One needed only to tug, and they would split entirely.

When Signa reached for another scone, Diana drew the plate

away with a thin smile that sharpened Signa's spine. She straightened, drawing her hand away in doubt.

Just eat it. Death's words were cold. *If you're hungry, eat the scone.*

But Death had no hold in society, no knowledge or stake in its politics.

Don't drink or eat too much, or too little. Only the right amount. Those were the lessons that her etiquette book taught. Signa just hadn't known what qualified as *too much*. Now she knew it was three scones. So despite Death's push, she didn't take another, even when Diana began prying again into the business of the Hawthornes, hunting for gossip she would undoubtedly spread. There was no room to relax in this conversation. She was more on her guard than ever, judging every inch of her body—from where she rested her pinkie to how quick her breathing was. Did she sip too quickly? Was the amount of sugar she added to her tea appropriate?

Exhaustion weighted her shoulders; socializing was going to take more getting used to than she'd anticipated.

For so long Signa had waited for this day; waited for the time when she would sit and chat with her friends as part of high society. For the time when others would show interest in her, and she might finally have the company she'd spent so long yearning for. Yet when Marjorie returned to the parlor, it felt as though an eternity had passed, and all Signa wanted was freedom and a good nap.

Charlotte was the last of the ladies to depart, and much to Signa's surprise, she refused to linger. Her eyes skimmed over Signa as a quick "I'm glad to see that you're doing well" passed her lips before she grasped her skirts and followed Marjorie out the door.

Tears burned Signa's eyes. Charlotte had recognized her. She'd recognized her, and yet... It meant nothing. Perhaps all that time together—all that friendship—had meant more to Signa than it had to Charlotte.

She'd forgotten that Death stood behind her until he grumbled, "Two of those girls behave as though they've just been let off their leading strings."

Swiping her eyes, Signa pivoted to him. "What are you still doing here?"

Again the shadows around him shifted, forming a table for him to kick his feet onto. "Good day to you, too. I came to see how you were settling in."

"I'd rather you didn't." Signa turned and paced the length of the parlor, not wanting him to see her so shaken. "How are you even here?"

He considered this, tipping back in his shadow chair. "You've spared Blythe for now, but that doesn't mean she's cured." The chair straightened, and he looked to her. "I'm here because she's still teetering on the bridge between the living and the dead. Because of that, when we are both near enough to her, it seems you can see me. I wasn't sure until today if that would be the case."

Blast this unfortunate connection of theirs. What she wouldn't give to cover the veil into the afterlife and never look upon it again. "And why is it I can hear your voice in my head?"

"Same reason you can hear my voice when I speak aloud, I suppose."

Were he corporeal, Signa would have shaken him. As it was, she spun on her heel and stepped toward him with a wrath that fueled her entire body. "Couldn't you see that I was busy?" she snarled. "This was *important* to me."

Death turned as though he could see the girls through the walls. "*Why?* I'd think such creatures only important to their mothers. Didn't you find it odd how two of them asked solely about your fortune and your family? They asked little about *you*."

True as it was, the last thing she wanted was to agree with him. And so she said stubbornly, "They're to be my friends."

"Your friends?" He stood, the table and chair he'd formed slipping back into the shadows. "Why? I've never seen you so . . ."

"So talkative?" Signa pressed. "Never seen me with company?"

They were nearly chest to metaphorical chest now. This near to him, Signa's skin buzzed not with fear but power. Determination. He was Death, and because of that she had no need to filter herself. No need to impress him.

Death bent so that his shadowed face hovered before hers, only a breath between them. "I've never seen you so demure, and so sickeningly stifled." A scone flew at her then, landing hard on her chest. She barely caught it before it hit the floor. "You wanted this, didn't you? Why would you let one person's opinion prevent you from having it?"

She curled her fingers into the flaky crust of the scone. "I was being polite. There are rules about these things—"

"What you were being was hungry. And if you're hungry, you should eat. Damn your rules." There was something dark about his tone. A sour disappointment that, to her frustration, gnawed at her.

"And what does it matter to you?"

The question ignited a burning rage in his eyes. An inferno that had him before her again, sucking the air from the room. "It matters because you're better than that. You were not made to be meek or wanting. If you embraced who you are, imagine the power you might wield. Imagine the things you could do."

"You mean the lives I could take?" Signa stepped closer. "Imagine the spirits I could speak to? The bidding I could do for the dead? I don't need to imagine it; I live it. That life consumes me, and it's not one I want."

"How do you know?" he demanded. "When all you do is run, how do you know what it is that you want? Would you rather spend your life pretending to be whatever it is you were with those girls?"

She threw the scone back at him, and to her surprise, it didn't slip through him as the knife had when she'd stabbed him. He caught it.

"Leave," she said once she'd managed to stifle her surprise. "You don't know me, and you never will. It's as you once said, we're both very busy people, and you're nothing but a distraction."

He scoffed, the sound so human. So male. "I came to offer my assistance. A murder would be significantly simpler to solve, I imagine, if you knew how to use your abilities."

"That won't be necessary," she said, not caring to consider the offer. "I can already speak with spirits—"

"So you see no value in an ability to walk through walls?" he demanded. "To alter your body so that others cannot see you? To become the very night itself, and submerge into the shadows? Imagine the spying you might do."

Those would be useful powers, yes, but accepting that meant accepting his help, and she had no desire to entertain him and his ego for any longer than necessary.

"All my life, I have wanted nothing more than to be rid of you." She squared her shoulders before the shadows that loomed over her. "I begged, night after night, death after death, for you to leave me alone. And now you want to offer me help?" There were not enough words. Not enough savageness within her to tell him the extent of what she thought of that. "I hate you, and I hate everything you've done to me. I will solve this, and I will do so without you."

All around them, the day winked out. The darkness was all-consuming as Death grew larger, his anger so palpable that it suffocated the room. Above them, the chandelier shook, its lights flickering like an approaching storm. The sunlight filtering in from the windows snuffed out like a candle.

"You no longer have a choice in this." Death's voice shook the walls, knocking two porcelain teacups to the floor. "I tire of these games. I know you better than you think, just as I know that you will never rid yourself of me, Little Bird. As I will never rid myself of you."

The shaking ceased, and daylight streamed back into the parlor as Death retreated to his shadows. "Our lessons begin at midnight. I'll see you then."

She was about to yell that he shouldn't bother. But the moment she opened her mouth to speak, a scone flew from the table and into her mouth, choking off the protest Death refused to hear.

SEVENTEEN

Balanced atop Signa's head was a book so heavy it was giving her a migraine.

"Balance, Signa," Marjorie instructed her. "Grace. Walk with grace."

From the corner, lounging comfortably upon a green velvet settee, Percy laughed. Given that he had no business being there, Marjorie flashed him a look, but Percy was far from vexed. He'd made it a point to announce that he'd come simply to watch his cousin attempt to learn manners—and that he was taking a great deal of amusement in those attempts. There was, however, something troubled about the furrow of his red brows, and the way his eyes flickered to the maids who rushed about the halls to set up for the party that would begin that evening.

He and Marjorie pretended not to notice them, so Signa followed suit, understanding why the party might be a sore spot for Percy.

"*Grace*, Signa," Percy repeated, drawing the word out with an overly airy tone. Signa never had a brother but imagined that if she did, he'd be every bit as annoying as Percy. It was almost as though he knew her politeness was a charade. Like he could see it in her face and was trying to pluck the truth out of her. She did everything in her power to ignore him, hoping to maintain the illusion that she was a respectable young woman.

Though after her run-in with Elijah the night prior, it seemed unlikely the master of Thorn Grove would care what she did or how she behaved. Assuming she didn't burn the manor to the ground, she doubted he'd bat an eye at her strange behaviors.

She was reminded of how Percy had waited atop the stairs observing his father with such longing. It was such a different version of him than she saw now—a relaxed Percy who kept a careless manner, a proper young gentleman without any troubles.

What had Elijah meant when he'd said he'd failed his son too many times? Signa was so distracted by her deluge of thoughts that she tripped over the Persian rug and watched the encyclopedia tumble from her head to the floor. Under her breath, she cursed, not realizing she'd said the word aloud until Percy doubled over with laughter and Marjorie threw her hands up in frustration.

"Language, Signa! I swear, you both are impossible today!"

Though Signa had the sense to blush and bow her head with an apology, Percy smiled coolly at the governess, far too charming for his own good. Signa fought the urge to roll her eyes as Marjorie's resolve crumbled beneath the boy's grin. The governess sighed and scooped the book from the floor.

"I don't know what's gotten into you today, Signa, but you are helpless." The comment was simply a fact, not meant to be unkind. "And you, Percy. I thought I told you yesterday to find something useful to do with your time."

He folded his hands behind him, chin proud. "Apologies, Miss Hargreaves. I just wanted to assure myself that my dear cousin felt welcome here."

The longer Marjorie glared at Percy, the more her eyes softened until, eventually, she relented. "Oh fine. Since it's obvious we'll get no further in our lessons, you may pay a visit to your cousin's room, Signa."

Percy perked up. "You're going to visit Blythe? Shall I join you?"

"Of course you should," Marjorie decided for them both. "Take some pastries from breakfast up to her. I'm sure that'll make her happy."

Signa prayed that Marjorie was right. She was going to need a peace offering after the way her first visit with Blythe had gone.

Percy matched Signa's pace, as eager to see his sister as she was. "If she's sick with the same illness that took my mother, the last thing she needs is to be holed away in her room," he said as they made their way up the stairs, taking them two at a time. "Everyone keeps telling her to rest. I'm sure she's bored senseless."

Signa didn't have to imagine the boredom or the loneliness it brought. If this visit went well, perhaps Blythe would allow her to visit more often.

"Did she and your mother both have the same symptoms?" Signa kept her voice low.

"Exactly the same, yes. Though Blythe's tongue hasn't yet begun to fester with sores, and her hallucinations are milder than my mother's were." Percy's tone had slipped to something colder, something pained, and Signa knew better than to press no matter how much she wanted to. It was a testament to her growth, she thought, that she was able to be sympathetic to the fact not everyone was as comfortable speaking about the dead as she was.

She listened while Percy shifted topics to rambling on about the portraits they passed, pointing out the male ancestors who had been in charge of Thorn Grove prior to his father. His chest was proud as he spoke, shoulders squared and confident. "What amazing men they were, to build such an empire."

Signa didn't think it was worth noting that a gentleman's club offered nothing different from the tea she'd had with the ladies that morning with its drinks, food, and gossip with people of a similar social status—only she hadn't paid a membership fee to participate. Regardless, she understood the pride in Percy's eyes. Grey's had done the Hawthornes well, and he was meant to continue that legacy.

After passing what must have been a dozen portraits of scowling men in suits, they knocked quietly upon Blythe's door and waited for permission to enter. Nothing in Blythe's sitting room had moved so much as a hair. The air was heady, pressing upon the two as they stepped inside and onto the plush rug. Though Blythe lived, her room was that of a ghost's.

A budding pressure in Signa's chest eased when she saw Blythe sitting upright in her bed, leaning against the headboard. Sick as the girl was, Blythe didn't scowl at Signa as she had last time. Rather, she looked to her brother and beamed.

"Percy! Where have you been? I've nearly begun to count the threads of the curtains, I've been so bored. What's that you've got there?"

Her grin stretched when he waved a scone at her, and she whipped out her hand to take it. "God, I've been waiting for them to make the lemon ones again." She bit into it and groaned as though it was the first thing she'd eaten all week.

Percy set the remaining pastries down and ruffled Blythe's straw-blond hair before pulling up a small iron chair to sit beside her. "I'll tell the kitchen to make them more often if you like them so much."

Signa waited at the threshold of Blythe's room, hands folded before her. She lingered there as Percy settled in, watching his Adam's apple bob as he looked his sister over—her pale, bony frame. Dead, dry hair. The bags under her eyes, and lips that were as pale as the crumbs she brushed from them. Percy took hold of her hand, so fragile a thing, and Signa noticed for the first time the starkness between them. Where Percy was freckled, Blythe was porcelain. Where his hair burned like a summer fire, hers was void of color. What they shared was the sternness of their father's mouth and the grim way their eyes squinted at the corners, like they were either always contemplating, as in Percy's case, or perpetually annoyed, in Blythe's. As different as they looked, when side by side there was no denying they were of shared blood.

"Is she going to come in," Blythe asked, "or will she continue to stand there and let in the draft?"

Percy leaned toward his sister conspiratorially, though his words were loud enough for Signa to hear. "Careful, Bee. You must remember to speak quietly when there are skittish fawns about. We wouldn't want to spook them."

Squaring her shoulders, Signa walked into the room with her chin held high. "I am no fawn."

The girl turned to her with a smile that nearly snipped Signa's breath straight from her lungs. The feeling was similar to what Signa had felt the first time she'd seen Blythe—like she and Blythe were linked by an unbreakable string. This must have been the connection that Death said happened when she'd unknowingly spared Blythe's life.

She barely knew this sickly thing who struggled to leave her bed, yet whose gaze could impale a person. All the same, Signa felt compelled toward her. She didn't know what it meant, or why she had these abilities. But what she did know was that she'd do everything in her power to save Blythe's life, and that started with figuring out the source of the poison.

"I want to apologize for the other night. It was . . . rude of me to say what I did. I've never been eloquent." Signa balanced herself atop the far corner of the bed, opposite Percy. She was ready to spring back up and flee at any moment.

The ice in Blythe's eyes melted as she licked the remaining sugar from her fingertips. "You ought to work on that." Her tongue was the faintest shade of pink. Almost white.

Goose bumps crawled across Signa's arms like spiders, and her stomach dropped before she noticed that the chill in the room was from an open window, and not because Death was lingering nearby. His absence might have given Signa hope, had she not known that Blythe was on borrowed time with a murderer still on the hunt.

"I won't thank you for saving me the other day, given that it was your fault I had an accident in the first place." Blythe's words were as cutting as Signa remembered them, each one its own knife. "But I won't refuse your company, either, for I've never had a cousin before. Will you be with us long?"

It was Percy who answered. "Father had the modiste prepare her a wardrobe for the season."

Blythe's face darkened. "I suppose I should be glad someone is getting his attention. Though if you are in need of gowns, you could have taken mine. I've no use for them anymore, and too many will go unworn."

"Blythe—"

"Oh hush, Percy. I don't mean it like that. They no longer fit me, and I doubt my body will ever be back to what it once was." With each word, the bite in her voice lessened. "Now tell me about work. Are there any updates?"

His grip on Blythe's hand tightened, and Signa got the impression that there was something more to this back-and-forth language of siblings that went beyond her understanding. "Uncle is on his way here right now to talk sense into the man, but I fear Father believes himself beyond reproach."

Blythe clucked her disapproval. "Surely, he'll bend one of these days. You must keep trying."

"He's not bent since the day you took ill, Blythe—"

"And when was that, exactly?" Signa hurried to ask, trying not to shrink under the weight of the eyes that turned toward her in surprise. "I ask merely out of curiosity. When did you fall ill?"

Blythe feigned a gasp. "I'm *ill*? Heavens, I'm surprised you noticed. No one dares to speak of it before me." She made a quiet, amused hum in the back of her throat before leaning her head upon the pillows. "About a month after my mother died."

Whoever was behind it, they'd wasted no time. Signa peered at a small pile of chocolates on Blythe's bedside table, next to a cup of tea. She crossed to that table and took one of the chocolates, trying to be discreet as she bit into it. Signa couldn't say whether she was relieved or disappointed to discover that it wasn't anything but normal chocolate, but she did take another bite. Her eyes fell to the tea next, and Signa reached for it before she could feign an excuse.

Blythe shot up, positively lethal. "Don't you *dare*! That's my medicine."

When Blythe stretched her hand out to take the dainty porcelain cup, Signa backed out of her reach and took a tentative sip. That was when she tasted it—barely more than a hint of the bitter berry, not enough to be noticeable to anyone who didn't have a tongue familiar with the taste.

This was it. This was how someone was keeping Blythe ill.

The cup was still nearly full, the liquid cold. "How long have you been taking this medicine?"

"Since the day I took ill," Blythe answered, glaring. "It hurts my stomach if I drink it too quickly. Put it down."

She didn't. Instead, Signa walked to the window and dumped the tea out.

"Are you mad?" Percy ripped the porcelain cup from Signa's hand. "For all we know, that could very well be what's keeping my sister alive!"

"On the contrary, it could very well be what's keeping her sick." Signa didn't want to let on that she knew what was happening, lest the killer find out and try other tactics. "Who gave this to you?"

Blythe's lips curled down and deep lines furrowed in her forehead. "My maid brings it every morning."

"And what's her name?"

"Elaine. Though I don't see why—"

Signa recognized the name at once as the servant who had been helping her dress. "Who prescribed this for you?"

"One of her *doctors*." Percy folded his arms across his chest. "And dare I say one more competent than you."

Even Signa knew that no doctor would prescribe belladonna in anything. Someone was sneaking it in—perhaps not in every cup but in many.

"I know this might sound strange," she began tentatively, "but, Blythe, I don't believe that you're suffering from any disease."

Percy took Signa's wrist in his grasp, gripping so hard that she flinched, certain she would bruise. "Do not fill my sister's head with nonsense. It's the same illness that took our mother—"

Signa tore her arm away and looked him hard in the eye. "This isn't medicine. I know because I've tasted it before. It's belladonna, from the berries that grow in the woods near here. Someone is poisoning her."

Blythe didn't move for a long moment, her mouth half open. "Percy," she began, and her brother only shook his head.

"One of the doctors would have realized it by now if it was poison." He was adamant in this belief, each word stressed. "Signa is merely guessing."

"I'm not guessing anything," she said with every bit of conviction she could summon. "I recognize the taste. And if you don't believe me, see for yourself. Blythe, the next time your medicine is brought to you, don't drink it. But don't refuse it, either, for you might alert someone of your suspicions. Wait until no one is around, and then find a safe place to dispose of it. Percy, you should be careful, too. Who's to say you're not next?"

His skepticism remained, evident in the creases between his brows.

"Shall I ask the doctor?" There was a fragility to Blythe's voice, but otherwise she was handling this better than Signa expected. "What about Father? He deserves to know, doesn't he? If there's a chance that what happened to Mother was no accident?"

Signa remembered how Elijah had shoved cake into his son's face, and the bags under his eyes, and how he was haunted and unable to sleep. His behavior was too erratic, too unpredictable. It wouldn't be safe to trust him, nor did she think it wise for anyone else—including Blythe's current doctor—to know that they'd caught on. Not to mention how suspicious it was that not a single one of Blythe's doctors had realized what was happening.

"The best thing we can do to help your father is to protect the two of you," Signa said. "Which means that, for now, this secret stays between us. Be careful with your meals. No jam. No berry reductions on your roasts. Drink your tea, but throw it out if there's anything odd about the taste. You must eat, both of you, and you must not rouse suspicion. But take extra precautions." She didn't dare mention that Sylas knew their secret as well. It didn't feel wise to mention him, and Signa still could use his help and his connection with Thorn Grove's servants—especially now that there was a lead.

Elaine.

Blythe sighed and let her head fall deep into the pillows, curling into the sheets as though to make herself smaller.

"We'll figure this out," Signa promised her, putting as much gusto behind the words as possible, trying to convince herself as well. "We're going to put a stop to this, and you're going to be okay. I won't let you die, Blythe."

She meant it. Blythe was given a second chance for a reason. Signa had linked herself to Blythe's fate, and she'd do everything in her power to beat Death once and for all.

EIGHTEEN

L
ATER THAT EVENING, FULL FROM SUPPER AND HER HEAD POUNDING
from the events of the day, Signa was relieved to find Elaine waiting in the sitting room to help her get ready for bed.

"Good evening, Elaine," she told the young woman, who could perhaps be only a few years her elder.

The maid kept her eyes downcast and her chin low, offering the smallest nod. "Good evening, miss." She had a cotton chemise laid out for Signa, who extended her hands to have Elaine work off her white kid gloves and help her into her nightwear, as she'd done every evening.

Signa's tongue burned with a thousand questions, but she needed to tread lightly to get the information she was after. *A Lady's Guide to Beauty and Etiquette* did little to instruct her on what sort of interactions with staff were considered acceptable, likely because anyone in the position of reading the book should already know. Her uncle had a handful of servants on staff and spoke to them very little, yet Signa didn't trust his tactic of pulling his shoulders back and holding his nose in the air, for what good would that do when she wanted Elaine to relax and be open with her?

"Have you been with the Hawthornes long?" Signa asked as she moved to her vanity, offering a friendly smile as Elaine took hold of an ivory brush and set to work combing boar bristles through Signa's hair.

"Not long, miss." The tension in Elaine's shoulders signaled that the maid was as hesitant to say the wrong thing as Signa was. It took Signa clearing her throat and waiting in an uncomfortable silence before Elaine added, "Missus Lillian hired me a little over a year ago, God rest her soul." She paused her brushing to cross herself.

"As her lady's maid?" Signa hoped there was enough genuine curiosity in her voice to steady the woman's nerves. If the pain of prying information from Elaine was any indicator, the servants and the occupants of Thorn Grove didn't often converse.

"Not hers," Elaine clarified, "but for the young miss, Blythe. The previous lady's maid left to retire by the sea."

"Thorn Grove is a rather dreary place, isn't it?" Signa mused. "I can understand why the sea would appeal."

"Aye, miss." Elaine's voice fell low and grave. "They say this place is haunted."

Ah, now they were getting somewhere. "My family's home was seaside," Signa told her, not needing to fake the longing in her voice. "It's called Foxglove. I remember very little of it, for I was a child when I visited. I do look forward to inheriting it, though I must admit that the idea of maintaining a home so large sounds rather daunting. I imagine it'll take ages to hire a full staff."

Elaine's hand hesitated for a single moment before she resumed her brushing, and Signa knew her words had done the trick. For who would choose the dreary Thorn Grove over the seaside Foxglove? If there was a chance for her to earn a place there, Elaine would want it. Which meant that Signa now had someone else on her side, whether Elaine realized it or not.

"You're quite skilled," Signa added. "It's a wonder you have time for both myself and Miss Hawthorne. I'm sure that's no easy task."

This time Elaine didn't hesitate. "Thank you, miss. Though I admit that the young Miss Hawthorne does not require much these days."

Signa searched the maid's face in the vanity's mirror. A tiny, concerned crease knitted between her brows. Her sadness seemed genuine, and Signa realized that in the entire time Elaine attended her, she hadn't once believed she was speaking with a potential killer.

"No," Signa said with a sigh, already feeling as though her lead was slipping through her fingers. "I suppose she doesn't. Just help dressing, and her medicine, I presume?"

Elaine nodded. "It's easy enough to get her ready. Her tea and meals are made in the kitchen. I merely drop them off. So don't worry, miss. You'll never be wanting for my time."

Though that did little to comfort her, Signa smiled and asked, "I know the rumors of the late Mistress Hawthorne. But tell me, Elaine, are there rumors of any other ghosts at Thorn Grove?" It was a passing thought, but one that grew with severity the longer she held to it. Why wouldn't there be more spirits at Thorn Grove when the Hawthornes had owned it for generations?

When Elaine made herself small and set the brush down upon the vanity, Signa felt her suspicions confirmed.

"The servants talk about seeing a man in the library," she said. "They say the books fall from the shelves on their own, but I've never been inside to see it myself."

Signa hadn't even known Thorn Grove *had* a library. But if there was another spirit in Thorn Grove—perhaps one who could talk—then it could be worth paying it a visit.

Once Signa was deemed ready for bed, Elaine made her way to the sitting room to retrieve a tray with a piping-hot teapot, a tiny pot of honey, and a biscuit. Just as Signa was reaching for her tea, a dark square slipped beneath her door.

Elaine's forehead pinched as she bent to pick it up, brandishing a black envelope with a beautiful golden wax seal. "Perhaps it's from one of your cousins?" Elaine guessed.

Signa took it, smoothing her finger over the delicate parchment. She somehow already knew that was wrong. "Or perhaps it's from Miss Hargreaves, detailing my lesson plans for tomorrow." That didn't feel right, either, but it was enough for Elaine to nod, satisfied.

Though Signa wanted more than anything to tear open the letter, she tucked the envelope into her lap and casually reached for the honey. "Thank you, Elaine." She kept her tone casual and polite, but full of what she hoped was obvious dismissal.

"Have a good evening, Miss Farrow." With a final passing glance at the envelope, Elaine bowed her head and saw herself out.

The moment the door shut, Signa tore open the letter. Written upon thick parchment in the most beautiful script she'd ever seen were three lines:

Meet me in the stables at the eleventh hour this evening, and dress warmly.

We ride to Grey's.

—S

NINETEEN

T HE PARTY WAS IN FULL BLAST THAT EVENING. MUSIC POURED FROM
the ballroom, with the trill of a grand piano reverberating against
the walls. It was as bustling as when Signa had first arrived at Thorn
Grove, the gowns as full and as dazzling as they'd been that night,
and the sweets passed around on silver platters just as luxurious.

Signa caught only glimpses of the festivities. The heavy wool
dress she'd changed into—with the exception of a corset, which she
was unable to fasten herself—was far from the imported velvets and
silks the others around her had donned. She sneaked around the
maids, maneuvering out of the vision of those who might question
her. Death had been right—this would have been so much easier if
she'd been able to call upon those blasted powers of hers.

But to put herself in that state would summon him, and after
what she'd said to him that afternoon, he was the last person she
wished to see.

She had every reason to hate Death. Every reason to be angry, and to tell him so.

So why did she feel so guilty?

Signa kept her head ducked low as she shuffled down the stairs, nearly clear of the house when her face collided with someone's chest. She stumbled back, noticing first the rosewood cane the man fisted tight, then shrinking beneath the weight of Byron Hawthorne's scrutiny.

One corner of his lip curled as he looked her over, pausing upon her eyes. The breath left him in a rush, a pallor overtaking his skin. "Lillian?" The words seemed to escape him before he could stop himself, and he shook his head. "No. You're that girl who was with Marjorie, aren't you? My brother's new ward. Where do you think you're headed, dressed like that?"

One wrong word, Signa knew, and he'd have her back up the stairs. She considered her lie carefully and decided it best to play into the role this man would expect of her—a young, foolish girl. "I—I just wanted to see the party, sir."

She swallowed, for although she was acting, her discomfort with this man was very real. He made a dismissive grunt and took her by the wrist as though he intended to haul her back up the stairs. They'd taken but one step when something down the hall caught his eye. Signa followed his gaze to see that it was Marjorie's strawberry-blond hair he watched as she escaped the party, making her way toward the kitchen.

Byron released Signa's hand. "Return to your room, girl," Byron demanded, though he no longer looked at her. "This is no place for children."

"Of course, sir." She nodded, but the moment he turned to follow Marjorie, Signa seized her opportunity to escape into the night, not daring to glance behind to see if she'd been spotted. Anyone who noticed her skulking off to meet a young man at this hour would think one thing, and if her etiquette book was accurate, it'd mean social ruin.

Sylas waited in the stables with the horses ready—Mitra again for Signa, and a stallion dark as the sky above for him, one that reminded her of the beautiful beasts that had picked her up from Aunt Magda's. Gundry sat at Sylas's heels, the hound's eyes a rich amber. His nose was lifted and his eyes alert, ensuring no company dared to venture too close.

"Took you long enough." Sylas glanced once at her wool gown and promptly unfastened his black cloak, draping it around her without waiting for permission. "Decide to stop for scones on your way here?"

"If only I were so lucky." Signa made a fist around the cloak, too embarrassed to thank him as he pressed Mitra's reins into her palm. Sliding her foot into a stirrup, Signa tried to pull herself up and onto the mare.

In no mood to waste time, Sylas reached for her waist and hoisted her up, checking to ensure that she was secure in the saddle. This time, she did her best not to flinch from his touch.

"It's half an hour's ride." He lifted himself onto his own stallion with admirable grace. "Keep close to Mitra for warmth—we won't be stopping."

"And might I ask why we're going to Grey's in the first place?" There was only an hour until she was meant to meet with Death. Although she didn't particularly care to see him, she had no desire to discover what he'd do if she was late for whatever ridiculous "lesson" he had planned.

"I was with the horses this afternoon when I overheard your governess speaking to Byron Hawthorne," Sylas told her, brisk. "Grey's will be closed for repairs tonight, and she is to join him there. There's something he wants to show her—something that he said will 'persuade her.' If we can outrun them, we might be able to figure out what it is."

That would explain the hunger in Byron's eyes when he saw Marjorie. "I saw them inside, heading for the kitchen," Signa said.

Sylas tightened his jaw. "They'll likely use the distraction of the party to take his carriage. We should hurry."

Gundry padded around the stallion's feet, amber eyes glinting and body tensed with anticipation. Signa wondered whether he was more dog or wolf. She was beginning to suspect the latter. "Is the hound coming with us?"

"Of course. Should we run into company, he'll alert us before they can see us. Now let's get going."

Though Signa had more questions—primarily how much trouble they'd be in if they were found—she was given no chance to ask them as Sylas gave his steed a gentle kick and took off. Mitra didn't wait for permission to follow. Wind stung Signa's cheeks and she pulled on the hood of her borrowed cloak. As it enveloped her, she was surprised to find it did not smell of hay and manure but of the wintertime woods, crisp and rich with pine.

She pulled the cloak closer as she followed behind Sylas, who seemed at ease beneath the starry night. He didn't shiver as she did but tipped his head back to face the sky. His black hair blew wild, as untamed and free as the way he rode. Beside him, Gundry ran at full speed, huffing with exertion and tongue lolling, loving every moment of the journey. Sylas caught the hound's eye, which sparked a grin of mischief from Sylas. He tipped his head back and howled into the night. Gundry joined in, the sound as beautiful as it was haunting as it echoed across the moors.

Watching Sylas, Signa softened. Every day, it seemed, there was another side of him to discover. So far, this was her favorite.

They rode in silence for a long while after that, the only sounds those of the beasts around them. Snorting from the horses, and heavy hoofbeats as they raced each other through the moors. Panting from Gundry, who never slowed even as the terrain shifted beneath his paws, grass turning into rubble and then cobblestones.

Sylas eased his horse to a stop, and Signa did the same. When they'd dismounted, Sylas tied the horses' reins loosely around a tree trunk. "We'll go on foot from here. Keep your hood on." Burrowed into the woodsy scent of it, she didn't argue.

Gundry ventured ahead to sniff out the streets. They were lined with hat shops and dressmakers and even a tiny apothecary, every building shut tight. Yet the lights of a pub farther down the street glowed bright, and it was better to take no chances.

"Byron and Marjorie. Do you think one of them could be behind the murder?" Her whisper echoed across the empty cobblestone street. It felt odd to be out at such an hour—odd to be out in town at *all*, but Signa felt no fear. She'd spent too much time with the night to be afraid.

And so, it seemed, had Sylas. Though, given his hulking size, it felt more likely that the night would be afraid of *him*. Sylas's walk was confident, his body long and chin lifted. "I'm not sure. But if someone's targeting the Hawthornes, there has to be a motive. Byron certainly has one—Grey's is the Hawthornes' source of income. It's their legacy. As for Marjorie—"

"There's something going on between her and Elijah," Signa said, earning a surprised blink from Sylas. Spotting it, she arched a brow. "Do you think you're the only one who can manage some sleuthing?"

Sylas set a hand on her shoulder, steering Signa to the side of the street so that they hugged the buildings. "Keep to the shadows, sleuth. If anyone sees you out at this hour, they'll think you've something to sell."

"But I've nothing in my—oh." Her cheeks warmed. "And they wouldn't think the same of you?"

"They'd think it scandalous, but you would withstand the worst of that social branding. If I were of higher status, it would be expected that I marry you. But you are lucky in this world, Miss Farrow, for you have the resources to care for yourself regardless of what society deems for you. Most people are not so fortunate." He looped his arm through Signa's and pulled her toward a greystone building—the tallest in the street, one with a massive bow window near the front entry.

Signa couldn't manage a more thorough look at the building,

for her entire face was on fire. Such a touch was in no way socially acceptable. From their difference in status, to the fact that they had no familial relation, this intimate link was nearly as scandalous as selling herself on the streets. It didn't matter that she had money; she didn't wish to *buy* people's affection. She wanted them to truly like and respect her. And yet... she'd never known that a man's arm could be so firm. That shoulders could feel so solid, and hands so strong.

Sylas was perhaps one of the most irritating creatures upon this earth, and yet she could not look away from him.

Whatever locks were on Grey's, Sylas wasted no time crouching before them, picking them with unnerving ease. He strode inside, gloved hands slipping into his pockets. "I've had practice," he said when he noticed that she'd stepped away from him, staring incredulously. "The padlocks on the stalls jam all the time, and we can't very well keep the horses stuck inside."

Signa nodded as she crossed the threshold, though it felt like her bones had been locked into place. How foolish she'd been to come. To agree to travel half an hour from her home in the dead of the night with a man who was practically a stranger. A man who had dismantled a lock as though it were a mere suggestion.

Where, she wondered, had he learned such a skill? And how much danger was she in? Perhaps she'd been a fool to trust Sylas— though she supposed she shouldn't worry too much. Should Sylas try anything, Signa needed only to summon her powers. To summon Death and end Sylas's life. Her hand went instinctively to her pockets, but they were empty.

She'd left her belladonna berries in the pockets of her day dress.

Sweat formed upon her brow, and her breathing grew uneasy as Gundry's sudden whine pierced the night, joined by the clunking of hooves and carriage wheels on cobblestones. Without missing a breath, Sylas shut the door and took hold of Signa's hand. There was no time to ask what he was doing—no time to look around—before she was shoved into a coat closet. Sylas stumbled in after her, hissing as he hit his head on something she couldn't see in the darkness. "Make room!"

Signa gathered her skirts closer, though there was little room to be spared. They were half on top of each other as he pressed in. He tried to brace against a wall, only for the leather of his gloves to brush against Signa's waist. She gasped and kicked one of his boots.

Sylas hissed, "Give me some credit, Miss Farrow. If I was trying to seduce you, my methods would be much more pointed."

His words were cut short as a door opposite the one they'd entered from rattled. Shooting Signa a glare to silently signal her to behave, Sylas eased the closet door shut.

Signa was convinced there was no part of her body that Sylas wasn't touching, and there was no part of him that she wasn't trying very hard not to think about. That she'd ventured out without a corset amplified the situation, for every brush against her felt that much more jarring, and the pressure of his body all the more perilous. It was an inopportune moment for such a fervent feeling to awaken in her, and yet awaken it did, quickening her pulse and making her mind wander. She wondered what it might be like to curl her fingers through his soot-colored hair, or how his lips might feel against hers. What his body might feel like beneath all the layers—

"Someone's here," Sylas whispered, and Signa nearly kicked him again.

"Obviously." Pulled from her stupor, she tried to peer through the thin wooden slats in the door. Though it was too dark to see his eyes, she could have sworn that Sylas was watching her before he leaned in and did the same, looking through the slats above her.

When the handle of the front door rattled, Signa drew a breath and held it, afraid that if she made so much as a sound, they'd be found out. Oh, what a fool she was to let Sylas drag her here, hiding in a coat closet of all places.

The two shadows entered without a sound, the larger of them bending to light one of the oil lamps, bathing his face in a dim ember glow. Through tiny slivers, she could see that Grey's floors were made of obsidian, as was the bar top stretching along an entire wall. There were glass tables scattered throughout, with plush leather chairs around each one. On the opposite side of the room, leather sofas surrounded the largest hearth Signa had ever seen.

"We'll have to be quick," Byron grumbled, voice rough as a carriage tumbling down a gravel road. "Should anyone discover a woman's been allowed in, we'll have even more of a headache than we do now."

"You beg me to come yet condemn me the moment I walk in?" Marjorie sounded haughtier than Signa had ever heard her. "I am perfectly content standing outside and sharing our discussion with the world if my feminine wiles offend you. Or perhaps we could take it back to the carriage, so that I may return home?"

Signa couldn't quite make out his response, though she thought it was something to do with how Marjorie needed to see this place for herself, to understand what he was trying to save. Taking a seat at one of the tables, Byron slid something across to her—papers. "Look at these and you'll see that liquor has not been ordered in weeks. And at these, which show we'd have no food for guests had I not realized our shipment was late. Elijah's not booked any entertainment, our cigars are no longer being imported, and yet it's he who holds the ledgers. It's he who refuses to offer this company any coin. He who refuses to pass his work on to me, and even worse, on to Percy! That boy has been here every day this week begging to work, Marjorie, and I am running out of excuses to give him."

Signa wished she could see Marjorie's face. Wished she could see *anything* as Marjorie answered, "I've done everything in my power, Byron. Yet even in her death, Lillian still holds his soul. I cannot get through to him."

"Then *change that*." There was such resentment in his tone that Signa flinched, glad for once that Sylas's body was there to steady her. One of his hands found purchase on her waist as he leaned over her to watch the scene unfold. Now that she'd noticed it, she struggled not to focus on every twitch of his fingers and shift in his body and to instead pay attention to what was happening outside the closet.

"Have you lost all your charm, woman?" Byron set his palms flat upon the table and leaned in. "Should he let this business fail, Percy will be left with nothing. He will be made a laughingstock and left with no prospects. I can't watch that happen to him, and I know you feel the same. Elijah has children—two, still, no matter what he may think. We must get him to realize that, before I can no longer fix his mess."

"Have you forgotten Lillian so easily?" There was a chill in Marjorie's voice that stole heat from the room and rendered Byron silent. "I know you haven't—the entire town knew your feelings for her."

"Lillian is unforgettable." Byron's voice dropped so low that Signa had to press her ear against the door to hear it. "Even so, we cannot allow my brother to throw everything away and chase after her."

"He must mourn her—"

"He *has* mourned! It's time for him to dust himself off before he damns this family. There's little I can do when he refuses to offer so much as his signature. If he won't give the business to Percy, convince him to give it to me. I'd take better care of it anyway, just as I would have taken better care of her."

Every muscle in Signa's body began to quiver at the heavy silence in the air. There was sweat along the back of her neck and down her back, but she paid it little mind.

"What," Marjorie inquired at last, "are you asking of me?"

There was no hesitation in Byron's response. "My brother is a lonely man, Marjorie. And lonely men are . . . susceptible. Especially to a woman's wiles."

"What are you implying?" Her fingers curled against the table. "Speak straight with me, Byron."

Byron ran a thumb and forefinger down his dark mustache, taking the time to gather his wits. "You and my brother have had

172

relations in the past. I'd have thought you'd jump at the opportunity to be with him—he could make quite the life for you."

The chair screeched against the obsidian floor as Marjorie stood. "How dare you? You may have spent your life pining over a lost love, Byron, but I will not degrade myself to such shame."

"I'm sorry if I've offended you—"

"Offended me?" Marjorie's laugh was like the shot of a pistol, sharp and halting. "You have called into question my very virtues. You have implied I am little more than a whore, and Elijah a puppet to be played with. You've more than offended me, sir. For the sake of the children, I will continue to try to speak to Elijah, but it won't be to help you. I want you to stay away from Percy."

Byron rose as well. "I will do no such thing. If you care about that boy, then you'll do as I ask. There's more than one way to ruin him, Miss Hargreaves."

There was a beat before she responded, her words shakier now. "Percy has done nothing wrong."

Byron rolled his shoulders back, preening in his victory. "I will not see my family's legacy fall over the death of some woman. Elijah must stop neglecting his duties."

"How callous you've become, Byron. God, how I wish she could see you now."

The slap was so loud that Sylas covered Signa's mouth and pulled her against his chest as she gasped from the surprise of it. Signa could only imagine how much it must have burned, and every part of her ached to throw open the closet door and go after Byron. To hurt him for hurting Marjorie.

On shaky feet, Marjorie clutched her cheek in one hand. With the other, she took hold of her coat. "It's time you grow up and stop competing with your brother. Lost as he may be right now, he will always be the better man." She spat on the floor, then left. Signa desperately hoped she would take the carriage and leave Byron stranded, but Byron cursed and followed after her, slamming the door shut behind him.

Signa was too numbed by surprise to move as the silence settled into her bones. Had Marjorie and Elijah been together before? It would explain their familiarity. Whether it had happened before Elijah was married or after, it was a scandal nonetheless. Even so, Signa was beginning to understand the appeal of illicit attraction. After a moment, her thoughts returned to the firmness of Sylas's body against hers, and to imagining things she had no business imagining, especially when it was already so hellishly hot in the tiny closet.

Fortunately, once they heard the rattle of a carriage rolling down the street, Sylas popped the coat closet door open and Signa burst out in desperate need of fresh air. She wanted nothing more than to strip out of her clothing, sweat slicked and stuffy, but settled for removing the cloak and tossing it at him. Signa had never been more grateful for the dark as she wondered whether he was thinking about her body as much as she was about his.

"I feel like we really bonded in there." His tone was teasing, confirming her suspicions. "I daresay I now know you better than I've ever known anyone." And then he stilled, as if realizing he'd given away a piece of information he didn't intend to, and he turned away while clearing his throat.

"He hit her," Signa whispered, dazed and eager for a change of subject.

Sylas nodded, adjusting his gloves. "He did."

"Do you think she'll be okay?"

"To be frank, I think it's wise to fear more for Byron's well-being than for Miss Hargreaves. I find that nothing is as terrifying as a woman scorned. And did you see her face? Positively murderous. Now"—he held out a hand—"enough of that. While we're here, let's find out what other secrets this place is hiding."

TWENTY

ESPITE THEIR SITUATION—OR PERHAPS BECAUSE OF IT—SIGNA couldn't stop the thrill that surged through her as Sylas took her hand and pulled her deeper into Grey's. Just that morning she'd been sipping tea, living out her dream of participating in high society. She'd expected that gathering to fill the lonely void within her, yet all it had done was make her realize how much harder she had to work, and how much more she had to learn and mold herself to be acceptable. Yet with Sylas, her shoulders finally eased and her body thrummed with life.

With him, there was no worry of anyone scrutinizing her every move. She could just *be*.

Their night together felt like a restart. Like filling her lungs with a deep breath. She let Sylas lead, trying to settle the pattering of her heart as he picked up an oil lamp and led her to the office. She needed to get ahold of herself—in addition to their differing statuses, she barely knew Sylas. Rather than let her mind stir with thoughts of handsome young men, she needed to focus on the task at hand.

Elijah's office at Grey's was similar to the one he had set up in Thorn Grove. A large mahogany desk and plush chair sat in the center, atop a rug of a burnished red. Someone had designed the room to have the air of masculinity, with a leather couch that sat in front of bookcases that took up a whole wall. Though Elijah had allegedly not been to the office in some time, there wasn't so much as a speck of dust upon the shelves, and the black leather ledgers were organized neatly on his desk.

Upon first glance, one would think everything about the office standard. But something urged Signa to look deeper, just as Sylas appeared inclined to do as he threw himself into the seat behind the desk and tried the top drawer. It didn't budge.

"Think you can manage to open it?" Signa asked, recalling how easily he'd unlatched the door to Grey's.

"I can try. These are fickler things, though. Harder to mask that you've been toying with it. Which is why—" He stood and crossed to the bookcase, inspecting the spines of old leather books and various knickknacks. He even shifted furniture around until, hidden beneath a lamp, he discovered an ornate silver key. "I would prefer to find one of these." Had his head not already been so inflated, Signa might have admitted she was impressed. He certainly waited for the praise and scoffed when she only nodded for him to open the drawer.

The contents were far less exciting than she had hoped. Old bills for imported alcohol and cigars were scattered throughout the drawer, as were letters left from patrons. *To the ineffable Mr. Elijah Hawthorne*, one writer began, spewing nonsense for two pages about how pleased he was to have the opportunity to seek membership at

Grey's, and how much he valued the qualities of a gentleman. Elijah must have kept the letter for his own amusement. There were more just like it, perhaps a dozen or so, each of them as indulgent as the next, written in the hope of getting into Elijah's good graces and claiming a membership.

She set the letters aside and began to riffle through the drawer once more, until she drew out a handful of photographs.

Sylas gave a hiss of protest. "Careful. We are merely ghosts passing through. We must leave no marks."

Signa ignored him. Elijah was now a shell of the man he'd been in the photographs of him and his family. Though only a moment captured in time, his laughter in the first picture in the stack was infectious. He beamed bright as a star, arm wound around the waist of a beautiful woman. She was sunlight incarnate, radiant, with flaxen-blond waves that cascaded down to her waist.

Lillian. She looked far from the haunted spirit that Signa knew—not yet a woman tormented by her death and helpless to change her daughter's fate.

Standing before them were two children: Percy, perhaps ten years old in the photo, and a young Blythe before him. Blythe looked every bit like her mother, though her expression was more cunning. In the miniature portrait, Lillian had her hand upon Percy's shoulder as the boy stared at the camera. Percy's expression was severe, small hands on the lapels of his suit jacket, as if to ensure he looked proper. It seemed not much had changed over the years.

Signa would have liked to steal the photograph to tease him with but didn't dare risk being found out. She started to put the photo back into the drawer when her thumb brushed across a thin edge on the back of the photo—there was something stuck to it. With the tip of her nail, she eased a slip of parchment from the back of the photograph. It was yellowed with coffee stains, and its dark ink blurred from a liquid spill.

"It's a letter," she told Sylas, who loomed over her.

I implore you, Elijah, to think of our son.
No matter what you may feel for Grey's, it is all he knows.
I understand your relation to that place is fraught, but we must remember that our son is not you. Whatever qualms you have are not to be taken out on the boy. Percy was born to inherit the Hawthorne legacy. It is all he wants, Elijah. Please, do not let your pain—do not let your selfishness—get in his way.

There were more words that had been blurred and stained beyond legibility, but there was no denying it came from Lillian, prior to her death. All along, Signa had been under the impression that Elijah had taken Grey's away from Percy *after* his wife's death. But according to this letter, Elijah had been having qualms about letting Percy inherit Grey's for far longer.

Another puzzle piece. Another bit of information to tuck away for safekeeping.

Sylas leaned over Signa's shoulder to read the letter, too close for comfort. "Poor bastard. Seems like Elijah's serious about running this place into the ground."

Signa tucked the letter into the back of the photo once more and returned it to the drawer before giving voice to a passing thought. "What could have made him change his mind so suddenly? What could make him want to give up his family's legacy? I thought it was his way of mourning."

"That's what everyone seems to believe." Sylas glanced out the window at the dark sky. It had to be well past midnight by now. "I don't think we'll find anything more tonight, Miss Farrow. We should hurry back, before someone takes notice of your absence."

Given the party, she doubted anyone would. Still, it was unwise to risk being found sneaking in for the second night in a row. She relented, doing a sweep to ensure everything was in place before she slipped away from the desk.

"Merely ghosts passing through," Signa said, no longer shy as she looped her arm through the one Sylas offered. His touch had awoken something within her that she had no interest in quelling. A lingering curiosity to experience the touch of a man beneath her fingertips.

It was, as she was discovering, a feeling she quite enjoyed.

TWENTY-ONE

AN HOUR AFTER SYLAS HAD DROPPED HER OFF IN THE TUNNELS, WITH directions to take the first right, the second left, and go straight until she arrived at the pantry, Signa was still wandering alone, her right hand pressed against the wall to guide her. Turn after turn, she was met with darkness and a maze that seemed to shift and ebb beneath her.

Music from Elijah's party was a distant thrum against the tunnel walls. Signa chased it all the same, clinging to the noise in the darkness. But no matter how far she chased, there was no end in sight. Turn after turn, tunnel after tunnel, the pressure in her chest mounted. It was like the day she arrived at Thorn Grove, when she'd roamed halls that had seemed endless, taunted by portraits of all who had lived there before her time.

Someone or something was toying with her, but knowing that did nothing to ease her shallow breathing. Each of her footsteps grew more desperate, each breath tighter, until she stumbled into yet another dead end.

She smacked the wall in frustration. "Who's there? I've no time for games."

A voice came from the darkness, low and taunting. "On the contrary, Little Bird, I think you could use more games in your life."

Signa had never been so relieved to hear that voice. She turned to face him, able to see Death even in the tunnels, for his shadows were darker than the night itself. He loomed larger than usual. "You," he said without softness, "are late. I hoped you might try to walk *through* the walls rather than play by the rules of this tunnel, but you are more stubborn than I imagined."

"And you're an arrogant fool." She had not forgotten his promise of midnight lessons, though never would she have guessed he'd stoop to petty games as punishment. "I don't have any berries with me, you ridiculous heap of shadows."

The darkness gathered around her. "A ridiculous heap of shadows, am I? Well, Miss Farrow, I'm afraid this heap of shadows is your only help at the moment, and you'd do well to remember that. Especially if you intend to save your cousin."

Despite her fear and her nerves and the anger boiling within her, Signa tipped her head back and laughed. It was a bitter, unnatural sound. "And I'm supposed to trust you?"

The sigh he blew between his lips became the wind in her hair. "What will it take for you to accept that I am not your enemy?"

"You not killing everyone around me would be a good start." She squared her shoulders. "And you could answer my questions, too, without the riddles."

Though still faceless and nothing more than swaths of shadow and the bleed of night, the darkness shrank until Death was a shadow shape of a man that bent to her. "Ask me, then, and I will answer."

She flattened her expression, careful not to show her surprise. Though he made no comment on the lives he'd taken, she knew better than to lose this opportunity. "If I have the powers you claim, why did they fail me when I got stuck in the fence?"

His shadows brushed close to her skin as he answered without hesitation, "Because you fear them. Because you fear me and my world, and that you may somehow be becoming part of it."

She bit the inside of her cheek, betraying nothing. "I don't belong to that world."

"No? Then why is it that I've never met another soul that shares my power?" The shadows circled around her. "Since the creation of life itself, there has been Death to balance it. And in all that time, I have never once been able to communicate so clearly with another living soul."

She dared not look away from the reaper, but instead tried to peer *through* the shadows protecting him. What might he look like with his shadows stripped away? Would he have a face? A body? Oh, what she wouldn't give to catch Death blushing. To catch him feeling as small and bare as she did.

"How did you feel," he asked suddenly, "when you used my powers last night? Did you like feeling its burn against your skin? Did you find comfort in the darkness and the shadows?"

She had, though it was a truth she'd tried not to admit even to herself. All her life, she'd hated Death. And yet she'd spent her years chasing after him like a moth to a flame. As difficult as her life had been because of him, she should have despised him. Why, then, was it that whenever she was with him, something within her seared hot and fervent?

Before Death, she should tremble. She should fear. And yet the more time she spent with him, the more that fear was beginning to slip away as curiosity festered in its absence.

She didn't hate Death, not truly. And God, what a fool that made her.

Death's shadows tilted, circling her. As they did, the air in the tunnels grew tighter and more fraught, and Signa let it turn her fingers to ice and her lungs to frost. There was a limit, though, to that coldness. Too much, and it burned.

Yet no matter how much she pretended otherwise, Signa craved that burn.

"Ah yes." Death's voice was a purr in the night. "That's what I thought. I have the power to help you, but I won't force myself on you. You must come of your own bidding. My touch is fatal, Little Bird. Just a brush of my skin, and you'll be behind the veil again, able to access your powers until your body repairs itself." He held out his hand. "No more pretenses—I want to show you our world. Say the word, and tonight I'll teach you to access your power without the belladonna."

The memory of their time in Lillian's garden surged, and Signa recalled the slice of the cold metal gate through her body. The pressure on her unmoving lungs as they sat frozen in time. There was something else she remembered, too—the freedom. The *power*.

What would it mean, though, if she acted with Death's wrath? If she allowed herself his power—what did that make her? There was a darkness waiting to embrace her, waiting to drown her. It was the side of herself she'd fought tooth and nail against, for should she give in to such desires and embrace the powers within her, just what might she become?

"Do you know which tunnel leads back to Thorn Grove?" she asked.

Death replied coolly, "I do."

"And can you lead me there?"

"I will not." Signa noted his choice of words with annoyance. "You have abilities that are unheard of, Signa Farrow. You are no ordinary human, and it's time you stopped acting like one. If you would embrace the power that I see in you—"

"It doesn't matter what *you* see!" Her words rang too loud, piercing in her own ears. "What if I *want* to be an ordinary human? I'm tired of you following me wherever I go. I'm tired of people dying!"

Though she saw no nose, Death looked as though he were pinching the bridge of one. "If you'd let me show you what you could be—the power that you could wield—you might change your mind. Perhaps you think an ordinary life will suit you now, but what happens when that's no longer enough? When there is a void in you that cannot be filled by tea and gossip?

"I have *tried* to leave you alone," he continued. "I have tried not to care. To not get involved. But we are connected, you and I. Our fates—"

"Fate can sod off!" Her temples pulsed with a blossoming headache. "I can determine my own fate without your help."

There was a smile in his voice. "If I ever see Fate again, I'll let him know you feel that way."

Signa stilled, though this shouldn't have surprised her. If Death was real, then why shouldn't Fate be?

Death noted her curiosity. "Tell me, do you truly wish me gone? Because I have tried to leave you. Yet every time I do, it seems you find a reason to pull me back. Say the word and I will try again if that's what you want."

When he drew a step away, Signa reached out instinctively to stop him. "Wait!" He stilled without hesitation, and the tension in Signa's chest eased some, and she told him, "I would prefer not to have everyone around me die, yes. But . . . I don't want to be stuck in here alone."

Again, Death reached out his hand. "My offer still stands, but you need to make a decision. I'm a busy man, remember?"

"Yes, I'm sure I'm preventing you from a dozen deaths as we speak."

He scoffed. "Souls are not patient creatures. Whether I go to them or not, they'll find me soon enough."

She rolled her eyes but knew there was no changing his mind. "Fine." The word came through gritted teeth. "Make me a promise, and I will play your game."

His empty, waiting hand clenched tight. "I don't make promises I cannot keep."

"Good. Then promise me you'll leave everyone in Thorn Grove alone. I'm tired of making bonds, only for you to take them from me."

The air grew even tighter, her lungs colder. When Death spoke again, all amusement—all his curiosity—had evaporated. "You had an uncle who ignored you. Who stole from your fortune and kept you locked away in a room so that he could bring the entire town to his bed. You had an aunt who abused you and another guardian who you never had to meet because he was someone who was not fit to ever be left alone with young girls, Signa. And as for the one who died in the bathtub? She had a scheme to marry you off to her friend's son so that he could take over your fortune and help them obtain wealth.

"I kept hoping that the next would be better than the last," he continued, "but greed turns people into monsters. Was it truly so terrible to have yourself freed from them?"

She'd never considered her life and all its upheaval in such a light. She'd been so young, and in too many strange situations to know what was normal and what wasn't. He was right that her guardians had all been cruel to her. All but one. "I had a grandmother who did none of those things," Signa argued. "What about her?"

The shadows around him jerked, irate. "All those who live must die, Little Bird. You know as well as I do that it was her time. I came for her while she still had her dignity."

Signa ground her teeth, wanting so badly for her frustration to only grow, never ebb. "Because of you, I've had a life of isolation. It was one hardship after the other because everyone around me believed that I was cursed."

Death snorted. "It's not my fault you've been surrounded by pious vultures—"

"Vultures or not, I would have at least enjoyed some company every now and then! You said yourself that life and death must maintain balance, yet you seem to be doing a lousy job at following that rule. Am I mistaken, or did you not tell me how important it is that I recognize my powers and don't go around accidentally killing people, so that we might maintain some fragile balance between life and death?"

His shadows stilled, and Signa found herself looking up at this strange man—at death incarnate, at the bleed of the night—with her heart in her throat. When he spoke, his voice was the sound of hooves upon cobblestone, low and choppy. "Perhaps it was more selfish of me than I realized, but I couldn't stand by and watch how they treated you."

He'd effectively stolen Signa's bite. It wasn't right, what he did. All those people, as awful as they'd been, hadn't deserved to die. Yet Signa couldn't help the way her stomach fluttered at his admission. "You . . . You took them to try and help me?" She didn't want to believe such a thing could be true. No one had ever stood up for her. No one had ever tried to protect her. So why had he?

"Of course I did, you ridiculous girl." He fisted his hands and drew a breath, as though attempting to summon his patience. "Does that satisfy you?"

It took her a moment to right herself, barely understanding what he meant. Because . . . no. She'd never realized she could be so *unsat-isfied*. Hadn't realized her lips could tingle or her stomach ache with a desire that she knew should not exist.

She should hate him. But to know there was someone watching her—someone protecting her and caring for her—it was all she'd ever wanted. And even though it hadn't been in the way she'd expected, even hearing those words felt far better than it should have.

"I accept your offer." She forced the words out before she could change her mind. "Show me how to access my powers without belladonna and get me out of here."

The words unbound him. When Death's shadows wrapped around Signa, she didn't flinch. Though a small part of her warned that this was wrong, that she should be afraid, she leaned into his caress. She could feel his shadows now. Could feel them along her skin, brushing against her neck and lips. Igniting parts of her that she'd never known could be awoken.

His fingers clasped around hers, and it was a true hand, soft against hers and pale as the moon. He pulled her in close. Signa drew a breath—he truly was more than the darkness and shadows he lurked in, then. He had shape.

"All those I touch," Death whispered, "die." His other hand pressed against her cheek suddenly, and he breathed out a wondrous sigh so heavy that Signa's entire body warmed. "Except for you, Signa Farrow. When I touch you, I feel you. On you, my influence is temporary."

Signa yearned to lean into that touch. He sounded nothing like himself, dark voice now breathy and wondrous. Slowly, he let his hand drop from her cheek, though the fingers of his other hand remained curled tight around hers. "Should we break our connection, you'll be corporeal once more," he warned her. Signa nodded and fastened her fingers around his, never wanting to experience being stuck within something again. Death made a low sound in the back of his throat as she pushed closer.

The longer they touched, the more she could feel her temperature plummeting. The weight of her body grew light as gravity slipped away. Ice cleaved through her, and her thoughts darkened as that power slipped in, assuring her she could do anything. That she was invincible.

She tipped her head back, relishing the feeling. This world was hers to take.

"How do you feel?" Death asked with a knowing lilt.

"Like the world I've known is suddenly insufficient." She didn't realize it until she'd spoken the truth aloud. Something about Death—something about when she was like this—made her brave. Made her confident in a way she otherwise dared not be.

"For you, this world *is* insufficient." Death led her through the tunnels. There were no walls to block them nor any doors to change their path. The world was open for their bidding.

"For you," Death continued, "the world could be infinite." They passed from one tunnel to the next, the world bowing to their whims. "Whether you welcome this power or not is your choice, but this feeling—this world—could belong to you. You need only to take it."

She shut her eyes. There was a pressure in the back of her skull that she soon realized came from the lonely souls calling to her, wishing to pass on. Then came another pressure upon her that she recognized as an approaching death—someone ready to be reaped from this earth calling to her.

When Signa opened her eyes again, they were wet. "Is it sad?" she asked. "What you do?"

The muscles in his hands flexed in surprise. "There are times I wish things could be different." It wasn't a direct answer, but Signa figured it was the best she'd get. "There are times I wish I could warn people of their choices. Lives I must take at too young an age or when they're surrounded by people who are not ready for them to leave. I am hated and feared more than anything or anyone in this world. So at times, yes, it can be sad. But it's who I am.

"There's good in it, too," he went on. "I am the first person people see when they draw their last breath. I am the messenger who can deliver them to those they've missed. I am the one who assures them not to worry, or who delivers a swift death to those who are not welcome into the afterlife. I am many things, but what I am not is ashamed."

"You must be lonely, though," she said, her chest aching a little at the thought. At the familiarity.

"Yes," he admitted. "For many years I was alone, forced to spend my days watching the lives of humans, never able to interact."

"But you can interact with me."

"Ah," he said, "so you see why I enjoy teasing you so. I am not so lonely anymore, Little Bird. Not so lonely at all."

She wanted more information—to know what this connection between them meant, and why she was able to see him. But when she turned to ask, he was surrounded by translucent blue orbs that danced around him, lighting their way.

"Despite what you may think, my world isn't so dark at all." Death inspected the orbs—souls, Signa realized. Impatient souls; the ones he promised might find him. They lit his cowl, and Signa caught the smallest glimpse of a face beneath his hood of shadows.

Just a trace of hair silver as the stars, and a flicker of a smile as he reached his hand out to the souls that flocked to him. Some flocked to Signa, too, spinning around her dress and through her tresses, though they swarmed back to Death when he cleared his throat.

"They're in need of ferrying," Death told her. "It's as I've said all along, I am a busy man." He pulled her through the tunnels with haste until they were in Thorn Grove. With every wall they passed through, Signa stopped worrying some, relaxing into this power she could very well get used to. They were up the stairs and to her room in no time at all.

Too soon, in fact.

I must be on my way, but I'll be back tomorrow night, for there is more to teach you. He took his time drawing his hand away.

Gravity settled upon her. Her lungs seared, empty fingers burning, as life sank back into her bones. She clutched her throat, the feeling worse than she remembered. "Stay out of my head," Signa grumbled, though there was little bite behind the command.

Not until you learn how to talk to me. Death laughed, though it was short-lived as the souls gathered closer, doubling, tripling, more demanding than ever. He swatted at them with a hiss.

"Good night, Death." Signa watched him escape through the window, the souls pushing him out faster than she would have liked.

Good night, Little Bird.

She leaned against her window and stared at his retreating figure until he disappeared with the night. Only then, curled up in her bed and ruminating over the night's events, did she realize that she couldn't remember ever feeling less alone.

TWENTY-TWO

S IGNA AWOKE BEFORE DAWN—AT AN HOUR WHEN THE SKY WAS still dim and the servants were her only company—and journeyed to the kitchen for an inspection. She pored over the pantries and the tea supply, through the honey and the jams and the flour with fervor, all while the head cook watched her with a grim frown.

"You'll not find any rats in my kitchen," the head cook barked. She was an old woman, her face well wrinkled and soft looking, though her eyes were stern. Signa told the woman that she was certain she wouldn't, adding that one could never be too careful these days. Then she made up some excuse about how she wanted to practice for the day she would run her own estate.

The cook grunted, clearly unenthused about having Signa poking through the entirety of the kitchen with such scrutiny but approving her intention. And so Signa searched, testing and tasting and scouring everything. She found the containers for tea and a small glass of what she presumed must be Blythe's real medicine, and there wasn't a hint of belladonna in any of it.

Signa was scowling by the time breakfast rolled around nearly two hours later, and Marjorie told her as much. Not wanting anyone to ask questions, Signa tucked her frustration away for after her lessons, when there'd be more time to think through her next steps. Perhaps Sylas would have an idea, or perhaps he'd found a lead.

She ate under Marjorie's scrutiny, careful to take small bites when the governess was looking. And when she was done eating, Signa followed Marjorie to the parlor to begin the second half of her morning—the half that still concerned itself with the living, and with the life she was to have once her time at Thorn Grove came to an end.

And in that new life, if Signa was ever meant to take her place in society, she would need to learn how to dance.

"I understand why this lesson is necessary for *you*," said Percy, who stood to greet her, straightening his shirt collar so not a single wrinkle marred the fabric. "But why am *I* here?"

Marjorie took a seat on the piano bench in the corner of the parlor. Her hair was pulled back into a beautiful spiral of curls, and she looked as elegant and proper as Signa had ever seen her in an ivory cotton wrapper. "If she's to learn properly, Signa will need both music and a partner. And if I am to be the music, I need you to be the partner."

Signa would have wagered that her directive also had to do with how Percy had taken to meandering around Thorn Grove, sighing and pathetic in his attempts to find something to do. She'd heard him outside earlier that morning, requesting a coach to be readied to drive him to Grey's, only for a groom to inform him that Elijah had banned him from traveling there, and that they were under strict orders to comply. She hadn't seen Percy's reaction, though she'd heard the door he'd slammed behind him.

Signa pitied her cousin. She'd known him for nearly a month now, long enough to realize he was a Hawthorne to his core. A proud, gentlemanly Hawthorne who'd had his legacy torn from his hands.

Percy peered down at her with his fox-like eyes. This close, she noticed that his eyebrows were rather bushy, though they were so pale a red that it appeared from a distance as though he had very little. His eyelashes, too, were pale as snow. "Are you any good at dancing?" Percy asked, to which Signa responded with an indignant, "Are *you*?" too quietly for Marjorie to hear. His laugh was little more than a puff of breath.

It wasn't that Signa was a poor dancer, but one without practice— unless the nights she'd spent alone in her room counted, when she'd pretended to dance with a handsome prince who'd sweep her away from her current hovel. Signa hadn't known any true steps back them. She'd learned them over the past week, when Marjorie had spent hours beating them into what the woman had so kindly referred to as Signa's "thick, stubborn head." This would be her first time practicing with a true partner, and she couldn't deny Percy was the perfect choice. He was made for society, an aristocrat born and bred. He'd likely be able to do any dance backward, should someone request that he do so.

Percy extended a freckled hand, and as Signa took it, the piano-forte came alive with a waltz.

Signa's gaze dipped immediately to her feet, counting her steps. She could say them silently in her head but felt it better to whisper them as she danced, to ensure she wouldn't miss any. The concentration stilted her steps so that they were almost mechanical.

"Oh, dear cousin." Percy snorted. "You dance as though you were made of wires and gears."

She shushed him so sharply that his neck retracted like a turtle's. He tripped over the rug and winced when it caused Signa to stumble, stepping on his toes with the heel of her boot. She didn't apologize as he pulled his foot back with a gasp—it was his fault for interrupting her after all—and continued her counting.

"If you're going to attempt to court men with those moves, the least you could learn to do is look up so you don't trample them," Percy hissed. "Whoever you dance with will be expecting a *lady*, not a mathematician. Look *up*."

Signa lost her count. She jerked her eyes up to him, a sneer ready when she realized that her body was still following the steps.

Percy's face spread into a victorious grin. "Ah, there we go!" He tightened the grip of one hand and braced the small of her back with the other as he hastened their pace to spin her around the parlor floor.

"Percy—" Marjorie warned him, speeding up the tempo as he surpassed it, pulling Signa along into his shenanigans. His laughter was so light and infectious that Signa found herself joining in, dissolving into a fit of her own as he kicked an ottoman out of their way and twirled her across the rug. They tripped over each other, nearly tumbling to the floor several times but always righting themselves in the end with some dramatic flourish.

"Still full of gears and wires?" she taunted him.

"Oh absolutely," he shot back. "If not for me, I'm certain you'd still be crawling along the dance floor, counting from one to three."

Signa stepped purposefully upon his toes.

So lost in their fun were they, delirious with their quips and laughter, that neither noticed Elijah Hawthorne had stepped into the parlor until Marjorie stood and the music came to a sudden halt.

Elijah's eyes were unlike Percy's. They were the blue of forget-me-nots, their spark hollowed out and concealed beneath shadows. Yet when he looked at his son and heard the young man's laugh, a light shone from behind that dark shroud. A break in the storm.

Elijah opened his mouth to speak, but was interrupted by his butler, Warwick, who hurried into the room. Footsteps echoed behind him, as did a low *thunk-thunk-thunk* of something heavy against the mahogany parlor floor. Byron Hawthorne strolled in behind Warwick, shoulders rolled back and a scowl upon his lips. Signa dared a look at Marjorie, who clenched her jaw and gripped the edge of the piano tightly.

"My apologies, Master Hawthorne," Warwick began. "He insisted—"

"Where are our shipments, Elijah?" Byron demanded, removing his gloves and handing them to Warwick. In his grasp was the same walking stick Signa had seen him use when she'd met him:

rosewood, with a brass handle carved into the shape of a bird's skull. Byron smoothed his thumb over it as he addressed Elijah, scratching a fingernail into its wood. "Grey's will be out of food before the week's end. If you don't want to sign the checks, then sign the deed and be done with this game."

Elijah held up a hand. He nodded to Percy and whispered, "Go on. Continue."

Percy drew away from Signa. There was a hunger in his eyes. Determination in the sharpness of his jaw. "Let me fill an order." His voice didn't waver. "I have contacts that can expedite it. We'll have everything no later than Wednesday."

Elijah ignored him. "I want you to continue." His eyes landed on Signa with such severity that she felt compelled to obey. She reached out to Percy to take him by the arm, hoping to ease the situation. The last thing she wanted was another cake incident.

But her cousin's focus was locked on his goal. Percy clenched his fists and took three steps toward his father. "I promise I can take care of it. I know what to order, and I know where to get it. I'll see to the delivery myself and ensure its quality upon arrival. If you'd only let me try, you'd see—"

"I said continue, boy!" Elijah's voice sliced through the air like a blade. "Or has your head filled with so much air that you cannot hear me? Have you forgotten that you are dancing with your cousin right now? You have an obligation to her, not to some order slips. Do not ignore her for talk of work."

They'd gotten a little practice in already, and what Signa wanted more than anything was for Percy to be happy. Seeing how much

Grey's meant to him made her want it *for* him; her dancing could wait. But before Signa could speak, Marjorie intervened.

"Sir, we were nearly finished," she said. "Let Percy take care of this matter. Compared to a dance, it's far more pressing—"

If Signa didn't know better, she'd think from the chill that tore through the room that Elijah himself were Death. The look he flashed Marjorie rendered the entire room into silence. Signa didn't dare to so much as breathe until Elijah took a seat in a plush emerald chair and folded one leg over the other.

He didn't look at his brother again, and Byron instead gave Marjorie a look of warning that had her brushing a hand tenderly against her cheek, as if she was recalling where he'd slapped her.

"You will come to regret these choices of yours, brother." Byron's hostility carried across the room. "I thought when Lillian died that you would step up. Yet look at how she pulls you down with her even now, six feet under. That woman will be your death, mark my words. She is not worth this."

"Had she agreed to be yours, you'd have thought otherwise. Now"—Elijah turned to Percy and Signa—"continue."

Defeated, Marjorie slumped into her seat as Warwick set one hand upon Byron's back. Byron shrugged him off, cursing his brother, but he didn't struggle as he was ushered out of Thorn Grove. With no room left to argue, a scowling Percy took Signa by one arm. She winced as he yanked her back into position, fingers digging into her skin.

Again the music around them swelled, and they danced. This time, neither missed a step.

TWENTY-THREE

SIGNA SLIPPED AWAY LATE THAT AFTERNOON.

Marjorie had been so tense that, after missing countless keys on the piano, she'd ended the dance lesson early. Elijah hadn't stayed for its entirety; he'd disappeared without a word halfway through one of the dances, with Warwick following behind him. It must have been difficult, Signa thought, to serve someone as volatile as Elijah.

Though she tried to speak with Percy after the lesson, he'd grabbed his gloves from the desk and his top hat from the rack, then disappeared out the door without once stopping to acknowledge her. Signa couldn't blame him, not really. She'd been an infant when she'd lost her parents, and she hadn't a single memory of them to miss. Percy was grown and full of memories when he'd lost his. And the worst part of it all was that one of his parents was still alive.

Signa didn't pry or chase after him but gave Percy his space as she took the stairs, dragging her exhausted legs to the second story and down the dreary hall. Past the gilt-framed portrait of the redheaded man with his whippet and the one of a beaming Lillian that hung across from Blythe's room. When Signa poked her head in, Blythe arched a fine blond brow but said nothing. She'd grown used to Signa's frequent visits in the past weeks.

"Evening," Signa said, keeping herself stoic so as to not reveal her worries over Blythe's brittle frame. Her cousin shouldn't still have been ingesting poison—she should have been getting better. And yet Blythe looked like a dried maple leaf, ready to crumble in the first gust of wind.

Blythe's dinner of roasted chicken and buttered potatoes was on the table beside her bed. Though she wasn't able to inspect all of Blythe's meals, Signa checked as many as she could. She bit into the chicken with great care, then the potatoes, and sighed with relief. There was no belladonna in the food, nor was there any in the oolong.

"What happens if the food is poisoned?" Blythe asked with a frown. "Won't you become just as sick as I am?"

"Not quite." Signa set down the tea and handed the plate to Blythe. "I recognize the taste. I'll spit it out before it can affect me."

Blythe leaned back, placated by the answer. Signa, however, was anything but as she observed her cousin, so thin and frail. Now that Blythe knew to be cautious, Signa had hoped the girl would recover quickly. So used was Signa to her own fast recovery that she had no concept of how long or painful a process recovery was for others. Perhaps it was normal for improvement to come at a snail's pace.

"I heard music." Blythe dipped her head back against the pillows. Her lips were as white as her skin—worse than ever. "Is there another party?"

Signa took a seat upon the bed's edge and grasped Blythe's hand. The girl made no protest as Signa curled her fingers around hers, feeling for the pulse in her wrist.

Slow. It was so, so slow.

"I was learning to dance," Signa offered, keeping her face free of worry. If Blythe was to get better, then she needed to believe she could. "I'm hoping to debut soon if I can convince Miss Hargreaves that I'm ready. You'll be joining in the season as well, won't you?" It was a shiny bobble she dangled at the end of a rod, hoping to give Blythe something to look forward to.

There wasn't so much as a glimmer in her cousin's eyes. "I was meant to debut this year," Blythe admitted. "I've spent years delaying it, but the moment I turned nineteen, Marjorie was insistent. No longer having to participate in the season is perhaps the one silver lining of my illness."

Signa balked at her cousin's words. "You don't wish to join society?" She'd never heard such a statement. Never thought that anyone might want anything different. To debut was expected—it was what the etiquette books instructed, and what society trained young women for.

Blythe leaned forward at Signa's bewilderment. "Do tell me you've considered what it will mean to take a husband." She took Signa by the wrist, her brows drawing together. "You hold your family's fortune, Signa. But should you marry, it will no longer be yours alone. You'll be giving everything—your wealth, your wants, your power—to a man who will hold more influence and respect than you as a woman will ever be able to garner for yourself in this world." Blythe's lips were thin, hard lines. Her grip slackened after a moment, and though her energy was depleted enough that she had to lean against her pillows, there was a hardness in her stare.

Signa hadn't been so naive as to dismiss such thoughts, yet they'd never seemed as important as Blythe made them sound. What use did she have for money when she was spending her days alone? Thus far in her life, what benefits had she gotten from her family's fortune? What reason did she have to hoard it?

"I will not marry," Blythe announced eventually, her voice a touch weaker. "I've enough money and status to do whatever I wish without sharing myself with a man." Her chin was knife sharp, and although Signa had never heard such a claim before, she believed her cousin.

Drawing her legs beneath her, Signa settled into the bed and asked, "What will you do then, with all your time?"

"Whatever I wish." A light sparked in Blythe's glossy eyes. "I will paint, and travel, and wander the halls at night so that I may sleep until the afternoon should I desire. I will have a hound, or three, and I'll spend my mornings riding horseback with no one to care for but myself. There are no limits to what I might do, for I will be wholly in charge."

Signa supposed it would be grand to do whatever one wished, without any responsibilities. It was a marvelous freedom, and yet she wondered... "And you'll do all these things alone?" The idea made her wilt a little.

Blythe looked affronted. "Of course not. I do have friends, you know. I'll visit them when I get bored, and Percy, and... you, I

203

suppose." The last few words were spoken softly, as though they'd surprised even her. She looked away before she could see that Signa leaned back, struck by the weight of those words.

Since the day Signa had unknowingly saved her cousin, she'd been able to feel the bond that tethered them. Every day it grew beyond those confines, into something more tangible. A fragile flame that Signa wanted nothing more than to nurse. To protect and stoke, to warm herself as she watched it burn.

"I'm glad to hear it," Signa whispered, still clutching her cousin's hand in her lap. "Though I must admit that I met some friends of yours—and to be frank, the idea that you'd seek some of them out for company is astounding."

It was in that moment Signa heard Blythe's laugh for the first time. It was warm and rich, so unlike the cold and severe self she portrayed. The toll of wedding bells, or the very first trill of a piano. Blythe was difficult to look away from, beautiful and fascinating, someone who'd likely draw every eye in a room. Signa wondered what her cousin was like before the illness; what she had been like when her family was whole and she was healthy. If that laugh was any indicator, Signa very much wanted to meet that girl someday.

"Few are true friends," Blythe said with mirth. "Most are unfortunate acquaintances."

"What about Eliza and Diana? Are you not close with them?"

"When I fancy some gossip, they're the first ones I seek. We're not close, though. That's the thing about society, cousin—there are vultures who will wait for the moment you stumble. And when you do, they'll sooner pick the skin from your bones to serve themselves rather than help you back to your feet. It's too easy to become prey."

Signa averted her attention, focusing on her lap and on the deep lines on the palm of Blythe's hand. She'd heard there were people who could tell your fortune from those lines, and she wondered what they might see in Blythe's. Could a life like the one she spoke of—free but alone—truly be so fulfilling?

"What of Miss Killinger?" Signa asked eventually. "I knew her once, you know. Long ago, she and I were close friends. Is she a vulture, too?"

Blythe's smile was small but bright. "Charlotte is wonderful. She's the only one who's bothered to visit me since I've been ill, and when my mother passed. We've been close for years, ever since she and her father took residence on some land across the woods so that she would have a better opportunity to find a husband. She's kind and smart, and a fantastic cook. She makes all sorts of jams and marmalades and syrups from things she grows in her garden, and she brings them to us as gifts a few times each year."

That kindness did indeed sound like the Charlotte she knew, and Signa was glad of it. Glad that if society truly was more like what Blythe warned of than what she'd envisioned all this time, there was still some good to be found within it.

Signa hadn't realized she'd been silent for some time until Blythe patted her on the thigh. "What about you, cousin?" she asked. "I did not mean to steal your excitement. Tell me, is there someone you've got your eyes on?"

Signa clawed at her memory for the name of the eligible bachelor Eliza had given her during their tea. "It seems Lord Wakefield is a popular choice."

The reply earned pursed lips from Blythe. "He's handsome enough, I suppose. Honorable and titled, which makes him a fine match. Though I never would have guessed he'd be your type. He's very . . . proper."

"You think I can't be proper?" Signa laughed, letting herself imagine for a moment what Lord Wakefield might be like. He'd have broad shoulders, she thought, and would look quite dignified. But the more she fleshed out an image of him in her mind, the more the image began to shift, until she saw smoky eyes and a man as tall as a willow. Until she saw Sylas. Her thoughts strayed to the feeling of her body against his when they'd been hiding in the closet at Grey's. Yet the more she thought of that, the more she thought of her past night spent hand in hand with Death—and of how natural it had seemed. She remembered the thrill that seared her veins when they'd touched, and the curiosity that kept her thoughts wandering back to him.

So thoroughly did these men fill her thoughts that Signa moved to the open window to cool the heat upon her skin. What was *wrong* with her? It was Lord Wakefield she should have been thinking about. For if a gentleman like him was to call upon her, Signa could guarantee her place in society, and a life full of good company and grand, joyous balls. Yes, that was what she should think about, indeed—security. Not late-night trysts with Sylas or midnight romps with Death. She needed to get a hold on herself.

Signa chose to focus instead on what she needed—to pry at the dam of the Hawthornes and see what information she might be able to break free from it. To learn something that could help save Blythe.

"It's Percy that the ladies are truly after. He was helping me learn to dance today when your father walked in. Forgive me if this is not my place, but I've been here for a few weeks now, and it's becoming increasingly clear that the two do not get along."

Blythe curled her fingers in the sheets, and Signa held her breath, wondering if she'd already pushed too far. She remembered how it'd felt to have Eliza and Diana prying at her, scavenging for gossip they could take and spread to whoever might listen. Blythe would be a fool to believe that Signa—a girl she hardly knew—wouldn't do the same. But Signa had no mind for gossip. She wanted only to save Blythe, and for the puzzle pieces in her head to begin their assembly.

Blythe, it seemed, recognized this. "For twenty years, my father and uncle raised Percy to take over the family business," she began. "When my mother died, my father became a different person. He forbade Percy from ever working at Grey's again. My father no longer spends his days there but instead holes up in his study, as though he's *trying* to let the business rot. Should Grey's burn down, I don't think he'd so much as bat an eye. It's more than our livelihood—it's how our family maintains its status. And as for my brother, it's always been his future."

The bags under Blythe's shut eyes were like two purple bruises as the conversation took its toll on her. She had to force the next words out, speaking softly. "My father won't tell us why he's taken the business away from Percy, but I think it's clear that my mother's death has rotted his mind. He's no longer thinking logically."

If Blythe was saying that her father didn't take the business away until after Lillian's death, that didn't at all match up with what Signa had found in the letter at Grey's. There was a piece to the puzzle that she was missing. She wanted to pry, but Blythe's chest was rising and falling in a steady rhythm. The girl had dozed off, and Signa had no choice but to hold her questions. She adjusted the blankets around Blythe, protecting her cousin from the cold that bit the air and sank into her bones. A cold, she realized too late, that was entirely unnatural.

Signa spun around to see that Death was behind her, his shadows stretching to cover her mouth before she could make a noise. The touch stole her breath and stilled her heart, putting her into that strange zone between the land of the living and the dead. It lasted mere seconds before he pulled away, and her body ached as her heart started up once more.

Shhhh . . . he whispered inside her mind. *You'll wake her.*

Signa wished to bite, to sink her fangs into Death and let the poison spread. But for the sake of letting Blythe rest, she jerked her hand toward Blythe's sitting room and motioned for him to follow. Her footsteps were slow, careful to avoid any creaking planks. "Leave now," she said the moment they were past the threshold. "God help you, I will not let you have her."

Relax, Little Bird, Death said smoothly. *I'm not here for her. Though I fear it won't be long until I do come to claim that poor girl's soul. I came to warn you. Should that girl not rid the poison from her body, I'll be back for her before the week's end. And her death won't be a kind one.*

Signa had half a mind to slam her fists into his chest and demand that Death leave Blythe alone forever. But Death didn't lord over her or threaten her with the chill of his shadows. The air didn't pull from her lungs with his nearness. It almost seemed like . . . like Death was trying to help her.

Signa stared deep into those fathomless shadows, leaning forward in an attempt to find a face. To find the eyes he must have had. But she saw nothing. "Why are you helping me?" she asked, hugging her arms tight around herself. "Isn't this your job, to reap the dead from this earth?"

I understand I've not been kind to you. Death hesitated, shadows shifting around his feet. *Because of me, your life has been harder than I ever meant for it to be. I didn't think of your future, Signa. I did not think of anything beyond how you were being treated in the moment by those who were meant to take care of you. And for that I am . . . sorry.* The last word sounded strange upon his tongue, as though he didn't care for the taste of it.

I cannot spare her forever, but if we can help her, then she may not have to die so soon. There's nothing I can do to prove myself to you. But if my word counts for anything, then you must trust me.

"*We?*" She'd never thought that this man—that Death incarnate— could ever seem so unsure.

"I'll be searching, too, and I'll let you know if I find anything to help her." Death spoke aloud now, in a watery voice that sent shivers up Signa's spine. She'd forgotten how much she liked that sound.

"Thorn Grove has a library," she said suddenly, pulling her thoughts from the space they too often liked to venture when he was nearby. "Perhaps I can find something there about an antidote."

He nodded. "See what you can find there tonight. And in the meantime, I'll do some sleuthing of my own."

"Thank you," Signa whispered, shivering as his shadows fell still and the air around them plummeted at least twenty degrees. "For your help, and for telling me."

"You're welcome." Again, the words sounded strange, like he struggled to even form them. "Our lessons will continue once you find something to expel that poison."

She nodded as Death disappeared into the shadows that stretched to claim him. Only when she was certain that he was gone did Signa peer around the door back at Blythe, watching the slow rise and fall of her chest. Then she clutched her own, her heartbeat like a caged beast. She checked her cheeks, too, placing a palm upon each of them only to discover that both were hot to the touch.

All this, over Death. Over someone she'd spent her life hating.

What in God's name was wrong with her?

TWENTY-FOUR

THORN GROVE WAS WELL ASLEEP BY THE TIME SIGNA REALIZED SHE hadn't the faintest idea where the library was.

She paced the floor of her sitting room, nightgown trailing behind her and curling at her ankles as she strode back and forth through the room. Consulting the library was the simplest way she could think of to find an antidote for Blythe, and while Signa preferred to conduct her search away from prying eyes, it wouldn't do to be found roaming the halls after being caught by Elijah once already. She'd investigated the entirety of the second floor and most of the first by this point, which left only the third story.

Signa was formulating her plan—and an excuse, in the event she was caught—when she heard the glass doors leading to her balcony rattle. Though her chest went cold, she realized soon enough that a spirit would have no need to knock, and that Death lacked enough manners to even consider doing so. So when the sound came again several moments later and sounded like someone tapping against the glass, she figured it could be but one person.

She pulled her robe around herself as she opened one of the doors for Sylas. He appeared to have climbed up the branches of a willow to get there, leaves still in his dark hair. "Evening." His grin gleamed bright in the moonlight. "You couldn't sleep, either, huh?"

She had half a mind to shut the door and let him climb back down. "What on earth are you thinking? You can't be here!"

Despite his size, he was graceful as a feline, not making so much as a noise as he slipped past her and into the room. "I saw from below that you had a candle lit, and your shadow kept pacing across the glass. I wanted to check that you were all right."

This boy would be her ruin if they weren't careful, though Signa had to admit that her blood rushed a little quicker with the thrill of a late-night visit. She didn't even necessarily mind that she wore only a robe over her nightgown, more curious about what he might think of it and what reaction she might get than embarrassed. Sure enough, Sylas's eyes lingered upon her body for a beat too long when he thought she wasn't looking, and he quickly cleared his throat and turned his attention to the ceiling when she turned back. Signa tried not to grin, warm with satisfaction.

"I'm as well as one can be, knowing my cousin is still as ill as the day I met her." She folded her arms across her chest and resumed her pacing. "If you're going to be in here, keep your voice down and tell me whether you've found anything useful."

"Hardly." He took a seat on her floor, leaning back against the wall. "I looked through the kitchen and the servants' quarters but couldn't find anything incriminating."

She feared as much, but hearing it aloud made it all the more aggravating. She ran her hands through her hair, tugging at the ends. "We must find something to help her. I hear there's a library in Thorn Grove, and I'd like to check it to see if I might find an antidote. Something herbal, to ward off poison."

"Poison?" he echoed, brows lifting. "That's a new development. I suppose if there's a chance to find anything about that, your best bet truly would be the library. It's massive."

"You know where it is, then?" Signa grabbed Sylas by the arm and hauled him to his feet. "Could you take me there?"

"Right now? In the middle of the night? Dressed like that?" When Signa didn't let go, he grinned and said, "How scandalous you are, Miss Farrow. If you insist, then follow me at once."

He led the way out into the hall. The walk up to the third story was achingly slow. Signa took each step with the utmost caution, bunching her nightgown in her fist so that she wouldn't trip over the long hem. She trailed behind him, finding it odd that a stable boy knew the house so well. Then again, Sylas hadn't always been a stable boy. Perhaps whatever job he'd had while Lillian was still alive allowed him occasional time in the massive estate. She made a note to ask him about it—later, though. Once they'd found something to help Blythe.

For now she asked, "Do you come here often?" her curiosity besting her.

"I've only had the opportunity to tour the house a few times." He walked with a confident ease, appearing far less worried about them being discovered than she was. "The staff have spoken of it enough, though. They don't journey up here much if they can avoid it, and even then they come only in the day."

Elaine had said the library was thought to be haunted, and if the staff went to such lengths to avoid it, Signa hated to imagine the spirit that awaited them inside. For years she'd avoided spirits, though if it was possible this one knew anything about Thorn Grove or Lillian's murder, it was too much of a lead to pass up. But with Sylas here, she'd no idea how that was feasible.

"You should leave once I'm there," she told him. "Nothing good will come of us being seen together."

He cast her an irritated look over his shoulder. "Two sets of eyes are better than one, and besides, even if I'm fired, you said yourself that I'd be taken care of."

She tried not to roll her eyes, for while he might be safe, she certainly wasn't. And the last thing she wanted was to have to hire Sylas if he ended up being responsible for any wild rumors or allegations about her. Still, he had a point. Death's warning was nothing to scoff at, and if she wanted to save Blythe, having Sylas's help was worth the risk.

The library was easier to find than she'd expected. Two oak doors with heavy brass handles led to a tremendous room with towering mahogany shelves stuffed full of books. There were rows upon rows of them, and in the center of the space were writing desks and plush leather reading chairs that looked comfortable enough to spend a day in. The room was lit by windows that bathed the room in pale starlight. Bright enough to see shapes and the vastness of the library but too dark to read the titles of the books.

Signa breathed in the musty scent of old parchment and ink. "We'll need to find a light." No sooner were the words out of her mouth before a candle upon one of the desks lit itself.

She made no move to grab it immediately and instead looked at Sylas, nervous he would run. He opened his mouth only to clamp it shut again. There wasn't a single excuse to explain a flame igniting of its own accord, and neither of them tried to offer one.

"Well." Signa cleared her throat. "At least we know all that talk of a spirit wasn't just a rumor."

Sylas's brows were to his hairline, yet all things considered, he was handling this remarkably well. Probably, she imagined, for her sake. "At least whatever's in here doesn't appear to be malicious?"

At least not yet, Signa thought as she squinted through the shadows, wondering where the spirit might be hiding. It was unnerving that she hadn't seen the spirit so far. She'd spent years ignoring them, hiding and pretending not to see, and she certainly didn't favor having the tables turned.

Sylas picked up the candle. "So we're looking for books on . . . botany?"

"Yes. Preferably something that discusses the medicinal uses of plants."

Across the library, a shadow whipped through the darkness, and Signa realized it was a book only after she'd stumbled into Sylas, biting back a yelp. It came from many rows ahead of them, and when the two of them simply stood there, another book flew from the same shelf.

Setting one hand on her waist to steady her, Sylas held the candle ahead of them.

Signa squinted through the glow of the flame. "Do you think . . ."

"I do," Sylas said, voice flat. He started toward the shelf the books had flown from, stopping to hover the candlelight over one that had been thrown. It was a thick leather-bound book on botany.

They turned the corner to another row of bookcases, and Signa seized Sylas by the arm, fear catching her breath as she saw who was helping them. The spirit was an older man with translucent blue skin, a full white beard, and spectacles that sat low upon his wide nose. Seeing that Signa had noticed him, he stood a little straighter.

"Are you all right?" Sylas asked her, steadying the candle. The spirit watched it with deep concern, and when it looked as though it might tip from its holder, he hurried to press a glowing finger against its side to steady it.

"*Careful,*" warned the spirit. "*Books are fragile things.*"

"Quite well." Signa leaned against the edge of a shelf, hoping her words were enough to satisfy both Sylas and the spirit. Only when it was clear that this spirit was not volatile like Lillian did her shoulders loosen. It wasn't malevolent, nor was its death so gruesome as to alter its appearance. "Do you know anything about the spirit that's rumored to haunt the library?" she asked Sylas.

"Not much. I heard he was a scholar who married into the family and died in one of those chairs. He fell asleep reading and passed away peacefully. Some say he was trying to read every book in the library."

"The chairs have since been changed, actually," the spirit noted. *"And my name is Thaddeus. Thaddeus Kipling. I'd have read every book in here by now, except they keep bringing more in."*

A spirit tethered to life by its desire to read! So novel was it that Signa almost laughed.

"He seems helpful enough. Not nearly so malicious as I feared," she noted.

Thaddeus sighed and thanked her, muttering about how everyone was too afraid to visit anymore, though all he ever did was try to help. *"Though I suppose fewer interruptions do make for more reading time."*

Again, she had to hold back her laughter. For nineteen years she had avoided spirits, blaming them for her being different and blaming that difference for keeping others away. But she rather liked Thaddeus, and for the first time she didn't feel remotely afraid in the presence of a spirit. If she'd given more of them a chance, would she have liked others just as well?

"Do you really think any of these books will tell us about poison?" Sylas held the candle up to a book to inspect the spine, effectively steering the conversation away from the spirit she couldn't blame him for not wanting to discuss. Every time Sylas leaned the candle too close to the book, Thaddeus would suck in a nervous breath and hold it until Sylas eased the flame away again.

"It's not the poison we need to read more about." Signa's eyes skimmed to the spirit, ensuring he was listening. "It's the antidote. I'm certain something in here must have some mention of it."

"Arsenic?" Thaddeus guessed, his eyes sparking with interest.

Signa checked that Sylas was occupied reading, then quickly shook her head.

Thaddeus hummed under his breath. *"Cyanide? Thallium? Strychnine? Atropine?"* He stopped when she very swiftly nodded. *"Ah, atropine! Someone's being poisoned by belladonna, are they? Well, that's easy, the antidote—ah. It wouldn't do you any good if I just told you, would it? I suppose you'd like to see the information for yourself. Here."* Thaddeus floated to the next bookcase, then stooped to point at a book from the bottom shelf. It was an unassuming thing; some sort of scholarly journal that Signa likely would never have selected.

"It's been a while," Thaddeus said as Signa stooped to pick it up, *"but I believe you'll find what you're looking for around the hundredth page. Interesting read, that one. Dry but informative. Do take care of it, won't you?"*

Signa thumbed to the hundredth page, then through a few more until she saw the word she was looking for—*Atropa. Atropa belladonna.* She clutched the book to her chest so fiercely, she thought she might cry. "Thank you, thank you, thank you," she said so loudly that Sylas nearly dropped the book he'd been skimming through.

"You found something already?" He scratched the back of his neck, perplexed. "What luck. I expected we'd be here all night."

Signa beamed at Thaddeus, whose chest puffed out a little. "I believe I did, though we had some help. Come." She dragged Sylas to one of the tables and spread the book before them. Even with the candlelight, they had to squint to see the small print. They read several pages of jargon Signa didn't understand before she found mention of treatments used on patients.

"Here it is!" She pressed a finger to the page and bent forward. Sylas followed suit, trying to peer over her shoulder.

" 'While the plant itself is toxic,' " she read aloud, the words like silk in her mouth, " 'the alkaloid content of the Calabar bean has proven an effective remedy for *Atropa belladonna.*' "

She grew giddier with each word. She tugged on Sylas's arm, shaking it as her excitement bloomed. They had a solution. Though Signa hadn't the faintest idea where she might find the non-native plant, there was at least a *possibility* now, which was far more than they'd had before.

"Too much of it, and Blythe could die," Sylas warned her as he read further. "You're to grind up a small dose of it and administer it in a liquid."

The only problem was how to get it. They certainly wouldn't find such a plant in Lillian's garden, though Signa did remember another possibility.

"There is an apothecary in town! I saw it the night you took me to Grey's. . . . Do you think they might have it?"

A grin spread wide across Sylas's face. "How brilliant you are. An apothecary is likely our best chance."

It was all Signa needed to hear to shut the book and hug it to her chest again. She felt light enough to dance upon a cloud. She was going to save her. Really, truly this time, Signa was going to save Blythe.

"Thank you," she whispered, grabbing hold of Sylas's shoulder and squeezing tight. "Thank you, thank you, thank you. And thank *you*, Thaddeus!"

She didn't look back at the spirit, nor at Sylas as he blew out the candle and whispered, "Thaddeus?" Instead, she clutched the book tight and hurried out the door.

"I'll go first thing in the morning," she said to no one in particular as Sylas nodded and shushed her gently. She listened for his sake, but Signa no longer cared who heard her now because everything was going to be fine. No—it would be better than fine. It was to be wonderful because first thing in the morning she would gather the antidote, and Blythe would finally have her life back.

Soon, all would be well again.

TWENTY-FIVE

WHILE ADDING CREAM TO HER CUP OF TEA AT BREAKFAST THE NEXT morning, Signa overheard Warwick telling Elijah that Blythe's tongue was beginning to fester with the same sores that Lillian's had in the late stages of her "disease." Blythe had been sick throughout the night, unable to keep any food or drink down.

Signa gripped her knife tight, trying not to let her frustration draw attention to herself for fear that Elijah might suddenly come to his senses and not allow such a conversation at the breakfast table.

Death's warning had been fortuitously timed, and now that a cure was known, Signa had only to get her hands on it. But she couldn't help wondering why Blythe was still so ill. Signa had instructed her not to drink anything but water. Had told her to dump her medicine when no one was watching. Signa had checked Blythe's room that very morning while her cousin slept; she'd inspected the cold tea and pastry left at her bedside, both of which were fine. But because her tongue was starting to show signs of poison, Signa knew that, somehow, she was still consuming belladonna.

"The doctor doesn't think it wise for her to have visitors today," Warwick told Elijah, who was scraping butter across a muffin in an angry manner Signa had not known someone holding a muffin could be capable of. "He and Percy were able to break the fever this morning, though she had a bout of delirium." Signa was glad, at least, that Percy had been there to supervise the doctor when she couldn't. She tried to steal his attention across the table to tell him as much, but Percy kept his tired eyes low as he stirred his untouched porridge.

"What did she see this time?" Elijah was as brash as he was disheveled, graying hair sprouting from his head every which way. He wore spectacles low on his nose and was still wearing an emerald robe with matching slippers while Signa already wore her corset and a pinstripe wrapper, with her hair twisted into an elegant knot at her neck. She'd have to change into a wool visiting dress before leaving the house, as to do otherwise would be met with immediate gossip and ridicule. While Signa had spent so many years longing for a place in society, she found herself becoming a bit...tired. And immensely jealous of Elijah's lack of care and decorum.

"It was Mother." Percy was the one who answered, still not looking up. "Blythe claimed she was in the garden with our mother."

It made no sense that after months with both Blythe and Lillian ill, no one had suspected poison. Was the doctor truly so incompetent? "Perhaps company is exactly what she needs," Signa said in her rage. The signs were there—the delirium, the sores, the sour stomach, coughing up blood. It was all there. It was true she knew a fair bit more about poison than the average person, but still.

"Miss Farrow—" Marjorie, who wore more rouge than usual upon her cheeks to conceal that one side of her face was still swollen, seemed ready to chide Signa before Elijah waved her off with his knife hand.

"Let her speak freely. Any rules we maintained in this home ended long ago." He ate nearly half the scone in one bite. "State your piece, girl." Despite his erratic behavior, Signa found she rather liked Elijah and his bluntness. In a world revolving around forced niceties and bending to the whims of others, it was refreshing. Still, she could not simply tell him that she knew of an antidote for Blythe's illness—she had to tread these waters lightly.

"In this state, it would be a burden on her mind to be left alone with such thoughts," Signa said. "If you don't mind, sir, I'd like to head into town to see if I can find something that might lift her spirits. Just a small gift, should you allow me some money and your permission."

Percy, who'd been glaring into his porridge as though it was the source of all his troubles, finally peered up at Signa with interest. Marjorie, however, was having none of it.

"If the doctor doesn't recommend she has company," Marjorie said, grasping a fork firmly in one hand, "we should abide by his suggestion." As a governess, she was welcome to sit and dine with the family, but she spoke too openly for any household that hadn't abandoned the strictures imposed by society. Too freely, and without anyone reprimanding her.

"As we did with Lillian?" Elijah asked coolly enough that several at the table shivered. "A lot of good that did my wife."

Signa collected Elijah's words and stored the memory away to add to her collection. One day soon, she would gather up all the pieces and lay the entire puzzle before her.

"Percy!" Elijah's voice boomed with authority. "You will go with your cousin. See that she is safe and has what she needs."

Percy sat straighter. "If we're to go into town, with your permission I'd like to stop by Grey's and check on the orders." His voice was flat and factual, lacking even a hint of emotion to betray his earlier desperation to visit the club.

The corners of Elijah's mouth twitched. "You will accompany your cousin on her errand, and then you'll return." He spoke with finality.

Percy seemed to feel it, too, for while it was clear he wanted to argue, he settled in his chair and gripped his teacup, knuckles white. "Yes, Father." When he sank lower in his seat, Signa dared not look at him, guilt heavy in her chest. "Of course."

Percy was far from entertaining company.

As he preferred not to ride horseback, a coach was readied for the journey into town. It wasn't too long a ride, but Signa had never been more uncomfortable. Even traveling with Sylas, an unrelated stranger, had been easier to navigate.

Signa missed the way Percy had been yesterday, before Byron

had shown up with the news of Grey's to spoil the mood. She missed his laughter and jesting, and the feeling of his spirit vibrant with life. The Percy she was with now was not the sly and teasing man that she'd been getting to know, but one who was rigid and proper and sharp. His thumb traced circles over a leather coin purse as he glared out the coach's window, chin jutting with great severity as he observed the passing landscape. Signa bit her tongue. It was cruel, she thought, that Elijah would not give him a chance. That he chose to ignore his son's suffering no matter how deep it was.

"I found something, cousin," she said, hoping to lift his spirits. "We're not here to find Blythe pretty new gloves or stationery. We're going into town because I've found her a cure."

Only then did he rouse. "What do you mean you've found a cure?" His eyes were narrowed. "There hasn't been a single doctor who's been able to help my sister."

"None of them knew that she was being poisoned. But we do, and I've found an antidote. There's an apothecary in town, and—"

"An apothecary?" His brows shot toward the ceiling. "Signa, we cannot trust my sister's life to an amateur. There has to be a medicine that will help her. We can speak with more doctors—"

"If the doctors haven't caught on now, they're either all fools or someone's been paying them off."

Any retorts died on his tongue. "You think that's possible?" His Adam's apple bobbed. "Even if that is the case, some apothecary's cure isn't something we should be playing around with. There are safer ways to go about these matters."

"I understand your frustration, but nothing else is working,

Percy." She took his hand, squeezing tight. "But this will, I promise. I need you to trust me."

He looked to the carriage roof as though it held the answers and sighed when it did not share them. "Very well. If there's a possibility, then of course we must try it. Though we cannot allow ourselves to be seen there—the entire town will talk."

"Of course."

Signa's smile was not reciprocated as Percy turned his attention to the rattling cobblestone streets that were so much brighter and more open in the daylight than when she'd been here with Sylas several nights before. Now the shops that lined the street were fully awakened. Through immaculate windows, Signa spotted women in gloves and bonnets, draped in cashmere gowns as they took their tea or filtered into a shop to order warm clothes and decorations for the approaching winter.

When they passed Grey's, Percy leaned over Signa and slammed the curtains shut. She reeled back. There was no humor in Percy's face. No hint of anything but severity.

Signa dared not speak another word.

Percy was the first one out of the carriage when it rolled to a stop in front of a tiny green shop. Ivy stretched up and over the walls, and a window display showcased an assortment of vibrant plants hung from woven canopies. Signa was so busy staring that it took Percy clearing his throat for her to notice he was holding out his arm. Passersby surveyed them with curiosity, turning to gossip with one another and likely theorizing over Signa's presence. Percy adjusted the small gold button on one of his brown leather gloves and paid them no mind.

There was likely nothing anyone could do or say that would make Percy come across as anything but a gentleman in the public eye.

Inside the shop, they were greeted by a frail elderly woman with white hair. One look at her and Percy's nose turned upward.

"Don't dawdle," he whispered. "We get whatever you need, and then we get out."

For a fleeting moment Signa wished she'd stepped on his toes harder the day before, though she refused to let his negativity sit with her when they'd entered such a wonderland. Jars of tonics and bottles of herbs sat upon shelves riddled with tiny wooden bobbles. There were small containers of living moss, and dainty baskets of dried herbs that smelled so fragrant Signa wanted to bathe in them.

The middle of the shop was full of live potted plants. Most of them were types Signa had never seen before, with trailing vines or large bulbous flowers. She resisted the urge to stroke her finger across their petals, awed that such a wondrous place could exist. Had she enough money, Signa would have been tempted to buy out the entire store.

"Can I help you find something, miss?" the shopkeeper asked. Signa was glad to see that she paid Percy's snobbery no mind.

His eyes darted to Signa, a dark warning brewing within them that signaled her to take caution with her words. The moment they left the apothecary, gossip would ignite. Though it was possible that whoever was harming Blythe was already aware they'd been found out, Signa and Percy didn't need to risk adding fuel to the fire, or word getting back to Elijah that his wife's death could have been prevented had someone been playing closer attention to her strange symptoms.

"I've a friend who ate something sour," Signa offered the shop-keeper. "I'm looking for a Calabar bean to help rid her body of some toxins from it. And perhaps something to soothe her stomach after, too."

The woman squinted her small eyes in assessment, then made a noise in the back of her throat as she hobbled with Signa toward a back shelf full of small plants and glass vials. Percy followed behind them, making a point of appearing disinterested as the woman inspected the shelves.

The shopkeeper muttered under her breath as she searched, growing more frustrated with her findings row after row until she found what it was that she was looking for and uttered a quiet "Aha!" She produced a small vial with a strange brown nut within it. The Calabar bean.

Signa reached for it, but the woman pulled the vial out of reach. She leaned toward Signa and whispered, "Are you sure it's what you're looking for? It's highly poisonous, and it won't help a sour stomach."

Signa knew the Calabar bean was a risk, but if Signa did nothing— if she took *no* risk—then Blythe would die, and Signa would spend the rest of her life wondering if she could have saved her.

Signa nodded and put her faith in Death. "Yes ma'am. It's pre-cisely what I need."

The woman dared a quick look at Percy, and said, very softly, "Are you safe, girl? If it's something for him that you need, I have a few things a little more ... inconspicuous."

Signa blanched and set her hands upon the woman's at once,

hoping that her earnestness was enough to confirm her sincerity. "That's not it at all, ma'am, I assure you. This will do just fine."

With reservation, the shopkeeper hummed and handed over the vial. "Crush it into a powder. Then, put about half of it into a glass with water to induce vomiting." Vomiting, Signa hoped, that would help rid Blythe of the poison.

The woman shuffled over to the back of the shop, skirts brushing against the dusty oak floor. For a long moment she searched, eventually producing a small jar filled with tiny brown seeds that she brought back to Signa. "Caraway seeds," she told her, placing the jar in Signa's palms. "To help settle your friend's stomach."

Percy's agitation grew with each person who wandered by the foggy, dirt-crusted windows of the shop and took note of his presence within it. His long fingers refused to cease their tapping upon his thigh. He watched the woman hand over the caraway seeds, keen as a hawk. "Do you have any more of the Calabar bean?"

"It's no easy plant to find," said the shopkeeper. "This is all I'll have for some time."

He grunted, dissatisfied, and produced his coin purse. "Very well. How much do we owe you?"

The woman flinched with surprise at his severity but said firmly enough, "A thruppence will do."

Percy pressed a shilling into her waiting palm. "For your discretion."

The shopkeeper fisted the coin with a snort, then dropped it into a pocket of her skirt. "Get out of here, boy, before I give you something to be discreet about."

There was no need to tell him twice. Signa tucked the vial away in her pocket as Percy tugged her out of the shop she easily could have spent a full day in, chatting to the shopkeeper about every beautiful thing within it. Her fingers curled tenderly around the jar of caraway seeds. Signa had the vague impression that Percy believed the apothecary might suddenly infect him with the plague.

He darted a look around to ensure no one was watching as he pushed open the door. "There is a madness within that woman," he said. "I don't trust her."

Signa bristled. "She is a *healer*."

"She's a witch," he scoffed. "I still don't see how some seed will help my sister when nothing else could."

Witch. The word sent Signa's mind reeling back to the night of Magda's death. "Don't call her that. If a berry is powerful enough to hurt your sister and kill your mother, then who are you to say a plant cannot heal with that same power?"

He had no response to that. She could feel the fear rolling off him in waves. She knew that if she were him, she wouldn't want to let herself hope that this tiny seed would somehow fix everything, either. Because if it didn't...

"Let's make haste," Percy muttered. "We'll need to get back to the carriage before—"

"Miss Farrow?" called a voice from down the street. "Miss Farrow, is that you?"

Dread sunk its claws into Signa when she saw that Eliza Wakefield and Charlotte Killinger approached, accompanied by a handsome gentleman with light brown skin and a head of wheat-brown curls. He wore a fashionable olive-green topcoat and a hat that he tipped toward them with a smile so charming that Signa's heart fluttered.

Sweat beaded upon Signa's brow as Charlotte noticed the shop they'd emerged from. It was good fortune that she was too polite to speak of it, though the same couldn't be said for Eliza.

"Oh, it *is* you," Eliza said as she lowered herself to a curtsy before Percy. "I thought it might be. Have you come from the apothecary?"

Percy took on an entirely new air before Signa could bat an eye. "And have ourselves cursed by a witch? Never." He spoke in a light, jovial manner that made Signa's jaw tense.

Eliza matched his grating smile, giggling as though he was most humorous. She waited for Charlotte and the man accompanying them to echo the laugh, but both kept their faces smooth. Eliza—finally able to peel her eyes from Percy long enough to remember herself—inclined her head and took Signa by the hand. "My apologies," she said. "This is my cousin Lord Everett Wakefield, son of the Duke of Berness." Eliza held his arm with a smirk upon her lips.

Signa did not remember ever meeting a lord before. He held himself proudly enough that she wondered whether he was first in line to inherit or last. She remembered from the conversation at her welcome tea that he was the most eligible bachelor in town next to Percy, and that he was the potential suitor she'd spoken with Blythe about the prior day.

Even if he were without money or title, Everett was a man who'd garner attention for his looks and for the regal way in which he held himself. His shoulders were rolled back, chest proud, and his face was full of youthful spirit. There was wealth in his imported clothing, and a glint in his eyes as he observed Signa. Everett Wakefield was one of the most handsome men she had ever seen, and her mind lost all coherent thought when he smiled at her.

"Cousin," Eliza trilled, "this is Signa Farrow, the one I've been telling you about."

Charlotte observed with a blank stare as Everett bowed his head low, the flecks of gold in his hazel eyes dazzling as they flicked up to watch her beneath impressively long lashes. "I'm well aware of who the Farrows were—I met your mother once, long ago."

Signa's spine tingled with tiny zaps of electricity as he pressed a kiss to the back of her glove. "My mother?"

Everett's smile gleamed bright. "Our parents were once acquainted, though I'm afraid I don't remember your father. My memory's a bit hazy, as I was a young boy, though I do remember how the whole house would laugh when your mother arrived. She was a pistol, and my family adored her. I'm sorry for your loss, Miss Farrow."

Signa had to remind herself to incline her head, too lost in her thoughts and a million questions she wanted to ask the man. She'd never expected her mother to be called a pistol. If the etiquette book she left behind and the stories Signa's grandmother had shared were right, surely Lord Wakefield was thinking of the wrong woman.

"It's lovely to see you again, Miss Farrow," Charlotte interjected, though to Signa's surprise, she looked more ill than she did enthused, her hands folded tightly before her. "And you as well, Mr. Hawthorne. I'm afraid we haven't long to chat as we've an appointment at a tearoom—"

"Oh dear, Charlotte, thank you for reminding me!" Eliza clapped her hands. "Do forgive me for being forward, but we'd be delighted if you were able to join us."

Signa didn't miss how Charlotte's eyes darkened when she said, "I'm not sure we'll be able to add more to our company with such short notice—"

"Nonsense. No one would deny two of the town's most prominent gentlemen." Eliza aimed her hopefulness at Percy. "I'm certain they will make an exception if you'd be so kind as to accompany us?"

Percy's fingers tapped at his side, and he cast a sideways look at Signa.

Tea, as Signa was learning, never really was just *tea*, and accepting an invitation meant every bit as much as requesting one did. It wasn't formal for Eliza to make the request herself, but having her cousin on her arm had made her bold. One couldn't exactly refuse tea with a lord, and though Signa knew what it would mean to decline, all she could think about was Death's warning ringing in her ears and that she desperately needed to get the antidote to Blythe. "It's a kind offer, but perhaps we could join you another day? We wouldn't want to impose."

Eliza didn't so much as acknowledge that Signa had spoken. "Everyone has been raving about this place. Trust me, Mr. Hawthorne, it'll be impossible to get in once the rest of the town catches wind. Everett and I absolutely insist that you join us today, don't we, Everett?"

He grinned down at Signa. "We'd be offended if you didn't." And though his tone was teasing, she knew the battle had been lost.

Blythe would have to hold on a little longer.

TWENTY-SIX

HAD THE CALABAR BEAN AND ALL IT SYMBOLIZED NOT BEEN WEIGH-ing down her pockets, the day would have been a lovely one for a promenade. Eliza looped one arm through Signa's and the other through Charlotte's, the three of them walking well ahead of the men. "What a coincidence it is to find you here. I had so hoped you'd have the chance to meet Everett prior to the spring. You're still planning to join the season, aren't you?"

She still had to speak to Marjorie, of course, but it made sense enough to debut in the spring that Signa nodded. "That's the hope."

Charlotte's smile was polite but thin. "It seems everyone and their mamas will be out this season."

"How right you are." Eliza laughed. "What a challenge it'll be to find a husband, especially now when we'll be competing with Miss Farrow." She said the last part in a conspiratorial whisper. "You will be the prized pony that all the men will bid on. It's fortunate for us that only one of you from Thorn Grove will be out this season, for it will be the same when Blythe makes her debut. And it's fortunate for me that the one I've got my eyes on is your relation."

Though Eliza's incessant gossip was tiresome, she was quite pretty, and her family was affluent enough that Signa knew without asking him that Percy would be equally interested in her. But would Eliza's interest continue if Percy didn't inherit Grey's?

"If you'll excuse me"—Eliza peeled herself away from the women—"I believe I'll get a head start on that." She moved back in one quick stride, taking her place at Percy's side and tilting her head back, laughing at whatever he said.

Left with Charlotte, Signa asked, "Is what Miss Wakefield said true? I never thought that my debuting would be a problem for anyone." Surely, that couldn't have been what soured Charlotte's mood the last time they'd spoken. Yes, Signa had money, but there would be others far better suited for maintaining a home. She didn't want children anytime soon, and her piano playing and skill with a needle were abysmal. Not to mention that there would be more beautiful women out for the season, like Charlotte, whom anyone would be lucky to have as a wife.

"It's not that it's a problem." Charlotte kept her voice low enough that Signa had to strain to hear her. "But it makes things more difficult for those of us who must secure a strong match. If Blythe weren't sick, it would've been the same situation. The men will flock to those with the highest prospects first, and the rest of us will get their scraps and will be expected to be happy for it."

"What of a love match?" Signa asked, not having a taste for such a callous stance. "Surely, it wouldn't matter how many ladies are out each season if one was to make one of those?"

Charlotte dipped her chin and peered at Signa as though seeing her for the first time. "Ever since my mother died and we were forced to move after the scandal, my father has been struggling to keep us afloat. He never had a son, so it's my duty to find someone who can support our family. I don't have the luxury of a love match, Miss Farrow. In fact, you will find that most of us don't. If that's what you're after, then I wish you luck, but I care only for securing my future. So do forgive me if I'm not enthused that you're joining the fray my first year out."

Charlotte's words stung like a wound. Signa knew she could carve out her own future, but she'd never considered that some women would *have* to be with a man not of their own choosing, simply to exist. It was the last thing she wanted for her friend, especially.

Signa wanted a love match. She wanted someone to dance with, and to laugh with late into the evening. Someone whose company she wouldn't tire of years from now. She wanted the same for her friend, too.

Signa wanted to ask Charlotte if there was anyone she *did* fancy, but she fell silent as they came upon a small tearoom. Another time, then. They'd have the discussion another time.

Everett held the door open, and one by one they filed inside.

The tearoom was clean and quaint, with a large, circular mahogany table already prepared for them. It was set with a beautiful arrangement of gilded petits fours, peach and chocolate scones, golden crumpets, miniature glazed fruit tarts, and delicate cucumber sandwiches. Signa's stomach betrayed her by growling, wanting to sample everything. It was unfortunate, the way societal rules could hinder a person. How much simpler life would be to not have to think about what she was expected to eat, and in what order. She strongly preferred Death's philosophy of simply wanting something and taking it.

Everett pulled chairs out for Signa and Charlotte, the latter of whom sat with more grace than Signa thought herself ever capable of. Percy followed suit for Eliza, who unfurled a black fan that she fluttered to conceal a blush Signa was certain wasn't there. It seemed there was a language with these fans—one Signa did not understand but had Percy entranced as Eliza fanned herself with slow and deliberate flicks of her wrist. The more she fanned, the more Signa wanted to reach across the table to throw the beastly thing out the window, for it wasn't even hot out and the fan's wind kept blowing baby hairs into her face.

Everett must have shared similar feelings; he screwed up his face and tried not to laugh at the sight of his cousin. When he caught Signa looking, he smirked. Charlotte glanced away in silence, spooning sugar into her tea.

"Have you been at Thorn Grove long, Miss Farrow?" Everett asked as he took a seat, waiting for the women to take their savories from the arrangement before doling his own onto a small porcelain plate.

Percy placed his napkin upon his lap, then set a scone upon both Signa's and Eliza's plates. Who was Signa to refuse a perfectly good scone? She spread lemon curd and clotted cream across it in the most graceful way she knew how, concealing her eager eyes with a mask of calm demure. "About a month, now," she said, hoping he'd pause from questions long enough for her to take a bite. "Thorn Grove is a beautiful place. The Hawthornes have done me a great kindness by allowing me to stay with them."

"Nonsense," Percy chided her. "You're family. Having you with us has been our delight."

Signa bit into her scone to spare him from her retort. Where was this kindness earlier, when he'd rushed her out of the apothecary, or when he'd criticized her dancing?

"Signa's birthday is in the spring, you know," Eliza said. "She'll be making her debut this season."

"I suppose that means we'll be seeing each other quite often, as I intend to remain in town throughout the upcoming season, as well." Everett's smile was far more charming than it had any right to be. The scone Signa had been chewing lodged in her throat. She swallowed a mouthful of steaming tea to help it pass. The drink scorched her tongue, and she was reminded of one of the rules in *A Lady's Guide to Beauty and Etiquette*: One must enjoy their tea in the smallest of sips, and should never take to blowing on a drink, no matter how hot.

"A coincidence, indeed." Signa couldn't tell if it was her heart fluttering or nerves getting the best of her stomach. Everett was, on paper, everything Signa had ever wanted—handsome, charming, kind, and an evident socialite. She didn't care much about his status but supposed that it could only be beneficial if the attention of those who sneaked sly, interested glances at them was any indicator. But good God, if just having tea was such an exhausting feat every time she had to do it, Signa hadn't a clue how she'd manage becoming the socialite she'd always dreamed of being. She wished, vaguely, that she were able to ask her mother how she'd done it.

Signa took another too-hot sip and sampled a cucumber sandwich before spreading butter across a crumpet, letting Percy do the talking while she took care of the food—the sooner it was gone, the sooner they could head back to Thorn Grove and Blythe, and the sooner she could get out of her own head.

Percy put on a display of gentlemanly behavior, flattering Eliza and wooing her in a way that delighted the young woman. He seemed every bit the lady's man that his father had allegedly been, asking Charlotte and Eliza of their hobbies and whether they'd seen any performances at the opera recently. He refilled Eliza's teacup with the utmost attentiveness, dripping with more charm than Signa had thought him capable of. Charlotte, meanwhile, spoke to Everett of his many travels.

Signa listened with great fascination as they discussed parties and sporting events she hadn't been privy to, and joined the conversation when Everett pressed for information about her interests and what she and Percy were doing in town. Percy, of course, came up with a lie before she'd been able to answer. All the while, Signa was too aware of the rigidness of her spine and how her neck ached from trying to keep it so straight. She was certain she'd broken several dining etiquette rules—like what foods to eat in what order, when to put the sugar into her tea, how many fingers to use when she held the cup to her lips—but fortunately, no one mentioned any quibbles, though she did catch Eliza gaping at her a few times. While the rules were embedded somewhere in Signa's brain, the practice of them felt unnatural. Eventually, she ceased eating and drinking altogether, as to not offend everyone in the room who watched her at Lord Wakefield's side.

The rest of the afternoon passed in a blur. Signa asked few questions, unable to fully relax for fear that she'd do or say something wrong. Perhaps it was silly to worry so, given that Eliza was too thoroughly enamored with Percy and her own fan waving to care about the number of scones Signa consumed, and that Everett and Charlotte were nothing if not cordial. Still, stress was summoning hives across her skin, and her stomach was queasy.

Finally, as the tea ran cold and the food disappeared, Percy set his folded napkin upon the table and stood. Everett followed suit, helping Signa and then Charlotte out of their chairs. When they were all standing, he offered Signa his hand.

A moment of panic surged through her before she took it and allowed him to escort her outside.

"It was a pleasure to meet you," he said, his smile gleaming with the straightest, whitest teeth Signa had ever seen. "I'm looking forward to getting to know you better, Miss Farrow, over the course of the upcoming season."

For years Signa had imagined a moment like this. In it, however, she'd never envisioned that she'd have sweat along her back or that her dying cousin would be waiting for her to come and deliver her a cure. It was too much for Signa to even think about, which was why she detached herself from Everett and grabbed on to Percy, hoping her smile looked convincing. "I'm looking forward to it as well," she told Everett, discreetly digging her fingers into Percy's arm until he clasped his hand over hers and smiled.

So genuine was Everett's smile that Signa's stomach twisted with guilt. Yet she knew there was no time for that, for there were matters far more pressing. With a final goodbye, she turned and hauled Percy to the carriage that waited to take them home to Blythe.

TWENTY-SEVEN

PERCY DREW THE CURTAINS SHUT THE MOMENT THEY WERE IN THE carriage, exhaling as he sank low into the seat. "I can't believe we were almost seen in that apothecary." His lips pinched tight, he appeared so much sterner than he'd been minutes prior. The severity of the quick change in his demeanor gave Signa whiplash. "Especially in front of the duke's son."

Signa wished the carriage would go faster. "Does it truly matter if they saw us?" she asked. "I'd expect anyone with half a heart might understand our desperation and be open to considering alternative remedies for Blythe."

"I'd hope that, too," he said. "But it may also make them suspicious."

Her defenses were rising. "What do you mean, *suspicious*?"

"I mean that the longer I think about it, the stranger I find the convenience of you just happening to know what's ailing my sister, let alone finding an alleged antidote." His green eyes narrowed. "I want to trust you, cousin, but I must admit that I find your sudden interest in Blythe quite odd. She's been worse ever since you arrived, and I'm finding it difficult to deny that you might be the reason."

It was dread that Signa felt then. Cold, icy dread leaking into her stomach. The look in Percy's eyes wasn't one she'd seen before; it was distant, venomous. But she understood it, for Blythe was his sister, and Signa had no doubt that she'd be willing to do whatever it took to protect her own sister, too, had she had one.

But she didn't know how to convince him of that. The Calabar bean itself was, technically, poison. It would do her no favors if he found out. "I'll sample the antidote myself, should you need proof," she said at last. "Would that satisfy your concerns?"

Percy stilled at Signa's declaration, leaning back against the leather seat as he considered her. When he'd gathered his wits enough to consider her proposal, he nodded—for as far as he knew, there was perhaps no better proof in this world. "Very well."

"Then consider it done." Signa set her hands upon her lap and counted the passing minutes. She didn't want to care about his hesitancy; Thorn Grove, odd as it was, was the best place she'd ever lived, and its people were growing on her. She also didn't want him to see how much his negativity about the apothecary had affected her, for Percy was the symbol of high society through and through. His reaction, as well as her own discomfort at tea, was a clear acknowledgment of how poorly Signa fit into that milieu.

She could become like clay and mold herself. She could wear the gowns and pin up her hair and pat rouge upon her cheeks—she could even feign interests if she had to. From the time she was a young girl, this had always been the road she'd been meant to take. Her grandmother had told her as much. Had told her to marry, and of the parties she'd attend. Had told her she'd be like her mother, and Signa had believed her because it was all she ever knew to want. But there was something else now. A curiosity. A darkness that had been brewing within her all these years that was perhaps not so dark as she'd once believed. She'd felt power. She'd felt the heat of her skin beneath a man's touch. She'd felt what it was like to sneak out and ride horseback beneath the moon.

And she liked that darkness more than she cared to admit.

She stewed in the silence of her thoughts for the entirety of the ride, then while in the kitchen as she ground up the Calabar bean, and then on her journey up the stairs, through the hall, and into Blythe's room with Percy at her side.

The moment the door opened, it felt as though someone punched her square in the chest. Death hung like smog in the air, suffocating.

The sole relief was that he was not yet present. He didn't stalk the shadows, waiting for her, and Signa understood that the feeling of his lingering presence in this room was a warning. If she was to save Blythe, she needed to move fast. Percy must have felt the urgency, too, for he barely glanced at his sister before his steps faltered.

Blythe was flat on the bed, as lifeless as Signa had ever seen her. Her breath slipped from her lips in tiny gasps. When Blythe heard them enter, her eyelids fluttered open, though she was unable to keep them that way for long.

Signa took a seat beside her without waiting for permission. She picked up a glass of water from the bedside table and stirred in the ground Calabar bean until the liquid turned a milky white.

Before she could make another move, Percy got hold of her arm. There was fire in his eyes. "You first," he said.

Her stare locked with his, Signa lifted the glass to her lips and took a swallow.

It wouldn't be long until her stomach protested the drink, so she steeled herself and didn't waste another moment on Percy.

She slipped her arm under Blythe's neck to help her sit up. Only when the drink was to her lips did Signa hesitate. Blythe was as weightless as a feather, her head lolling against Signa's arm. Whether she would be able to handle the substance was a mystery. The life was draining from her fast, and the Calabar bean was another poison; it would make her throw up, though it was also meant to counter the effects of belladonna.

"This will be hard," Signa warned her, "but you must fight. If you feel yourself about to vomit, let it happen. It will help."

Blythe said nothing, but the fluttering of her eyelids led Signa to believe that she understood.

Percy stood beside them, eyes anxious. "Will she be all right?"

Signa could have killed him for that question, and she flashed a look that warned as much. Blythe was sick, but she could still hear them. "This should help her tremendously," Signa said without adding: *Should her system tolerate it.*

She goaded Blythe into drinking half the glass, then took a basin from the floor for when the moment arrived that they'd need it. "I'm sorry," she whispered, sitting close, smoothing the damp, stringy strands of Blythe's pale blond hair off her forehead. "I must have missed something. I thought only the medicine was poisoned, but I'm not so sure anymore."

"Or perhaps one of us slipped up and gave away too much information to the wrong person." A hint of accusation lingered in Percy's whisper.

Signa *had* told someone, admittedly far more easily than she should have. But Sylas had helped her; he'd shown her the library and taken her to Grey's. If he wanted Blythe dead, surely he wouldn't have been so helpful. "No one slipped up." She spoke with confidence. "I must have made a miscalculation. We'll have to monitor what she consumes more carefully."

"And what of your remedy?" He nodded to the remnants of the milky-white drink. "Will you have enough, should this happen again?"

Signa nodded. "For one more dose, yes. Though let us hope she won't need it."

"Let's pray that you're right." Percy's brows were severe as he watched Signa work with the caraway, preparing it for after Blythe lost her guts, which didn't take long.

"I'll stay with her," Signa said, thankful for quick reflexes as she got the basin to Blythe just in time, helping again to smooth the girl's hair back from her face. Her own stomach was cramping, nausea rolling over her as cold sweat prickled her skin. She refused to let on in front of Percy; the nausea would pass soon enough. "We'll need water," she told him with stern authority. "Go ask the kitchen staff for some bread. She needs to eat something easy on her stomach once we've gotten through the worst of this. And please, be discreet."

Percy nodded and cast one last look at his sister. She'd never seen his cheeks so hollowed out, or his eyes so empty. He turned on his heel without so much as another word, the sound of his boots clicking as he disappeared down the hall.

It was late into the evening when Blythe began to settle. Signa hadn't been certain that her cousin would make it when Blythe's labored breathing tightened and her skin became feverish. But somewhere during those long hours, there'd been a turning point. Blythe's flushed cheeks cooled, and her stomach was no longer so eager to empty itself. She lay back in the bed, her hair pulled into a loose braid Signa had woven between emptying the basin and fetching Blythe more water.

Blythe's breathing was deep now, and her eyes were finally managing to stay open.

"Are you with me?" Signa asked, easing her shoulders when Blythe nodded. Picking up a loaf of sourdough from the tray Percy had brought them, Signa tore off a small piece and handed it to Blythe. "Try to eat this. You're going to feel weak for a while, but I think you're going to be all right. We're just going to have to be careful with whatever you put into your body."

The bread slipped from Blythe's fingers; she was too weak to hold it. She faltered at the realization, tears welling, but Signa would have none of that. She picked up the loaf, broke it into even smaller bites, then set a small piece in Blythe's mouth. Piece after piece Signa fed her, letting Blythe's head fall upon her shoulder, letting the girl's tears flow freely until she became too exhausted to eat another bite or cry another tear, and she fell asleep.

As Blythe slept, Signa smoothed a hand over her cousin's hair, willing strength into her. "Don't worry," Signa whispered. "I'll find whoever did this to you. I promise."

From the threshold, a quiet voice said, "How were you able to help her?" Marjorie was watching them with glistening eyes.

She looked to the glass on the bedside table, the evidence still there. "Just an old remedy I found in the library," Signa whispered, not knowing what else to say.

Signa understood Marjorie could likely banish her if she wanted to. She could deem Signa a witch and throw her out of Thorn Grove. But instead, her eyes softened. "You should get some rest, too."

Signa's skin prickled at the mere suggestion of leaving Blythe alone, or in the hands of another. But for now, Death's presence had dissipated from the room, his warning retracted. Again, Blythe had been spared.

Whether Signa had been able to save her one final time, they could only hope.

Signa eased Blythe's head down upon the pillows before slipping from the bed. On the bedside table she'd left small pieces of bread and two glasses of water. In one of the glasses she'd added ground caraway seeds to help settle Blythe's stomach. For now, it was all she could do.

"The best thing we can do for her is let her sleep," Marjorie told her, and Signa knew it was not her place to argue. Even if she'd helped Blythe, Signa was still little more than a stranger to the Haw-thornes. She was also a woman, and a young one at that. No matter how much she wanted to hole up in Blythe's room to watch over her at all hours, such a thing would never be allowed when the family had proper doctors employed.

So for now she took her skirts in hand and followed Marjorie out the door, letting the woman lead her through the candlelit hall and back to her own room.

Marjorie slowed, forcing them to linger in the hallway. "You are fitting into Thorn Grove better than I ever expected," she said. The darkness of the night covered the memory of Marjorie's injury well. In the dim glow of the iron sconces, all Signa could make out was a fading bruise upon her bottom lip.

"Thank you," Signa said before she allowed herself to relive the memory of seeing that bruise inflicted. Her hands clenched at her sides.

"It's been a pleasure to see you getting along well with other ladies your age." The heels of Marjorie's boots tapped loudly against the hardwood floors. "You wish to debut this season, don't you?"

It was perhaps a strange time to be talking about such a thing, but Death's presence in Thorn Grove had been long and tedious, and Signa had learned that when Death claimed your every waking moment, mundane conversations felt like a reprieve. Perhaps Marjorie felt the same.

"I don't mean to bother anyone with it," Signa said. "I'll be leaving Thorn Grove for a home of my own around the same time. I can debut once I'm gone—"

"There's no need to apologize, Signa. You've been doing a wonderful job with your lessons, and I think having your season this spring is a good idea. Besides, no one will stand for you debuting yourself without any proper chaperone. It's unheard of."

Signa sucked in her cheeks. "You think it's a good idea?"

"I do. And I'll speak to Elijah about it tomorrow." Signa did not miss the casual use of his name. "In the meantime, we'll be having a ball this Christmas, and you will attend. It'll be a good experience for you."

Blood rushed to Signa's cheeks. All day she'd spent caring for Blythe. Her back ached, her eyes kept trying to shut on their own, and she was certain she smelled sour. Yet despite all that, Marjorie's words had her buzzing with excitement. This was her chance to prove to herself as much as anyone else that she was fit for a life outside the shadows. For the life she'd always been meant to have. To be like her mother, or like Lillian—someone everyone told stories about and adored. Someone whose name alone could soften a voice.

"I . . . would love that."

Marjorie smiled. "Then I will arrange all the details. It's about time Thorn Grove started hosting proper parties again—perhaps this will be exactly what everyone needs."

TWENTY-EIGHT

SYLAS WAS WAITING FOR SIGNA IN HER SUITE. SHE NEARLY DARTED back into the hall at the sight of his head bobbing up from the side of her bed, smothering the surprised yelp that burned in the back of her throat.

"How is Miss Hawthorne?" was the first thing he said. The question was enough to soften the sharpness of her tongue.

"The antidote worked," she answered, glancing down the hall to ensure they were alone before she shut and locked the door. Coolness flooded the room when she stepped in, and she scowled when she noticed why. Sylas had climbed the willow tree again and had left the balcony doors open for a quick escape.

"One of these days we're going to get caught." There was no place for iciness in her voice. Exhausted though she was, Blythe had been saved, and it was thanks to his help.

"We haven't been found yet." Sylas grinned as he took a seat upon the edge of her bed. Signa's stomach warmed at the sight of him there. She tucked her hair behind her ear, suddenly aware of the smell of sickness upon her, and of how in need of a bath she was.

"I want to thank you for your help," she began, skin sweltering despite the cold. "I know I'll be paying you, but even so it means the world. It's a precarious situation, and my cousin can use whatever help she can get." When she sat upon her chaise for fear that sitting too close to him might inspire certain...*ideas*, Sylas stood and moved to the chair before her.

"I've pulled the logs of all those employed at Thorn Grove, as well as any who were let go within the past year." Sylas motioned to a thick stack of papers that he'd already placed upon her writing desk. "I was unable to find anything in the ones I looked through, but perhaps your luck will be better. Take care not to have them found. I imagine it'd be difficult to try and explain how you acquired them."

Signa nodded, and though she was eager to get started on poring over them, it was a task that would have to wait until after a night's rest. Should she try to read them now, she doubted she'd be able to see straight. She wanted only a bath and to change out of her heavy attire prior to Death's midnight arrival. But before that, while Sylas was present, there was something she'd been wondering about ever since Percy's accusation.

"Why is it that you agreed to help me, anyway?" The words came out in a flurry, and Signa wasn't certain why her heart was pattering so hard beneath his observation. "Even with the money, do you not worry for your reputation? Nothing good would come of you being discovered."

It didn't take so much as a moment of consideration before he answered. "Speaking frankly, Miss Farrow, there's not much left of my reputation to maintain." He watched her eyes as they fell to his boots, wondering at the polished leather of such fine quality. He shifted his feet to one side, as though doing so might retire the boots from her inspection.

"I am not a selfless man," he admitted. "I would not put myself in this position unless there was something more concrete for me to gain. Just know that, by helping you, I will obtain the resources I require to help someone that I care for very deeply."

Signa wished she had water to quench the sudden parchedness of her mouth. There was such fervency to the way Sylas spoke; such a raw passion that Signa immediately stewed with jealousy for whoever could command such affection. She gave her cheek a quick pat, trying to will some of the heat from her skin. It wouldn't do to allow herself to be so taken with Sylas when there was another who held his affection already. She couldn't help that she found him handsome, or that she enjoyed his company. They'd simply have to be friends, then. Friends, and nothing more.

Besides, Sylas wasn't the only one who Signa too often found her thoughts wandering off to. There was another man she was anxious to see again, though it wasn't thoughts of friendship she had in mind.

"Whatever your reason, I appreciate it all the same, Mr. Thorly."

Sylas looked as though he were glowing from within at the praise. "Just Sylas is fine," he said. "And of course, there's no thanks necessary. I'll keep an ear to the ground and will be in contact should I hear anything informative."

There was more she wanted to ask, and more details she wanted to compel him to share. But with midnight a mere hour away, there wasn't time. She stood, and Sylas mirrored her example, taking the hint that this meeting was over.

"Have a wonderful night, Sylas." She folded her hands in her lap, wondering if she should try to look more affronted that he'd sneaked in through the window, and less like his doing so thrilled her.

Sylas made his way toward the window and hauled himself onto the willow tree as respectfully as one could do such a thing. When he was secure he turned back to her, moonlight glinting in his eyes. "Have a good evening, Miss Farrow. I'll be in touch soon."

TWENTY-NINE

WHEN MIDNIGHT STRUCK LATER THAT NIGHT, SIGNA WAS READY.
She paced the length of the sitting room as she waited for the darkness to pull inward as Death filled her room, bringing with him the chill of late autumn. Signa was glad for the slippers she wore and the robe she'd pulled over her thin chemise. The warning of the approaching winter hung in the air, it's chill bitter and biting across her skin.

"You did well. I'm glad you found a way to help Blythe." Death took in the dark tresses that Signa had brushed and the cheeks that she'd pinched life into. She'd spent the past hour since Sylas had left letting her mind whirl as she readied herself, thinking through everything she wanted to ask him. Everything she wanted to discuss.

"Only because you warned me." Signa wrung her hands. "Though the solution is temporary. Tell me ... are you certain you haven't any clue who could be behind Lillian's murder?"

Death took a seat on the arm of the chaise. "This is no elaborate scheme. It's as I've told you before—I'm limited in what I can see. When I touch someone, I claim their life. With that touch, I can see snippets of their living years, but I'm no psychic, nor am I all-knowing."

Signa sighed. While she'd expected as much, it would have been so much easier if he knew something.

"And what of your powers, Signa?" He rose from the chaise and prowled toward her. Every step he took caused a flurry in her chest, a cold burn creeping into her lungs. "There's something I've been curious about for a while. When you touched Magda, did you see anything?"

She'd buried the memory of that night deep, preferring never to think of what she'd done. But she did consider the question, and she shook her head. Death might have been able to see the lives of those he claimed, but Signa hadn't seen a thing when she'd touched Magda.

Death made a low hum under his breath. "While you do have my powers," he said, "it would seem that you're not able to use them to the same extent. At least not yet."

"What do you mean, 'not yet'?" Signa remained still as he drew a step closer to her.

The shadows swayed on the walls around him, a back-and-forth dance that lulled her into a sense of comfort. "It's merely a thought, though I wonder if you might be able to access your abilities better, Little Bird, if you were dead."

Finally, she had the sense to take a step back. "But I cannot die. I don't *want* to die."

"Exactly," he said. "You have a very long and full life ahead of you, rest assured. It's only a theory, but I do believe that when your life is over—and it will be eventually, Signa—these powers will be awaiting you."

Signa wrapped her arms around herself. "You think I'm like you." Her words were little more than a puff of air, fast and disbelieving. "You think I'm... What? Death?"

Death's shadows shifted, making him a touch smaller and less intimidating. "A reaper," he clarified in perhaps the softest voice she'd ever heard. A lake beneath the stars, still and quiet. "Yes."

It was a theory, he said, as though the idea wasn't enough to make her head spin. A theory, but one that had more merit than she cared to consider.

Suddenly, the cold was enough to make Signa shiver, though this time it wasn't because of Death's presence. She gripped the edge of a table to steady herself, and when that didn't work, she stumbled back into a chair as the idea pounded against her temples. "How would that be possible? Were you human once, too?"

He knelt before her. "No, I don't believe I was. It's impossible to remember everything, old as I am—though I'm certain I'd have remembered that."

It didn't make sense. Why, after all this time, would Fate decide that another reaper needed to exist in this world? Signa couldn't say with confidence that's what she was, but it was... a possibility. A damning one she couldn't quite wrap her mind around, but a possibility nonetheless.

"I think it'd be wise to test the limits of your abilities." Death spoke as though Signa were a child. As though she were a small, fragile thing that needed to be coddled. It didn't go unnoticed, and it wasn't difficult to think of where he might have learned to speak with a softness that felt so unlike the Death she believed had always existed. For so many years she'd seen him only as the reaper—a shadow with a lethal touch who'd pluck away any and every person in her life. But as he set a hand upon her knee with a touch that made Signa's heart leap into her throat, she realized he was something else entirely.

Death was the ferrier of souls; he was not a demon or a monster, but the one who guided wayward spirits. She'd seen how they clung to him. How they sought him out in anticipation. And for those who were afraid . . . Well, he had to have learned his softness somewhere.

His was so far from the life that Signa had imagined for herself. And yet, when he offered his hand and asked, "Will you trust me?" her body moved forward without hesitation. Gloveless, she touched her bare skin to his shadows, wrapping her fingers around his.

Ice tore through her veins, stilling her heart, and she didn't fight against him. He helped her up and onto her feet, and she felt the burn of her powers stronger than they ever were with the belladonna berries—steady and so potent that when Signa shut her eyes, she felt the reverberation of the earth beneath her.

He shifted so that he was behind her, trailing his hand up to brush it against her bare neck to maintain the connection. Signa bit back a gasp when she felt his chest press against her back, too often forgetting that Death was merely hiding beneath those shadows of his. Forgetting that there was a true man, chest and all, underneath them.

"Consider this the start of tonight's lesson." He whispered the words, steadying her. "What do you feel?"

Signa knew there were many ways she could answer: She could say that she felt the firmness of his chest and a heat in her belly as she imagined what that chest might feel like crushed against hers. Or she could tell him that her thoughts were wandering to just what Death could do with his shadows, but that was certainly more than she cared to admit.

She relaxed against him. As her shoulders eased, the world came into focus around her. She could feel it as though it were breathing—in the heat of the stars, leaves wilting from the trees, the chill of the earth as rain threatened from the heavy skies. Heartbeats, too—she could feel their final beats, too many each second.

"I feel . . . life," she said at last.

Death made a sound in the back of his throat, low and approving. "What do you hear?" His fingertips slid from her neck to cover her ears.

She'd never heard the world so quiet—like there was nothing else in all existence other than the two of them. But then the world slipped in piece by piece. She listened to final breaths and soft words. To the murmurs of love spoken to the dying, and though there was sadness there, there was also warmth for the lives that had led them to this moment.

"I hear their goodbyes."

Signa swallowed as Death slid his hands down to cover her eyes. When he leaned in, his lips brushed her ear. She shivered, wishing so badly to see that sliver of hair and the face he hid from her, and to finally look upon it.

"What do you see?" he whispered in a voice that made her knees weak.

The images came to her—the grass itself, beginning to shrivel from the cold. A family surrounding an elderly man as his heart stilled. She saw their faces, heard their voices, and there, dangling just out of reach, was a tether that Signa felt as though she could almost pluck from the air. One that would take her right to each of them.

Death eased his hands away, and Signa turned toward him at once. There was more to do, more tests to conduct. But in that moment she wanted only to look at this man who had spent his life seeing these things and embracing them. He was the first one the deceased saw after their eyes shut for the last time, and the weight of that settled into her.

"How do you handle this day after day?" Signa asked, one hand pressing to her chest. With his touch gone, life was leaching back into her skin, pulsing her stilled heart and forcing her blood to move.

"You become used to it," Death told her. "Some are patient in their deaths, and their souls will wait for me to come and claim them. Others are more persistent, as you saw a few nights ago. If I don't find them immediately, they'll find me. But I am never far from a lost soul, Little Bird, and I am not restrained to being in one place at a time."

He was close enough that she could imagine pulling down that hood of his, and finally looking upon him. There was a heat in her lower belly, for what she envisioned happening after that was far from chaste. Death stepped closer to take her by the shoulders, as though daring her to act on her impulses.

She was curious enough to do it, too. Not just to kiss him but also to explore other ways he might make her feel. Her robe and chemise suddenly felt like useless, flimsy things. She could feel every brush of his hands and gasped as shadows wound around her robe, sliding it down her bare shoulders and to her waist as Death crushed her closer.

He paused when she made no move to stop him, skimming his thumb along one hip. "Is this okay?"

The question broke Signa from her trance. She'd been too spellbound, too full of wanting, to even think through what all this meant. She hadn't debuted yet, and already she was this close to breaking the biggest societal rule there was for a woman—destroying her virtue. The rules in her etiquette book were limitless on this subject, and yet here she was, and with Death, no less. She understood him better now, but that didn't make him any less dangerous—though the danger made little difference to the ache of her body. She'd seen enough people seek out relations to know that the physical connection with a man was something she'd like to experience for herself, and by every indication of her body, she wanted to.

Besides, no one but she could even see Death—how would they ever know?

"H-how would that even work? With your shadows, I mean?" Signa asked. Rather than answer her aloud, Signa's skin burned as one of Death's shadows slipped beneath her nightgown and brushed against her inner thigh.

"Care to find out?"

Her body was screaming yes, ignoring the warning that rang deep within her mind. A tiny voice telling her to come to her senses and remember whom she was dealing with. Yet she stifled that voice and buried it six feet under. Listening to the most primal part of herself, Signa nodded.

Death unbound himself. His shadows wound around her, easing her down and onto the chaise as his hands lifted her hair, lips brushing so close that Signa arched toward him. He laughed, a raw and throaty sound as he lowered himself to her neck. Her eyes fluttered shut when she felt him there, trailing kisses from her ear to her collarbones—soft, peppered kisses, and every now and then a gentle suck on her skin that had Signa writhing, pulling him close. The shadows were enveloping her, brushing up her thigh in cold, smooth strokes that caused her to tilt her head back, offering herself to him.

She leaned into the feeling as Death's shadows brushed closer to where she wanted him. Where she ached for him. His lips were at her jaw, inching up as his shadows followed suit. Her heart was hammering, her breaths coming in soft rasps as she waited for his lips. For his touch.

But the warning rang again in her head, louder this time: If she let this happen with him, what did that mean? Did it mean she was ready to accept what she was? To embrace it?

Death stilled as Signa pressed her hands upon his chest to ease him away.

She wasn't ready yet. Wasn't sure what sort of life she wanted for herself.

And so she scooted herself back and said, "Tell me something you like," before she could change her mind.

"Something . . . I like?" He peeled himself from her. "I suppose I like you."

She nearly choked on her own breath. "What about hobbies? Or food—do you like food?"

"I don't eat much, though I've enjoyed what I've tried." He sat upon the edge of the chaise with a laugh, and as he'd done the night they'd met in the woods, Death made himself smaller. He did so for her, Signa realized. He was trying to be more presentable for her sake.

"You don't have to do that." She bit her lip as soon as she said it, wishing that she could just shut up for a minute and think about what she was doing. "You don't have to make yourself smaller. I'd rather see the true you, and not have any surprises."

She felt his eyes upon her. "Does this mean you no longer fear me?"

"It means I'm not sure." It felt wrong to say she was no longer hesitant around Death, or cautious of his power. But to say she feared him as she once had? After what he'd done for her—after he'd warned her about Blythe? That, too, would be a lie. She wrapped her robe around herself, avoiding his stare. The spell was broken now, and that tiny voice had freed itself and was screaming of virtue in her head. "I should get to sleep. Shall we continue our lessons tomorrow?"

Death nodded. "I want you to practice trying to speak with me. With your thoughts, not your words. You shouldn't need the belladonna berries to get in touch with me."

Halfway to her bed, Signa paused when he said, "I like animals more than most things." She turned, watching the last wisps of his shadows slinking out the window. "I like that they can see me."

And then he was gone, and Signa felt light enough to float.

THIRTY

Only a single night had passed since Blythe had taken the Calabar bean, and already she was making miraculous improvement.

"I've never seen anything like it," the doctor said as Blythe spooned porridge into her mouth. "What miracle is this?"

Percy stood with his arms crossed and eyes perplexed. "A miracle, indeed."

Blythe wouldn't be joining them for the Christmas ball or even a stroll around the manor anytime soon, but the antidote was working. And Signa knew that any day now, she'd find the one responsible for hurting her. She replayed Percy's words over and over again in her mind, relaxing into them. *A miracle, indeed.*

Signa slipped away from the sickroom to ready herself for breakfast, hoping to eat quickly and find a few moments to continue her search for the source of Blythe's poison and her research over the logs that Sylas had delivered. They hadn't proven helpful thus far, though she certainly knew more than she ever cared to about the staff and their behavior. Except for Sylas, of course. It hadn't slipped her notice that he'd purposefully left his logs from the stack.

Signa was seated at her vanity, not yet finished with her hair, when Marjorie arrived with a letter in hand.

"It's from Lord Everett Wakefield." She handed Signa a small white envelope. Signa's name was written on the front in careful, elegant script. Though Signa had anticipated excitement from her governess, Marjorie took hold of her hand and squeezed it. "Be careful" was all Marjorie said before she picked up a brush and combed through Signa's hair.

"With Lord Wakefield?" Signa asked, incredulous.

"With all of them."

Understanding the firmness in the woman's voice, Signa kept herself stoic as she drew the letter close to her chest and opened it without flourish.

Dear Miss Farrow,

I could not convince myself to wait even a moment longer to speak with you again. I would very much like to see you—today, if you'll have me? It's a lovely day for a ride upon the moors.

With regard,
Everett Wakefield

Signa looked up at Marjorie's reflection in the mirror. "He wishes to meet with me."

Marjorie gave no reaction as she began to pin Signa's hair back at her neck, twisting it into loose, flowing curls that cascaded down one shoulder. "And do you wish to meet with him?"

Signa brushed her thumb over her written name, surprised to realize she'd not thought of Lord Wakefield since they'd had tea. At first she supposed it was because she'd been so busy with Blythe and had plenty else to occupy her mind. Though that hadn't stopped her from thinking of Death, she realized. Or even of how she longed for another ride with Sylas. "I'll soon be twenty, and Lord Wakefield is a kind, successful man," she said, each word tense. "Shouldn't I want him to call upon me?"

"It's perfectly respectable to deny his request," Marjorie said. "We can blame your refusal on Elijah if you wish and tell Lord Wakefield that you'll not be receiving until your season. It would give you more time to ready yourself."

Signa leaned back in her seat, trying to collect her thoughts. "Do you not think I should see him?"

Marjorie was quick to admonish her. "I want you to be wise. All the men I've known were born with clever lies upon their tongues. They will speak dishonesties, or words sweeter than nectar, to take the things they want. You've a fortune to your name. It would be safer, I think, to debut and then host suitors here at Thorn Grove after you've come out for the season. You've no reason to come when called, and it would do you well to know your options."

There was no denying Everett's intentions. Had he arrived a month earlier, Signa would have allowed him to call upon her in a heartbeat. His was the face that Signa pictured when she shut her eyes and imagined her life in society. He was handsome and wealthy and charismatic. Together they would have a grand estate where they would host magnificent parties. And whenever they weren't hosting, they'd be expected to attend balls and the opera, and tea—and Signa would never again want for companionship.

So why couldn't she bring herself to accept his offer?

"Why didn't you ever marry?" Signa asked suddenly. Perhaps it wasn't the kindest question, and perhaps she was pressing her luck, but she needed another push. Another nudge to reassure herself that she wouldn't be dooming herself forever by refusing Everett.

Even if Marjorie hadn't a penny to her name, surely she would draw the attention of many respectable men. She was *beautiful.* "You were courted," Signa added, "weren't you?"

"My family wasn't high in social status, but we weren't horribly low, either. And I had my looks, and my hair, which many men have an eye for." Marjorie tousled one of her soft waves and chuckled quietly to herself. "So yes, Signa, I was courted wildly. And you will be, too. I won't tell you that you shouldn't marry, but there's no need for you to rush. Accept calling cards if you like, but whatever you do, proceed slowly with the men that you meet."

Signa didn't need to be experienced to know what Marjorie was alluding to, and she thought of all she'd almost done with Death the night before. Her etiquette book talked about relationships with men as though they were a transaction. As though she, as a woman, had to maintain each and every aspect of herself—virginity included—else she'd be thought of as impure. As *dirty.*

A Lady's Guide to Beauty and Etiquette was starting to feel less like her saving grace and more like a nuisance. A grim reminder that because she couldn't master the rules—because they exhausted her so—she would never be good enough, or perfect enough, or deserving enough. It was silly, she thought, for a book to make her feel such loathing for herself. She was better than that, *more* than that.

"Did you not like any of the men you met?" There was little avoiding the fact that Marjorie was an unmarried woman in service. It was a good living, but still. Someone with her looks, Signa thought, could have been the lady of an estate like Thorn Grove.

Marjorie took a seat in a reading chair. "On the contrary, I fell in love with a man who never had any intention of loving me back. And for that, I paid the price."

Signa recalled the way Marjorie behaved around Elijah. The way she'd touched his shoulder, and the way she spoke to him so freely. "What happened to him?"

"I believed we would be together for the rest of our lives," she said. "But he fell in love with another woman, and the two of them were soon engaged. I had given myself to him wholly, but he left me without explanation." Her eyes were distant as she wandered into the depths of her memories.

"Could you not find someone else?"

Marjorie folded her hands upon her lap. "In the eyes of society, I was already ruined. My parents rejected me. It was fortunate that

I was able to find work here at Thorn Grove when there were many worse places I could have ended up."

Marjorie had done nothing wrong by falling in love, and yet she was condemned for it. Tossed out of society like she was rotten, and like that rottenness might somehow spread. Like love or desire for someone was an infection. Would society do the same to her? If Signa made one wrong move, would she be forever cast aside by the people she was working so hard to please? And if the answer was yes . . . Did she ever really matter to them at all? She could follow all the rules of the etiquette book until her mind was numb and her will gone. She could masquerade every day, just as she had been, but for what reason? To be liked by those who would condemn her the moment she stepped out of line?

Signa set the envelope down upon her vanity. "And Mr. Hawthorne . . . he treats you well?"

With a smile, Marjorie stood. "Very well indeed, Miss Farrow, but enough about me. Have you made your decision?"

Signa returned her attention to the mirror, inspecting the glossiness of her hair and the fullness of her cheeks. Her time at Thorn Grove was doing her well, and there were more important things than to jeopardize it over a handsome face. And so she smiled up at Marjorie's reflection and said, "Tell Lord Wakefield that I'll see him Christmas Eve, for the masquerade ball."

THIRTY-ONE

A DAYTIME JOURNEY TO THE LIBRARY WAS FAR LESS EERIE THAN HER visit with Sylas had been two nights prior.

Signa took the stairs two at a time, easing the double oak doors open as to not frighten Thaddeus in the event that he was reading. "Thaddeus?" she called as she swung the doors open. "Sorry for interrupting. I wanted to thank you for your help—"

Her stomach lurched at the immediate sight of smoke. Clutching her skirts, she ran toward it. Thaddeus stood outside the row of shelves she and Sylas had been searching through. Handfuls of books lay scattered upon the floor, burning. It was a fresh fire, and if the flames weren't put out soon, it might gain enough momentum to burn all of Thorn Grove. "Who did this?" Thaddeus didn't answer. He watched his beloved books burn to cinders, flames reflected in his hollow, bespectacled eyes.

Signa wrapped her arms around her waist, hugging herself. This was her fault. Just two nights before she'd stood there, smiling and laughing and thrilled that she'd finally found a way to help her cousin. Someone hadn't liked that. Someone, it seemed, didn't want to give her the chance to find anything more.

She needed to fetch some water, or get help, or do *something*. If they put the fire out now, they could preserve most of the books. They could preserve the library.

Yet the moment Signa turned to run, the library doors slammed shut. Panic rose like bile in her throat as Thaddeus spun toward her. There was no warmth in his eyes. None of the smiles or kindness that there'd been before. His movements were jerky and his eyes like weapons; he appeared every bit as volatile as Lillian had been the night in the garden.

"Thaddeus, help," she pleaded, voice raw and scratchy in the growing smoke. "We can stop this fire from spreading any farther, but you have to let me go."

His expression remained hollow, untouched by her words as he stalked toward her.

Signa pressed her trembling hands against her sides to steady herself. "Thaddeus—"

He lunged, moving not *toward* her body but *into* it. A cold sharper than anything she'd ever felt numbed her limbs, freezing in the same way it did when Death touched her. And yet this did not feel remotely similar, for there was no power waiting for her. No connection to the world or her abilities as a reaper. There was nothing but ice.

She tried to blink eyelids that wouldn't shut. To move fingers that wouldn't close and feet that wouldn't walk. She couldn't so much as tremble, and she realized—distantly, for even her thoughts were beginning to haze at the edges—what this was.

Death had warned her that a spirit had the power to possess a person, though she'd never anticipated it happening to her.

The spirit was taking control of every inch of her, seizing hold of her body and even her mind, for her thoughts were now as wild and chaotic as his. His desires became her own.

Thaddeus wanted to toss more books into the fire and let Thorn Grove be consumed. But there was a part of him, too, that recognized help was available. That if they put out the fire now, everything needn't be lost. It was that hesitation—that tiny inkling stirring within him—that Signa clung to. It was the only hope, and so she tried to push on that thought. Tried to bring it to the forefront of their shared mind and unravel it ever so slowly, drawing him in.

She pushed and pushed, feeling like she was being sucked deeper into his rage by the moment.

She couldn't tell her thoughts from his when the library doors burst open and the world around them plummeted into a more familiar cold.

Signa had never been so happy to feel Death's arrival. To see his shadows slinking from the wall, pooling into a form that stood before her. Only faintly did she register that he was holding his hand out for her.

No. Not for her but for Thaddeus.

"Let the girl go." There was not a single note of gentleness in his voice. When Thaddeus didn't automatically respond, Death spoke again, low and vicious and seething. "Let. Her. Go."

And finally, he did.

Signa fell to her knees, trembling and so unnaturally chilled that she had half a mind to step into the fire.

Thaddeus paced before Death, a hint of light returning to his eyes. *"They came so fast. So fast, I couldn't do anything to stop them."*

It was Death who asked, for Signa's lips could not form the words: "Who couldn't you stop?"

Thaddeus flinched. He picked a book up from the table and then dropped it again, over and over. *"I was reading. I was reading, and I did not see. They came so fast. I was reading. I was reading, and I did not see."*

The fire was spreading. There was no time for Signa to let herself tremble. No time to succumb to the numbness of her body. She took a shaky step, the shadows helping steady her. Then another, and another, until they retreated to Death's side and she was starting toward the door as quickly as her body could manage.

"What will you do with him?" she whispered through quivering lips as she reached the hall, peering back over her shoulder to watch Death. His shadows spread like a blanket across the floor, as though he might somehow staunch the flames.

"I've told you already, I don't take spirits against their will." The room plummeted into darkness. Death's voice rang in her head. *Now hurry, Signa. Find help!*

And she did, stumbling down the stairs and screaming for whoever was there.

Elijah found her. He emerged from Blythe's room, a panic in his eyes when she told him of the fire. He and Warwick hurried to it, marshaling the staff to extinguish the flames.

Signa couldn't be certain whether he'd been sent or had rushed to her himself, but as one of the staff that had been enlisted to help, Sylas stood before her moments later. "What happened?" he asked as he took her by the shoulders and shepherded her away from the commotion, steering Signa back toward her suite.

At first, she couldn't answer. While the majority of the library was still intact, Signa's thoughts were lost to how Thaddeus had watched his favorite thing in the world burn away. So many books gone, just like that. Still, it was better to lose books than to lose their lives. What might have happened if she hadn't gone up there and noticed the fire when she did? Would whoever was behind the fire have been content to let all of Thorn Grove burn? She couldn't bear to think of it.

"I think," she said between chattering teeth, "someone is trying to send us a warning."

Sylas's grip on her tightened. "You look on the verge of fainting," he told her when they'd reached her door. "I'll find someone to come tend to you, but I need to go and help with the fire. In the meantime, promise me you'll try to rest."

"I promise," she answered meekly. It wasn't as though she was well enough to do anything *but* rest. Sylas held her for a moment longer before prying himself away. Signa watched his feet disappear back in the direction of the fire before she opened the door to her suite and dragged herself inside. Each step across the threshold was arduous.

It was most fortunate that Elaine soon appeared with a pot of tea and a tray full of scones. She pulled a plush chair close to the hearth and helped Signa into it, though it took Elaine some time to light the fire. The tinderbox in the kitchen had gone missing, and she'd had to scour the servants' quarters for another. Though fire was the last thing Signa wanted to see, it alone was able to soothe the pervading chill deep within her bones.

She sat in a chair by the hearth until sundown, trying not to think about how she'd let a spirit seize control of her body. It was a relief that Death had arrived when he did, though she hated that she'd had to rely on him to save her.

Elaine returned later to help her into a bath, and by the time she was clean, Signa was starting to feel like herself once more. The fog in her mind had cleared, and she had a new plan: She would learn to fend for herself, no matter how many nights it took of training with Death or how much she had to practice her powers. It would be worth it to learn everything, if only to avoid ever being possessed again.

And so later that evening, she sat in her bed with her hair wet and nightgown on, eyes shut. She had her window open, letting crisp air into her suite. It billowed the canopy above her bed, its chill sinking into the sheets as she bundled beneath the covers. A good chill, this time. Biting and stormy and *real*.

Her grandmother had always warned her not to leave the window open when her hair was wet, but it was a warning Signa preferred never to heed. She enjoyed the way the last tendrils of autumn felt against her skin, and she sought comfort within its cool grasp and the scent of dampened earth. It made her feel closer to the world around her. Like she was human.

It also, she realized, made her think of Death. She hadn't felt his presence since the library, and hour by hour her curiosity was mounting. Death had given Signa a challenge to communicate with him mentally. Now, she would finally try.

I'm glad you were there earlier. I don't know what would have happened if you hadn't arrived.

When the only response was silence, Signa scooted to the middle of the bed, folding her legs beneath her. *What's happened to Thaddeus?* She hadn't a clue if this was working; there was no guidebook for how to be a reaper. She shut her eyes and used the chill of the night to help her envision Death before her. Imagined that the cold was his touch against her skin. *Did you learn anything more from him?*

A spark within her told her he was there, listening.

He loved those books. It's my fault they've been destroyed.

Finally, his response came, and she couldn't help the thrill that ran through her. She'd actually done it. *Take a breath, Little Bird. You are no more at fault for the fire than I am at fault for the fact that people die. You did everything right—your cousin is still alive because of your efforts. Remember that.*

She worried her lip. While she recognized that there very well may have been some small modicum of truth in those words, it felt impossible to believe them.

Thaddeus is himself again, though I don't think he'll be long for this world. His voice was a cool burn against her skin. *What you experienced, Signa, is rare. It takes a lot out of a spirit to possess someone, and most decide to pass on not long after. Spirits don't have the ability to filter their emotions as we do, and they act on impulse. I'm sorry I wasn't there to help you sooner.*

She didn't want his apology; he was the last person she blamed.

All along he'd warned her to practice her abilities. To test her limits as a reaper. She should have listened.

Thank you, she thought. *For helping me, and for warning me about Blythe. I never would have known how dire a situation she was in had you not informed me.*

His response came after a long moment. *I would have taken her tonight had you not helped her. I fear our time to find the murderer is dwindling. She may be safe for now, but who is to say how long that will last?*

It was shame Signa felt, then. Shame for not finding the killer, yet. Shame for continuing on with lessons and musings over men, all while Blythe was deathly ill.

As if sensing that within her, Death said, *You are not responsible for her life. Nor will you be responsible when the time comes—and it will one day come—for me to take her. You must not allow yourself to be consumed so thoroughly by death. It's not selfish to live.*

She curled her toes in the sheets, combing fingers through her wet hair. How deep a nerve he'd struck, though it was one thing to be told that and another to believe it. *You were right to tell me that this would be easier if I'd rely on my abilities more,* she told him. *I think... I need you. I need your help. But I'm afraid.* It was easier to admit it from the safety of her bed, when he was not standing there before her. Even so, her cheeks heated all the same.

The silence between them grew, so loud it was grating. *It will come easier with practice,* he said at last, *and I will do everything in my power to help. I've taught you this much, haven't I? You have the power of the world within you, Signa Farrow. You need only to embrace it.*

The unspoken truth hung heavy between them—she would

be doing more than embracing her powers. She would be embracing *him*.

Her throat was too tight. She thought of their night together. Of how close she'd been to a decision there was no going back from. They'd stopped just in time, and that was a good thing.... Wasn't it? Because of course she shouldn't want that—shouldn't want *him*. And yet...

Stop worrying about society and playing its game, hoping that you'll be good enough, Death urged her. *There is no such thing as true goodness, there is only perception. So why not try my way of living? I think it would suit you just fine.*

It wasn't long ago that she'd held a knife in her hands and tried to plunge it through him. She'd wanted for so long to be rid of Death, but she was no longer so sure of that as she'd once been. Even the sound of his voice in her head warmed her. She felt endless curiosity about him. She wanted to pry him apart. To know his deepest depths, his likes, his wants. No matter how much she learned, she doubted she'd ever be satisfied.

The more she thought about him, the harder her toes curled into the bedsheets. But the chill of the wind was fierce, and it reminded Signa of what it'd felt like to be in his arms. There was infinite power in those arms, and an infinite power that came from being held within them. Never had she felt such stirrings within herself, such atrocities that Aunt Magda would have had her burned alive for.

Because she was having thoughts about Death. About *her* and Death. And they weren't the sort of thoughts that belonged in polite society.

I would come to you. His voice dropped lower, almost tender. *Should you call me, I will come.* There was something pressing about the way he said it—something fervent and searching.

Signa clutched a pillow tight to her chest.

She could do it. All it would take was a single word, and he'd be there before her.

But then what? Would she let him cure the ache of her lips? Tend to the heat of her belly? Would they continue where they'd left off the night before?

"Good" girls didn't want the things Signa was considering. For so long she'd had her plans, her hopes, and now he was throwing a wrench into all of them. She let loose of the pillow. It took everything in her not to summon him to her room. Not to speak the words that threatened her tongue. Instead, she curled into the sheets and shut her eyes, willing away the desire.

She had no doubt she'd dream of him. And for once, she was looking forward to it. *I'll remember that,* she told him, and left it at that.

He took it as a promise, his voice a rasp that made Signa believe he was having the same thoughts that she was. It was a sound she wouldn't soon stop thinking about. *Good night, Little Bird. You've done well.*

She wasn't certain he'd left her when Signa trailed a finger down her nightgown and smoothed her thumb over her inner thigh, imagining that the touch was his. She welcomed the night's chill into her bones, tilted her head back, absorbing it into her as though it was his embrace.

It would be another night, Signa was certain, when she wouldn't be getting much sleep at all.

THIRTY-TWO

IT'D BEEN YEARS SINCE SIGNA HAD A REASON TO CELEBRATE CHRISTMAS. The last time she'd celebrated was when her grandmother had been alive; they'd eaten mince pies and pudding every night of December and had decorated a tree with candles, fruits, and ribbons. The memories had faded some, but she remembered powdery snow outside the window and a fire burning in the hearth. She remembered the smell of pastries and gingerbread and oranges, and she recalled her grandmother reading her stories.

She held on to those memories when her grandmother had passed, nostalgic for the company and the warmth of stories and sweets. Her uncle had decorated their home, but Signa hadn't been allowed near the tree for fear she might somehow ruin it, and he'd spent his December nights with brandy and a lover, leaving Signa alone in her bedroom. None of her other guardians had done much to celebrate Christmas, perhaps cooking a turkey or setting up a tree, but there was never any warmth to it like there'd been with her grandmother.

After several years, Signa had stopped yearning for the past.

But once December rolled around at Thorn Grove, that nostalgia emerged with a vengeance. She sat at the top of the stairs, watching as the maids hung wreaths and garlands, decorating the manor for a ball that would not be held for another few weeks.

She lingered by the kitchen, where Percy worked off his boredom by raiding the pantries and pestering the cooks for sweets he shared with her and Blythe, insisting they'd put meat on his sister's bones. And then she'd watch, through frosted windows, for the first snowfall. When it came, she went directly to Blythe's room, helped bundle her up, and then led her and Percy downstairs for hot chocolate before they journeyed outside.

"I don't see why you're so excited," Percy said to Signa. He tried not to let his teeth chatter in the cold. He was becoming too used to the heat of the kitchen, and he was so fair skinned and prone to flushing that the tip of his nose and ears had turned red within minutes of being outside. "Why could we not drink this by a fire?"

Nestled in a wool gown and thick cape, its green velvet hood pulled up around her head, Blythe laughed. The sound reminded Signa of the toll of church bells: warm and safe and beautiful. Even Percy quieted upon hearing it, for her laughter was so rare these days. He watched with a hard expression as Blythe sipped from her hot chocolate, as though he worried she might disappear at any moment.

"A bit cold, Percy?" Signa teased, laughing, too, as he tucked his gloved hands under his arms to conserve warmth.

"We shan't count on him for making snowmen or snow angels," Blythe mused, leaning back on her hands to watch the snow falling upon the lawn before them. "My brother's never been fond of the snow."

"It's beastly weather, and wool itches like mad," he grumbled. "I'd much prefer to be seaside during the summer."

Perhaps it was because of her taste toward the cold, but Signa couldn't wait for snow to cover the fields and for the temperature to plummet. Autumn and winter had always been her favorite seasons. They felt quiet, like the earth was at rest, preparing itself for the warmer months ahead. She supposed she should start learning to enjoy the spring as well, now that she was nearing her debut—but there was something beautiful about the stillness of this time of year. Something wonderful and fragile.

Staring out at the moors, daydreaming of how lovely they'd look veiled in white, Signa caught a glimpse of Sylas in the distance. He was escorting a bay mare into the stables, and as though he felt her eyes upon him, he turned to steal a glance over his shoulder. He gave the tiniest wave when he caught her staring, and Signa turned away at once, skin burning hot from her mortification.

What was with her thoughts, betraying her by bouncing from him to Death? She and Sylas were friends and nothing more. Besides, it wasn't as though Death was a second choice by any means; she thought of him even more than she did Sylas. Though she wasn't quite sure yet what that said about her.

"I'm going inside where there is coffee and books and a hearth," Percy announced, glancing toward his sister. "Don't stay out much longer. The cold isn't good for your health."

Blythe nodded vaguely and waved him away, tipping her head back to gaze at the sky. Signa mimicked her, lying beside Blythe on the flat ground.

It truly was the perfect day for the first snow of the season. Gray, cloudy skies and the final tendrils of autumn retreating. Soon the trees would be bare and the entire ground would be covered in white.

"I wasn't sure that I'd see another Christmas." Blythe's voice was soft as snowfall, yet it struck deeply, like someone had twisted a knife deep within her stomach. Signa rolled to her side to look at her cousin, who looked back at her with the smallest smile upon her lips. "I must thank you, cousin. Not only for your help but because I feel that you are the only one who did not give up on me."

Tears prickled in Signa's eyes, though she refused to let them fall as she reached to take Blythe's hand. "I've never known a family. I will not presume to know what it feels like to have a sibling, though I do imagine it. And I imagine that if I had one, I would feel for them as I feel for you."

Blythe smiled again, the barest hint of emotion upon her face before she sat up and straightened herself, seemingly having no desire to revel in such feelings. "Come," she said, standing. "Percy's right that we should keep warm. Besides, there's something I'd like to show you."

Signa followed her inside and up the stairs. It was clear that being out this past hour had exhausted her. She clutched the banister as she walked, steadfast in her determination not to let her exhaustion show. Signa wished she *would* show it more, but Blythe was the most stubborn girl she'd ever met. So stubborn that she'd nearly cheated Death as many times as Signa.

When they reached her room, Blythe threw off her cape and took a seat upon the settee, skin flushed and clammy. "Do pull the bell for me, would you?" she asked, motioning toward the pulley that alerted the servants. "I'll need Elaine to help me get out of this gown. I'd forgotten how heavy wool is."

Signa did as she was asked, then noticed a thin white box adorned with a gold ribbon on the vanity. "Bring that here," Blythe said, exhaustion weighing down the excitement in her voice.

Signa took the box and joined her cousin on the settee, holding the box on her lap. It was remarkably light but too large to be any sort of jewelry or mittens—and far too small to be a gown. She started to give it a tiny shake when Blythe grabbed her hand.

"Careful, it's fragile!" she growled. "As much as I'd like to be there for the masquerade ball, I'm afraid that's beyond my limits. Next year, I assure you, my crinoline will be the largest by far, and my gown the boldest. But for now, this is the only way I can send a little piece of myself with you." She motioned to the box, her smile growing. "Open it."

Unable to recall the last time she had received a gift, Signa peeled the ribbon off with care, as if fraying it would somehow destroy the gift within. Inside the box was a mask that Signa gingerly lifted from a cocoon of tissue paper.

"Go ahead," Blythe urged. "Try it on."

She did. Gilded branches curved like vines around the right side of Signa's face and her honey-colored eye. Delicate, sculpted petals of lilac and deep green ivy wove around those branches, spilling over her head and past her blue eye. It was a gorgeous, mythical thing that Signa set back down at once, afraid she'd break it.

"It's for the masquerade." Blythe's words were a little too quick, and she kept searching Signa's face for a reaction. "I had it designed for you, as a Christmas gift. Do you like it?"

Signa held it upon her lap, staring down at one of the most beautiful pieces of art she'd ever seen. Somehow, it was *hers*. Someone had thought of her as they had this made, and that was by far the kindest compliment she'd ever received.

"I adore it," she whispered, returning the mask to the box with gentle hands. "Though I'm not sure how to wear such a thing. It deserves to be framed."

"Nonsense." Blythe *tsk*ed. "If you think it a work of art, then wear it and become the art yourself. I know how much you're looking forward to the ball, and if I cannot be there to steal all the attention, you must do so for me."

Signa laughed. "I suppose I've no other choice." There was a warmth in her heart that she'd not felt in some time. "This is the most extraordinary thing anyone has ever given to me. Thank you."

Blythe waved her hand in gentle dismissal, her nose scrunching up a little. "It's you who deserves all the thanks, for Thorn Grove has been altered since your arrival. I'm out of my bed. Father is smiling once more. It's not perfect, but it's more progress than I ever thought we'd see, and it's you we have to thank. You are valued, Signa. I want you to hear that from me before some vulture of a man starts filling your head with sweet words. I care for you not because you're polite or skilled at social graces, but for all the oddities that make you who you are. And someone else will, too, I assure you." She took the mask and held it to Signa's face, looking it over with a smile before she set it back into the box. "I know how society teaches us to be soft and dull and compliant, but you will not be any of those things, do you understand? Do not change the parts of yourself that you like to make others comfortable. Do not try to mold yourself to fit the standards someone else has set for us. Those are the rules for wearing this mask."

Signa clutched the box tighter, trying to commit the words to memory, for they were everything she was feeling. Everything she was fearing. "It's exhausting," Signa said as she looked down to her lap, "to pretend you are something—someone—you're not."

Blythe took her by the hand. "Then do not spend your life exhausted."

Signa felt as though she were standing on a precipice, teetering with one foot in a world she felt called to but was afraid to know, and the other in a world that she'd spent her life wanting, only to discover that perhaps it was not meant for her. She didn't have the answers—didn't know what she wanted. But she hoped to figure it out soon, and so she nodded, even though she wasn't certain that she meant it.

Blythe's eyes narrowed, but before she could ensure Signa's nod meant that promise, there was a knock on the door.

"Miss Hawthorne?" It was Elaine, carrying a tray. Signa met her at the threshold to Blythe's suite and without asking permission, lifted the porcelain teacup to her lips. She drew a sip, ignoring Elaine's surprised protest.

"Miss Farrow—"

Signa didn't wait to hear the rest of that sentence. She set the decidedly poison-free cup down on the tray and said to Blythe, "Enjoy your tea."

"Remember what I said, cousin!" Blythe's voice was a faint trill as Signa headed out the door and down the hall, slipping the mask from the box to stare at it as she went.

Soon. She would figure out what she wanted soon. But first, there was a ball to prepare for.

THIRTY-THREE

S IGNA SPENT THE FULL DAY WITH BLYTHE, MEMORIZING THE NAMES of every respectable gentleman and lady who would be in attendance at the Christmas ball. Signa's head had been swimming by the end of it, but Blythe had seemed in fine spirits when Signa left her early that evening. Signa expected, however, that Blythe would be at her window all night, watching as men and women filtered into Thorn Grove in plush gowns and extravagant masks.

Now Signa stood before her mirror, dusted with powder and rouge, her hair combed and styled so that the dark tresses were pinned at the nape of her neck. The girl who looked back at her was everything she was meant to be—a vision of beauty, poised and elegant.

Her full lips were a deep crimson, and with hair as glossy as a crow's feather and fair skin that had begun to glow over the past weeks, Signa thought she looked quite pretty. Meals at Thorn Grove had done her well; she'd never known she could have curves, nor had she seen herself with hips or a pleasing softness to her belly. Signa knew she could play her societal role well that night. What she wondered, though, was whether she could make her performance last. Even now, Signa's body felt too heavy, wrong in its own flesh. She'd never realized how weak she was, either; when not using her powers, she felt like little more than a leaf in the wind. Like the Little Bird that Death called her, pushed and pulled, aimless and susceptible to the will of the breeze.

Signa fought clammy skin and pulsing nerves as she waited for Elaine to bring the dress Marjorie had teased her with all week, refusing to show Signa anything of it but promising it would be a pleasant shade of lilac. She cursed those nerves—she was human. A perfectly normal human who should have no troubles at a ball. A girl who should want to practice for her season so she could step into the next phase of her life.

But the more she thought about it, the more Marjorie's and Blythe's warnings crept into her head. What was the purpose of it all? She'd marry, and then she'd . . . What? Have tea on Tuesdays and Saturdays, and any other blasted day of the week, while catering to the whims of her husband and hosting company? She wanted more than gossip and tea. More than maintaining a house, and ensuring her script was nice and her piano playing tolerable.

What had Death done to her to make her wonder if such a life could be enough?

"Miss Farrow?" A knock came at her door, and Elaine entered carrying a brilliant gown, bold as blood. Signa's breath escaped her. She fell a step back as the maid set the gown upon her bed, unable to look away.

Signa had never worn such a shade—had never dared be so bold. She brushed her fingers over the smooth fabric. The gown was the loveliest thing she'd ever laid eyes upon, and definitely not the promised shade of lilac. "This is for me?"

"Aye, miss," Elaine said with a small smile. "We ought to hurry you into it, so you don't miss any more of the party."

It was an effort to refrain from tearing off her clothing and being quick to let the woman fasten her corset and help her into the gown. The gown was satin with a bustled skirt and fitted bodice with cinched lacing along the back. It fit like a glove to all the new contours of her body. The color was unfamiliar on her skin, and it made Signa feel as though she'd freshly emerged from a sea of blood. It was so rich a shade and so exquisite that it had no need for loud embroidery to draw the eye.

The gown was somehow made even more divine when Elaine helped Signa don the gilded mask Blythe had gifted to her. "If you're ready, miss," the maid said as she looked Signa over with a smile, "Mr. Hawthorne will be your escort."

Signa hadn't expected that to mean Percy, but he waited outside her room in a fine black suit and a silver fox mask with a pointed nose. He bowed upon seeing her, offering a genuine smile.

"It's a shame that you've been locked away for so long." He held out his arm. "Come, cousin. Let us show society whom they've been missing."

The lead in Signa's stomach weighed something fierce, but she took Percy's arm and rolled her shoulders back. Together they descended the stairs.

Musicians played in the ballroom below, the cry of the violins and a piano welcoming her into a room so beautiful that she believed herself to be in a dream. It certainly smelled like one, with the scent of roasted chestnuts and perfumed bodies sweetening the air. The paneled walls were gilded, and the grand ballroom had a marble floor and matching pillars that reflected the crystal chandelier above their heads, casting a buttery haze over the room. Evergreen garlands were strung along the walls, and holly wreaths adorned the pillars.

Well-dressed strangers twirled about in masks of lace and jewels, plucking plum pudding and bubbling champagne from silver platters offered by servants in trim black suits and tidy white gloves.

Signa felt Percy stiffen as his father approached. Elijah Hawthorne was almost unrecognizable, his shoulders squared and his chin proudly lifted. His face was clean-shaven and exquisitely handsome, his blond hair styled neatly. He wore a mask adorned with holly crafted to look as though the tips of the green leaves were frosted over. In one hand was a glass with no bubbles, nor any of the amber spirits Signa might have expected. It seemed that he was drinking... water. In this state, Signa could see the bachelor who had once been known to steal the hearts of many. She could see the man behind the sorrow, and he was lovely.

"Marvelous, isn't it?" Elijah asked.

"Marvelous." Percy's voice held a bitter edge.

"It's nice to see you cleaned up, son. And you—" Elijah took hold of Signa's hand and gave her a twirl. "Absolutely radiant. You look so much like your mother dressed up like this."

Mid-turn, Signa froze. "I do?"

"Oh yes. A true firecracker, that one. There was nothing she hated more than people, and nothing she loved more than attention. A true conundrum."

Signa pressed a hand to her throat, searching for the words to voice a question that had lingered on her tongue for too long. "How did my mother favor society and all its rules?" Guilt weighed upon her the moment the words were out, for asking the question aloud felt like denying each and every one of the stories her grandmother had told her.

All her life, Signa had imagined her mother in a particular way that she struggled to emulate. But from the way others spoke of Rima, Signa's mind couldn't help but to wonder. To question.

"Rima was like the sun." Elijah spoke with great conviction. "All wanted to be near her. But those who ventured too close? They would burn. Rima did what she wanted without apology, and she was beautiful for it. I'm sorry you never got the chance to know her, Signa. If it means anything, Blythe sometimes reminds me of her."

Signa swallowed down the emotion that made her throat thick. Nineteen years she'd obsessed over that etiquette book, secretly wishing to become a pleasant, proper young woman who might make her mother proud.

Nineteen years, and now Signa didn't even know whether her mother would have cared about such efforts.

She bowed her head. "Thank you, Elijah—"

Elijah cut her off as soon as she began to speak. He set down his glass and took Signa's gloved hands in his own. "It's you who deserves to be thanked." He squeezed her palms. "So deep was I in my sorrow that I am ashamed to say I'd begun to lose all hope. I owe you a great deal of gratitude for what you've done for my daughter, Miss Farrow. For you, this ball is my first gift of many."

Percy went stiff beside her. "If you'll excuse me, cousin, I'll find you later on the dance floor." He straightened his tie, then the buttons on his gloves—and he was gone without another glance toward his father.

If Elijah was bothered, he didn't show it. Signa tried to mirror his lack of concern, not letting Percy's feelings about his father sour her own mood. It was a relief to feel welcomed, a relief to see that Elijah was in no hurry to rush her out of the manor. Signa couldn't remember the last time she'd felt so comfortable in a home. Couldn't remember the last time she hadn't looked forward to leaving.

"I hope that one day soon we will be standing here at a party to celebrate Blythe," Signa said.

Elijah's grip on her hands slackened, and though she couldn't say for sure, given the poor lighting, Signa thought she saw his eyes well up. "Indeed," he said softly. "I would like that very much." He straightened then, dropping her hands altogether. "Now, don't waste this night with an old man like me. Go on and find someone to dance with. Find *fifty* people to dance with, should you wish."

So Signa did. Into the dizzying, swaying bodies she ventured, lingering close enough to appear interested in a dance—but not close enough to get trampled by heels or whipped by flying skirts. With dreamy eyes she watched two women dance with each other as though they were floating upon a cloud, silk dresses swirling around them. She watched with a flutter in her heart as a handsome man offered his hand to a young lady while hoping the next one would choose her.

But the next handsome man Signa saw did not offer his hand, but stole her breath instead.

On the outskirts of the ballroom, Sylas Thorly sipped from a flute of champagne. Signa's heart stuttered at the sight of him, for in that moment he looked little like staff, or like a young man who worked in the stables, but every bit a proper gentleman in a well-fitted suit of deep onyx and a mask that appeared as though it had been carved from fine metal, crafted with intricate carvings. She had to do a double take to ensure she wasn't mistaken, but Signa knew she'd recognize those smoky gray eyes anywhere.

Though she knew full well that she shouldn't be so attracted to him and that she should instead be trying to figure out from whom he had borrowed such a fine suit, Signa couldn't help but to stare at him for a beat longer. God, he was handsome. Though the very moment she thought it, she forced herself to glance away. Already she was treading a very fine line with her relationship with Death and didn't need any additional considerations to add to the mix. Not to mention that Sylas had made it clear that he had someone important to him already. Signa needed to get her head on straight.

Still, she felt compelled to know why he would dare risk coming here, even if it was a masquerade. It wasn't as though she could approach him directly. So, instead, she made her way to a display of sweets nearby, making a show of inspecting them. When her eyes caught Sylas's from above a beautifully glazed fruit tart, he finished his champagne and set it upon a table as he made his way to the display. "That color suits you," he said with a wry smile. "You look beautiful."

Signa steadied herself, not about to be bested by surprise and let him see her trip up. She cleared her throat, quick to right herself, though she had no idea how long she'd be able to keep up with this charade of examining each and every available sweet. That lesson had obviously been missing from her etiquette book.

"What are you doing here?" she demanded. "You could be caught!"

"Relax," he said as he plucked a mincemeat pie from the display and took a bite. "Dressed like this, I'm certain no one will recognize me. Besides, this is precisely where I need to be. If someone is trying to harm the Hawthornes, the distraction of the night is a perfect time for them to strike. I want this solved just as much as you do, so I'm keeping an eye out."

Signa no longer bothered with pretending to select a sweet but held his stare directly and asked, "And why is that, Mr. Thorly?" Surely it couldn't be for the money alone, could it? Or was there something he needed it for that desperately?

Sylas's jaw tensed. "It's no different than I've told you already, Miss Farrow. There is a woman I care for immensely, and by assisting you and taking your offer, I'm caring for her in the only way I'm capable of at the moment."

She wanted to press for more—to know who this girl was and in what ways their deal helped her—though Sylas was spared from answering by a familiar voice that called suddenly from behind Signa, "What a *wonderful* party!" It was Diana Blackwater who spoke, taking hold of Signa's arm. Eliza Wakefield was at her side, fanning herself with a frilly white-lace fan. Signa supposed it was meant to look expensive, though it reminded her very much of a tea doily.

"I've always heard the Hawthornes' parties are legendary, but I daresay this one rivals even my imagination." Diana's voice was so grating that Signa felt as though her ears might suddenly bleed. Signa turned to glance back at Sylas, and sighed upon seeing that he was already making an escape, not about to let himself get involved with the new arrivals. She supposed she'd just have to get answers from him later.

Diana held her hostage, eyes not on Signa but wandering to the crowd, ensuring that others were looking and would see that she and Signa were—allegedly—close. Signa supposed they were, given that she knew almost no one else at the ball. But Diana doled out quips as though they were compliments, and Signa hadn't yet forgotten how eager she'd been to gossip about the Hawthornes when she and Signa first met.

Eliza, too, was something else entirely. She held an overly jeweled mask to her face with a long white stick, and she was dressed in a soft lilac gown—the very shade Signa had been meant to wear until she'd been surprised with the gorgeous red gown she wore now.

"I thought you were wearing green?" Signa asked, glad the girl at least had the decency to hide her blush with her mask. "Though the lilac does suit you. Tell me, have either of you seen Miss Killinger?" She searched for her old friend through the swaying bodies and masks.

"She's likely off somewhere brooding over Lord Wakefield," Diana scoffed, voice thick with mirth.

Signa straightened her mask with great care, treating it like the most fragile artifact. "Why would she be brooding?"

Diana arched a brow. "We all thought that he and Miss Hawthorne would be matched this season. But with Blythe out of the picture, poor Miss Killinger probably believes she has a chance with him."

Signa didn't join in when Diana began to giggle, the sound bitter and ugly. She instead scanned the crowd, relieved to see that Charlotte was far from sulking in the shadows. Her gown was a rich sapphire, gorgeous against her warm brown skin, and her curls were pinned up to show off her delicate neck. The mask she'd donned shimmered like a glittering snowflake.

Charlotte spoke to Percy, who was grinning as though she'd just told the cleverest joke. Charlotte was beaming, too, and soon enough they set their glasses down and took to the dance floor. Diana and Eliza truly were gossipmongers; despite their talk, Charlotte appeared to be having a grand time.

"Her pining will end soon enough," Eliza said in too airy a tone. Her gaze trailed behind Signa. "My cousin already has his eye on another."

Signa turned to the man who came up behind her. Even in a mask, she knew from height and hair that it was Everett Wakefield. He was handsome in a fine black suit with a white-and-gold mask that was designed to look like it was cracking. It covered only his eyes, and Signa wondered if he'd done that purposely, so that others could still see the strong cut of his jaw and his smooth brown skin. If he had, then the ploy was working. Young women flocked to him, introduced by eager mamas or simply standing nearby and fanning themselves dramatically in the hope of being noticed.

Signa was glad to see that Everett was polite to those mamas and blissfully ignorant of the surrounding women, though she was unsure how she felt when it became clear that he was watching only her.

"We meet again, Miss Farrow."

She imagined that his voice should have kicked up a flutter in her chest and frowned a little when it didn't. "So we do." A servant offered them each a beautiful glazed tart, and Everett mirrored Signa's choice to refuse the offer. Her stomach was so sour with nerves that she wasn't certain she could eat anything without being sick. "I'm glad you could attend, Lord Wakefield."

What must it be like, Signa wondered, to have an ensemble flocking to get your attention? If she were to walk into a party on his arm, would people rally to speak with her, like they did to him? Signa hated that she wondered. Hated that she *cared*. What did it matter what others thought of her? It was all starting to seem so ridiculous, and yet she couldn't help the bitter curiosity that festered within her.

"I apologize for intruding during my last visit," Everett began in a voice light as gossamer. "I didn't realize you weren't yet receiving."

She blushed; with all that had happened since, she'd completely forgotten the note and his request to call on her. "There's nothing to forgive. I was flattered."

He smiled. "Is that so? Well then, Miss Farrow, how would you feel about flattering me in turn by allowing me your first dance?"

She dared a look around him first. Sylas was nowhere to be seen, and it wasn't as though there was anyone waiting in the shadows for her, so she cleared her throat and lifted her head to reply. "I would be delighted." Signa discreetly wiped her clammy hands upon her dress before she took hold of Everett's as he led her to the center of the dance floor, where the jovial music of a gallopade swelled.

Everett bowed, and Signa responded with a curtsy before

stepping forward and placing one hand upon his arm and the other in his hand. She swallowed when his hand came around to the small of her back, and they began. It was a fast dance, one with quick footsteps that had everyone weaving from their partners and to the next group over before circling back again. Joyous laughter filled the ballroom. Signa and Everett twirled and wove back and forth, growing flushed and clammy but too delighted to care.

Everett was a skilled dancer, the steps ingrained so deeply within him that he didn't falter when Signa missed one. His grip on her tightened, helping correct her with not condemnation or embarrassment but a grin.

"Selfishly, Miss Farrow, I'm glad you came to Thorn Grove." His smile was infectious. The kind that made her cheeks ache without any clue why. And yet, joyous as the dancing was, his arms did not feel right beneath her hands. He wasn't the one she wanted to dance with. He wasn't the one she wanted to see her dressed up like this, bold and striking and beautiful.

She grew breathless as they turned about the room once more, her hand coming up to set before his as they circled each other. When she didn't respond, he leaned close. "I'm looking forward to the spring."

He'd spoken quietly enough, but Signa caught the tail end of murmured conversations that sounded very much like gossip as too many eyes observed them. She wondered if he noticed it, too, and if it bothered him. So distracted was she that she lost her footing, and he caught her before she could stumble, just in time for the song to end.

His brows creased, forming deep lines upon his forehead. "Are you all right?"

She wished that she had Eliza's hideous tea-doily fan so that she might hide her warming face. "Quite well," she said, following suit as the women around her curtsied to their partners. "Thank you, Lord Wakefield. You're a lovely dance partner."

He bowed, and though the lines on his forehead didn't smooth themselves fully, he didn't press her. "As are you. I hope this won't be our final dance this evening."

"No, I don't imagine it will be."

It was as though he'd shattered some invisible barrier with that first dance. She only made it a few steps before someone begged her pardon and made introductions. Soon her dance card was filled, with the exception of the last spot. No one dared take the final waltz from Lord Wakefield. He and Signa caught each other's eyes several times throughout the night as Signa danced and spun and twirled with more men than she could count. Ones older and younger, wealthy and hungry to elevate their status.

Though she'd expected to enjoy her time and conversation, the more people she met, the more drained she became. While most of the men had decency, there were too many who made Signa's skin prickle, and even one—an older man with a shrewd mouth and wiry frame—whose hands lingered far lower on her back than appropriate.

She caught sight of Charlotte twirling in the arms of men Signa had never met, and then again with Percy. She and her cousin laughed and whispered, eyes gleaming. Signa's heart warmed at the sight, though Eliza watched from the sidelines, her mouth tight and her fluttering fan almost lethal.

Everyone else certainly seemed to be enjoying themselves. Now that some hours had passed—accompanied by many drinks—the laughs came easier and the mood was even lighter. It was amusing to people watch, though Signa soon found herself wanting to sneak away to her bedroom with grand illusions of lighting some candles and drawing a late-night bath. For weeks now she had been trying to keep herself together. To play pretend, and tell herself that finding her footing in social circles would get easier. But the rules were stressful and unforgiving, and Signa's chest felt as though it might burst if she could not escape to the shadows to catch her breath.

But just as a dance ended and she began her retreat, all heads turned to watch a new guest arrive.

Signa was certain she'd never seen the man before. Hair silver as starlight was tied at the nape of his neck, while his attire was a black suit of rich imported fabric and boots of the finest dark leather, as were his gloves. On his face was a mask of pure gold—one that had everyone in the room buzzing with whispers. It was a far more gruesome mask than anyone else had dared to wear, almost devilish in its severity, with two long horns spiraling from the base of the skull. He was impressively tall and well-built, and as he stepped forward, people parted for him. He didn't acknowledge them as he crossed the floor to stand before Signa, nor did he say even a word when he offered his hand to her.

She took it before she knew what she was doing. The music disappeared with his touch, and she knew at once who it was that pulled her into his arms.

"Hello, Little Bird. Care to dance?"

THIRTY-FOUR

THE LIGHTS AND LAUGHTER OF THE BALLROOM FADED AS SIGNA eased from Death's grasp.

"What are you doing here?" Her heart thundered as she looked past him to faces still as statues. "Can they see you?"

"I'm wearing a mask, Signa. Whatever they think they see is merely an illusion." She didn't need to hear the mirth in his voice to know that he was grinning because she could see it now. Full pink lips that curled into a grin, and a cut of cheekbones—the only parts of his face that weren't covered by the mask.

One by one the unblinking eyes that observed them evaporated like smoke as the ballroom sank away. Somehow they were in the garden now, bathing in the moon's pale glow. The ground beneath Signa's feet grew damp, and the air was heady. Snow crunched beneath her feet and the sky spun into a canopy of stars.

"You look even more beautiful than I imagined." Stepping closer, he brushed a gloved hand against her hip, inspecting the gown's fabric. "Do you approve of my gift?"

Oh, she could make a home in that voice of his, for it was sweeter than any nectar. Signa felt as though she'd been laid naked before him, exposed in a way she'd not known possible. "It's the loveliest thing I've ever seen." Her breath was tight. She should have known such a dress would never have come from Marjorie. Only if she'd been able to claw her way into the depths of her own soul would Signa have been able to pick such a gown for herself.

He made a noise of agreement, a rasp of a sound that had Signa leaning in. "I could not be the first, so let me be your last of the night. Dance with me, Little Bird."

Death was perhaps the most powerful being in existence—more powerful than any king. He was as fearsome as the night, as unstoppable as the wind or the rain. And yet, though subtle, there was a tremor in his request.

Every fiber of her being was screaming to run. But when he stretched a hand to her—not shadows, a true hand—her body burned. How was it that after she'd spent so many years of her life fighting him—fighting that part of her—she now craved his touch?

Death's hand tightened on her hip and she bent to his touch, letting him lead. His movements were fluid and graceful, and the longer they danced, the more Signa felt the weight of her body disappearing. She was a feather and he was the breeze, gliding her upon the wind.

"You are more than just shadows." It took effort for Signa to find her voice.

He faltered for a step but was quick to correct himself. "I can be, when the purpose serves me."

"You have a form." She leaned closer to try to peer beneath the shadows and golden mask that obscured him. He missed no steps but did well at keeping Signa at a distance. "What do you look like beneath your mask and your shadows?"

He clucked. "So forward a question at a masquerade. Perhaps I'll show you one day."

Something in his voice was softer then, the wall between them slipping away. It was the moment Signa needed to sink her nails into that wall and tear it down. "Do you not like the way you look?"

His laugh was a rustle of the leaves, the soft caw of a crow at dusk. "I'm confident you'll find me incredibly handsome. I simply prefer not to use my true face often. I can alter my appearance to give people what they need in their final moments. But my image—my *true* image—I reserve. I don't want my face to be the last one this entire world sees before they die."

Signa yearned to see that face. Only a few hours earlier, she'd been in Everett's arms, considering a life with him in high society. Now she was wondering how Death's lips might feel against hers.

With him, Signa no longer wanted to wonder. She wanted to *know*.

Death dipped his head low, words brushing against her ear. "I have waited for you for a very long time, Signa Farrow."

Breathless, she couldn't find the words to respond. So instead, she lifted up onto her toes and pressed her lips to his.

The world disappeared as seconds spun into moments long

enough for her hands to wind around his neck. For the cold to sink into her bones and Death's surprise to give way to desire. He leaned her against a tree, kissing her back not with politeness or constraint but with a bone-deep hunger breaking free. His hands were in her hair, undoing it from its pins so that it tumbled over her shoulders. They were on the cut of her jaw, on the small of her back, on her neck.

The darkness enveloped them as he pushed himself against Signa, who made no move to stop him. The moment he'd kissed her, she'd become his, every part of her unwilling to turn away. Unwilling to stop herself. His shadows enveloped them, as though Death intended to consume her entirely, and she shut her eyes, ready and willing. *Wanting* to be consumed.

The shadows dissipated as Death tore away from her, and Signa's entire body shuddered. He was, as far as she was concerned, the very embodiment of the devilish mask he wore. Her eyes were wild as they searched for him, not wanting this to be the end. If he laid her upon the ground right then, she'd continue what they'd started that night in her suite.

But he said, "It's nearly midnight. You're expected back at the ball," and that was the end of it. Death trailed his fingers down her arm and to her hand, and as they spun once more, the world around them began to reappear. Stars disappeared, replaced by gilded walls, and where Signa had stood on moss, she now walked upon marble. The sound of the pond became the boisterous laughter of strangers, and Signa found herself longing for the quiet again.

"I could come to you later." He didn't look at her when he spoke.

"You need only open your window, and I will come." He swept his fingers through her unbound hair, then disappeared.

Within seconds the ballroom was exactly as it had been before. But the time was all wrong. It was nearly midnight.

"There you are!"

Signa spun to find Marjorie hurrying toward her with relief. "Lord Wakefield has been asking for you, and not one of us had any idea where you'd gone off to." She looked Signa over. "What on earth are you wearing? And what did you do to your hair? Oh, never mind. There's no time to fix it. Come." Signa was too distracted by her swollen lips to care that Marjorie took hold of her arm and escorted her out of the ballroom. She didn't pay attention to whatever the governess was prattling on about Everett, too busy trying to memorize the way Death's lips had felt against hers.

The crowd gathered as the countdown to midnight began. A Christmas tree towered in the center of the foyer, decorated with giant red and gold bobbles, fruits, and lit candles. Signa caught sight of Percy next to it, laughing with Charlotte as she handed him a glass of champagne and took one for herself. Eliza was there, too, trying to slip closer to the duo. A man in a crow mask clasped Percy by the shoulder. Signa wouldn't have recognized him if not for the walking stick in his hand—Byron. It was with relief that she noticed Percy smile. He spoke low to the man, patting a yawning, departing Byron on the arm as he threw back his champagne.

Everett Wakefield was near the front of the crowd. His smile was small and confused when Signa caught his eye, for she'd missed the last waltz with him. She averted her attention and hated herself for it. He was a kind man, yet with the brush of Death upon her lips, it didn't matter how kind he was. Death was her poison, and all she wanted was to consume more.

She thought she caught a glimpse of Sylas, too, and had half a mind to hurry to him and ask if he'd seen anything, but Elijah already had a flute of water raised by the time Signa walked into the room, finishing a speech for his guests. Signa caught only the tail end of it, thrust into a cheering crowd as he said, "And may this be a merry Christmas, indeed!"

The crowd around him echoed those words as midnight struck. Someone shoved a flute into Signa's hand and she accepted it with a laugh, sipping the champagne as others toasted and wished one another a merry holiday. They were strangers, but in that moment it didn't matter, for her body hummed with happiness.

Had the chatter been a little louder, Signa could have remained in that happiness, for she might not have noticed the sound of shattering crystal and the gasps that followed. The ballroom might never have fallen into silence as all eyes turned to the tree. And she might never have registered that, beside her, Marjorie was screaming, and Sylas had suddenly appeared beside her, gripping her wrist.

"Shut your eyes," he whispered, low enough that Signa couldn't be certain she wasn't imagining things. "You don't need to see this, Signa."

But she didn't shut her eyes, and she *did* have to see this, because a body had fallen into the Christmas tree, sending it crashing to the ground as the decorations shattered on the floor. And that body was Percy, whose eyes had rolled back in his head as he lay, unconscious, in the mess of his own blood and vomit.

THIRTY-FIVE

I T WAS FORTUNATE FOR PERCY THAT SIGNA HAD A SINGLE DOSE LEFT of the Calabar bean.

They left Warwick in charge of escorting everyone from Thorn Grove. Signa had never disliked people more than when she'd overheard whispers that perhaps Percy had been too taken with liquor, like his father. She bristled at the very thought of it, for how rude these people were to cast judgment upon the man who had invited them so graciously into their home. Surely, their gossip was not that of *polite* society; Elijah hadn't so much as had one drink that evening.

Holed up with her in Elijah's room, away from prying guests, Marjorie and Elijah allowed Signa to work without protest when she said she could reverse Percy's illness just as she'd reversed Blythe's. Her anger made it easier for Signa to beat the rest of the Calabar bean into a fine powder, which she'd stirred into a glass of water and administered to a trembling, gasping Percy as thick beads of sweat rolled down his neck. Marjorie and Elijah watched with grim eyes, neither daring to speak.

Percy, fortunately, was quick to throw up the poison, and within the hour he was breathing easier. Death, who'd been crouched at his bedside all the while, still and waiting, finally nodded once and then was gone. Instantly, the tension in Signa's shoulders eased.

"How did this happen?" Elijah looked to Signa and the remnants of the milky-white antidote on the nightstand.

Signa had no answer. She'd seen Sylas for only seconds before she followed Elijah and Marjorie into the room, though in that time he swore he'd seen nothing out of the ordinary. No matter how she twisted her brain to rearrange the pieces, it was a puzzle that made no sense. One by one the Hawthornes were falling ill from belladonna—but why? For their money? Signa had been suspicious of both Byron and Marjorie since the night she and Sylas went to Grey's. Yes, Byron wanted his brother to cease his hold on Grey's, but would he hurt Percy to do it? And what might Marjorie's involvement be?

Signa raked her fingers through her hair as her frustration mounted. Percy had been fine when he'd escorted her to the party, and she'd seen him smiling and dancing. Even in those final moments before his fall, he'd looked happy, chatting with Charlotte and Eliza. But Byron had been there too. Byron, whose words Signa recalled from that night at Grey's with Sylas.

If he won't give the business to Percy, convince him to give it to me. There'd been such bitterness in those words. Such rage. *I'd take better care of it anyway, just as I would have taken better care of her.*

"Where's Byron?" Signa asked. "He and Percy were together moments before he collapsed."

Elijah sat on his knees at Percy's bedside, watching the slow rise and fall of his son's chest. "You think my brother is responsible for this?"

Signa couldn't be sure, and she knew it was best not to answer rashly. Byron had made it clear that he wanted nothing more than for Grey's to stay in the family, and though he'd been advocating for Percy that night, could there have been more to his interest?

"It's possible he saw something." The truth sat on the tip of Signa's tongue, daring to be spoken aloud. She *wanted*, very much, to tell Elijah and Marjorie the truth about what was happening. Yet the more people who knew, the more likely the information was to get out. It also wasn't out of the realm of possibility that they might know more than they were letting on. Too many times Signa's mind had wandered to Marjorie and the strange situations her governess shouldn't have been in. Situations that made no sense, no matter how much Signa rearranged the puzzle pieces in her mind.

She needed answers—quickly. Before it was too late.

"I'm just glad this remedy is working," Signa said. "It's meant to cure ailments of the stomach, but that was the last of it." She felt fragile admitting it aloud and hugged herself. They nearly lost Percy tonight. One more incident, and that would be the end of him, Blythe, or whatever other Hawthorne might be targeted next.

"This is no disease, is it?" Elijah said. "This is no coincidence. Someone is targeting my family."

Elijah was delicate as crystal. Not wanting to give him a reason to shatter, Signa whispered, "Anything is possible."

Marjorie said nothing as she tucked the blankets around Percy and placed a dampened cloth on his forehead. Worry was etched into every line of her face.

All Signa could think of was Percy's laughter as they'd danced together during her lessons. How he'd taken to bringing her scones and pastries late in the evening, when he couldn't sleep or was making himself sick worrying over Grey's. There was Blythe to think about, too. Blythe, whose laughter Signa wanted to hear more often. She was tired of seeing Blythe struggle—for breath, for comfort, for life.

It was time to put an end to this.

"There's nothing more I can do for him tonight." Signa stood, skirts in hand. "He needs rest."

Elijah nodded. "I'll find a way to procure more of this medicine," he promised her. "Marjorie, see if you can find Byron and bring him to me. We might as well see if he knows anything."

"Of course, sir." Marjorie's eyes were glossy as she watched Elijah lean in, his hand trembling as he pressed it gently upon his son's cheek.

Whoever was behind the poisonings was clever, always one step ahead. Now it was time for Signa to be cleverer.

THIRTY-SIX

T HE DRIED BELLADONNA BERRIES FELT LIKE WRINKLED PRUNES AS Signa cupped them delicately in her palms. Still in her gown, she sat cross-legged upon her bed with the window open beside her and the bitter cold pressing against her skin as she recalled her lessons. It wasn't enough to simply pass through objects. She needed to avoid notice, to befriend the shadows and make herself invisible, just as Death did. With a steadying breath, she focused on her intention—to shed her corporeal form, to join the ghosts of Thorn Grove for just one night—and pressed ten dried berries to her tongue.

Within moments the room around her was spinning. Her temples throbbed, ears ringing as though a pistol had just fired beside her.

Signa? Death's worried voice cleared a space in her mind and steadied her.

Wherever you are, you don't need to come, she told him. *I'll be fine. Watch over the others.*

When she opened her eyes, she was still in her body, yet it felt lighter. She reached her hand out to the shadows in the corner of the room. They obeyed at once, swirling around her feet and wrapping around her arms, masking her in their darkness.

A thrill of power surged through her blood as the world opened itself for her bidding. Signa moved to inspect herself in the mirror. No face of a ghost peered back at her, for Signa wasn't like the spirits. She was swathed in shadows, the darkness of the night itself—just like Death.

She'd done it.

You're not breathing. Death's voice was hard and icy. *Why aren't you breathing, Signa?*

I told you not to worry. With new conviction, she passed through the door to her suite without opening it. *I'm going to finally put an end to this.*

Signa wasn't convinced at first that no one could see her, but she willed her invisibility stronger than she'd ever willed anything, and she barely managed to dance out of the way before a maid passed through her. Her hands and feet were bare, and though the shadows protected her, this wasn't the time to test her fatal touch.

Signa had checked for clues everywhere in Thorn Grove but the bedrooms. She made her way through the rooms one at a time, searching for secrets and lies—anything to fill in the pieces to her incomplete puzzle.

There were ledgers in Warwick's room, boring leather-bound books filled with notes on what household goods needed restocking and details about each of the servants and their work ethics. When Signa reached for the ledgers, the shadows obeyed her silent command, flipping through the pages for her. She almost laughed, confidence blooming as she called her powers to her and scoured each room. They weren't much different than the logs she'd already been reading, and she was disappointed to again find no notes on Sylas. There were more ledgers to be searched, but for now there was no choice but to move on.

In one room she found a servant muttering under her breath about curses and ghosts while packing a travel trunk, and in another she found two who were doing everything *but* worrying over the mysterious disease plaguing the Hawthornes. Cheeks warm, Signa hurried through a wall without looking.

The room she came to next was decidedly feminine, with walls a soft shade of green and a dresser adorned with bottles of amber perfume, a hairbrush, and rouge. She knew the room belonged to Marjorie when saw lesson plans on the desk with Signa's name on them and brief notes about her progress.

The notes were simple upon first glance, but Signa knew in her gut that there was nothing simple about Marjorie. There had to be *something*, and so she riffled through her desk until she came across a small leather-bound journal buried at the bottom of a drawer.

She perched on the edge of Marjorie's bed and set the journal upon her lap. Hands trembling, she flipped to the first page.

October 22, 1852

I'm not sure I will ever belong at Thorn Grove.

How many days will I sweep the kitchen or launder the sheets before she allows me to see him?

Perhaps she's right and I shouldn't tell him. Perhaps he will not accept my love after all that has happened. All the same, it is cruel to force us apart. If not for Lillian, all would be as it should. All would be well.

Signa turned to the next page, dated a little over a week later.

November 1, 1852

Lillian has eyes everywhere. I feel them upon me more than ever, watching my every move, ensuring I don't get too close to him.

But today she took Blythe into town for new dresses for the season, and I found him in the stables, admiring the horses. He's an excellent rider—he's excellent at everything he does, really.

Perhaps I should not have told him, but I spent twenty years believing that the truth would set us free. Yet I fear Lillian was right to demand my silence—no one has ever looked at me with such contempt.

Perhaps if I'd listened, my heart would not be breaking.

ℰ⟶

January 10, 1853

I never imagined what would become of Lillian once the truth was out, but I do not pity her.

This is what she deserves, and when she's gone, Elijah will be free. This family will be free.

April 11, 1853

Lillian is gone, but I fear she has taken my Elijah with her.

I pray for the children. I pray for Lillian, God rest her soul, and that she will soon be nothing more than a memory to us all.

I pray that, finally, we can be a family.

Signa couldn't flip through the journal any faster. There were pages upon pages detailing Marjorie's affection for Elijah, and for the children—and how different life would be had she been the one to raise Percy and Blythe. Marjorie wanted Lillian out of the picture, and by the sound of it, Lillian wanted Marjorie gone just as badly. But if that was the case, why hadn't Elijah simply sent Marjorie away?

Signa skimmed the pages for anything about belladonna, or even a single hint of poison. But if Marjorie knew anything of it, she knew better than to write about it in her journal.

The entries weren't proof that Marjorie had harmed Lillian, but they were a clue. Perhaps the poisoner wasn't Byron after all. Either way, Signa needed *more*.

She closed the journal and let the shadows wrap tight around it. If someone wanted to take it from her, they'd have to pry it from her cold, dead fingers.

From top to bottom she tore through the room, searching for anything to confirm her suspicions. She groaned, shadows yanking a drawer from Marjorie's armoire and throwing it across the room in frustration when she still hadn't found anything more than the journal.

She pressed two more berries upon her tongue, her rations running low since she'd last stocked her supply the night she'd visited the garden. There had to be something more concrete elsewhere in Thorn Grove, and she needed more time to find it. Room by room she hunted for answers. The longer she remained under the belladonna's influence, the more natural it felt shifting through the walls and walking by people who didn't spare her so much as a glance.

Eventually, Signa came to the room across from Blythe's, where Lillian's portrait stared at her expectantly, urging her to take that next step forward. She heeded the call.

The sitting room was even larger than her own, outfitted with mahogany furniture and walls of soft blue and cream—all covered in a thick layer of dust. It was clear no one had visited in some time. Probably, Signa thought, not since Lillian's death.

Only the room wasn't as empty as she'd first believed.

Signa startled at the sound of footsteps in the attached bedroom before remembering that she could not be seen. Gathering her shadows, she floated through the wall and found Marjorie inside. She sat upon the dusty bed, her breathing labored as she held a small black-and-white photograph. Signa stepped around Marjorie to peer over the woman's shoulder.

The photo was of Percy with his mother and father. Given how young Percy looked, Signa guessed it was taken before Blythe had been born.

Signa didn't expect the tears that welled in Marjorie's eyes, nor did she know what to do when Marjorie ripped the photograph in half. She flung open the window nearby and sent scraps of the photo scattering into the snow as she held in her sobs.

Signa had half a mind to abandon her snooping and retrieve those scraps for Percy, knowing he'd never have a chance for another portrait like that one. But she fell still at the sight of Marjorie's hands. Her fingers were bare, the tips stained a deep plum.

Signa looked down at her own hands. The fingertips were the same: stained the color of belladonna.

Signa stumbled back against the bedpost. To her dismay, she did not fall through it but hit it hard, making the bed groan. Marjorie whirled around, and Signa used every ounce of her focus to control her ability to conceal herself in the shadows once more.

"Who's there?" Marjorie's eyes darted across the room, searching for a body she couldn't find. Signa made herself small and prayed the belladonna would last long enough for her to leave unseen. She had readied herself to silently flee when Marjorie spoke.

"Is it you, Lillian?" There was a coldness to those words, more frigid than the presence of Death himself. Marjorie spun to search the room, her face glowing amber in the light of the single candle she held before her. "Am I so insignificant to you that a lifetime of torment was not enough? Do you need the afterlife as well? God, what I wouldn't give for you to just *leave!*" Marjorie listened to the silence for a moment longer before she sank to her knees, setting the candle aside and cradling her head in her lap. "I'm sorry," Marjorie whispered, voice like a prayer. "I'm so, so sorry."

Slowly, puzzle pieces were snapping together. Marjorie's infatuation with Elijah was no new thing. Elijah was the young man she'd spoken of, the one who had left her. She loved him, and she'd believed that he loved her back.

Perhaps she wanted that second chance. Perhaps she wanted a taste of the life she could have had if not for Lillian.

Signa's chest burned with the pain of breath flowing back into her lungs. She curled a hand upon her throat, head heavy with questions she wanted answers to—but there was no time left to get them.

She didn't dare risk being caught with the journal in hand. Signa pushed through the wall without sparing Marjorie another glance, feeling the weight of her body seize her once more. She barely managed to stumble into the hallway before the belladonna faded from her system; her heart restarted and sent the shadows slithering away from her. Skirts in her hands, Signa ran as quickly as she could along the hallway, past the framed portraits with eyes that followed her back to her room.

She slammed the door shut behind her and fell against it, breathless. There was no opportunity to rest, for Death waited before the window she'd forgotten to shut, in the form of his shadows once more. Yet he was not here to make good on what he'd promised her after their dance. The world around him grew tight in the anger she could feel rolling from him in waves, like he was siphoning oxygen from the air.

"What is it? What's wrong?" Signa asked. The question shattered like ice between them, and he turned away.

"It's Blythe."

THIRTY-SEVEN

BLYTHE WAS ON ALL FOURS ON HER BED, YELLOW BILE POURING FROM her mouth. She choked on it, struggling to find breaths between heaving.

Elijah held her by the shoulders. "Help her! Please!"

Signa curled her arms around herself; there was nothing she could do. They'd used the last of the Calabar bean to spare Percy. The familiar prickle of Death's presence against Signa's neck filled her with dread. He stood there in the corner, watching them, waiting. A reaper ready to strike.

It's time, Signa.

She turned away, refusing to acknowledge him.

Blythe heaved again, vomiting on the corner of the bed. Elijah scooped his daughter's hair up in tender hands.

The door flew open as Marjorie rushed in, her hands gloved and her breathing labored. She wasn't two feet past the threshold when Signa blocked her.

"Not one step closer." Signa tried to mimic the ferocity Blythe was so skilled at, yet she couldn't keep her voice from trembling. "You need to stay away from her." With Blythe dying and Percy following in her footsteps, there was no longer time to tiptoe around. Clutching Marjorie's journal tight in one hand, Signa said, "Take off your gloves."

Marjorie's face was pale as the moon. "Where did you get that?" She reached to snatch the journal with shaky hands, but Signa pulled it out of reach.

Signa wasn't sure how Marjorie administered the poison, but the woman had enough access to the household that the possibilities were infinite. Marjorie wanted a family. She wanted to be with Elijah. Perhaps that meant that any memory of Lillian had to go.

"There is poison upon her fingertips," Signa said at last, wishing to tear the leather gloves from Marjorie's hands.

Marjorie, who she'd spent so much time with. Whose company she enjoyed, and who'd tried to advise and guide her. Signa remembered how fondly Marjorie had looked upon the children. How tender her hand had been as she stroked Percy's hair and set a damp cloth upon his forehead. There'd been such love in her touch, but Signa had read the journal for herself, and she'd seen the stain of belladonna with her own eyes.

"You think this is my doing?" Marjorie's fists were clenched so tightly that they trembled at her sides.

"Look at her right hand," Signa told Elijah. God, how foolish she was for not realizing what was going on ages ago. If only she'd checked the bedrooms sooner. "You'll find it stained with belladonna. It's what poisoned Blythe and what killed Lillian. I didn't want to say anything until I knew who was behind it."

Elijah was a shell of a man, hardly seeming to recognize the words as he watched his daughter with hollow eyes. Only the quiver of his bottom lip and the shaking of his hands gave away that he'd heard her, though there was no time for his attention to fray.

Blythe had nothing left in her to heave up. She convulsed, gulping desperate gasps of air.

In the corner, the reaper stepped forward.

Signa spun to him. "Don't you dare." She had never wished for anything more than she wished for Blythe's safety in that moment. She wanted to tell Death he owed her for all the pain he'd forced her to endure. But that wasn't quite right. Death owed nothing for his existence. And already Blythe had lived longer than she was meant to. Still, it wasn't long enough.

"Give her one more chance," Signa whispered instead, not caring who was watching or that they might think her mad. "I'm going to stop this. Give *me* one more chance."

In that moment it was just her, the reaper, and a room cold as frost. The temperature stole movement from her limbs and she dropped to her knees.

Death is not something to be controlled. You need to learn this, Signa. You need to understand.

"I know you can do it." She was pleading, and she didn't care. "We saved her once, and we can do it again. Just one more time, please."

Is there someone else who deserves death more?

The words were a test. If she wanted to spare a life, she needed to take one in exchange. Perhaps it would be a random one. Perhaps it would be one of her own choosing. Whoever it was, Signa would not allow Blythe to die that night. Rising back to her feet, she pushed through the searing cold and the shadows that urged her back—and put herself between Death and her cousin.

Don't be a fool. You're cruel to make her hold on like this. There was truth in what he said. Blythe was a walking corpse, ghostly skin clenching desperately to protruding bones. She couldn't so much as tilt her face to look at Signa, her body too exhausted to continue this fight.

"It's okay" was all Blythe whispered, over and over again, the softest, tiredest refrain. "It's okay. It's okay if I go."

Sweat slicked across her neck and down her back, her clothing damp and sticking to her skin. It didn't have to be like this. Now that they knew Marjorie was the poisoner, Blythe could finally heal.

It would take only two words. One single command, and Blythe would have another chance.

"Do it." Signa's words were firm, meant not for her cousin but for the reaper who looked on. "She's not dying today."

Do you understand what this means? There was no judgment in his tone, only dedication to ensuring that she understood the gravity of her decision. *You are toying with Fate, Signa. You're playing God.*

"I don't care," she said, and she meant it. "Do whatever you must, but if you care for me at all, then help her."

He cast one long look at Blythe, the shadows around him thinning as he bowed his head.

Very well.

At once, Blythe's breathing began to steady.

The reaper disappeared, and in his wake, he left a sleeping girl, a baffled man, a red-faced woman, and a girl who had just damned another soul without a moment's hesitation. One who stood before all of them, power thrumming through her blood.

Signa could get drunk off that power. Could drown herself in it, it felt so good.

"Are you a witch, girl?" Marjorie asked, voice shattering like a fallen teacup. "What have you done?"

Signa needn't say a word. Elijah was beside her, his eyes wild and face purple as he shook with anger. "Show me your hands." It was he who must have taught Blythe how to wield her words, for had the estate been smaller, his voice alone would have brought it to shambles.

Marjorie drew a step back. "Elijah, I'd never—"

"Take off your gloves and show me your hands!" He crossed the floor, each step more murderous than the last, barely restraining his rage. Marjorie drew several tentative steps back, and Signa quickly flattened herself against the wall as he took hold of her wrist and yanked off the glove. He took one look at her fingers and dropped her hand, disgust and pain written clear across his face.

"You've never cared for Blythe." His words dripped with venom as he leaned into her, so close his chest pressed against hers. "You never cared for her, just as you never cared for Lillian. She was a good woman, Marjorie. And these children are innocent. How dare you lay a hand on them? On *Percy*?"

The noise that came from the back of Marjorie's throat was a strange one, something between a gasp and a snort. "The fact that you think I did *anything* to them is ridiculous and you know it. I'd never lay a hand on them!"

His jaw clenched, and he pointed to the door. "I want you to leave."

Marjorie gripped the door's frame as if to stake her claim upon the room. "You can't do that."

"I can do whatever I please." The flickering of the oil lamp shadowed Elijah's face, hollowing his cheeks. "I don't want to see your face near Thorn Grove. Leave now, or I'll call for the constable."

Marjorie's chest caved in as though the wind had been knocked from her, and she scowled at Elijah as if he were the devil himself. "You're making a mistake." Marjorie spun to Signa, whose blood turned cold. "And *you*. You've no idea what you're doing, child. You know nothing at all."

A young woman followed by Death didn't easily feel fear. But in that moment, the feeling sank deep into Signa's core, forcing goose bumps like a rash across her skin.

Fortunately, Marjorie was gone the next time she blinked.

The moment the door shut behind her, Elijah's knees buckled. The sound that tore through him was warped and broken. It was enough to shatter Signa's heart and make her hands ache to reach out to him, to tell him that all would be okay. Blythe had survived the latest attack of this poison, and soon it would be out of her system. But this level of heartbreak was something she'd never experienced, and something that could never be put into words. The man before her had shattered, and there was no picking up the pieces.

324

THIRTY-EIGHT

Lijah didn't ask for an explanation. He asked only to be left alone with his sleeping daughter, and Signa was more than willing to oblige.

The veil over what she'd done began to dissipate, clarity sinking in. Percy would recover, and Blythe would live to see another day. The murderer was found, and all would soon be well again at Thorn Grove. But to make that happen, Signa had condemned another soul to death. She'd sacrificed another life in place of Blythe's.

She chewed her nails to the skin as she paced down the hall, mind reeling. She knew she should care more, she should have regrets. But she'd make the same choice again and again if she had to.

God, what was she becoming?

When she reached her suite, the chill warned her that Death waited inside. He was pacing the drawing room floor when she opened the door, shadows dragging behind him like a cloak. The moment he caught sight of her, the shadows in the room rushed forward, hovering mere inches from her.

"Come with me." It wasn't a question, yet hesitation laced the command.

"Where?" was all she could think to say.

"It's time for you to see what I do." He extended his hand, beckoning. "It's time for you to see that there's more to death than you believe."

The hand he stretched toward her meant so much more than just a hand. She knew that taking it would mean opening herself up to him and his world. It would mean accepting what she'd done and embracing this side of herself once and for all.

This wasn't Death the killer who stood before her. This wasn't the demon she'd built up in her head, spending too many years hating. This was the man who ferried innocent souls to their afterlife. This was Death, whose powers she shared. Who understood her better than anyone else ever could. She was tired of running from him.

Signa laced their fingers together as she tipped her head back to observe the souls floating around them. The more she watched them, the more she could make out glimpses of faces within. "Why don't they look like typical spirits?" She gripped Death like a vise. He was bending the space around them as they moved, shifting to somewhere new. It felt like slipping through a pond and emerging dry.

"They would have that form had I reached them sooner," he said. "They're eager to pass, and traveling is simpler as a soul. Spirits are weighed down by the emotions and memories they cling to. Spirits linger, souls pass on."

"Pass on to . . . here?"

Wherever they were, it wasn't Thorn Grove. They'd crossed over into a place where time stood still. Signa was glad she no longer had to breathe, for the air here was too thick. It sat upon the base of her throat, making it impossible to swallow. She stumbled over soil as Death pulled her ahead. The farther they pressed forward, the antsier the souls around them became. They no longer hovered so tightly around Death but rushed ahead before inching back, fearful of getting lost in the forming mist.

They came to a magnificent blue-and-white bridge built over an endless lake. Though it was covered by fog, the sheer number of souls that were crossing over shone a hazy light upon it.

Some floated along in small spheres while others shifted back into their spirit selves, hurrying through the throng toward the call of something wonderful that waited for them on the other side. Something that Signa felt deep in her core, warm and rich and consuming.

She started to follow them, needing to find out what it was, but Death gripped her tightly. "Cross that bridge and you'll no longer be of this world," he warned her. "It's not your time."

They sat upon the bank of the lake, watching the souls from a distance.

It'd been ages since she'd visited a church, and she didn't remember any lessons about the afterlife. She'd always believed it was a dark, lonely place. But whatever resided beyond the bridge didn't feel like an end-all—it felt like a beginning. Like a journey beckoning to be taken. "What happens once you cross?"

"There are many possibilities." He loosened his grip and leaned back to watch her. Perhaps it was to avoid spooking the spirits, but Death was softer here. "Some souls choose to give up the memories of their life on Earth and to be reborn as someone new. Others keep their memories and remain in the afterlife, awaiting those they left behind."

"What of those who do not live a just life?" she asked. "Is there a punishment?"

Death's voice was dark when he spoke next. "The afterlife is my domain, Little Bird, and I take care of my people. It's no easy decision, but I do not welcome those who will taint my home. I claim those souls for myself, and I get rid of them. For them, there will be no afterlife. There will be nothing."

It was a cold fate, but Signa already felt a fierce protectiveness of this place, and knew without even seeing it that she, too, would do whatever it took to preserve all that waited across the bridge. "Do you know everyone there?" she asked as she watched one of the souls bob across the bridge.

"I've met all residents of the afterlife." There was pride in those words. "Though I admit that some stand out more than others. Your mother is one of the many reasons I don't care to journey into that place often, you know. All she does is pester me with questions about you."

Signa curled her fingers in the grass, a smile warming her lips. "Everyone's been making her sound so fierce. I always imagined her a bit like Marjorie, I suppose."

"Like a murderer?"

Signa swatted him on the chest. "Of course not! I meant someone who always seemed very proper."

Death nodded, considering. "She has more manners than you, certainly, but that's not saying much." This time when Signa went to swat at him, his shadows caught her hand and tossed it back at her with a laugh. "Your father is a kind and tender man, very soft spoken. Rima is more like you, so loud with her opinions and always butting in. She knew her position in society well and abused it for her benefit. With as much money and influence as your family had, no one dared to criticize them, for fear that they might lose the possibility of an investment by the Farrows."

Signa leaned against his shadows that stilled for her, soft as she imagined a cloud would be. "You seem to know a lot about them."

"Of course I do," he said with such seriousness that Signa stilled. "They're your parents. I wanted to know everything I could about them. And you're just as brazen as she is, you know. In all my years, no one has ever spoken to me with such hostility as you do, but she comes in a close second."

Perhaps her mother wouldn't be so disappointed in her after all. All the years Signa had spent obsessing over fitting into a particular mold—into what she'd believed everyone expected of her—perhaps it was all for naught.

He couldn't know how grateful she was for him in that moment. He couldn't know that, as glad as she was to hear him speak of her parents, she was reminded deeply of her own loneliness. But at Death's side, slipping her hand in his, she realized she needn't endure that alone. There was no pretending. No lying about what she wanted or molding herself into someone else. With Death, Signa could be wholly herself.

With him, she wasn't so lonely.

She lowered her head upon her shoulder, smiling as Death tensed with surprise. "Tell me what it's like across that bridge."

He rested his chin upon her head. "If you really want to know, I'd be more than happy to invite you in and keep you to myself for eternity." When she nudged him on the shoulder, Death laughed. "It's a place that's kinder than the living world. There are no needs, no wants, no fear."

"So why don't you spend more time there?"

Death brushed his thumb across the back of her hand, and her skin burned with want. "I will do whatever I must to protect that place and its people. But being there for too long is exhausting. I cannot share in their pleasures, Little Bird. There is no family waiting for me, and it's possible some of my wants will never be settled, no matter where I am. Seeing them—being in that place— is a reminder of that. Besides, I find the living world far more entertaining."

As someone still struggling to find her place, Signa could relate. Death was the most hated man in the world, and even here in the afterlife, he didn't fit in. It was no wonder he came across as so prickly. She probably came across the same way.

"I chose a man in his eighties." Signa knew at once what he was referring to, and the words were a bruise upon her mind. "He would have had another ten years, though they would've been ones wrought with pain in his bones. He's there, on the bridge." Death nodded ahead.

Signa didn't want to look at the man she'd condemned to save

Blythe, but he deserved at least that much. She hugged her arms around her stomach and forced herself to acknowledge the stout, short man whose life she'd stolen. Ten years was a long time. Even with pain, what things might that man have done with his life? What memories might he have made? What joy might he have felt?

"I don't like doing that, Signa." The shadows drew around them like a curtain, shielding the bridge from view. "We're toying with Fate, who is not someone to be played with. Do not ask me again to take the life of someone who's not ready to be claimed."

The words sank into her and burrowed deep within her soul. She became smaller, curling in on herself.

"I'm sorry I asked that of you." She trembled when she spoke. "But if you hated it so much, then . . . why did you do it? Why did you listen to me?"

When he turned to her, the moonlight shone upon him in a way that reminded Signa of a painting, wisps of shadows like brush-strokes upon a canvas. "Because I have waited an eternity to meet you, Signa Farrow." The words were a balm she clung to, relished. "To me, you are a song to a soul that has never known music. Light to someone who has only seen the darkness. You bring out the absolute worst in me, and I become vindictive toward those who treat you in ways I don't care for. Yet you also bring out the best in me—I want to be better because of you. Better *for* you.

"In all my existence, I've asked only for one thing—for one person who might understand me, and whom I could let myself touch. When I touch someone, I see the life they've lived in flashes of memories as they die. But the first time I touched you, it was your future

I saw. A glimpse of you in my arms, dancing in a beautiful red dress beneath the moonlight." He tilted her chin up and Signa shivered, savoring the touch.

"You are what I want." He drew his hand away. "I know I cannot force you to want me in return, but say that you do, and I promise that I am wholly and unequivocally yours. Say that you do, and I will make this world everything for you, Signa."

The words struck hard. For so long she'd wanted nothing more than to be a normal girl, without Death lingering in the shadows of her life. She'd dreamed of how sweet it would be, only to find the taste bitter on her tongue. She could spend her life at Everett's side, keeping one ear out for gossip, feeling trapped and weak and stifled. And all the while she would remember that there was something—someone—that had once made her feel so alive.

A normal girl wouldn't be able to save her cousin's soul.

A normal girl wouldn't be able to sit upon this bank, staring at the bridge into the beautiful afterlife.

For so long she'd been fighting who she was, in favor of who others wanted her to be. She'd had enough.

The answer was there—it had always been there. She turned her head up to him, lips a breath from his. "I believe that I have always been yours, Death. As you were made for me, perhaps I was made for you. For I want to feel the way I feel when I am by your side forever. I want to feel the way I feel when you touch me."

He let out the softest breath as the darkness within him ignited, and he became the night itself.

He was the fire of the stars. The dazzle of the moon. The

darkness of the shadows, and the caress of wind against her skin as that darkness drank her in like she was the finest wine.

Signa knew before she wound an arm around his neck—before she pressed her chest against his—that there would be no turning back. When they kissed, his touch broke something within her. Something small and timid. Something that had been holding her back for too long.

It didn't matter who other people believed her to be. It didn't matter what they thought of her. *This* was who she was, and she was ready to embrace it.

"You are no soft thing to be coddled." His voice was soothing as the season's first rain, and she shivered from the way it glided upon her skin. "You are bolder than the sun, Signa Farrow, and it's time that you burn."

Death pulled her into the forest and laid her upon the cold ground. His lips kissed down the length of her neck and to the top of her corset. She tried to steal a look at him, but the mist and the shadows obscured him. She could have tried harder, but in the end it didn't matter to her what Death looked like. What she felt for him— how she wanted him—was bone-deep and aching.

In her almost twenty years, she'd never felt so alive. She was without abandon, her hands slipping through the shadows to curl in his hair and on his shoulders, her lips on his mouth, his neck, every bit as starved for him as he was for her.

Lace by lace her dress was undone, the silk slipping from her skin. He leaned back to admire her laid bare beneath the stars, dark hair unbound and spilling over her fair shoulders.

Never had Signa been so exposed, yet she didn't hide herself from him, nor did she shy away from the shadows that encircled her bare thighs. Signa guided his hands over her waist. Over her breasts and her hips, and then lower, shivering with pleasure beneath his touch.

"You're sure you want this?" he asked, almost as though he couldn't believe it. As though he expected her to come to her senses and force him away.

But Signa no longer viewed Death as someone dangerous. He was thrilling and freeing, and she wanted him more than she'd ever wanted anything.

"I have never been more sure of something in all my life." She cupped her palm against his face, easing him down so that his body covered hers. Her kiss was tender but firm in her desire, hoping she could ease his worry. That she could show him she wanted this every bit as much as he did.

Whether it was the kiss or the words that undid him, he groaned and kissed her full on the mouth. He didn't hesitate after that. His lips were on her thigh at once, kissing up the bare skin until she gasped, head falling back as her body melted beneath his touch.

His shadows traced her hip bones, slipping to the sensitive place his lips had once been. She exhaled a soft breath, any tension she'd felt loosening itself. Every touch was fire upon her skin, searing into her and commanding her attention. For once nothing else mattered. No inheritance, no spirits, nothing but his body as it covered hers, and the deep aching of want that filled her.

He groaned as he pressed into her, and Signa soon felt herself coming unbound. *She* was the darkness of the shadows, now. The one making him bend and stretch and twist, taking all he offered, all she wanted.

She wrapped her legs around him as the yearning built, keeping him close as something within her mounted. It wasn't just *him* she felt. It was the night itself, shadows and darkness and stars that exploded within her as she came undone.

A growl escaped his throat as she arched beneath him, and he fisted her hair in one hand. His muscles tensed as she pulled him close, kissing his neck and lips and all she could get of him until he growled her name and lost himself within her, shadows curling around her as he collapsed beside her.

Signa unwrapped herself from him, satisfaction on her lips. *She* was the one who made Death twist to her whim. She was the one who made him whisper her name as she tipped her head back to the sky, and she rather liked that.

Signa laced her fingers through his, and he brushed his thumb over the back of her hand in long, content strokes.

"I have waited for you for millennia, Signa Farrow." There was a silky husk to his voice now, too pleased for his own good. "Since the dawn of this earth, I have waited. You are mine, and I am yours. And together, this world is ours."

THIRTY-NINE

Both Signa and Elijah sat at the breakfast table well before daylight, poring over theories and motives, neither of them willing to speak the truth aloud—that Marjorie couldn't have been acting alone. That her reaction was too surprised. That her love for the Hawthorne children was too genuine.

But the stain of belladonna upon her fingertips and the entries in her journal didn't lie. She had wanted Lillian gone, but that wasn't enough. Hands could be washed and poisoned cups cleaned, so they needed proof. They needed answers. And thus, they had gathered to try and find them.

Signa was relieved that Elijah spoke frankly with her, and he listened to her suspicions with the utmost attentiveness. When she suggested Byron as Marjorie's accomplice, he didn't balk or tell her she was mad. He leaned his chin upon steepled fingers and said, "I'm sure we'll have the chance to speak with my brother soon."

He was right, though Signa didn't ask how he knew Byron

would appear. It was hardly sunrise when he hammered the knocker loud enough to rouse the dead.

"Let him in, Warwick," Elijah called out to the butler. His throat was scratchy, voice on its last dregs. It felt like so long ago that he'd been a burst of starlight upon the ballroom floor, grinning and sober and *happy*. Before her now, Elijah had his slippered feet drawn up into a chair as he sipped on black tea he'd poured far too much milk into. The bags beneath his eyes were heavier than Signa had ever seen, and he did nothing to tame the disheveled hair that was strewn across his forehead and into his eyes. His facial hair had regrown, now a shadow across his face.

Breakfast had been brought out moments prior, and Signa took spoonfuls of porridge as she listened to the *thunk-thunk-thunk* of Byron's cane against the hardwood. Byron didn't wait for permission, or for Warwick to escort him into the dining room before he threw the door open, face flushed such a shade of crimson that he appeared close to bursting. He took one look at Signa and growled, "Get out of here, girl."

Elijah held up a hand in her defense. "Signa will stay." He motioned to a chair opposite her. "Sit, Byron."

"If you think I'm going to—"

"I said *sit*."

Signa looked to the corner of the room, in the darkest shadows, half expecting that Elijah had somehow summoned Death with that tone.

Byron smacked his tailcoat to the side and sat. His fists were clenched tight as he set his hands upon the white lace tablecloth.

"What have you done, Elijah? A broker arrived at Grey's this morning, rambling nonsense about the sale of the business."

Elijah took a spoonful of porridge, scrunched up his nose, then added milk and a cube of sugar. "Of course there's a broker. Did you expect I'd let my family starve?"

God help Byron and the man's poor heart. He turned from red to purple, so angry that he'd forgotten to breathe. Signa thought he would pass out, or yell at the very least, but he drew in a breath and settled his mounting anger. "If you want to sell the business," he began with an admirable level of calm, "let me purchase it. We can work out a payment plan, or a percentage of the monies for you to collect. You'll never have to touch another ledger."

Elijah requested Warwick to alert the kitchen staff they were in need of more tea. The silence was a weight around them. Signa felt as though her crawling skin might jump from her bones at any moment. Sitting silent in the midst of the two men's bickering was a unique form of torture.

Byron seemed to think so as well. "Elijah." The name struck like a hammer on a nail. "Is that offer agreeable to you? You know I would never let your family suffer."

Elijah's jaw screwed tight. "I never intended for my family to suffer, either. Which is why I'll ask you just this once, Byron—were you working with Marjorie to harm my family?"

Signa didn't dare blink for fear that she'd miss his reaction. Yet she didn't know how to read Byron's retracted neck and creasing brows as anything other than surprise.

"Have you been drinking again," Byron demanded, "or have you gone mad? What are you raving about?"

Elijah raised a porcelain teacup to his lips and watched his brother through the billowing steam with an astounding level of calm. "Do you know what happened to my son?"

Byron slammed his teacup onto its saucer, splattering a few drops of tea onto the ivory tablecloth. "Elijah, no more games. What's happened to Percy?"

Signa wanted Byron to be guilty. She wanted answers, or even to use her new abilities to follow him home and confirm for herself what his involvement was. But Byron's concern appeared genuine, and while part of her was relieved, she couldn't help but grit her teeth as her frustration mounted over the lack of information.

Elijah's face hardened. "He fell ill moments after you left the party last night. We found Marjorie with poison, and I have reason to suspect the two of you may have been working together."

"Poison?" As though his intent was to stand, Byron pushed from the table with his walking stick in hand. At the last moment he seemed to think better of it and settled back in his chair. In a smooth, cold voice, he said, "We have had our differences, Elijah, but why in God's name would I hurt anyone in your family?"

"You likely have more reasons to harm me than I can count," Elijah began, ticking them off on his fingers. "It's no secret you want Grey's, but perhaps it goes deeper than that. Perhaps it's because of what Lillian meant to you. Perhaps you killed her because you were tired of seeing her with me. Or perhaps you wanted me to feel the same hurt that you did when she chose me. Or perhaps—"

"Enough!" Byron gripped the edge of the table, knuckles bone white. Signa sank low in her seat, wishing to disappear. Family arguments were a new experience, and certainly not her forte.

"The fact that you would even *suggest*..." Byron's words trailed off with the shake of his head. "It's true I loved Lillian, as it's true that I want Grey's. But that's because you're running it into the *ground*, Elijah. Did you know that Percy came to my home last summer, begging me to speak with you? For you to believe that I would harm your family is ridiculous. I love those children, you fool." He did not have the same passion or fervor that Elijah had, yet Signa found herself believing every word.

"It's unlikely I will ever marry or have children of my own," Byron continued. "To me, Percy and Blythe are as close as I will ever get to that. Percy and I especially have grown close, as you'd see if only you opened your eyes. When you dismissed him, it was me he confided in. I want him to succeed. I want to see him take over Grey's, to marry, to be *happy*. I would never lay a hand on him."

"But you would lay a hand on a woman." Signa wanted to pinch herself for speaking.

Byron's attention snapped to her, as if noticing her for the first time.

Elijah's jaw ticked. "You were the one who hurt Marjorie?" Signa hadn't realized that he'd noticed. "Why?"

Byron set his walking stick to the side. "You've been alone for too long, Elijah. I know you had feelings for the woman once. I thought that perhaps you might still."

Elijah's laugh was bitter. "You thought what? That if I bedded her, I might forget the death of my wife? That I might revert back to my old behaviors and begin to work at Grey's once more? It's you who's the fool, brother."

"There's a lady at the table, Elijah—"

"Then she can cover her delicate ears if I offend her. You're too old-fashioned, Byron. It's no wonder Lillian never loved—"

"Finish that sentence," Byron hissed, leaning forward to wag his finger at Elijah, "and you'll be sorry."

"Will I? Heavens, how I tremble to think—"

"Oh for the love of God, I've heard enough from you both." Signa slammed her chair back and stood, unable to withstand a moment longer of them squealing like pigs. "You are behaving like children. If you can't have a civil conversation, then sip your tea and I'll ask the questions."

So similar were the two men with their blanched faces and owlish eyes. Signa could see their resemblance now, in a way she never had before. The same stern brows and cut jawline. Tawny skin, a few shades darker on Elijah. Byron was more severe, like Percy, with a longer nose and sharper angles, though they were remarkably alike.

"We don't know if Marjorie was acting alone, and we need proof of her involvement," Signa began, keeping her words snappy and precise. "Poison upon her fingers isn't enough. Byron, if you know why she'd poison the Hawthornes, you must tell us."

Byron's bark of laughter was the last thing Signa expected. "You truly think Marjorie would make them ill? You're a fool, girl. That woman would never harm Percy."

Elijah brushed two fingers down both sides of his lips, smoothing his returning scruff. "Tell me about the journal you found, Signa. The one you confronted her with."

"She wrote about a time she found you in the stables," Signa answered. "She wrote that she told you of her feelings, and you rejected—"

"Whatever you're speaking of did not happen." Of this, Elijah was firm. "Are you certain it was me she named?"

"Of course I am! She said she wanted to have the family she was always meant to have. She said . . . She said . . ." Signa realized then that, no, Marjorie had never once referred to Elijah by name as the one that she loved. But she'd seen the way the woman touched him, and how freely she spoke while in his presence. So if not him . . . "Was there someone else? Someone else here that she loved, and felt she owed the truth to?"

Elijah's pallor was so apparent that Signa feared his soul had already departed his body before she could get an answer. Byron's face followed suit, and the two shared a look that Signa could not for the life of her interpret.

The night before, she'd been so sure of what she'd read. So certain that she'd started to piece the puzzle together. But from the expression on their faces, she was more doubtful than ever.

"There's someone else she might have been referring to," Elijah finally answered.

"Elijah—" It was the first time, in her memory, that Signa had heard a protective edge in Byron's voice as he watched his brother.

"It's fine, Byron. Though I'm not certain whether this girl is an angel or the devil himself, she has saved my children more times than I can count. Besides, if what she says is true, it's not like he doesn't already know."

"Know *what?*" Signa pressed fingers to her temples. She thought her head might explode if she didn't get answers soon. Fortunately, the Hawthorne men took pity on her.

"Marjorie didn't remain at Thorn Grove because she loved me." Though they were alone in the room, Elijah spoke so quietly that Signa strained to hear him. "She stayed because she had a child."

The puzzle snapped together.

In the eyes of society, I was already ruined. Marjorie had warned Signa to be careful with men. She'd had a child out of wedlock, and because of it, society brushed their hands of her.

Blythe looked so much like Lillian. They had the same sunburst hair, the same small features. Yet with two blond parents, Percy's harvest-orange hair and freckled skin had always seemed out of place. How had she not seen it sooner?

"Percy is your and Marjorie's son," Signa said, head in her hands, "isn't he?"

Elijah didn't hesitate. "We kept it quiet, as much for Marjorie's sake as Percy's. I'd just gotten engaged when she found out, and I had no idea she was pregnant until she appeared on our doorstep with him one day. Marjorie had been disowned by her family and left with nothing. No money, no prospects, and no one who would so much as look at her twice if they knew she'd birthed a child out of wedlock. So she asked Lillian and me to raise Percy as our own, and I said yes. Of *course* I said yes. He's my son, and I wanted him to have the world, not a life on the streets."

"And Lillian was fine with that?"

"Lillian never treated Percy as anything other than her own son," Byron said with startling conviction.

Elijah nodded. "We struggled to have a child of our own for some time, and while explaining to my new wife that there was a child I had known nothing about is not an experience I wish to ever relive, I think she viewed Percy as a blessing. From the moment she saw Percy, she loved him."

It was as though someone had dumped an entirely new puzzle across the table. Signa pressed a hand to her temples again, sorting the pieces. "And what about Marjorie?" she asked. "Was she fine with this arrangement?"

"As fine as she could be, I suppose." Elijah stirred his tea, recalling the memories. "I gave her a respectable job, a home to live in, and the chance to watch her son grow up. But Percy couldn't know the truth of his lineage. There was too much I wanted for him, too much that he'd not be able to get, were it discovered that he was born a bastard. Marjorie and Lillian, too, would have been gossiped about wherever they went."

"He'd be no more ridiculed than he is now," Byron interrupted with a scowl. "You're making a mockery of him and the entire Hawthorne family by ruining his prospects."

Never had she seen such a snarl as the one Elijah flashed at his brother. "I'm not trying to make a mockery of my son; I'm trying to *protect* him. Just as I'm trying to protect you, you fool. For years we gave ourselves to our jobs, missing sleep, missing birthdays, missing memories. And for what? To miss my wife's final days so that overly entitled men might spend their days gambling and drinking? For the money to afford me a lonely house that grows quieter with each passing day? My son deserves to be better than I was.

"You are not married, Byron, because you put too much of yourself into a job that means nothing, just as I did. I had to learn that lesson the hard way, brother. I believed the doctors would make my wife better, and so I continued to spend day after day at the club. I could've been there to help her. I could have made things easier for her, and yet I chose my work. I won't have my son making the same choice. He will not inherit Grey's, nor will I sell it to you and damn you for the rest of your existence. Let some other poor soul have it. We'll keep a percentage, and we will need for nothing."

Signa wished Percy were awake to hear his father. She hoped he'd be relieved to know that it wasn't Elijah's hate or mistrust keeping him away from the family business. It was love. And perhaps if Percy knew that, they could begin to repair the fraying seam between them.

If Byron was any indicator, however, there was far more to repair.

"Don't you understand what this will do to your reputation?" Byron asked. "The moment you sign those papers, it disappears."

"Then call me a magician." Elijah waved away the worry. "I have all I need. The rest is a game I wish to play no longer."

Byron slid listless fingers through his hair and tugged at the strands. "Perhaps *you* no longer wish to play, but that is not a choice you get to make for all of us. I'm set enough in my life that I know what I want, and it's Grey's."

345

They would, undoubtedly, argue their point until both were blue in the face, but Signa was distracted by her memories of Marjorie's tenderness toward Percy. Of the adoration and fondness in her eyes, and how easily she gave in to him.

She could understand Marjorie wanting Lillian out of the picture. Blythe's poisoning, too, she could understand, for the girl likely didn't fit with Marjorie's idea of the family she was meant to have. But why had Percy fallen ill?

There was still one piece missing. One final piece, and the puzzle would finally be solved.

Signa. The brush of cold against her skin was so sudden she gasped, though in their bickering, neither of the Hawthorne men noticed. *Come quick. Something's happening with Percy.*

Signa pushed up from her chair without hesitation and sprinted toward the door. The Hawthorne men abruptly ceased their arguing and Elijah called out, "Where are you going?"

"To Percy's room!" she called back. She didn't turn around, but she heard the legs of their chairs screech against the floor and knew that they followed.

FORTY

Percy was standing near the window when Signa stormed in, his eyes bloodshot as he clutched the ledge. It was a miracle he had the strength to stand, though Signa got the impression it was not will but adrenaline fueling him.

She wrapped her arms around herself as howling wind billowed into the room from the open window. Death loomed behind him, observing the scene in silent curiosity.

"Percy?" Byron called, huffing from the hurried climb up the stairs. He leaned his weight upon his walking stick, cursing his arthritic knee.

Percy's hollowed eyes passed over each of them as though they were ghosts. His face shone with perspiration, skin sallow and gaunt.

"Son, what is it?" Elijah asked. "What's happened?"

"What in the heavens is he looking at?" Byron asked.

Signa looked not at Percy for an answer but to Death. *I didn't see what happened,* he told her. *I felt a spirit here and saw him opening the window when I came to check on him. He's been staring out it ever since.*

Signa crossed to her cousin and took him by the shoulders, easing him away from the window and into his bed.

"We should call a doctor at once," Byron began, already starting out the door when Elijah reeled him back.

"No doctor can fix this. He's having hallucinations. Warwick!" he called out to the butler, who had hurried after them, though Signa hadn't realized it. "Bring him some tea and something to eat—"

"No tea!" Percy's body buckled with a violent shudder. He fell back into the bed, lips chapped and shivering.

Signa pulled up the linen sheets for him, trying to draw his attention away from the window. "Whatever you saw, it should be gone by the morning. Would it help if I stayed with you for a while?"

Percy's haunted eyes flitted around the room, unable to rest anywhere for long. "I saw her." He didn't stammer, and though he still shook, there was a clarity about those words that struck Signa. "Mother. She was here."

Percy's eyes fluttered shut, and she knew he was experiencing the same exhaustion that settled into Signa's bones whenever she had a run-in with a spirit. It was enough to confirm her suspicions, which Elijah echoed in a wondrous whisper.

"It was Lillian. It's as I've thought all along—she's here, watching over the children." He trembled like a reed in the wind.

"Lillian is dead, Elijah." A vein in Byron's neck pulsed. "This is nonsense. Nothing more than a bout of delirium."

"That was no delirium." There was no severity in Elijah's voice. He believed Lillian was there, and that was all that mattered. "My wife is still upon this earth."

It would have relieved Signa to share just how right he was. But there was a veil between the worlds of the living and the dead that was better left uncrossed. So she said, "Perhaps," though Elijah was too lost in the valley of his own thoughts to pay her any mind. He took a fleeting glance at his son to ensure that Percy was still breathing before he hurried out of the room, muttering about his wife.

Perhaps he intended to search for her. Or perhaps he intended to return to his drinking, in the hope that he'd find solace at the bottom of a glass.

She was glad when Byron, after one more hard look at Percy, chose to follow his brother, perhaps to stop him from doing anything reckless.

Signa settled into the chill of her skin as Death came closer. "It may have been Lillian you took, but the one who truly died has been left here upon the earth." She pitied Elijah. Pitied him so deeply that it felt as though a hole were burning through her heart.

"Signa." Death spoke the way one might when they were trying not to spook a wild animal. "All who live must die. That is the way of the world."

But oh, how she wished it wasn't. How fragile a life seemed when she watched one after another shatter before her eyes. "I cannot bear watching him." The hole in her heart had grown too large, gnawed away with each passing second. "All of these people . . . How do you do it? How do you live, leaving broken people in your wake?"

Signa covered her mouth at once, hating that she'd voiced the question out loud, but Death merely sank into Signa, resting his chin upon her head.

"A human life is a beautiful thing," he said. "You humans . . . you *feel*. You feel so deeply that it consumes you. There were humans I kept a watch over, though I would blink and they'd be fifty, sixty years older—and the time would come for me to meet them. For the longest time, I pitied them for their short lives. And I admit, Signa, that I have grown more callous with my age. But I have also grown to admire humans. They've such a short time to experience their lives, and so they *must* feel deeply. They must experience in one life-time things it's taken me an eternity to experience. When I see men like Elijah, rather than feel guilt for what I've done, I remember that he feels sorrow because he loved so deeply. And were I not real, Little Bird, were I not Death, he would never have experienced that love. So which is better? To live forever, or to live and love?"

Death's hands slid down her arms, and he took hold of her hands. "Don't fear me." His tender voice brushed against her ears. "Don't resent me when I've only just gotten you, please, for I am what makes this world beautiful."

Try as she might, she did not—could not—hate Death. She supposed he was right in a way, but that didn't change that she was still but a human. If it was as he said—if humans felt so deeply and loved so greatly—was that why her heart ached for this family and all it had become to her? Was it because she loved them?

Hand in hand with Death, she let the thought consume her. Let it lighten her heart and harden her resolve.

Yes, she loved them. And because of that love, she would do any-thing to save them and make this family whole once more.

FORTY-ONE

DAYS AT THORN GROVE WERE NO LONGER STRUCTURED AFFAIRS. Gone were the lessons and any remnants of etiquette, replaced by a somberness that fell upon the house like a mourning veil. For its part, Thorn Grove as a whole was eager to return to some semblance of normalcy. It was obvious in the way the servants kept their heads ducked low, and how no one dared speak of what had happened during the ball, or of Marjorie's sudden disappearance three nights prior.

Without a governess to oversee her teachings and with all the Hawthornes in a state, Signa was left with little supervision and an abundance of time. Mostly she found herself sleuthing through Thorn Grove and poring over the remaining staff logs with Sylas by candlelight, investigating the estate's inhabitants as she tried to find a way forward. Tried to find some sort of clue to show her where to look next.

Elijah had taken to drinking again. He spent his days with his sick children and his evenings pacing the halls, searching for a wife he'd never find.

Blythe was recovering alone in her bedroom, still so sick that she refused all company but her father's. And while Signa wished more than anything to pay her a visit, she knew that if Blythe still had the mind not to want visitors, then she was at least faring well enough to be coherent and self-conscious.

Percy was finally walking without assistance, but he remained shaken from his mother's appearance. While his skin had warmed with color and light had once again found its way into his eyes, he ate and drank so little that his skin clung to his bones, his face skeletal in its gauntness. He spent his days like his father spent his nights, pacing the halls and muttering to himself, so lost in his own thoughts that Signa only watched and dared not speak. She supposed his behavior was normal enough. Percy believed himself visited by his mother's ghost. Just how *was* someone expected to deal with that?

What Signa didn't expect was that Percy had taken to disappearing for long hours in the evening when he thought no one was watching. From her open balcony, she would hear him leave, and watch as he journeyed to the stables, then to the woods on horseback minutes later. He returned late in the evening and with enough dirt on his hands that Sylas had sent a note the evening prior, detailing Percy's appearance.

"You should take a break," Sylas told Signa when she joined him in the stables after Percy had disappeared one evening; she was determined to discover exactly where her cousin ventured. She was haggard, her hair sticking up at odd angles and her eyes weighed down by deep purple shadows. "You've done so much for the Haw-thornes already. Look at what this is doing to you."

Signa leaned against a wall, pinching the bridge of her nose as she waited for him to ready the horses. "I don't care what it's doing." She had to bite her tongue to stop herself from spitting the words, not angry with him so much as she was frustrated by the entire situation.

There was more to this puzzle that she wasn't seeing, and there could be no relaxing until she knew the truth of it all. The Haw-thornes were the closest thing to a real family she'd ever had. If it meant a thousand more sleepless nights until she was able to ensure their safety, then so be it. "Would you please just ready the horses?"

"What do you think you're going to find tonight that you won't be able to find tomorrow?" Sylas insisted, sterner this time. "You need to take care of yourself—"

She pushed him aside and headed to the tack room to get the saddle herself. Her body buckled from the weight of it, and though Sylas was right there—arms folded as he glowered at her—he didn't lift so much as a finger to help. When her mouth tightened and her eyes narrowed, he merely shrugged. "Figure it out yourself if you're doing so well."

She had half a mind to drop the saddle on his foot. Such a brute was he that it would serve him right, though Signa couldn't deny that he was a brute who was nice to look at, even through the haze of her headache. Even with all she felt for Death, there were moments with Sylas—with his broad grin and annoying muscles and disheveled hair—when slivers of doubt crept in. A tiny, niggling curiosity about what could have been with Sylas, instead.

Not that it meant anything, of course. He had told her already that there was someone in his life that he cared for deeply, and now it was the same for her. She only wished she knew *who*, exactly, it was who had captured his heart. For now though, it was a trivial curiosity. There were far more pressing matters that demanded her attention.

"Are you going with me or not?" she asked at last, shoving aside those thoughts as she let herself into Mitra's stall and hauled the saddle up and onto her back. The horse nudged her nose into Signa's hand.

Only then did Sylas sigh with the realization that this wasn't a fight he'd win. "Of course I am. Step aside." He took a bridle and finished readying Mitra, everything about him exasperated. She tried not to let herself smile.

They left soon after, Gundry on their heels. Sylas led the charge through snow-covered moors, toward the woods that stretched ahead with branches waiting to snare them.

"It's likely he's gone to the garden," Signa said as she peered down at hoof tracks in the snow that made a straight line toward the trees. "Has he ever said anything to you while waiting for a horse?"

"Your cousin isn't one to speak with the help," Sylas mused. "Too gentlemanly, that one."

Signa followed the tracks through the clawing trees into the belly of the woods, where they converged with something that gave her pause—a new pair of boot tracks in the snow, too small to belong to Percy.

Sylas slid off his mount and stooped to inspect them. "Whoever these belong to may still be here." His voice was barely a whisper. "The print is clearly defined, which means it's fresh."

Signa scanned Percy's tracks again. He wasn't in his right mind since being targeted with the poison, and for his own safety, these new tracks couldn't be ignored. "Follow Percy," she said. "See if you can find out what he's up to, and make sure he doesn't try anything reckless. I'll follow these footprints. Perhaps they'll lead to Marjorie."

It was clear in the tension of his shoulders just how displeased Sylas was with this decision. Dragging a hand down his jaw, he sighed and pulled himself back onto his mount. "We meet back at the stables in an hour," he said firmly. "If you're not there, I'm coming to find you."

"One hour," she promised, giving him a hard look as she gripped the reins. "I'll see you then." And with a gentle kick to Mitra's side Signa left him, following the tracks as they led her along a path she'd yet to explore.

Deeper and deeper into the forest she went, until the footprints disappeared beneath dirt and bramble and all that coated the forest floor. The woods were denser here. An area less traveled, where vegetation would be flourishing if not for the snow. Signa eased herself from Mitra, crunching twigs beneath her boots as she held the reins tight.

There was something peaceful about winter; a stillness that Signa often felt herself falling into. But this deep into the woods, with her head still pulsing, it was unnerving. Goose bumps rose along her skin as she pressed against the warmth of Mitra's side, uncertain how much farther they could safely venture. She was bending to see if she could push some of the bramble aside to clear a path when a voice called from behind her, soft and familiar, "Careful. The bark is poisonous."

Signa whirled to find Charlotte, breath pluming the sky. She was dressed in a thick emerald cloak and carried a wicker basket in her hands.

"It's called a poison sumac," Charlotte told her, beckoning Signa away. "It'll give you a nasty rash if you or your horse so much as graze it." With a smile, she added, "I learned that the hard way a few years ago, when I was first discovering these woods."

Of *course* the prints belonged to Charlotte. Signa remembered Blythe telling her that Charlotte lived on the opposite edge of the woods, though she couldn't imagine why the girl might be out in this weather. Signa's eyes wandered to the basket in her hands. When she squinted, her head pulsed and her vision created little shapes of light in the snow beneath her feet. Signa must have swayed, for Charlotte reached out to steady her.

"Are you ill? The last thing you need to be doing right now is riding alone," Charlotte admonished her. "Go on and take a seat here on this rock."

Signa shut her eyes for a moment against the spinning world, then allowed Charlotte to help her sit. "It's only a headache. It'll pass soon enough."

When she opened her eyes, Charlotte was frowning. She flipped the lid of her basket open to reveal an assortment of foraged goods. Chestnuts, pinecones, tiny little mushrooms of strange colors, and a piece of bark she handed to Signa. "Willow bark," she said by way of explanation. "Better as a tea, but if you chew on it, that should help ease your headache."

Signa stuck the bark in her mouth without question and began to chew. She'd do anything to get rid of the pulsing aura that swam in her sight. "What are you doing out here?" Signa asked between chews, scrunching up her nose at the bark's bitterness.

"I could ask you the same thing," Charlotte said. "After the Christmas ball, I didn't expect I'd see you or any of the Hawthornes around for some time. And certainly not here of all places."

"You hardly see me anyway." Signa surprised even herself with how bluntly she spoke. "I would have enjoyed seeing you that night. Or anytime, really. It feels as though a wall has been built between us."

"It does feel that way," Charlotte admitted. "Though it's by no fault of yours. You've seen the vultures that surround us, Signa. If any of them ever knew my past—if they knew what happened between my mother and your uncle—I would never hear the end of it. We came this far to rid ourselves of the scandal, so imagine my surprise when you showed up, only months before my season." She sat down on the rock, warm hazel eyes meeting Signa's. "It's been a long time, and I didn't know what kind of person you had become. I just want to make a good match, and to take care of my father."

Perhaps it was the bark, or perhaps it was the conversation, but Signa was already feeling a little better. Frustrating as it was, she was glad to know that she and Charlotte felt similarly. "I understand," she said. And she meant it, for she'd felt similar worries upon seeing Charlotte at Thorn Grove.

"I would have thought you'd have given up foraging with your approaching debut," Signa teased her, fingers curling around some moss. "Some would call you a witch for this wonderful remedy of yours."

"It takes a witch to know one," Charlotte scoffed. "You think I didn't see you coming out of the apothecary? You've always enjoyed plants as much as I've enjoyed discovering what the woods have to offer on any given day." She shut her basket tight and lifted her chin high. "It's nice to have something to do that doesn't require getting all dolled up or parading myself around, but mostly I continue because the willow bark helps my father with his arthritis."

"That's kind of you," Signa said, hoping that if she softened her tone, Charlotte would realize she meant it.

In the end, Charlotte did relax a little. "What about you?" she asked. "I'm surprised you were allowed to ride alone. What are you doing out here?"

"I have an escort," Signa told her, teeth aching from all the chewing. She delicately picked a sliver of bark from her tongue. "We ended up separated, though. Percy's been coming out here lately, and I've been worried about him. Have you seen him?"

Charlotte was slow to choose her next words. "He and Blythe used to help me with foraging, and I'd tell them all about what was edible and what wasn't. But as we grew older, it was improper for us to spend time alone with each other. I see him sometimes, like tonight, but only in passing. He seemed in a hurry. I think he was going to visit his mother."

She said it so casually. Signa had never been aware of him visiting the garden, and Sylas had never mentioned Percy visiting the stables to request a horse until the past few days. "Does he do that often?"

"Well she *was* his mother," Charlotte answered, speaking more

358

freely in the woods. More like the old friend Signa had once known. "Of course he does. Blythe used to as well, before the garden was locked and she took ill."

Signa spat out the rest of the bark as she mulled over those words. "Are there others who visit?" Signa wasn't certain what she needed to know, but there was a curiosity to be quelled. She stood as Charlotte did and followed her in the direction to the garden.

"Lillian didn't entertain guests there, no," Charlotte admitted, scratching Mitra's neck as they walked. "But Mr. Hawthorne did prefer to have someone escort her there. Usually, a servant, or a groom from the stables."

Electricity shot through Signa's spine. As much as she enjoyed Sylas's company, curiosity ate at her, and she couldn't shake the questions that piled on one after the other: How was it that a stable boy would have such nice boots and gloves? Why was it that the day he'd been meant to escort her to the garden, he'd chosen to ride the unruliest horse and get himself lost in the woods? Had he wanted to prevent her from getting inside?

He knew about the library, too. He knew how to get there despite being a stable boy. He'd also been the one to show her the secret passages.

And before that, after she'd found the garden, he'd been so quick to accept her offer of money and a position should he waver in his loyalty to the Hawthornes. He claimed it was to help someone he cared for, though Signa couldn't for the life of her figure out who that might be.

She *liked* Sylas—more than she liked most people in fact. She was comfortable around him. She'd chosen him to be her confidant in her quest to solve the mystery of Lillian's death.

But what if she'd chosen wrong?

"I should be getting back," she decided aloud, the urgency in her voice enough to make Charlotte jump.

"Of course," Charlotte said, looking a little uneasy upon sensing Signa's panic. "Do you know the . . . Signa, do you see that?"

A plume of gray smoke filled the sky ahead of them.

Dread filled her. In the middle of winter, it could be no accident. "Hurry to Thorn Grove and get Elijah," she directed Charlotte, then hurried Mitra toward the rock and used it to lever herself up and into the saddle. "Tell him to hurry."

"Signa—"

"Percy could be in there!" Sylas, too, though Signa did not dare admit her suspicions aloud. Did not dare admit the possibility. "Please, just go!" She didn't linger to see if Charlotte followed her command. Clutching Mitra tight, Signa rode straight toward the smoke. Toward the garden, and toward the answers that waited.

FORTY-TWO

MITRA BOLTED THROUGH THE SNOW AND THE GNARLED BRANCHES
that scraped at them. There were eyes in the woods, concealed
in the bramble and the shadows. Eyes that were forever watching,
waiting to see what might happen. Lillian was nearby, luring Signa
closer. Wind ripped through her hair, burrowing in her ears and rattling her brain. The dead could be bitter. They could be depressed,
or restless. But the spirit that pulled Signa toward the garden was
spiraling more wildly than any she'd ever felt.

A few yards ahead, shredded ivy littered the ground, torn from
the iron gates—now thrown open—that barricaded the garden.
Sylas's horse waited outside, ears flat, hooves scraping at the ground.
Signa was off Mitra and hurrying through the garden gates before
she could second-guess herself.

The fire was still contained to the garden, though it was growing by the second. Flames devoured whatever vegetation they could

find in the melting snow. The flames stretched, embers seeking purchase in a bush that flared to life beside Signa.

Sylas shoved her to the side before the fire could singe her clothing. She hadn't even noticed him approach. "It's too much!" he yelled, his words nearly drowned out by the roar of the flames and the croaking frogs that fled past their feet. "Get out of here!"

She ignored him. "Where is Percy?"

"The fire had already started by the time I arrived. I haven't seen him—"

Signa gripped him by the coat, effectively silencing him. "Just who are you, Sylas Thorly? Was it you who started the fire in the library?" God, she was annoyed when her voice cracked, though no more so than when his shoulders slumped.

"Of course not—" He grasped hold of her wrist, trying to pull her from the garden, but Signa yanked free.

"Don't touch me!" Anger festered inside her. Hot, senseless anger that didn't care about the smoke or the garden, or anything other than whether he had betrayed her. Whether he was destroying the Hawthornes.

If Sylas was the culprit, his face revealed nothing. "I'm not involved, Signa, I swear it! Now stop being so damn stubborn and get out of here!"

Gundry panted at her side, pawing and circling, eager to flee. But even if Signa wanted to run, her body wouldn't allow it. She was trying to decipher whether she believed his concern was genuine when coolness seized hold of her—Lillian's spirit grounding her to the garden.

"She wants me here," she told Sylas, breathless. "I can't leave."

Sylas took hold of her hands, but this time she didn't try to pull away. There was no obvious doubt on his face, or any sign that he thought her mad. With everything in her, she wanted to trust him. "Take the horses and get out of here," she whispered.

The flames were mirrored in his smoky eyes. "Signa Farrow, you are a fool if you believe I would leave and allow anything to happen to you."

Heat licked her skin, the smoke doubling by the second. It wasn't enough to choke them yet, or to stop them, but enough to turn Lillian's shadow ghostly where she floated above her burning grave. Her black eyes wandered to where another figure stood, obscured by the smoke.

"Who's there?" the figure called, and Signa nearly sagged with relief at the sound of that voice.

"Percy!" Signa ran to her cousin, whose eyes were wild and haunted. His hair was mussed and filled with leaves, and he wore his nightshirt still. "We saw the smoke, and . . ." Something glinted in his palms. "Is that—Percy, is that a tinderbox?"

He ran his thumb along its side and tucked the tiny silver tinderbox into the pocket of his trousers. "I had to take care of the problem."

The wind picked up, lashing embers at Signa's sleeve. From her grave, Lillian snarled.

"But this is your mother's garden," Signa reminded him. He was too far into his own head to pay her any mind, but she couldn't stop herself from saying it. Not with Lillian watching. "It's where she's—"

Realization struck. "What was it that you needed to take care of, Percy?" Signa swallowed her rising dread and reached for Sylas, for she already knew the answer.

Something in Percy's expression cracked. "She won't leave me alone." His voice betrayed no sadness or fear. No remorse. "You see her, too, don't you? Is that why you're here? Did she send you to Thorn Grove to haunt me?"

"Signa—" Though soft, Sylas's voice cut like a blade. "We shouldn't be here."

He shouldn't be. But Signa Farrow was not made of the same flesh and bone. She was made of the night, so she did not cower. "You were poisoned, cousin." She held her hands up, as though placating a toddler. "It's normal to hallucinate. Your mother loved you very much, but she's gone—"

"She's not my mother!" The yell burst from him like a tempest. "She was never my *mother* because my mother is a governess. She's a whore who fled her home because she was an embarrassment to her family. My father was a fool for ever allowing her to set foot in our home—"

"She only ever wanted what was best for you," Signa argued, remembering the pages upon pages she'd found in Marjorie's journal, all of them about Percy. She remembered the way the woman had watched him, always with a smile upon her lips. Always with fondness.

"If she wanted what was best for me, she should have stayed out of my life!" Free from the eye of society, he spoke with abandon. "If anyone found out, I'd be ruined. It's not like it's *hard* to tell we're related. Just look at us—anyone who saw us side by side could surely piece it together sooner or later."

Signa would have given anything for him to allow her to take him home and be done with all of this. Her heart ached worse than she knew what to do with because, for all his faults, Signa had begun to view Percy as she imagined one might view a brother—with unrivaled annoyance, certainly, but also with love. She'd wanted Elijah to come to his senses and let him inherit the business. She'd wanted Percy to be happy, as he was when they'd danced, laughing and teasing each other with every step.

But when she looked at him now, she saw with sudden clarity what he was: a murderer. "You poisoned yourself," she whispered, thinking aloud as the puzzle pieces snapped together. "You knew I'd save you."

"What I knew was that you still had one dose left of the antidote." Never had she heard a voice so bitter. "I searched for it everywhere, but I could never find it. I needed it gone."

"And the fire in the library?" Her voice cracked. "Would you truly have burned Thorn Grove to the ground?"

"Of course not," he seethed. "I would have saved it after a few books burned. *I* would have been the hero. But you had to go and ruin that, too."

So numb was her body that she'd hardly registered Sylas's hand squeezing hers until he leaned in with a whisper that was nearly stolen by the crackling flames. "You don't have to do this. I'll take care of him. When I let go of your hand, run."

He freed her hand, but Signa couldn't run. Lillian loomed behind her son, eyes damp with bloodied tears. Rage had hardened her sadness. With every inch of space she closed between them, the snow melted and the earth beneath her wilted.

The force of her anger brought Signa to her knees, and Lillian bent before her, eyes full of an apology she could not speak. The spirit reached her hand forward, commanding but not forceful, and there was a plea in her eyes. A plea Signa understood at once.

Lillian was going to possess her—but only if Signa let her.

She wanted to say no. Wanted to forget the memory of that deep, awful cold burning within her. But who else would ever allow Lillian this chance? Who else *could*?

She steeled herself and took hold of Lillian's hand.

Lillian stepped within her. Signa's eyes rolled backward as the spirit seized her. Her body felt as though someone had taken a spoon and hollowed her out. As though she were nothing more than a shell of herself; like she was living out a night terror, unable to move or command her own body.

Why?

It wasn't her own thought, but Lillian's that blossomed as an endless pressure in her head. Signa couldn't move. Couldn't scream.

WHY?

She'd experienced pain like this only once before, when she'd watched her grandmother die. It was bone-deep and soul cleaving. No matter how hard she tried, Signa couldn't shut herself away from it. She was a vessel, and Lillian the driver.

"Why did you do it?" she cried out, the words bubbling from her throat. Every time she tried to clamp her mouth shut, her lips seared with white-hot pain.

Percy started. "It's none of your—"

"It's not Signa who's asking!" Though the words came out of her mouth, it was Lillian who voiced them. Her body shuddered with chills so relentless that she wanted to throw herself into the flames. "It's your mother."

Percy went rigid, face pale, throat drawn in like he was holding his breath.

"Tell me the truth." Signa wouldn't have been certain she spoke the words aloud had Percy not flinched. "Tell me why. Tell me what I did to make you hate me."

Lifting his chin to look into her eyes, Percy said, "You were never the one meant to die."

FORTY-THREE

I MEANT FOR IT TO BE MARJORIE." THERE WAS NO HESITATION IN HIS words, no guilt or denial. "Did you think no one would ever realize the truth? The entire town already whispers about Father likely having bastard children roaming about. How long did you think it'd take before someone figured out that I was born to the governess?"

"Marjorie only ever wanted what was best for you," Lillian spoke through Signa's lips, hoping that her son might say something to redeem himself. That she'd still find love somewhere deep within him. But Signa saw only a callous young man who believed that she and Sylas would burn that night. It was the reason he spoke so freely.

As many times as Signa had been spurned, the realization still cut like a knife. She'd trusted him. Danced with him. Relied on him. And for what?

"If Marjorie wanted what was best, she never would have told me the truth." There was no extinguishing Percy's anger. No soothing the rage that burned in his voice. "She didn't want what was best—she wanted a relationship. If I allowed that, then how long until she wanted others to know of us? How long until word got out that I was a bastard, and my prospects ruined? Don't you see? I had to protect myself and this family from shame."

Lillian wanted nothing more than to forgive her son, and Signa had to gather every drop of energy she had to push against Lillian and remind her of the truth. Though the spirit resisted at first, Signa could feel her understanding in the way her body wilted, shoulders caving in as Lillian asked, "Then why was I the one who ended up dead?"

"You tell me!" Percy seethed. "I put belladonna into a pot of tea that was meant for Marjorie. But you drank it, didn't you? I didn't realize it until you grew sick, and by then it was too late. You were dying, so slowly that you had the manor descending into chaos. So I gave you more berries, always in the tea, to help you pass on so that everyone might end their suffering. But it was never enough. I was getting them to you too slowly, and your body was developing a tolerance too quickly."

Signa noticed then that Percy was shivering from the chill of communing with the dead. She wished it were enough to freeze him. It was a bitter thought, though in that moment she hated Percy so deeply that she'd have taken Death's scythe and cleaved him in two herself. He had no remorse. No sympathy. He spoke like he had that day at the apothecary—with the cold calculation of someone who cared only for how others perceived him. How fast a person could fall into that trap and let themselves be ensnared.

"And what of Blythe?" Signa was surprised when her own words were spoken aloud. Lillian's grasp on her was weakening.

She registered the smoke growing closer around them and Sylas's shadow on the hard ground beside her. God, she never should have gotten him into this mess.

Percy turned his face to the flames. "I had to do something to bring Father back to his senses. He wanted to ruin this family. I needed to bring him closer to me—I thought that we might become closer through our suffering. Yet ever since you arrived"—he glared venom at Signa—"he's only gotten closer to *her*."

"So you made yourself sick as well," Signa added. "Not just to get rid of the antidote but because you thought you could—what? Scare him into keeping Grey's? Have him offer it to you out of sympathy?" The puzzle pieces were finally locking together.

"I wouldn't expect you to understand." Percy spoke too easily. Too confidently for the situation, slipping back into the role he so often played in high society. "My father took away everything I've spent my entire life working toward, all because he was too deep in his mourning to make sense of anything. I did what I had to do. He left me no choice."

"You had *every* choice." It was Lillian who spoke again, a tremor of exhaustion in her voice. "Your father didn't take the business away because he hates you. He did it because he *loves* you, Percy. Because he regrets spending his life working and never seeing his family. He didn't want the same for you, don't you see?"

A shadow crossed Percy's face, and for a moment Signa wondered if the words hit their mark. If there was any light left in his soul. But the darkness crept over Percy's eyes again as he shook the idea free, refusing it.

There was no time for discussion. No time to argue. There was fire at his heels. "None of it matters anymore." He locked eyes with Lillian. With Signa. "This fire will consume your body, and I'll be free from you at last. And this time, Signa, you won't have the chance to save anyone."

The flames caught the glow of steel in Percy's palm—a pocket-knife. Small, sharp, and ready for blood. He aimed for Signa's throat, but his swing went wide as Sylas shoved her to the side, hard enough for her to lose her breath, and he buried the knife in her shoulder.

Signa felt each of Lillian's emotions, even sharper than the thrust from the knife—the sorrow, the pain, and most potent, the realization that there was no coming back for Percy. She lifted her head to steal one last look at her son, to forever remember him as the baby placed in her arms twenty years before, and then Lillian turned to Sylas. "He is yours to do with as you will. I cannot protect him anymore" was all she said, each word cracked and broken, and she dropped her hold on Signa's body.

Signa fell upon all fours, clutching her chest and gasping from her returned breath as Percy brought the knife down again. Before it could strike, Sylas stepped in front of her and caught the blade in his palm. Percy gasped, eyes wild as he tried to lower his hand. He pushed down upon it without success, attempting to get the knife to budge. To cut. To do anything. "What is this?" His lip trembled, skin ashen. "What are you doing?" Percy looked to Signa for an explanation, trembling like a leaf caught in a storm.

Sylas didn't waver as he held the blade. Signa waited for the blood to come. For him to wince from the pain. But there was not so much as a scratch upon his glove.

It was as though all the air had been pressed from her lungs when she heard him whisper, "This wasn't how I intended to do this. I'm sorry, Little Bird."

His shoulders were blurring, bleeding into the night. Signa understood the sorrow in his voice as shadows built around his feet and engulfed him until he was no longer Sylas but the reaper of the night. The bringer of death. One by one the stars winked out, until the night turned black and the only light came from the seething flames that glistened upon the snow and bowed at his feet. He pulled the night into him, claiming the moon for his scythe, and pointed its tip at Percy's throat.

Death stood before her, and Signa could not breathe.

Sylas had been the one to bring her to Thorn Grove. To help her, step by step. He'd led her to Grey's, to the garden, the library. It was him she'd ridden with in the moonlight. Him who made her question her feelings for Death.

Death and Sylas were one and the same.

She couldn't ask why. Not yet anyway, for Gundry stood at his heels. The hound was no longer of this world. Just as the shadows had wound around Sylas, they spun around Gundry as well, lengthening his maw and sharpening his incisors. He tripled in size until he stood at Death's shoulder with paws larger than Signa's head, eyes as crimson as blood as shadows dripped from his panting mouth. *Hungry*, Signa realized. He was hungry.

"This is where you make your choice." Death spoke to her with words like nectar. Like honeyed wine she could drown in. "*This* is where you decide what world you are made for. There are but two options: let him run and hope that he will be a changed man, for if you send him to trial, he will surely be hanged. Or . . ."

"Or?"

Death touched her shoulder, where the knife wound had already stitched itself back together. He pulled her up to her feet so her back pressed against his chest, and so she faced Percy and the flames that charred Lillian's grave. "Or you claim his life as your own and give his remaining time to Blythe. You are not cursed—you are a reaper. You are the night incarnate, the ferrier of souls. You are the bridge between the living and the dead—a caged bird that's ready to fly. So spread your wings, Signa Farrow, because you are limitless. Spread your wings, and oh, how we'll fly."

How right it sounded. How simple, like something deep and pulsing within her knew that was the answer. That it was right.

You are no soft thing to be coddled. The words Death had once told her played in her mind, over and over again. *You are bolder than the sun, Signa Farrow, and it's time that you burn.*

He was right. She no longer feared what brewed within her, and she was done making apologies for who she was. Signa would not just burn; she would ignite. She would blaze hotter than a star at Death's side and would finally claim all that she was. All that was hers.

She leaned against him and let that thrum of power course through her. It was ice in her veins and fire in her heart. Gone were her worries, her fears, for as she let the power consume her, she understood those fears meant nothing. She no longer claimed them. She was to be the ruler of the night. The bringer of death. A reaper. And she would start her reign now.

"Are you certain?" Death's voice was a caress amid the chaos.

Signa had never been more certain of anything in her life. She had cared for Percy; had begun to love him. But she understood now why Death had done all that he did. Understood why he'd given people an early end, all because he'd been selfish. All because he'd wanted to protect her.

For Blythe, she would do the same. For Elijah, for Thorn Grove, she would be selfish. Percy had made his choice, and now it was time to make hers.

If Percy would not feel remorse for his sins, Signa would ensure that he came to regret them.

When Signa faced her cousin, it was with the night itself in her eyes and hair silver as starlight. She didn't need to speak. She simply thought of her desire to raise the dead garden beneath him like a cage, and the world bent to her will. Dead bramble tore through the snow and flames, roots ensnaring Percy, whose nails ripped at them in desperation, trying to tear himself free. "Release me!" He gaped at her through the barbed trap of thorns and vines. They snaked around his wrists, securing him to the ground. "What in God's name are you?"

For once, she had an answer. "I am free." And then she turned to Gundry and let the hellhound have his feast.

FORTY-FOUR

SIGNA DIDN'T WAIT TO SEE THE FATE OF PERCY'S SPIRIT. WHETHER HE chose the afterlife or to linger, or whether Death claimed Percy's soul as his own, she had no desire to know. She sat with her back against a tree just outside the garden and barely felt the bite of the snow sinking into her clothing or the smoke still in her lungs, even as the garden fire was snuffed out.

It was over. After all this time, the Hawthornes would be spared from their torment. Or at least those remaining would, though Signa didn't want to think about that. She curled her arms around her knees, trying to process all she'd seen and done, and only looking up when two pale, translucent feet appeared before her.

Lillian sat down beside her, no longer so terrifying. The wounds around her mouth were healing, and her eyes were no longer so hollow. She was more a woman than a spirit. A young, mournful woman with damp eyes that watched the smoke dissipate in the sky.

"Thank you," Lillian said. The words were soft and a

little scratchy from disuse, as if she struggled to remember how to form them. Signa turned to peer at the spirit, who set a hand upon her arm.

Signa felt her hesitant touch like one might feel the brush of the wind against skin, gentle and a little cold. "You have nothing to thank me for." Her voice was harsher than she intended. "I couldn't save them both."

Even as the sound of Percy's laughter as he'd spun her across the parlor rang in her head, she couldn't regret her choice. Percy's remaining years would go to Blythe; it was the least he owed her. But the callousness of the decision had surprised her. She'd known what to do so quickly, so easily, and she hadn't once hesitated.

Signa truly was a reaper. And though she didn't know what it meant for her or her future, there was no going back.

Death emerged from the garden gates, his shadows slipping away to reveal the form of Sylas, only with silver hair in place of black. Her eyes drifted to the earnestness in his eyes, and she glanced away. She'd talk to him soon, but with Lillian here, it wasn't the time. Death scratched the back of his neck, understanding that simply enough. Nothing in his expression revealed Percy's fate. Perhaps Signa would ask about that, too, someday. But not yet.

Death extended a hand toward Lillian's spirit and asked in a soft, smoky voice, "Are you ready?"

Lillian's brows pinched together, and she started to lift her hand until her attention was pulled to the sound of hoofbeats fast approaching. She whipped her head to one side, letting out a soft gasp as Elijah appeared in a wild-eyed haste atop his mount. His eyes found Signa's immediately, for she was the only one he could see before he turned to the smoke.

"The garden." The sound Elijah made as he looked to it was something between a choke and a cry as he slipped off his horse and stumbled to the gate.

Lillian turned to her husband, clutching her hands over her chest. Over her mouth. There was a quiver in her bottom lip as she stepped toward him ever so slowly and set a hand upon his back.

He drew breath at the touch. Spine stiff, eyes wet, he turned to Signa and whispered, "Is she here?" Every word was fragile. Every breath threatening to break him. "My wife, is she here?"

Nineteen years Signa had spent avoiding the truth. Avoiding all that made her different. But no longer did these powers of hers feel like such a bad thing. It seemed there could be beauty in them, too.

"Yes," she told him as Lillian pressed her forehead against her husband's back, winding her arms around him. "She's right here."

Elijah reached a trembling hand toward where Lillian's arms wound around him, his body shaking. "I knew you were. All this time, I knew you were still with me."

"Yes, my love." Lillian spoke clearly, the only hesitation in her words coming from a tremor of emotion that she was barely keeping down. "I've been with you this whole time."

Though he couldn't see her, probably couldn't even hear her, he dipped his head against the garden gate and shut his eyes as they poured tears. "I should have taken better care of this place," he said. "I never should have shut these doors."

A breeze picked up, easing the gates fully open. There was no sign of Percy inside. No sign of anything but snow and charred trees, and wisps of smoke still fading into the night.

"So open them now," she whispered against the back of his neck. Her body was beginning to disappear at the edges. Signa knew she'd remain forever if she could, but there was no time. Her spirit was wisping away like the wind itself. "Open them and enjoy my garden. Visit this place and think of me."

Death took a step forward. "There's not much time left if you wish to pass on," he said, not sternly but with finality. Whether Lillian chose to go or not, her spirit was not long for this world.

Lillian clutched her husband tighter. "I am still with you, my love, and I will always be. When you wish to see me, look at the child of our love, and there I'll be. Take care of her, as I will take care of our son." She drew away until her hands fell to her sides.

As though he were able to feel her absence, Elijah spun around. "Stay. I will do better by you, I swear it. But stay, Lillian. Stay. I don't know how to be without you."

Through her tears, Lillian smiled. "Then you will learn." She took a long, final look at her husband and then turned to stroke Mitra's mane and plant a final kiss upon the horse. Mitra's ears flattened.

"I was happy in this life," Lillian told Signa. "I was the happiest I've ever been here with him, and I wouldn't change any part of it. Tell him that for me, would you?"

Signa bowed her head, her eyes hot. The two before her had the sort of love she'd spent her life dreaming about. It may not have been perfect, but it had been true. She looked to the shadows beside

Lillian where Death waited, and she wondered what an eternity with that love might feel like. "I will," Signa promised her, earning Elijah's attention just as Lillian took hold of the reaper's hand.

Death cast one final look at Signa as Lillian took her final steps in this world. *I'll be back soon. And I'll explain everything.*

Signa looked forward to it; she was tired of puzzles. But for now she turned to Elijah, and she told him gently, in the softest voice possible, "She's gone, Elijah. She's finally at peace."

And then she held him as he fell to his knees outside the garden gates and cried.

FORTY-FIVE

B Y THE TIME SIGNA AND ELIJAH RETURNED TO THE STABLES, DAWN
had crept into the sky.

She was relieved that Elijah hadn't pressed her about the garden.
That he'd not yet asked about Percy or how she'd known Lillian was
truly gone. She was glad for the moment of peace his silence gave
her. The opportunity to sink into her bed just before the sun awoke.

She felt Death before she saw him, that familiar cold slipping
into her bones. That icy chill she'd come to anticipate drawing her
eyes open and her attention into focus.

He was not his shadow self but the stable boy she knew, a hound
at his side. Gundry took one look at Signa, jumped into her bed, and
circled a few times before curling up at her feet.

"I understand if you don't want to speak with me," Death
said—or was she meant to call him Sylas now? "But I promise that
I'll answer your questions with nothing but honesty, if you're ready
to ask."

Of course she was ready to ask. There were a million questions spinning in her head. "How long have you been at Thorn Grove?" was her first. "How long have you managed this charade?"

He kept his head dipped low. "I was never truly at Thorn Grove," he admitted, grimacing when Signa rubbed her temples. "As far as anyone else here knows, Sylas Thorly never existed. To anyone but you, I was invisible." He took a seat on the edge of the bed next to Gundry but stood swiftly when she gave him a pointed kick. She had no intention of letting him relax for even a moment.

She took her time responding, letting him stew as she thought through all that had happened in the past weeks. When Elijah had sent for her at Aunt Magda's, she'd certainly thought it odd that he'd have her travel with a young man who was not a blood relation. At the train station, too, he'd walked ahead without communicating with anyone, and he had let her catch up. But everything at Thorn Grove was strange, and she merely thought Sylas rude. "The sweets on the train," she said aloud, remembering how he'd devoured them. Tasting them for the first time most likely. "Elijah doesn't seem like the type who would have gifted me those."

Sylas let his shadows form a chair beneath him. He lounged upon it, so comfortable that Signa glared until he righted himself. "I couldn't help myself. I was so angry when I picked you up that day, Signa. You looked half starved."

She had been, but that didn't mean she had to be grateful for all his lies. He'd led her to the garden after that . . . Where he'd gotten lost just so that he could appear as Death and help her get inside. He'd been the one to help her at Grey's, too, and with getting into the library. With each step—whether he was in this form or made of shadows—he had been there to help. But... "Were you truly helping me?" she whispered. "Or did you know the truth all along?"

Beneath the glow of the moon, his eyes were no longer dark and smoky but the shade of starlight, like his hair. There was still a darkness within them, though, like swirling galaxies had made their home within those eyes. Signa understood then that this was his true self—the face he never revealed to anyone. He was more beautiful than she'd ever seen him. "If at any point I knew the truth, I would have told you." It was a firm, earnest answer. "I never wanted you to lose Blythe. I never wanted you to lose *anyone* else. When Lillian died, she didn't know who killed her, and so I did not know, either. That was up to you to figure out. And you did a brilliant job, Signa. You saved a life."

"Yes, but I had to take another one to do it." Even as Signa said the words aloud, she couldn't get them to bite the way that she wanted them to. She'd meant to repair the Hawthornes, and yet she'd taken another child from Elijah. Even so, the guilt wouldn't come. Percy's death, as far as she was concerned, was just. And in exchange, Blythe would get to live a long, healthy life.

It was a life taken for a life gained, and without a body... Perhaps the Hawthornes need not ever know what had happened to Percy.

"I want to know why you did it," Signa said suddenly. "Why use this form at all if not to fool me?"

Death looked like a sculpture, the dim light casting deep hollows into the contours of his cheeks as he flexed his jaw. "I know you're no fool, Little Bird. I had no intention of mocking you, nor did I realize what I was getting myself into or the ruse I was creating until it was too late. For that, I apologize. But as for my reason, I admit that it was merely out of a selfish desire to discover who you were. It's as I've told you already—I've spent the entirety of my existence waiting for you. Waiting for someone I can talk to. Someone I can feel. When I realized that was you . . . I needed to know who you were.

"Then you asked for my help," he continued, "and I wanted to be there for you. But I knew that I could not help you in the form you were familiar with because you were afraid of me. You said once that you hated me, and so I remained as Sylas. Not just to get you to Thorn Grove but to spend time with you and help you, without the stigma. Without the fear. Had I approached you in my shadows, you never would have trusted my help."

He was right, and although she was angry about the lie, part of her was relieved, too. Relieved that he'd stayed with her, no matter the form, because Blythe was still alive. And in the end, that was all that mattered.

He stood and took hold of her hand. "I won't pretend to understand what you're going through, as I was not born as you were, and have never been human. But I will be here with you every step of the way, assuming . . ."

"Assuming what?"

The stars were a canvas behind him, glowing as brightly as those silver eyes of his. Even the moon seemed to pull her closer to him as he asked, "Assuming you'll have me?"

Death had told her once that people's fates were predetermined, and she wondered if perhaps she was finally looking hers in the face. For so long she had resisted it. For so long she'd fought against this part of her—and oh, how exhausted she was. She was tired of the pretending. Tired of making herself someone she was not while running away from all that made her feel good and whole. Tired of questions and puzzles and guessing.

She just . . . wanted to *be*.

She knew who she was now, and she would no longer hide. She was a reaper, she was Death, and that darkness was her home. *He* was her home.

And so she curled her fingers around his. "Neither of us will ever be alone again."

FORTY-SIX

I T WAS A SLOW PROCESS, GETTING BLYTHE TO HEAL.

It was a fate Signa wished upon no one. Blythe spent days of agony curled in her bed with thin breaths and swimming vision. Nights spent withering away, skin stretched over brittle bones, unable to keep anything down. Signa and Elijah took turns at her bedside, sometimes offering stories. Sometimes chatting on Blythe's better days. And sometimes Signa would simply sit quietly, staring at the corner of the room while Blythe slept, trusting that they needed only to have patience.

Eventually, the improvement came. Her vomiting stopped within two weeks, and one late winter morning, Blythe managed to rise from the bed on her own so that she could watch the snowfall from her window. Like a newborn colt, she could hardly hold herself upright. But if there was one thing Signa had learned in her life of solitude, it was patience. And as she was waiting for her parents' old home, Foxglove, to be readied for her arrival, she had nothing but time.

Blythe didn't take well to needing assistance for the first several months, often insisting that Signa hurry up and leave now that she was twenty and had inherited her fortune. Insisting that she didn't want the help, didn't need it. But Signa had learned by then that Blythe was all talk, and because she'd spent too much of her life wishing someone would be there for her, Signa refused to leave Blythe's side. It took many long days to slowly put meat on her bones and rebuild her strength, but by early spring Blythe was walking on her own two legs once more.

Elijah couldn't have been happier for his daughter, whom he watched with a keen eye. The parties at Thorn Grove ceased entirely, replaced by time spent together in the garden. Never would Signa have guessed that father and daughter were so similar if she hadn't seen the proof of it each morning at breakfast, both of them wearing slippers to the table and making grand declarations for why whichever flavor scone they were eating at the time was the best. One morning, Blythe had demanded that Warwick gather the cook, who laughed with rosy cheeks as she listened to Elijah and Blythe prattle on about how they simply must have lemon or rose or chocolate scones for their next tea.

So spirited were they now that it took Signa some getting used to. It was as though someone had taken a broom to Thorn Grove and was sweeping away the cobwebs and the darkness—pulling back the curtains and letting the light filter in.

There was not a day when they didn't think of Lillian, just as there was not a day when Signa didn't think of Percy and his fate. She kept the burden of that knowledge to herself, unwilling to shatter Blythe's and Elijah's hearts again when they were only just rebuilding. Both Percy and Lillian were gone from Thorn Grove and would never be back.

Life at Thorn Grove was changing for the better, but there was still one thing left that Signa had to take care of.

Marjorie had returned one afternoon. They'd searched for her to no avail, but at the news of her son's disappearance, she'd come seeking answers. She and Elijah locked themselves away in his office, and though Signa had tried her best to eavesdrop, she was shooed away by Warwick. She waited impatiently after that, pacing the halls as Marjorie disappeared into her former bedroom. Signa lingered near it, bouncing on the balls of her feet until the door cracked open and Marjorie stood with a travel chest in her arms.

Marjorie took one look at her, and her lips tightened. "Hello, Miss Farrow."

"Good morning, Miss Hargreaves." Everything Signa had planned to say tumbled from her head all at once. She was left standing in an awkward silence, her hands clasped with worry in front of her. "I was hoping that I might have a word?"

Marjorie was no longer the prim-and-proper governess Signa once knew. She instead was a woman with dark circles beneath her eyes who likely would have given anything to escape this conversation. Signa didn't blame her, but she was relieved when Marjorie sighed, set down her chest, and invited Signa inside. Her room was bare. She motioned for Signa to sit in a straight-backed chair with a yellow-floral stencil, then took a seat opposite her.

"I'm glad to see you're safe," said Signa, pulling the reluctant words from herself. "We looked for you for quite some time."

"I'm aware." Marjorie's voice was cool, but Signa was relieved to find that it had no hardness. There wasn't much affection, either, but Signa supposed she could live with that. "I came only to get news of Percy, and to gather my belongings. If you've got something to say, best do it quickly."

Signa drew in a deep breath to gather her words. "I owe you an apology. I wanted to keep Blythe safe, but I didn't have the evidence I needed before accusing you. I'm sorry."

Marjorie accepted her apology with a nod, though nothing about her expression softened. "It's quite all right. I admire your affection for the Hawthornes, and we both know it was not a baseless accusation."

Signa chewed on her bottom lip. Marjorie was right—though the woman was innocent, there'd been the belladonna stain upon her fingertips.

"I found the berries right before you accused me," Marjorie said.

Signa sensed that the final puzzle piece dangled before her. She hadn't told anyone the truth about Percy. Instead, she told anyone who asked that she'd never found him in the garden that night, and never saw who set the garden on fire. She said Percy had fled, fearful that someone was trying to kill him and spurred on by his anger at his father's plan to sell Grey's. With the help of Death spending his nights at Thorn Grove, subliminally whispering the story into every sleeping ear, all in the manor came to terms with the new reality. A large portion of the staff had been culled in the hope that the reduction would remove whoever was poisoning the food, and although Signa did feel guilty about the departures, Death was keeping his eye on the staff to ensure that all landed at suitable positions.

When Blythe began to heal, Signa let Elijah believe that he'd gotten rid of the perpetrator once and for all. He'd alerted the authorities, who'd begun an investigation, but without any proof or confessions, the case had been slowly fizzling. Though he was dissatisfied with having no definite conclusion, Elijah made it clear that he cared more about spending time with Blythe than pressing the issue.

"So you knew the belladonna berries belonged to Percy?" Signa asked Marjorie, having no desire to dance around the question.

Marjorie's red hair was tied back at the nape of her neck, and freckles dusted the skin beneath her tired eyes. She looked so much like her son in that moment that Signa's stomach twisted.

"I never said where I found them."

"You didn't have to." Signa turned away, unable to stare at their resemblance for a moment longer. "I know it was him. I'm the only one who does, and I have every intention of keeping it that way. The Hawthornes don't need another heartbreak."

Marjorie's relief came in the form of a swallow and a quick exhale of breath. "Please understand that I didn't have even a moment to gather my thoughts or decide what the best course of action was when I realized what was happening. I wanted to speak with him. To spare him if I could. He's my son, and I needed time to think."

"Time was a luxury that Blythe didn't have." Signa wrung her skirts in her hands. "I was wrong, but when you hesitated, I took action. And that action is what saved Blythe's life. I'm sorry for accusing you—I truly am. But please understand that I also thought I was doing the best thing I could with the options that were before me."

A vein in Marjorie's forehead pulsed as she smoothed out her dress. "Elijah tells me that Percy has gone." There was more she wanted to say, the hint of a question lingering at the edges. "Will my son ever be back, Miss Farrow?"

Signa had been confident when she decided to claim Percy's years for Blythe, and she was confident now as she lifted her chin and looked Marjorie in the eye. "He will never again return to Thorn Grove. Of that I'm certain."

Marjorie didn't wait a breath before she stood, eyes damp and resolute. "Then it's time for me to go. I've a train to catch, into the country. It's time I begin a new life, away from this place."

Signa vowed then to forever keep the truth of Percy's feelings toward Marjorie to herself. It was better to lie, wasn't it? To let Marjorie believe that he loved her. That he hadn't wanted her dead. "Then I wish you well," Signa said with a small dip of her head. "I hope you land somewhere magnificent."

Marjorie nodded, and with a bow of her own, she disappeared into the hall and out the doors of Thorn Grove.

Signa gave the empty room one last look before she stepped into the hall and shut the door behind her. With the last piece of the puzzle set into place, it truly was time for her to move on.

You did well.

A familiar chill trickled up her arms and down her back as Death appeared behind her, wrapping his arms around her waist.

She leaned into his touch, lulled by the comfort of it. "You were watching?"

"Not to spy," he answered aloud, bending so that his words brushed against her ear. His grip on her tightened, lips peppering small kisses along her neck. Signa wondered vaguely what she might look like to anyone who happened down the hall, but she couldn't make herself care. It was Death who pulled away with a throaty chuckle. "How about we move this to your room?"

"Is that why you came here?" she teased him, taking hold of his hand. She didn't need to be asked twice. All week she'd left her window open as she tossed under her sheets, waiting for him to join her. And each night he'd ignored the invitation.

She led Death to her room as the shadows dropped around him, and he was but a young man with silver hair and galaxies in his eyes. He sighed his content as Signa kissed up his neck, along his jawline . . . He pulled away before she could reach his lips.

Signa drew back. "Do you not want to? I can stop, if—"

"Signa Farrow, the last thing I want is to stop. But there's something we need to discuss." He took a seat on the edge of her bed and whispered, as though tender words might somehow make them better, "It's going to be harder for us to see each other from now on."

She sat beside him and folded her legs beneath her. "What do you mean?"

"I mean that Blythe is healing," he said. "You've solved the murder, and Thorn Grove is well. You can only see me when the veil between our worlds has been lifted and death waits nearby."

"But I have the belladonna berries," Signa argued. "I can see you whenever I want."

He lifted one hand from her lap and cupped it in both of his own. "Sometimes maybe. But I will not be another cage in which you spend your life, Little Bird. I do not want you to rely on such things just to see me."

"But I *want* to see you." The dread in her stomach sank lower. "What is it you're suggesting?"

Her worry was so palpable that he scooted closer and nudged his shoulder against hers. "One day we will be together without barriers," Death promised. "And we will still see each other until then—our paths will cross, as they always have. But I want you to live. I do not want you to grow to regret your days in this world, but to look fondly upon them."

She had only just settled into this life—into the knowledge that her destiny was different than what she'd spent so much time trying to make it. She'd only just embraced the darkest parts of herself, embraced *him,* and now he was—what? Trying to warn her away from him? "If that's what you want for me, then you will not leave me again," she said sternly.

"It's not by choice." He squeezed her hand tight. "I won't be able to see you every day, and I want to be realistic about that. I'll not have you eating those berries just so we can have five minutes together." Signa tore her hand from his, wanting nothing more than to curse at him. But she bit that swelling emotion down, for there would be time for it later.

"I have already chosen you." There was steel in her voice. "Don't you dare try to be diplomatic now. This is a big world, and I'm certain that there will be ways for us to find each other."

"There will be," he agreed. "But when everyone you know is gone, I will still be here, Signa. This is not easy for me, either; I've wanted nothing more than to be with you. For you to want me. But I don't want you so focused on the world of the dead that you forget to enjoy that of the living. Do you understand?"

She did, perfectly well. But Signa had no intention of giving up another person she'd grown to love. "I will live my life," she told him, "and I will find you in those stolen moments. My decisions are mine to make, and what I'm deciding is that we'll figure it out. We will *try*. And in the meantime, I'd like to make use of the time we have left."

Death swallowed as Signa shifted upon the bed. It was fortunate she was still in a tea dress—one without a corset, which she could easily undo herself. Her eyes flicked to his with a silent question, and Death responded by twisting to pull her onto him so that she straddled his lap. "Are you certain?" he asked. "Even knowing that it may be some time before we see each other again?"

"You are the one thing I am certain of." She brought his hands up to the laces of her gown, guiding his fingers between them. "We'll find a way." Only when his fingers slid through the silk laces, undoing them, did she shut her eyes and let the gown glide off her, trying to memorize the feeling of those fingers against her skin, trailing from her neck to her hips. The feeling, a moment later, of his chest pressed against hers. His thumb as it traced gentle circles against her inner thigh.

No matter how long it took, she would wait for him, and whenever she doubted, or whenever she missed him, she would remember this moment when he laid her down upon the sheets, and how the night itself had consumed her.

EPILOGUE

SIGNA SEARCHED FOR DEATH EVERYWHERE THESE DAYS.

He no longer came to her in the night. Nor did he come to her when she visited Mitra in the stables, where another stable boy had taken his place, as though Sylas had never existed. Death did not come to her even when her thoughts strayed to the press of his body against hers, or when she craved the power that thrummed through her blood along with it. Nor was he there now, among the dancers and gossipers at Thorn Grove. She looked for his black suit against the gilded walls. His devilish horned mask weaving between the guests. As she had at every party since her debut, she searched for him over the rim of her champagne flute, unsettled when the hair along the back of her neck remained flat and her spine was warm rather than chilled.

I want to see you. She was glad, at least, that she could still communicate with him. As frustrating as it all was, he was still a reaper, and wherever he ventured, death was sure to follow. And Signa had to admit that she'd grown quite comfortable with her life at Thorn Grove and those who were part of it. It was about time her world settled.

His answer came in a honeyed voice. *Shall I bring about a plague? We would get to see each other quite often, then.*

Signa snorted and took another sip of champagne, about to warn him not to threaten her with a good time, when a deep voice came from behind her.

"It's a pleasure to see you again, Miss Farrow." She'd not heard from Lord Wakefield since the Christmas ball four months prior, when she'd missed their promised last waltz. It was her hope that he'd lost interest, though the glint in his eyes signaled she'd been mistaken. Like all suitors, though, the sooner she could scare him away, the sooner she could begin her life as a proper spinster whose only companion was the night itself.

On that night, however, she and Everett had no choice but to reacquaint themselves. "Allow me to introduce my father," he said, "His Grace the Duke of Berness, Julius Wakefield." Beside Everett stood a man who looked every bit his blood. He was a full head taller than Signa, with deep-set eyes and broad shoulders. He had an air about him that made her skin prickle, for the way he looked at her reminded her of how one might inspect a show horse prior to placing their bets.

The idea of curtsying to anyone who looked at her like that was enough to make her skin crawl in protest. And yet she did curtsy, for this man was the new owner of Grey's, set to take control the next month in a deal that would have him splitting the profits with the Hawthornes. Elijah had been dancing through the halls since the deal was made. Even Byron wasn't quite so cranky about the decision as one might have expected. He'd still be getting paid, and his family would be forever taken care of and remain in its bolstered status. A family that he now planned to have, if him courting his way through the ballroom was any indicator.

As this occasion with Everett and his father was a celebration of the transfer, Signa bit her tongue and lowered her head to Lord Julius for Elijah's sake. "It's a pleasure to make your acquaintance, Your Grace," she said, making her voice buttery. It took everything in her power to maintain her smile when he continued to inspect her for too long a moment before clasping Everett upon one shoulder.

Only then, apparently having deemed Signa worthy enough, did the duke grin. "The pleasure is all mine, Miss Farrow. My son has told me much about you. You look so very much like your mother, you know." There was a hardened edge to his words. "Though your eyes are most unusual."

Signa sipped from her champagne flute. "They're most unusual indeed, Your Grace. For with them, I am able to see spirits." When she allowed her lips to stretch into a coy grin, Julius exhaled a rumble of laughter from somewhere deep in his belly.

"Am I missing all the fun?" Elijah appeared behind him, drawn to the laughter. He was practically glowing from within. "Charming the duke, are we, Signa?"

"Your niece seems to be a fine young woman," said Julius. "Not that I expected anything less. My Everett is quite taken with her."

Everett looked ready to melt into a puddle and forever disappear into the earth. Signa, cheeks warm and neck clammy, was prepared to join him. The two looked to the gilded walls and the crystal chandeliers, to the floor and the dancers, and to anywhere but at each other.

Will you be able to visit me tonight, should I die of mortification? Signa asked Death, who had chosen now of all times to go quiet.

Elijah, bless his beautiful soul, was quick to catch on and steer Julius's attention away from Everett and Signa. "I think it's about time for us to prepare our toast. Come with me, and let's get ourselves another drink first." He led Julius into the crowd so that Everett and Signa stood alone, both of them staring at the floor and trying to form words that would not further their embarrassment.

"What a riveting conversation," Everett said, clearing his throat and scratching at the back of his neck.

So charming was his bashfulness that Signa smiled. "How have you been, Lord Wakefield? It's been some time since we last spoke."

While she'd anticipated he would laugh and play coy with her, he answered with deep confusion. "It certainly has been. Though—and forgive me for being so bold—when you did not return for another dance with me that night of the Christmas ball, I assumed my interest was . . . unrequited."

He was right, for while dancing with Everett had been lovely, it had not compared with dancing in Death's arms. Still, Everett was a kind man, and she didn't wish to hurt him. "I apologize. The excitement of the night got the better of me, and I lost track of the time."

Unfortunately, Everett didn't quite get the hint, for his face lit up. "Dance with me tonight, then."

Signa wasn't certain how she could say no. Flustered, and with guilt rising in her stomach, she offered him her dance card, and Everett promptly filled in not one but two spots. Later, she'd have to find a way to let him down gently. But, for that night, she hoped Death wasn't paying attention.

Eliza Wakefield, however, was very much paying attention. When Signa noticed, Eliza glanced away quickly and turned her attention to laughing at whatever those around her were saying. Signa cringed. She'd hoped that she wouldn't have to speak with Eliza or that mousy friend of hers, Diana—both of whom she'd declined tea with twice now. But it was impossible not to see her, given the abominable tea-doily fan that Eliza waved about.

Everett caught her staring and creased his brow, for Signa was making a rather displeased expression that she had little control of. "Is something the matter?"

She shook her head. "I was simply admiring Eliza's dress. Such a beautiful thing it is, so bright and . . . yellow."

"Father thought it wise for her to wear something bold. He's eager to see her married, I think. He's been taking calls from gentlemen all week. I believe she may soon be promised to Sir Bennet." He nodded discreetly to a man across the ballroom floor. Signa had to bite her tongue not to say anything. Sir Bennet was not an unattractive man, but he was quite old, with a head full of white hair and wrinkled skin around his eyes. He hunched a little as he walked, shoulders rounding in on themselves.

"Not the most youthful man," Everett said, guessing what Signa was thinking without her needing to say a word, "but very respectable. He'd give her a good life."

He certainly would, assuming Eliza's goal was to become a wealthy widow within the next handful of years. Regardless, Signa did her best to nod—about to ask what the rush was when Eliza was still so young—when a beautiful winter-blue gown of a dazzling silk with a fitted corset top caught her eye. Blythe looked every bit a princess as she swept onto the ballroom floor. She basked in the stares and the whispers of her name as though half starved for them. There was youth in her suntanned skin again. A glint in her lively eyes.

When she caught Signa staring, Blythe beamed and glided over to take her cousin by the hand. "Oh, this is magnificent," she crooned, darting looks at the trays of sweets and champagne. She didn't care one bit that she was stealing Signa away from Everett.

Everett cleared his throat. "Good evening, Miss Hawthorne."

"Oh, hello, Everett." Blythe didn't look at him long enough to register his surprise at being addressed so informally but instead took in all the women in their gorgeous gowns as they buzzed about the ballroom. It was like a shimmering veil had been placed over the party as Signa watched Blythe observe the other women. Everything felt a thousand times lovelier. Signa had done the unspeakable to protect her cousin, but it had all been worth it. Deeply, irrevocably worth it.

Blythe's hungry eyes scanned the crowd, lighting up when they landed upon a woman who was coming their way—Charlotte.

Signa's chest tightened. She'd spent the past several months avoiding Charlotte and those questioning eyes of hers. She'd been in the woods the night of the fire, and if there was anyone who might disbelieve her story about Percy, it was Charlotte.

"Blythe, I am glad to see you well," Charlotte said, beaming and beautiful as ever in a silk gown pink as a peony. She took Blythe by the hands, her smile thin but genuine. "Was your brother able to make it this evening?" And though her question was to Blythe, Charlotte's eyes slid to Signa.

"There's been no word from him yet," Blythe said, her light dimming. "Though I'm sure that he'll send word once he's settled."

"Of course he will." Charlotte squeezed Blythe's hands, though Signa could see the doubt in her face.

It was a relief when Elijah tapped a crystal flute to draw the crowd's attention. The guests began to quiet, even Eliza, whose laughter ceased when Julius glared at her with a look that had Eliza promptly lowering her fan.

"We want to thank you all for joining us tonight," began Elijah. Byron stood to his right, with Julius just behind him. "Grey's has been in my family for four generations. We Hawthornes have run it with pride, and we have immense respect for the institution. So much respect that, as it's grown beyond us, we were not so foolish as to believe we alone could keep up with it. As of this day, we would like to welcome His Grace, Julius Wakefield, into Grey's, and to announce our official partnership with the Wakefield family. We'd also like you all to bear witness to this moment as we embark on a new legacy that we hope will continue for many years to come."

Elijah held up a contract with such flourish that several guests began to clap. He presented it to Julius, who stepped forward with a quill in hand to sign the document. After adding his name, he addressed the clapping crowd with a practiced grin. "I look forward to this new venture," he said, "and to our partnership!"

Elijah's beaming could not have been any brighter. And though less enthused, Byron raised his glass for a toast. "Cheers to our partnership," he said. "And to many more years to come."

Signa raised her flute with them, as did the rest of the revelers, all clinking glasses with a bright exuberance that ignited the ballroom.

Julius made a show of finishing his champagne in one go. Three things happened then:

First came the gasping breath of Julius, whose eyes bulged as he clutched his chest and clawed at his throat.

Second came Eliza's scream as the man fell, blood pooling in his mouth. Everett rushed for him with a desperate cry, and Signa followed.

And third came a chill that stole Signa's breath and brought her to her knees at Julius's side, where Death loomed over him. He looked down at Signa with a sigh. "You should be careful what you wish for, Little Bird." And then he plucked Julius's spirit straight from his body.

That spirit looked to Signa. "*Ah,*" Julius said, his head tilting as he observed her. "*It seems you were telling the truth about those eyes.*"

Oh, she could *kill* Death. Yet there was no chance to because the bodies around her began to slow, freezing in place. Death moved beside her at once, tense as a figure she'd not noticed stooped beside them—a young man with deep bronze skin and eyes of melted gold.

He inspected the shattered flute that had fallen out of Julius's hand, picking up a broken shard and holding it up to the light. A few drops of liquid clung to it, and Signa's breath ceased as she realized that the color was a tinge too blue. There was something wrong with the scent, too. Something bitter beneath the alcohol. Something that smelled of bitter almond.

It was no belladonna, but Signa knew poison when she encountered it.

"Fate is a funny thing, isn't it?" The man's voice sounded as ancient as the earth itself, the words such a low rumble that they caused the flutes of champagne to quake. Signa leaned back into Death's grip as those golden eyes turned to her, unable to look away. She realized at once who they belonged to.

"What a pleasure it is to finally meet you, Signa Farrow," Fate whispered. "It would appear that you have another murder to solve."

ACKNOWLEDGMENTS

The journey of taking a book from an idea in your head to a tangible story that readers get to hold in their hands is a feat that takes a small army of amazing people who deserve all that thanks.

So thank you to Pete Knapp, the best agent I could ask for. Sometimes it feels like you are literally the other half of my severely type A brain, and I can't even explain in words how wonderful that is. This industry is like being on a train that's veered off course, only to end up on the tracks of a never-ending roller coaster. Which is to say that it's ridiculously challenging to navigate, and I'm all the more thankful to be able to fully trust my business partner in all of this, and to know you're always going to have my back. You are a wonderful agent—please never leave this industry. I am spoiled, and I will simply perish without you.

At Little, Brown Young Readers, thank you to my editor Hallie Tibbets for giving Signa and Death's story a fabulous new home. You are a line-edit wizard, and this story is so much stronger and tighter because of you.

Deirdre Jones, thank you for swooping in and taking this story under your wings. I'm so excited to be working with you on the sequel.

Alvina Ling, Megan Tingley, Jackie Engel, Marisa Finkelstein, and Virginia Lawther, thank you so much for your hand in raising this book up and helping debut it out into the world.

Robin Cruise, for your copyediting wizardry, and for teaching me that not everything needs a comma. I will try my best to internalize that lesson moving forward, though I make no promises that the commas won't somehow weasel their way in.

Proofreaders Chandra Wohleber and Kerry Johnson, for your sharp eyes and help catching even the most micro details.

Designer Jenny Kimura, art director Karina Granda, and illustrator Elena Masci for giving this book the most gorgeous, stunning, perfect cover I could have imagined. It was everything I had hoped for and more.

On the marketing and sales side, thank you, Stefanie Hoffman, Shanese Mullins, Savannah Kennelly, Christie Michel, Shawn Foster, and Danielle Cantarella, for supporting and hyping up this book, and for all your work getting as many eyes as possible onto it.

To the UK team over at Hodder & Stoughton, thank you, Holly Powell, for being there from the very beginning with your brilliant editorial eye to help bring this story to life. Lydia Blageden and Teagan White, for giving the story a beautiful face in the UK with such a spectacular design. I'm very spoiled to have two of the most gorgeous covers. Natasha Quereshi, Callie Robertson, Kate Keehan, Sarah Clay, Matthew Everett, it's so great to get to work with this team, and I sincerely appreciate you championing this book.

At my agency, Park & Fine Literary and Media, thank you, Abigail Koons and Ema Barnes, for working so diligently to get

Belladonna into as many hands as possible all throughout the world. Stuti Telidevara, thank you so much for all your help with planning and organizing and being all-around wonderful. Emily Sweet and Andrea Mai, for your strategic minds and meticulous work.

Abby Ranger, your input during the story's earliest stages was instrumental and very much appreciated.

Debbie Deuble Hill, film agent extraordinaire, thank you for your unwavering faith and confidence in this story, and for your dedication to finding it the perfect home on screen.

Nicole Otto, magnificent human, thank you for being the first to ever pick me out of the slush and for letting me send you all my panicked publishing texts. You are a gem and I can't wait to see your face again.

To the friends who were instrumental in the creation of this story, and whom I'd never survive publishing without: Rachel Griffin, Adrienne Young, Kristin Dwyer, Shelby Mahurin, Diya Mishra, and Haley Marshall. I am fully aware that I am A Lot. Thank you for putting up with my shenanigans. You are some of my absolute favorite people in this world, and I am forever grateful to have you.

Bri Renae, thank you for being one of the earliest readers, and for making me truly believe this story was something special. Also, for introducing me to the idea of Shadow Daddies and Scones. One day we will make it a thing.

Jordan Gray, thank you for your kindness and enthusiasm, and great editorial eye. The bombazine gown at the beginning of the book is all you.

Shea Standefer and Tomi Adeyemi, for the faith in me and for the KBBQ. Always for the KBBQ. ,

To all the authors and reviewers who took the time to read and blurb *Belladonna* early on, I am eternally grateful. I love this book so much, and it means the world that you loved it, too.

To the street team: I cannot thank each of you by name, but please know that I truly appreciate every single one of you. All your excitement, your hype, your beautiful photos. You have made this journey so incredibly special.

Peter Gundry, it would feel wrong not to thank you. I listened to your music every single day for years as I worked on this book. I'm sorry that the only one I could name you after was the dog, but you got to admit that he's pretty cool.

Josh, to say that it's been a journey to get here is putting it lightly. Thank you for sticking by my side through all the stress, the late nights, and the long weekends, and for being a great partner.

Mom and Dad, I really wish you wouldn't read this one, but alas, I know you will and I appreciate it. Thank you for always believing and supporting whatever preposterous thing I decide to do next.

Pookie and Rowdy, this was our final book together, and I will forever miss you both poking your wet noses in my face and trying to distract me from writing every single day. Don't worry, Mooka and Meadow are doing a great job picking up where you left off.

God, for giving me the story and the words, and for putting this book into all the right hands along the way.

And finally, to all the readers who have made it here. You are the reason I get to do this. Thank you, thank you, thank you.

Adalyn Grace

ADALYN GRACE

is the *New York Times* bestselling author of *All the Stars and Teeth*, which was named "2020's biggest YA fantasy" by *Entertainment Weekly*, and its sequel, *All the Tides of Fate*. Prior to becoming an author, Adalyn spent four years working in live theatre, acted as the managing editor of a nonprofit newspaper, and studied storytelling as an intern on Nickelodeon Animation's popular series *The Legend of Korra*. Local to San Diego, Adalyn spends her nonwriting days watching too much anime and playing video games with her two dorky dogs. She invites you to visit her on Instagram @authoradalyngrace or her website, AdalynGraceAuthor.com.

THE STORY CONTINUES IN

FOXGLOVE

Turn the page for an
exclusive deleted chapter from
the author's original draft of

MARJORIE HAD DEEMED HERSELF ESCORT FOR THE MORNING'S EXCURsions. She maintained her distance as Signa crossed a damp lawn, hiking up the hem of her wool dress to keep it out of the mud from the prior night's rain. It was getting cold enough out that she suspected that rain would turn to snow soon, and Signa was more than ready.

"Miss Farrow!" Everett called, waving his hands over his head as though he wasn't the only one waiting on the lawn and she might somehow miss him. He hurried over, carefully crossing the slog to reach her. The earth was protesting his declaration of the day being a fine one for a ride. The wind was bitter and the ground caked with mud and mossy puddles. Mist rolled in over the hills, shrouding the gray sky.

Despite it all, the sight of Everett's grin had Signa feeling fresh and warm as a spring day. He bowed to Marjorie in acknowledgment, then to her.

"You came!"

God, was he handsome. Dreary as the day was, Everett was a beam of sunshine in its midst. At his smile, Signa nearly forgot the cold nipping at her, seeking purchase upon any inch of bare skin. Maybe this wouldn't be so bad as she'd thought.... Maybe there *could* be something here between them. That would certainly make her life easier.

"Did you think I'd say no when you were waiting on the front porch in this weather?" Signa teased.

He scratched the back of his neck, having the decency to at least appear bashful. This was no small thing he was doing, to seek out Signa prior to her debut. "Regardless, I'm glad that you came.

I'm afraid I chose a piss-poor day for a ride, though. I promise the weather seemed much more mild from my window this morning. Are you still open for giving it a try?"

"I am," she agreed, though when she glanced toward the stables, her turning stomach did everything *but* agree. Sylas was in those stables. She could already imagine him taking one look at Everett's muddied shoes and turning up his nose, or making some snide comment about how opulent he was.

Though it was clear all three of them were meant to go into the stables, Signa's gut protested the idea so much that she hurried a few steps ahead of the others.

"Allow me to fetch the horses," she told Everett with such a false smile that her cheeks ached.

"I would be happy to—"

"I would like to ask the groom about a certain path. It's a surprise, though I want to ensure that with last night's rain, it's still a safe trek." She flashed Marjorie a quick glance. Though her chaperone's eyes were narrowed, there was nothing she could say on the matter. It wasn't as though Marjorie could be the one to gather the horses and leave Signa and Everett alone. She could insist none of them separate, but Marjorie seemed to sense the desperation in Signa's words and inclined her head to the girl.

Signa bit back a relieved sigh. "I'll only be a moment."

She hurried the rest of the way to the stables, only stopping when Mitra reached out to nip at her elbow for Signa's attention. Signa slowed then and turned to the mare, stroking her hand over her beautiful golden face.

"Hello there, pretty girl," she cooed. "Tell me, where is the horrible scowling man who feeds you?"

From deeper within the stables, Sylas cleared his throat. "If it's me you're looking for, I'm not sure I can help you today. I've a full schedule of scowling to tend to."

Signa pressed her lips together so that he would not get the satisfaction of her laughter. Three stalls down she found him, bent over and cleaning the hooves of a gorgeous red stallion.

She could not help where her eyes wandered, for it was not *her* fault that he was bent over. Nor could she control the flush of her cheeks as he straightened and peered at her from over his shoulder. With the back of his hand, he brushed away strands of rich black hair that had fallen into his eyes.

Despite the cold, Sylas had not bothered with a coat. He wore only a loose white tunic with the top buttons undone. Upon his skin was a sheen of sweat that trailed down the dip of his chest. Signa tried her best to pull her eyes from it—from him—but it truly felt like this man had been put upon the earth to challenge her. It'd been a week since she'd caught up with Sylas, and it was admittedly an odd feeling to see him again. As much as Death occupied her thoughts, it was as though the moment Signa saw Sylas, he took the place in the forefront of her mind.

It was a good thing, though, she supposed. At least Sylas was living.

It wasn't proper form for Sylas to have been dressed so casually rather than in his uniform, but Signa was beginning to enjoy that about Thorn Grove more than ever. The Hawthornes were so wealthy that no one cared whether their stable boy took off his coat or if the master of the house wore slippers to breakfast. Their wealth afforded them some provocativeness, for everyone just wanted a piece of them. To sink their claws into the family's fortune and leech whatever they could from them by proxy, no matter how they felt about decorum.

Signa was certain there must have been loads of gossip about the Hawthornes' behavior, but that gossip would not stop people from arriving to the extravagant parties, or from using the Hawthornes in whichever ways best suited them. In society, they were a well-enjoyed topic of conversation and interest. But Signa knew the gossip that happened behind closed doors and over porcelain cups. Eliza and Diana had been all too eager to soak up more of it.

Everett Wakefield, at least, seemed kind enough, though with Marjorie's warning to be wise with men ringing in her ears, it was impossible for her to fully settle.

Especially with Sylas standing there before her, his hair mussed and muscles taut from work. His back was so . . . broad.

So lost in her staring was she that, at first, Signa wasn't aware that Sylas had caught wind of what was happening. She didn't notice his folded arms, or that he'd tightened his lips to keep from laughing at her roaming attention. Only when she eventually glanced back up at his face, her eyes owlish, did he allow a pleased smirk to creep across his face.

"Can I help you with something?" he asked.

She shook her thoughts away and tried to stand tall before him. Fists bunched at her sides, she lifted her chin and said, "A ride. I am here to ride."

"A ride?" Oh, how his smirk grew. "You're asking for my help with . . . a ride?"

"Yes." Only when he began to laugh did Signa's mouth drop open as she gleaned the ridiculous male humor that must have entertained him so. "Oh, you beastly boy! I am here to ride a *horse*."

Before she could say anything more, Everett's voice sounded from the stable entrance. "Miss Farrow? Do you need assistance?"

"Just one moment, Lord Wakefield!" she called, dread seeping into her.

Signa didn't need to look at Sylas to know that she had piqued his interest. He bent toward Signa so that they were face-to-face, his voice low. "And is that just one horse, *Miss* Farrow?"

She looked anywhere but at his earnest face, and held up three fingers. "One for our chaperone, too, please."

With a snort, Sylas grabbed his jacket from a hook and tugged it on. He didn't hesitate to push past her and out of the stall, taking a long look at Everett, who was chatting with Marjorie and had no knowledge of being stared at. Sylas raked his hair back, his expression unchanged.

"How's Blythe?" he asked suddenly, back in the stall with her. "I heard she had a bit of a spell last week."

"She's doing much better." Better than Signa had ever seen her, in fact. The Calabar bean did its work well enough that, for the moment, Signa wasn't worried. "You've not heard anything else from the staff, I suppose?"

"Nothing yet," he said, as eager to fall into a different topic as Signa. "I'll let you know the moment I do. Now go on and hurry back to him." Sylas's smile was thin as a knife's tip. "I'll prepare the horses."

Though hesitant, Signa did as she was told. It didn't take long until the horses were ready. Only, Sylas did not bother to deliver them himself.

"What in God's name...?" Everett's brows shot up to his hairline as three fully saddled horses burst out of the stable doors. Mitra was the first, and Signa was able to grab the reins as the mare rushed straight toward her, nudging her head into Signa's chest. Marjorie caught the reins of the next horse with a surprised gasp, angry eyes darting toward the stables.

"My apologies, Lord Wakefield," she huffed. "There must have been a recent staff change. I've no idea what they're thinking—"

The third horse shot out then.

Balwin, the peculiar horse Signa had met during her first visit to the stables, burst from the doors. Unlike the others, he made no effort to approach the trio. He instead seemed to view keeping his reins away from them as a game, galloping around Everett and then lunging toward the woods.

"Where on earth is your groom?" Everett yelled as he, too, lunged. He ran after Balwin, able to grab hold of the horse's reins only for Balwin to become distracted by a mud puddle. He dipped one of his front hooves into it, splashing around in the puddle while Everett pulled on the reins. He dragged a reluctant Balwin back with his nose scrunched while Signa struggled to pull herself up into Mitra's saddle.

Perhaps Sylas was a little too comfortable at Thorn Grove now that Signa had offered him a secure future. She cursed him silently, glaring at the stable doors.

"I'm so sorry," she told Everett when she'd managed her way onto Mitra, grateful at least that he'd been too distracted to witness her complete lack of grace. "Balwin means well. He truly is a good horse."

Everett rolled his shoulders back and nodded, gentle as he pushed Balwin's nipping mouth away from him. "It's no bother. I've been around horses my whole life, Miss Farrow. I'm sure I can handle this one."

Signa's shoulders had just begun to sink with relief when Everett stepped into a stirrup to mount the horse, only to have the entire saddle come undone. He fell at once onto his back, gasping, and the saddle tumbled on top of him. Fortunately, the mud cushioned the blow.

"Lord Wakefield!" Marjorie screamed from atop her own mount. "Are you all right?"

Without the faintest clue what to do, Signa could only stare. Should she dismount and help him? Would that injure his pride? What good were her etiquette books if they could not help her in a situation so dire as this?

"It would be in everyone's best interest, Miss Hargreaves, if you discussed this recent staff change with your employer." Everett spit mud from his mouth, gritting his teeth. From the waist down, his backside was caked with mud. Signa covered her mouth; it was a sight ridiculous enough to laugh at, were she not so mortified. "Had that been your saddle, Miss Farrow, I would see to the matter myself." He managed to get himself upright without muddying the saddle. Taking hold of Balwin's reins, he threw the saddle back over the stallion, cinching it with fast, deft fingers.

"I suppose it's not proper of me to continue our ride while

looking as I do." Everett's gaze softened as his eyes sought out Signa. "But I won't say anything if you won't?"

She tipped her head toward the sky, the tension in her shoulders loosening. It took everything in her willpower to not shoot a glare at Sylas, who she was certain was watching them from the shadows. What was it with these foolish, jealous men in her life? His behavior was little different from Death's.

The joke was on him, though, because Everett took the complications in stride—and that was all the more attractive.

"I wouldn't dare tell a soul."

Relieved, he once again set to mounting Balwin, checking his weight in the stirrups this time. "A ride into town no longer seems a viable option," he mused. "Why don't we—" He never got to finish that sentence, for Balwin was not waiting for a decision. The horse took off, not at a walk but in a full canter. Everett, who had not yet settled himself, once again flew off the horse and fell, rump first, onto the ground.

Behind him, Signa watched as Balwin sank into the mud puddle he'd thrown Everett into earlier and rolled himself around in it.

Oh, she was going to kill Sylas.

This time, Signa did not hesitate to climb down from Mitra and rush to his side, followed swiftly by Marjorie. The entirety of Everett's back was caked with mud; it was now in his hair, too. On his breeches, coating his shoes . . . What he needed at that moment was a proper bath. A ride would have been too uncomfortable for them both, for whenever Signa glanced up to see the mud caking the tips of his hair and plastering it to his face, she nearly lost herself.

"I am so sorry," she said, trying to help him up. But Everett waved her away, muttering something about how he didn't want to soil her clothing.

Marjorie was there, too, brushing away some of the mud as though doing so would make a difference. "Should you allow us to take you back to Thorn Grove—"

"As much as I appreciate that offer—and believe me, I do—I fear my pride is too wounded to allow me within a mile of Miss Farrow's sight." When Signa chimed in to protest, Everett added, "I will get over it soon, I'm sure. For now, though, perhaps it's wise for me to return home. And the next time we go riding, it can be at my home. My groom is a bit more . . . well equipped for these things."

She steeled herself long enough to uncover her traitorous mouth, grateful that he was not angry. "So there will be a 'next time,' then?"

"I hope so." Everett's voice was soft, which was a good sign. After something like this, Signa couldn't imagine how mortified she'd be. "Though it seems I might have to share you with others by the time we next meet, which I must admit I am not keen on."

With the Christmas ball soon approaching, it made sense that he was here to steal her time away and make a good first impression. The ball was practice for her debut, and she'd be meeting many other men that night—though she was certain none would be so handsome or successful as Lord Wakefield.

The more she thought about it, though, the more the warnings rang in her head.

Perhaps Everett did have a true interest in her. He seemed kind enough, and being with him would be nearly as much of a social climb for her as it would be an investment for him. But if he'd only come calling to Thorn Grove so that he'd have the upper hand on the other suitors she'd soon meet, Signa was perhaps glad for the turn the day had taken.

"I'll take the horses back to the stables," she offered for lack of anything better to say, and she took the horses by their reins. When Balwin jerked his head back to try to tug away, Signa held steady and glared at the horse until he settled, admitting defeat with a sad swish of his tail. "Could you please see that Lord Wakefield gets to his carriage safely? And, Lord Wakefield, when I see you next, I have hope that it will be without all the mud."

Everett bowed his head, but Signa could not watch him. He looked far too ridiculous. "Of course," he said. "Have a good rest of your day, Miss Farrow."

She nodded, and only when he and Marjorie had crossed enough of the lawn that they would no longer hear her did Signa turn on her heel and stamp back to the stables, pulling the horses behind her.

"Very funny, Mr. Thorly!" She stomped into the stabled, seething. "You could have injured the poor man!"

She jumped when his voice sounded behind her, low and cloying. "He would've been fine. But now it seems we've got several horses here, all of which haven't been given the ride they were promised." Sylas's fingers curled around hers, which still held the reins tight. The leather of his gloves was cool against her warming skin. "Want to go on a ride with me, Signa?"

She tore away from him, hating that the press of his chest and her name on his lips were enough to scramble her brain.

"Take them out yourself." She shoved the reins into his hands and pulled away. "Lord Wakefield is a kind man, and you're lucky if he doesn't report you to Elijah. He didn't deserve that."

His eyes rolling, Sylas started to lead the horses back toward their stalls, which did make Signa feel a little guilty. She found some carrots in one of the food buckets and took a few to them as an apology for not taking them out as she'd intended. But she'd be damned before she'd ride with Sylas.

"It's not my fault if the man doesn't know how to ride a horse," Sylas said. Removing the horses' bridles, he shut the stall doors behind him. "You really ought to have higher standards."

"He is a *lord*," Signa shot back, surprised when that fact brought a hitch to Sylas's step. "And you know that him falling had nothing to do with skill."

"Are you implying that I sabotaged him?" Sylas flashed a smug look back at her.

"Indeed, Mr. Thorly. But what I don't understand is *why*. If there's something I should know about him, then tell me now. I'm to debut shortly, and Lord Wakefield has already made his intentions perfectly clear."

"It's got nothing to do with him." Sylas turned away, carrying Mitra's saddle to the tack room and dropping Balwin's on the floor to be washed. "I've never even met the man. Besides, it's a basic rule that one should always be responsible for checking their own horse. As a gentleman, he should have thought to double-check that Balwin's saddle was secure."

"Then tell me what it does have to do with!" Her words echoed through the stables, frightening the horses into stillness. Signa hadn't meant to come across so angry, but that's what it took for him to look at her. And when he did—when he looked up beneath those dark eyelashes, with anger in those smoky eyes, she lost herself and closed the space between them. Sylas drew a step back, pressing himself into a stall door as Signa grabbed a fistful of his shirt.

"You, Mr. Thorly, are positively boorish. Have you no decency? No manners?" She pressed herself against him, her tongue feeling particularly sharp, though she found that when the time came to speak again, her words ran dry. The two of them were...close. So close that she hadn't the faintest idea what to do with herself. Fortunately, though, there was no need to think, for Sylas took her by the shoulders and bent to press his lips to hers.

It wasn't a sweet, gentle kiss, but a crushing one that made Signa feel as though she were exploding from the inside out. She startled, which in turn made Sylas startle, breaking the kiss almost as soon as it began.

Sylas stumbled a step back, looking every bit as thrown off as she felt—like the gears in his mind were churning, attempting to piece together what he'd just done. "I...I'm sorry, I shouldn't have done that." He was toying with his shirt, suddenly very interested in its buttons. "I apologize for ruining your outing with Lord Wakefield....Though I'm certain you would have had a horrible time anyway."

Smoothing her hands out over her dress, Signa bobbed her head along in a continuous nod, keeping her gaze down so that he would not see the flush of her cheeks. This was entirely scandalous— enough to ruin her prospects and opportunity to ever join society.

And yet, in that moment, she could not quite bring herself to care about propriety anymore than she could stop herself from relishing the burn of her lips. "I will accept your apology so long as you ensure that both of those horses get a proper outing today."

His laugh was a dark, inviting thing. Chills slithered along her spine, and Signa found her lips feeling suddenly cold.

"That," he said, "I can do."

Though part of her very much wanted to remain there, doing so would be unwise. And though the repercussions would be consequential for her, it would mean the end of work for Sylas—and she knew better than to put him in that situation. No matter how she may have wanted to...

To what? To linger? To allow him to kiss her once more, and perhaps this time not stop? First Death, and now him—two people who were entirely wrong for her yet did not feel wrong in the slightest.

There were too few people in this world that Signa felt as though she could be herself around, yet Sylas, *charming* as he was, was becoming one of them. Had there been no society, no rules she was expected to adhere to, then perhaps he would be an option. But right then, with her approaching debut, society and expectations *were* factors, and she'd yet to make up her own mind on how she felt about it all. She had no choice but to ease away from Sylas, bowing her head low as she did so.

"Take care, then, Mr. Thorly."

"Yes, yes. Good. Take care, then, Miss Farrow."

She turned sharply on her heel, fingers pressed upon her lips, and did not once dare to turn back.

DISCUSSION QUESTIONS

1. Why does Death call Signa "Little Bird"? Is this a fitting nickname for her?

2. Loneliness pervades the novel and influences characters' desires and actions. How does loneliness affect each character? Is there any character unaffected by this emotion?

3. Many of the descriptions and idioms throughout the book incorporate references to death or dying, e.g., "Only the dead sleep at such an hour" (p. 74) or "Sounds like the devil himself is stomping around outside" (p. 81). How do such expressions and figures of speech set the tone in the novel?

4. When does Signa feel most like herself? When is she most relaxed? With whom does she speak the most freely?

5. Do you agree with Death's justification for why so many people around Signa die? What was his purpose in removing certain people from her life?

6. Blythe's views of standard societal customs differ from those of her peers. How do her opinions and plans change Signa's expectations for the future?

7. How might the novel be seen as a commentary on grief? When Death teaches Signa about the afterlife, how might his lessons be comforting to readers who are dealing with grief?

8. Death says to Signa, "You must not allow yourself to be consumed so thoroughly by death. It's not selfish to live" (p. 276). What does he mean by this? How might such a warning apply to all people?

9. After an eternity spent watching humans and crafting a philosophy on life, Death poses the question, "So which is better? To live forever, or to live and love?" (p. 350) What do you think?

10. Justifying his actions and explaining the balance of life and death, Death says, "... for I am what makes this world beautiful" (p. 350). What does he mean?

11. Are there moments of foreshadowing throughout the novel that hint at the ending? What hints did the author give that you understood only at the end?

12. How does the end of the novel mirror the prologue? What do you think happens after the last page?